ZANE PRESENTS

Man
SWAPPERS

Dear Reader:

Every once in a while, a book comes along that makes you pause and wonder how the author was able to pull off such a unique concept. Such is the case with *Man Swappers* by Cairo. A set of triplets who have both government names and freak-the-hell-out-of-men names. A set of triplets that have decided that their sexual liberation entails only sleeping with the same exact men at the same exact time. Wow! All I can say is that Cairo has stepped up his A-game on this one.

Feast your eyes and libido on these three fascinating women who might look exactly alike but have extremely different personalities, career goals, and sexual desires. One loves dominating men, one has an oral fetish, and one loves to play voyeur and pleasure herself...at least for a little while before she joins the festivities. What happens when one of the men starts to catch feelings for a particular triplet? What happens when another triplet falls for a complete stranger and decides to keep him all to herself? What happens when the third one becomes fascinated with a much younger man who is hung like a horse? Only Cairo can answer those and so many other wild questions in his latest erotic tome.

Thanks for giving *Man Swappers* support and I am confident that you will enjoy reading it as much as I enjoyed editing it. Make sure to check out Cairo's other titles: *The Kat Trap, The Man Handler, Daddy Long Stroke, Deep Throat Diva* and *Kitty-Kitty, Bang-Bang*. Thanks also for supporting the dozens of other authors that I publish under Strebor Books. We truly appreciate the love. For more information on our titles, please visit www.zanestore.com and you can find me on my personal website: www.eroticanoir.com. You can also join my online social network at www.planetzane.org.

Blessings,

Zane

Publisher
Strebor Books International
www.simonandschuster.com/streborbooks

ZANE PRESENTS

Man
SWAPPERS

A NOVEL BY

CAIRO

SBI

STREBOR BOOKS

NEW YORK LONDON TORONTO SYDNEY

Strebor Books
P.O. Box 6505
Largo, MD 20792
http://www.streborbooks.com

© 2012 by Cairo

ISBN 978-1-59309-387-7
ISBN 978-1-4516-5107-2 (ebook)
LCCN 2011938319

First Strebor Books trade paperback edition March 2012

Cover design: www.mariondesigns.com
Cover photograph: © Keith Saunders/Marion Designs

10 9 8 7 6 5 4

Manufactured in the United States of America

For information regarding special discounts for bulk purchases, please contact Simon & Schuster Special Sales at 1-866-506-1949 or business@simonandschuster.com

The Simon & Schuster Speakers Bureau can bring authors to your live event. For more information or to book an event, contact the Simon & Schuster Speakers Bureau at 1-866-248-3049 or visit our website at www.simonspeakers.com.

THIS BOOK IS DEDICATED TO
Sandy Gooden, Aaliyah Muhammad & Kat Torres;
three beauties who love the Cairo Juice so much
that they created Juice Lovas Review,
a Facebook book club for lovers of hot, juicy reads!

ACKNOWLEDGMENTS

Whew, what can I say? Two-and-a-half-years (and six books later) and this journey is slowly evolvin' into a movement. The Cairo Movement—lovers of great sex and hot, steamy, juicy reads by ya boy! Books flooded wit' the kinda sex scenes that'll set ya drawz on fire and keeps peeps horny; that keeps 'em on edge, and keeps 'em wantin' to fuck 'n suck! Yes, the movement is here! Let's keep embracin' the sexual revolution, responsibly and respectfully, and flyin' the freak flags high!

To my publicist, Yona Deshommes at Simon & Schuster: Your continued belief and support keeps ya boy on rock! And I love it when you crack that whip (inside joke)!

To the beautiful Allison Hobbs: You, my sweet, sexy vixen-friend, have made this journey more "Scandalicious" than I could have ever imagined. Real talk, I am honored to be in such great company and more proud to call you a true friend, baby!

To the Facebook Beauties and Cuties who splash their sweet, sticky cream up on my wall; and to the other lovers of the Cairo Juice (new and old), who continue to crave more of the heat wit' each sip: Thank you, thank you, thank you! On some real ish, I 'preciate YOU ridin' this wave wit' me!

A special shout-out to all the Beauties who tuck their men in at night, read 'em a few lines from one of my books as bedtime stories, then climb up on top of 'em and slay 'em down into the mattress: Now that's the kinda sexiness that keeps me nuttin' on myself. Thanks for the luv!

I continue to get mad luv from the ladies who read my books, but I am also startin' to get more dudes checkin' for my work as well; that's wassup! So it's only right I shout out some of the fellas who've hit me up and shown me luv: Eli Anderson, Mike Holmes, Kevin Jackson, Markeith D. Brown, Sr. (even though you get read to at bedtime—LOL), Charles Turnage, Shamar out in the ATL, BonaFide Beatz in Milwaukee, Calvin Andrews, Jeffery Roshell, Charles Carlos Carroll, Megel Sherman, and many others: Thanks, my dudes!

To all my peeps who come thru and chill wit' me in chat on Tuesday nights on Planetzane.org: Thanks for keepin' chat hot. I enjoy the vibe!

To everyone who continues to visit my website and blog (and who return for more doses of the juice): Thanks, and WelCum! And to the true members of *Cairo's World*, you already know how it goes down. Thanks for keepin' it real nasty wit' me.

To Zane and Charmaine: Grazie! Merci! Gracias! No matter what language I say it in, I can't begin to thank the both of you enough! Thanks for the mad luv!

And, last but not least, this acknowledgment wouldn't be complete if I didn't say wassup to the naysayers and undercover juice lovers who secretly crave to know what kinda nastiness I'm gonna write next. Deep down inside, you know I'm slowly becomin' ya guilty pleasures. LOL. Don't worry, I won't tell 'em I got you nuttin' on ya'selves if you don't; just keep lickin' them fingers while you spittin' out the hate. Ya boy, ain't goin' anywhere!

One luv—
Cairo

Pleasure

CHAPTER ONE

M y panties are wet and my body is hot and ready. I am so fucking horny watching my sister, Porsha, down on her knees sucking dick. I watch as she bobs her head back and forth, making swishy popping noises with her mouth as she slurps, gulps, and swallows the thick, eight-inch dick in front of her.

"That's right, Sis," I urge, grinning and sexily eyeing the six-foot-three, 220-pound, caramel-skinned stallion she's kneeling before. He palms the back of her head, eyeing me back. My tongue traces my cherry red painted lips. "Throat that nigga's dick, Passion. Rock his top, like Mommy taught you." She swallows him down to the base, juggling his balls in her hand. "That's my girl. You're making Mommy so proud of you."

Porsha, a.k.a. Passion, enjoys connecting with a man's inner spirit, empowering him to be less inhibited. She encourages him to relax, relate, release and...enjoy the moment.

I thumb my nipples and they pop up like chocolate Hershey kisses, eager to be licked, suckled, and devoured by his hot, hungry mouth. But, tonight, there'll be no touching. He is only allowed to look.

"You like looking at these pretty titties?" I ask him, seductively shaking them at him. I lift up my left breast and flick my long tongue over my nipple. He pulls in his bottom lip. I switch to my right breast, then do the same thing. "You wanna suck these nipples?"

He groans. "Ohhh, yeaaaah, baby...aaaaah, fuuuuck..." I can tell Porsha's head game is getting the best of him. He is straining to hold it together; struggling not to spill his creamy yogurt without permission.

"Motherfucker," my other sister, Persia, barks, snapping her whip. "You better not cum until I tell you to. You understand me?"

"Yessssssss...uhhhh, shiiiit..."

My sister, Persia—a.k.a. Pain, is domineering and commanding. Tonight, she is the mistress of ceremony, if you will. She enjoys creating scenarios and role-playing almost as much as she enjoys administering pain. Although she'll tell you, *quick*, that she is not a Sadomasochist, or a Dominatrix, she's the one who enjoys wearing the latex and leather getups with six-inch pencil boots and red nail polish and lipstick, dragging men around by collars and chains. And you can see the gleam in her eyes every time she causes a man to whimper and beg.

And, then, there is me—Paris, a.k.a. Pleasure. I am turned on by watching my two sisters bring a man to his knees as much as I enjoy having him watching me pleasure myself. I enjoy seeing a man experience intimacy, and allowing him to fulfill his hidden carnal desires while connecting with his fantasies. I am the one who lets them watch me fuck myself with fingers or toys, or a combination of the two, wishing it could be them lost in between the slick folds of my pussy. It is in the knowing that he cannot touch, that he cannot smell, that he cannot taste, the essence of my womanhood—unless, I allow him to—that brings me the most pleasure. I enjoy seeing a man experience sensual and sexual gratification. And, it is within the dark confines of his mind that my sisters and I transform deepest desires into flesh-to-flesh reality.

"Yes what, you sneaky motherfucker?" Persia barks, bringing my attention back to her. "Fucking your best friend's sister, you nasty motherfucker." She walks over to him and snaps a nipple clamp onto his left nipple.

He winces. And bolts of electricity shoot through my clit. "Aaaaah…yes, Mistress Pain."

"You like watching his mother, don't you? You like gazing at her big, wet pussy?"

Bitch, you wish. My pussy ain't big, I think, cuttin' an eye at her. I smack the front of my pussy, then spread my lips so he can see for himself how tight it is.

He licks his lips. "Yes, Mistress Pain."

"Tell your friend's mother how pretty she is."

Porsha sucks him ferociously, taking him all the way down in her throat while she smacks, pops and pinches her clit.

"Aaah, oh, shit…" he moans.

"Look at his mother," Persia says, turning his face in my direction, "and tell the bitch what a sexy whore she is."

The word *whore* slices through me. But I will play my position and let it go, for now.

"You real fuckin' sexy, ma," he says, gazing at me. He purposefully doesn't call me a whore, knowing it will bring him delightful consequences.

She grabs him by the throat. Her nails sink into his jugular. He winces, then grunts. Porsha's wearing his dick out, sucking it feverishly. "That's not what I told you to say, you defiant little shit. I said to tell her she's a sexy whore."

"Aaaah, shiiiiit…"

"You better not nut, you dumb fuck. Now say it."

I force a grin. Continue in the fantasy, leaning back on my right forearm, using my left hand to massage my clit over my thin silk panties while staring at Persia. Despite my annoyance that she is forcing him to call me a whore, I am still in awe at how well she flips into script and dominates, manipulates, and controls men. She is wearing a crotchless latex cat suit with cut-out breasts. Her chocolate nipples poke out like sweet pieces of double-coated chocolate malt balls.

He repeats her words, and she lets go of his throat, mushing him in the face. I can see the imprint of her nails embedded in his skin. He keeps his eyes locked on me, biting down on his bottom lip.

"You like fuckin' your friend's sister's throat?" Persia asks, clamping his right nipple. He snaps his eyes shut, pulling in a deep breath. "Open your eyes," she says, stepping up on the footstool near him and sticking her tongue in his ear. She bites down on his earlobe. Repeats the question; tells him to keep his eyes locked on me as I part my shapely legs so he can see my swollen petals around the crotch of my panties.

"Yes, Pain, baby. Her throat feels so fuckin'...aaah, shit... good."

Persia walks over to the table, draped with a black tablecloth, and grabs a wooden ruler. She walks back over to Emerson. But tonight he is being called Sammie—this is what he has asked for. To be a horny teenage boy who sneaks into a window to get his dick sucked by his friend's sister while he watches their mother masturbate. I am the mother who walked in on them, then started watching and playing with myself. A role I happily oblige. Persia glides the ruler over his muscular ass. She traces his ass cheeks with it, runs the edge of it down the crack of his ass, then without warning she whacks him with it. He flinches. She whacks him again, and again. Then, like a razor, she slowly slides it up his ass crack before lighting his ass on fire.

"You wanna nut, don't you, you nasty little fucker?"

"No, Pain. Only if it is pleasin' to you."

I moan, listening to the smacking sounds of Porsha's dick sucking. "That's right, suck the shit out that fat dick. Suck him how Mommy showed you." I let out a girlish giggle, then grind on my hand. "You have my pussy soooooo wet," I moan again, gazing at Emerson. "Sammie, you wanna smell my wet panties while you fuck my daughter's nasty little throat with your dick?"

"Yesssss…" he moans.

"You wanna taste 'em?"

He groans, then grunts, nodding his head as Porsha pulls his cock from out of her mouth and begins to coat it with a glob of spit. She jacks him off, then slowly starts sucking on his balls. "Aaaaah, yeah, baby…just like that…"

I lift my legs up in the air and slowly peel off my panties. I spread open my legs; give him a visual of what he can't have. His eyes widen as he drinks in the loveliness of my freshly shaven pussy. It greets him with glistened lips, smiling at him. He watches as I dip one finger, then two, in and scoop out my juices. I slip my fingers into my mouth and gently suck on them. When I have cleaned my fingers of my cream, I part my pussy lips and allow him to swallow in its pink center, lush and slippery.

I love my pussy. No, seriously…I adore it. The way it looks; the way it feels; the way it smells; the way its muscles constrict and contract—gripping and tugging at a finger, or tongue, or a neat little battery-operated gadget—when being teased, taunted and toyed with. Oh, how I love the way my cunt drips with its own sweet, sticky, delectable honey as it whines and begs and pleads for a deep fucking by a deliciously thick, pulsating cock.

Too bad—for him, tonight, there will be no fucking...by choice.

Emerson, uh Sammie, lets out another moan, keeping his eyes glued to my weeping pussy. He knows my cunt cries for his touch. Knows it begs for his thrusts. And I see the yearning in his eyes to give it what it needs, wants, and craves—his tongue, his fingers, his thick, veiny dick!

Porsha slides a hand between her legs, rapidly smacks her pussy and pops her clit a few times while throating Emerson's cock.

Persia removes his left nipple clamp, then twirls her tongue around it. She flicks her tongue over it, then nibbles on it before moving over to his right nipple and doing the same thing. I know she is about to allow him to bust his nut. And he knows it, too. She walks in back of him, drops down and starts nibbling and biting on his swollen ass cheeks. She kisses and licks where she has bruised. I watch as she parts his ass open, then runs her tongue in his crack.

"Oh, fuck...goddamn...y'all freaky-ass bitches fuckin' my head up..."

"Did I tell you to speak, you dirty, little maggot? Do you want me to paddle your tight ass until he bleeds?"

"No, Pain."

"Then you speak when spoken to. You understand?"

"Yes, Pain.

"Muhfucka," Porsha says, stroking his dick, "you can say what you want. You know you ain't ever gonna find another set of fly, freaky bitches like us who'll fuck you stress free. So you better shut the fuck up and ask Pain if you can feed us your nut."

"Pain, baby, may I have permission to bust this nut?"

Persia stops what she's doing. "You think you deserve to cum, you naughty little fucker?" she asks, smacking him on the ass again.

"Yes, Pain."

She walks around to the front of him, grabbing him by the neck, then pulling him into her and forcefully kissing him. I rapidly finger myself. My pussy explodes, watching him greedily suck the scent of his ass off of Persia's tongue. She pulls back from him. "You like how your ass tastes?"

Porsha wets his dick with more spit, then slips it back into her hungry mouth.

"Aaaaah, shit..."

"Answer me, motherfucker," Persia says, pinching and twisting his nipples.

"Mmmm, aaaahhh...yes, Mistress. I like how my ass tastes on your tongue. I love it when you eat my ass."

"Of course you do, you nasty little sonofabitch." She kisses him again, then walks in back of him, again, and squats down. "Keep fucking her horny mouth real good and I'll let you cum." He grunts as she pulls open his cheeks and blows into his hole. "You want my tongue back in your horny, tight ass?"

Porsha rapidly sucks and gulps his cock.

"Ohhhh, shiiiiiit...yessssss, baby. Fuck my ass with your tongue."

"Don't you nut, yet," Persia warns as she buries her face back into his ass and fucks him with her heated tongue.

He dips at the knees, grabs the sides of Porsha's head and face-fucks her relentlessly, moaning. It is all music to my ears. When he can no longer take the intense dick-sucking and ass-licking my sisters are giving him—or watching me play in my wet abyss, his body begins to shake. I watch as his head drops backward and his eyes roll up to the ceiling. He lets out a load, rumbling moan. His body starts to quiver.

It is time.

I smile, wiping my drenched pussy with my panties, then get up and walk over to him. I lick his left nipple, pull him by the neck toward me, then slip my tongue into his mouth. I suck on his tongue, his lips. Wipe his face with my cum-stained panties, then stuff them into his mouth. He greedily sucks and chews on them.

"Clean my panties, you nasty nigga," I say, running my hands along his chiseled chest. I allow my nails to lightly graze across his skin. I whisper in his ear, pulling my panties out of his mouth. I smell them. "Mmmm, my pussy smells so good. What do you think my son would say if he caught you fuckin' his sister's pretty little face and watchin' his mother play with herself?" I reach between his legs and grab his balls while Porsha continues bobbing back and forth on his cock. I roll them in my hand, then lightly squeeze.

"Aaaah, fuuuuck...he'd tell me how fucked up I am."

"He sure would. You ready to show him how fucked up you are?" I ask, dropping down to my knees next to Porsha. He will feed the two of us his milk while Persia eats his ass.

"Oh, yes...aaaaah..." Porsha releases his cock from her throat. He grabs it and rapidly jacks it, moaning. I am anxious to feel his hot cum splash up against my lips and tongue. He has two sets of eyes looking up at him, two wet tongues wagging in anticipated delight, waiting to be drenched by his cream.

Porsha and I both lap at his balls, then pull one into each of our mouths. "Aaaaaah, fuuuck...Yeah, suck them balls...aaah...you pretty bitches got a nigga's head spinnin'...aaaah, shit...I'm cummin'... ooohhh...here it comes...open ya mouths...come get this nut..."

He scoots back as Porsha and I open our mouths, and say, "Aaaaaaah," wagging our tongues, and flicking them at the tip of his swollen mushroom head. His body shudders as he pumps out a gushing stream of hot creamy nut. He swings his dick from side to side, sprays us with his sticky cream. Persia removes her tongue from his ass, then comes around and tongues him down again. He continues stroking his dick, squeezing out more nut, then allows me and Porsha to take turns sucking out the last few drops of his salty and sweet nectar.

"Daaaaaaaaaaaaamn…" he says, trying to catch his breath. "That shit was good as fuck. Y'all got a muhfucka's head spinnin'."

Porsha and I swallow his nut, standing up and licking our lips. We both take turns kissing him, then push him back on the sofa. "We ain't finished with you, nasty boy," Porsha says, rolling a condom down on his dick, then straddling him. "You fucked my mouth; now it's time to fuck my pussy." She reaches under for his still-hard dick. She strokes it at the base, allowing the head to brush up against the back of her pussy. She will not allow him to enter her until I am in position. I stand up on the sofa and look down into his glazed eyes. The eyes of a man seduced and pleasured by three beautiful women—sisters identical in every way imaginable.

Porsha slips his dick into her smoldering hole, then gallops down on his shaft. Persia is now on her knees, sucking on his balls.

He moans.

I straddle his face. Allow my smoldering slit to hover over his seeking mouth. He sticks his thick tongue out, rapidly flaps it back and forth. I lower my pussy, barely allowing the tip of his tongue to touch it. He reaches up for me with his hands. I grab them, pushing them up over his head. Pin them against the wall. Then slowly mount his mouth; give him access to my wetness. Grind on his mouth until I cum in it.

Tonight, we have brought this man before us to heightened

bliss. We have taken him on a sexual journey like no other. And have allowed him to explore a hidden desire without guilt or shame. Our motto is simple: What one has, the others share— including men. Yes, Porsha, Persia, and I have given this hunk of man a night he will soon never forget. And, together, we are man swappers—three sisters, three insatiable libidos—who share the same man, with one mission in mind. To fuck him—together, and take him to the edge of ecstasy, taunt him, then toss his ass over.

Porsha
CHAPTER TWO

"Girrrrrl, I almost shitted my drawers and gagged on Emerson's dick last night when Persia's crazy ass told him to call you a whore," I say to Paris, shaking my head at Persia. We're sitting in a booth at Je's restaurant in downtown Newark waiting to order their slamming breakfast. It's busy. But, fortunately for us, we picked a good day to come 'cause usually it's packed tight up in here, and the line is wrapped around the building to get in. "Baaaaaby, the look on your face was priceless." I crack up, knowing how much she dislikes being called *that*. Whores are sleazy and gutter-like to her.

She rolls her eyes at me. "Thanks for reminding me, heifer. Besides, you didn't have on any drawers, you were bare-assed with a mouthful of dick, remember?" I keep laughing. She glares over at Persia. "Yeah, bitch, you coulda at least told him to call me a *ho*. Damn."

Persia flicks her wrist at her. "Whore, ho, what's the difference? It was all a part of the fantasy."

She huffs. "Noooooo, the fantasy was Emerson having his boy's sister suck his dick while their mother watched; not you referring to her, *me*, as a whore."

"Ummm, excuse me. I know what the fantasy was. I was there. Or did you forget?"

"No, obviously *you* did," Paris snaps, picking up the menu and looking it over. She eyes Persia over the edge of the menu. "Don't call me that shit again."

"I didn't call you that, boo. Emerson did. And, technically, it wasn't you who was the whore. It was his boy's mother. The role you played."

"You know what the hell I mean," Paris snorts.

Persia smirks. "Oh lighten up. No need in getting your panties all twisted around your clit. It's only a name. Don't let it have so much power over you."

Paris sucks her teeth. "Whatever. Next time, use another word."

"Okay, then. How about slut? Would that work for you?"

I shake my head, knowing that this little situation is about to turn nasty if I don't intervene. For us to be so identical in our looks, mannerisms, and body-types, yet have three such distinctly different personalities is mind-boggling—and, at times, messy. Oh, wait…you don't know. We're identical triplets. Yes, who share each other's men, something we've been doing since freshman year in college. And as long as we don't open our mouths, we can fuck a man into oblivion and he'd never know which one of us he was fucking, first.

Anyway, Persia is clearly the most antagonistic and mean-spirited of the three of us. And she's a lot more aggressive with men than Paris and me. Whereas, Paris—who is so much more like our mother—is the calmer, more laid-back of us all. She's also the sneaky type who'd rather sit by the fire and sip chardonnay with a chenille throw draped over her shoulder while curled up reading a good novel. Then—in the still of the night, shimmy her fast-ass down the balcony when she thinks everyone is fast asleep to guzzle down a dick. And I'm the mixture of the two.

Cool, calm, collected and…oh so refined, one minute. Then ready to swing a bitch into a wall the next. And, when it comes to men, shoot, ain't no shame in my game. I'll fuck 'em every which way the sun shines.

"Okay, ladies," I say, waving the white table napkin in the air. "Kiss and make up. This is not the place, nor the time, for getting catty."

"Oh shut up," they say in unison. "You're the one who started this mess."

"Well, excuuuuuuse, me," I say, looking at Paris. "I'm not the one who called you a whore and said your pussy was a big-ass mess."

Persia snickers, "Girl, you are such an instigator. You know damn well I didn't say no shit like that. Well, not about her pussy being a mess."

Paris grunts, glancing over at Persia. "Mmmph, well, shit. You might as well have. You told him to look at my *big*, wet pussy; same difference."

"Oh, right. I sure did, didn't I?"

"I'll have you bitches know I have a nice tight pussy. I do kegel exercises twice a day."

I look at her, amused. "Oh, that's what you were doing when I walked in on you spitting out that big-ass tennis ball the other day?"

Persia and I laugh.

"Both of you hookers can kiss my sweet ass," Paris says, leaning up on her forearms. She whispers through clenched teeth the way our mother used to when we were getting on her nerves. "'Cause I'll whip both of y'all's asses. Now try it."

We bust out laughing, knowing damn well fist-fighting each other isn't what we do. We tease, we talk shit to each other, but that's where we draw the line. And it's always done with a whole lot of love.

"Anyway, speaking of Emerson," Persia says, placing her elbows up on the table. "Have either of you noticed how funny style he's been acting lately?"

I shake my head. "Not really, why?"

Paris purses her lips. "Well, I didn't sense him acting funny, but I did notice he seemed a little preoccupied the last few times he was with us, but I didn't really pay too much attention to it."

"Well, I have," Persia says. "And you do know what that smells to me, right?"

"Another woman," I say.

Persia smirks, raising a brow. "Exaaactly."

"Neither one of you know that for sure," Paris says, glancing at the both of us. "So let's not go there, yet. At least not until we have something more specific to go on."

Persia rolls her eyes. "I'll tell you this. We may not know for sure what or *who* he's doing, but he's doing something with someone, trust me. And he has one time to not return a call, or deliver the dick, and his ass is chopped. You know…"

She stops talking when our waiter finally comes over to our table. He stares at us, blinking his eyes. He's a tall, lean, mocha-colored cutie with deep, spinning waves and almond-shaped eyes. He's shocked at how identical the three of us are, and how similar our voice patterns are. The way he looks at us, tells us what we already know—he's mesmerized by our beauty, like so many others. We smile at him, slyly nodding at each other. We are all thinking the same thing: he's fuckable.

"Good morning, ladies. My name is Royce and I'll be your server today. Can I get you something to drink?"

Damn, I've never seen his fine-ass here, I think, eyeing him. I am pleasantly surprised at the sight of our waiter. And I can tell Persia is also. Paris tries to act disinterested. We're usually greeted and waited on by one of the females who either come off a little rough around the edges or look like they've been around the block a few times and back. Shit, a few of them look as if they've just been released from a jail cell. But, the food is good as hell. And judging by what's standing before us, today is definitely our lucky day. There's a hint of a Caribbean accent that makes my clitoris jump. I tightly press my thighs together to pinch off the flow of excitement swelling between my legs. There's something about hearing a Caribbean man talk low and dirty in his dialect that makes my pussy overheat. We exchange pleasantries, give him our drink orders, then watch as he walks off.

"Damn, he has a nice ass," Persia says, leaning in and lowering her voice while fanning herself. "I'd like to clamp my legs around his waist and dig my nails deep into that plump, golden-brown booty."

"And I'd like to suck the skin off his dick," I say, seductively licking my lips at the thought of being down on my knees sucking him senseless. "I bet he has some real good dick, too."

"Mmmp, mmph, mmph," Persia says, patting her chest, "there's nothing like some good ole juicy, Bajan cock."

An older gentleman wearing a Yankees fitted overhears us and smiles, shaking his head. Persia shoots him a look, and he turns his nosey ass back around. We keep on talking as if we're the only three in the restaurant.

"Yeah, but he looks too damn young," Paris offers thoughtfully.

"Chile, please," I say, flicking my wrist at her. "As long as he's over twenty-one, is single, and ain't packin' a little-ass dick, he can get it." We give each other high-fives, laughing.

"I know that's right," Persia agrees. Truth is our rules are simple. Any man we fuck has to be: one, single. Now we'll share a man amongst ourselves, but we ain't sharing another bitch's man; two, willing to fuck all three of us either together, or separately; preferably with us in the same room since that's what turns us on the most; three: he must be over the age of twenty-one; four, he must be able to nut more than one round; and, five: be open and honest about his sexual desires. If his ass can't be honest about what it is he wants and craves, then he's probably going to have a hard time being honest about other shit in his life.

"You ladies need a few more minutes, or are you ready to order?" our waiter asks.

"Is your family from the Caribbean?" I ask, allowing my eyes to roam the length of his body. I clasp my hands in front of me. He says he's from Saint Lucia. I smile, imagining him standing here naked with his long West Indian cock dangling in front of him, eager to be sucked. Shit, in my head, he's lying naked up on this table and I am drizzling warm maple syrup all over his nipples, down the center of his chest, and all over his dick and balls. My sisters and I take turns licking every inch of his sticky body, then mount his cock and face, and fuck him senseless.

"Ooooh, we love Saint Lucia," Persia coos, snapping me out of my mini-daze. "So, tell me, Royce from Saint Lucia, how old are you?" She's eyeing him like he's a thick, slab of juicy baby back ribs. She licks her lips.

"Twenty-three," he says, rubbing his dimpled chin.

"You involved with anyone?" I ask.

"Nah, not at the moment."

Persia grins. "Well, in that case," she says flirtatiously, "we'll have you to go."

He laughs.

"I'm dead serious," Persia says, tilting her head. She keeps her gaze locked on his. "Have you ever fantasized about being in a foursome?"

He shakes his head, blushing and visibly caught off-guard, shifting his weight from one foot to the other. He nervously glances around the restaurant to make sure no one is hearing this. But, of course, the nosey-ass fart across from us has his hairy ears all pressed into our conversation, ear-hustling.

"Oh, that's okay. You probably couldn't handle us, anyway. We'd eat you alive, baby." Persia and I laugh.

Paris sucks her teeth. "Listen, ignore her. I'll have French toast, scrambled eggs, hard, with cheddar cheese, and grits."

"Okay," he says, sounding relieved. He looks over at me. "Do you need more time?"

"Give me the same," I add. Persia rolls her eyes and orders pancakes and a vegetable and cheese omelet. When Royce returns with our food, Persia starts in on him again.

She reaches over and touches his arm. "Do you think we're sexy?"

He nods, grinning. "Hellzz yeah," he snaps excitedly before catching himself. He looks around the restaurant to make sure no one overheard him. Of course, the two nosey bitches sitting at the table next to us glance over at us.

Persia motions with her finger for him to lean in to her. She lightly blows into his ear, speaks to him in a low, seductive tone. "And we have real good pussy, baby. Imagine the three of us without clothes on, stretched out on a bed butt-naked, legs spread wide, mouths open, tongues wagging—all waiting on *you*. For you to experience anything you've ever wanted to experience. Do you think you ready for something like that?"

He smiles uneasily, taking the three of us in. I smile at him.

Paris stays focused on her meal as if she's not hearing any of this. His face becomes flush from shock and nervousness. For a moment, I think he's about to break out in a sweat. Although he tries to play it cool, Persia has put him on the spot. Something she enjoys doing to men.

"Listen," Persia continues, deciding to let him off the hook. "How about you slide us your number when you bring us our bill? Then we can talk more privately."

"Cool-cool," he says, grinning. "I gotta handle the rest of my customers, but definitely will."

"Make sure you do," she says, smiling at him. He turns to walk off and bumps into the back of someone's chair. We watch him walk off, chuckling. "You see his sexy ass grinning like he hit the damn Jersey Lotto?" Paris eyes her. She shrugs. "What?"

Paris huffs. "Just once do you think we can go out without you recruiting or tryna round up the next batch of dick? Damn."

"Okay, your point?"

"The point is exactly what I said. You need to stop being so damn extra with it. And exercise a bit more discretion. Geesh."

"Paris, puhleeze. Don't sit here and try to get all prudish on me," Persia responds incredulously. "We need to keep our options open. A freak has always got to be ready for new opportunities that may arise. And this freak stays prepared, okay? Thought you knew."

"Well, maybe a freak needs to learn when to open and shut her damn mouth sometimes, instead of inviting every damn Charles, Dick and Nut in."

Persia frowns. "Bitch, what the fuck's wrong with you this morning? I'm not bleeding and neither is Porsha, so I know your ass is not on the rag, either. So what the fuck is it with all this bitchiness?"

Paris sighs. "Nothing; let's drop it."

"No, let's *not* drop shit. If there's something you need to say, then say it. So we can address it and—"

I look around the room and notice a few people trying to get their ear-hustle on. I cut in. "*And* how about we not get into this right now." I blink, looking over toward the door. Two chicks walk through the door, and I roll my eyes. "Roach alert," I say, jerking my head over in their direction. Persia and Paris follow my eyes.

"Damn, this bitch," Persia says. "And her Road Kill."

I laugh. "That bitch looks like a damn possum." It's our cousin, Zena, and her friend, Ameeka, one of the sideshow rodeo hoes she hangs with.

Persia laughs. "Let's hope she doesn't see us."

"Nope, not so lucky," Paris says, throwing her hand up in a Miss America hand wave. Zena waves back, then says something out of the side of her mouth to Ameeka as they make their way over to us. Aside from the fact that she's still holding on to shit that happened in 2000—when we were seniors in high school, Zena has a love-hate relationship with us, particularly Persia. She's never gotten over the fact that the guy she had a high school crush on asked Persia to go to the senior prom with him. And Persia not only went, she fucked him, knowing Zena had a thing for him.

"Bitch, please. He ain't your man," Persia had told her when Zena had confronted her about it at our family's annual picnic.

"Yeah, but you know how I feel about him."

Persia bucked her eyes. "Well, does *he* know how you feel?"

"No."

"Exactly. So until he does, it's open season. So get on up outta my face 'cause I'm going. And if he acts right, I might let him hit it." The next thing I know, Zena slaps her and they start going at it. Paris and I stood and watched the two of them slap, kick, punch, and bite each other until two of our uncles ran over and broke it up. Then all four of us got whipped by our mothers for fighting. Well, they got their asses beat for fighting. Paris and I got ours tore up for watching. Now, here we are eleven years later, and this bitch is still holding on to the shit. And she ended up getting him, and eventually marrying his ass any-damn-way.

"Bitch, you fucking my leftovers," Paris reminded her the day Zena announced she was engaged, and demanded that Paris respect her relationship. "So, whooptie-doo! Big dick for sure, but the nigga can't fuck but for a hot second. So, enjoy!"

Needless to say, we didn't get an invite to her wedding.

"And the drama begins," I say, shaking my head as she approaches the table.

"Well, isn't this cute," Zena says, giving Persia and Paris phony-air kisses and waving at me, "the three of you over on this side of town. What brings you High-end Divas over on this end; *recruitment*? Y'all still doin' each other's men?" She says this as a dig, of course. Her friend snickers. We can't stand this bitch with her Cookie Monster face, either.

Persia eyes Ameeka. "Sweetie, I don't know what you over there snickering about when I saw your man two weeks ago all hugged up. And it wasn't with you. So looks like we aren't the only ones sharing a man"—she snaps her fingers—"okay?" Ameeka gives her a look of disbelief, opening her mouth to say something. Persia puts her hand up to stop her. "Save it. You can play stupid if you want. But what you need to do is handle your own situation before you try and snicker at us."

I can tell she's pissed. But the truth is the truth. "Zena, I'll be over at our table," she huffs, storming off.

Persia, Paris and I laugh. "Trick," all three of us say at the same time.

"I see why he cheats on her with that big-ass, oversized face of hers," Persia continues. She acts like she doesn't hear us. But the place is only but so big, so of course everyone up in the restaurant has gotten an earful. Most of the patrons look on with amusement; others with disgust and annoyance that we are disrupting their meal.

"Now, girls," Zena says, tossing her micro-braids over her shoulder. She has a forehead and hairline like that *Essence* chick, Susan Taylor. "That wasn't nice."

I eye Zena. "Girlfriend, you started it."

Persia rests her forearms up on the table, looking Zena up and down. She scrunches her nose up like Zena's a pile of hot horse shit. "And, since you came over here trying to be messy, tell me. Does your hubby know that that last baby of yours isn't even his?"

Zena's eyes pop open in shock. "W-w-whaat? Who told you that shit? I-I-I don't know where y'all got your information from, but you need to go back and check your facts."

"No, sweetie," Persia says. "You need to request a blood test so you can have *your* facts 'cause we already know what it is. How long was hubby over in Iraq? And how long was he home before you announced you were pregnant again? And how many months later did you drop that baby?"

"Mmmm, let's see," Paris states, counting on her fingers, "One, two, three..." She shakes her head. "It just doesn't add up. You said the baby was full-term, but he was born a month earlier. So how is that full-term if it's supposed to be your hubby's?"

"Y'all can sit here and think and speculate what the hell you want. All of my kids have the same daddy, and it's Aaron—*my* husband," she adds for emphasis, shifting her weight from one foot to the other. "You know what. I'm not even doing this with you bitches today."

Persia tosses her hand up at her, flicking her wrist, dismissing her. "Then don't. See ya."

Persia and I laugh as Zena walks off to join her low-budget-ass friend. It really pisses me off how bitches like her are so quick to judge us for doing what we do when they're worse than us. Shit, we aren't doing anything you and any other bitch hasn't been doing, or known to do—passing the dick around.

"I can't stand that bitch," Persia sneers as the waiter finally comes back over to see if we want, or need, anything else. Persia shifts her attention back to him, smiling. Her frown is immediately replaced with a warm, inviting smile. She tells him he can bring us our check, then watches him walk off. "I bet you his young-ass got some good dick."

"He might," I say, watching Paris ruffle through her bag, then pulling out a pack of Cobalt chewing gum. She offers us some, then tosses it back into her bag.

Persia continues, "But I bet you he can't handle one of us, let alone all three of us. We'd have that poor boy strung the hell out, and you know it. The last thing we need is a damn junkie on our hands."

"Yeah, girl," I agree, nodding. "We definitely don't need that."

In spite of her mood, Paris chuckles, rolling the stick of gum into her mouth. "My treat," she says, pulling out her AMEX card. "Y'all heifers are too much."

"But am I lying?" Persia asks, laughing.

Paris and I shake our heads and say at the same time, "Nope, not at all."

When he returns to our table with the check, Persia pulls out her wallet and tosses a ten on the table. I do the same. And as if on cue, the young Caribbean stud slides Persia his number written on the back of a card as she slides out of the booth.

She leans into his ear and whispers, "I hope you have a big dick," then heads for the door.

CHAPTER THREE

I'm not sure what the hell was going on with Paris and her moody ass this morning, but I was three seconds from screaming on her. Sometimes she can be such a fucking stick in the mud when she gets on her bullshit. Luckily, we're sisters and we're extremely close and, no matter what, I'm going to love her. But, damn it, sometimes she can be a real bitch! Well, shit, on second thought...so can I. So I guess we're even.

But that hooker Zena. She's a waste of space. If she wants to live in lies, then that's on her, but this sista here is going to always be true. And the truth is I *enjoy* fucking the same men as my sisters. I realize that a woman who doesn't understand our thinking is going to think it's nasty. That it's trifling. That it's downright despicable and repulsive. I get it. All the holier-than-thou-self-righteous hoes think sharing a man is sinful. Why? Because my sisters and I are open about doing it? Mmmph. Well, answer me this: Would it be better if we randomly shared a man, acting as if it wasn't happening, like so many other women do? Should we play dumb, and stupid, and settle for a man knowing he has other women on the side? Mmmph. No, I don't think so! What we women should do is take back our power. Hold them accountable for their behaviors, and stop making excuses for why they do what they do. Shit, it's obvious why they do what they do—because they can. So we have to stop letting them get all up in our heads, stressing about what (or who) the fuck they're doing. Because truth of the matter is a man's going to do what he wants no matter how hard we try to stop him, or control him. And cheating is one of those things that most men are going to do *at least* once.

Although having more than one woman is something most men only dream of, yearn for, there are plenty more men who actually do live it. So knowing this, my sisters and I have empowered ourselves to give men the opportunity to have more than one woman. So what's so wrong with that? Is it the fact that we're sisters connected by genetics and blood that makes it dirty? Or would it be more acceptable if we were simply three women fucking and sucking and fighting over the same man, acting as if we didn't know about the other?

Well, understand this. The difference between what my sisters and I do from what any other woman who has ever shared her man has done is this: we willingly and openly accept it for what it is. We allow men to indulge their animalistic need to mount and mate with more than one woman—*closely* monitored, of course.

Yes, we are the scandalous triplets in our family. And our own mother has the nerve to still be very *appalled*, as she called it, when she learned of what we were doing. And, even now—to this very day, she's not able to let it go.

"Girls," she had said, sitting down at the head of the dining room table with her arms resting on the table and her hands clasped in front of her. We were in our senior years at Howard University, almost twenty-one; and, in our minds, grown. "I'm hearing some very disturbing rumors…"

"What kind of rumors?" Paris asked, shifting in her seat.

"Things that I dare not believe about you girls. I didn't raise y'all to be no loose girls. So I'm hoping they're not true…"

My sisters and I looked at each other, already knowing where the conversation was headed. "You hope what isn't true?" Porsha asked, getting impatient. Our mother, love her dearly, has a way with dragging shit out instead of getting to the point.

"Well…" she paused, trying to find her words. A practice she rehearsed over and over to keep our father from storming up out of the house when she said something he didn't like. Out of the three of us, my patience level is the shortest. And when it comes to nonsense I am much more vocal about it than they are.

I huffed, glancing down at my watch. "Mom, will you please spill it already? Geesh. Say what you have to say and stop beating around the bush."

She ignored my irritation, squinting her eyes at me. "Persia, don't get mouthy with me. Now, like I was saying, I hope these rumors being spread about y'all are nothing but the devil and his lies."

"MOM!" I yelled, getting up from my seat. "This is ridiculous. Will you, please. Get. To. The Damn. Point."

"The point is your Aunt Lucky called here, then your Aunt Fanny, to tell me they heard the three of you have been sleeping with each other's boyfriends." Lucky and Fanny are two of her gossiping-ass sisters, Lucille and Francine, who enjoy rattling off everyone else's business, except their own. They are always somewhere meddling. The only aunt who had any sense was my Aunt Penny—my mother's youngest sister. She packed up and moved to Arizona, far away from all of their asses.

I rolled my eyes up in my head. Paris and Porsha glanced over at me, shaking their heads for me not to get into it with her. "That's old news."

"*Old news?*" she repeated in disbelief. "What in the world do you mean, it's 'old news'? It's new news to me. And y'all know how I am about gossip and rumors."

Yeah, you like dishing it, but can't stand to be on the receiving end of it. "Well, what we do isn't a rumor," I informed her. "It's a fact. I thought you were gonna say some mess about one of us being pregnant, or having a disease or something."

Porsha and Paris snickered.

"Oh, good Lord," she said, getting up from her seat. "Say this isn't so." She looked around at each of us, waiting. "One of you had better open your mouth and tell me right now that your aunts have been calling here with a bunch of hot trash lies 'cause I *know* damn well none of my daughters would be so goddamn trifling to do some ho-ass shit like that."

My sisters and I blinked, blinked again. It was very rare that we heard our mother use that kind of language. Out of her four sisters, she is the prim, proper, prissy one, despite being born in Newark. Despite being raised in the projects. She was the one who made sure her three daughters went to private schools instead of public schools, and moved us far away from the hood because she wanted better for us. Always a lady; always turning the other cheek—for most things, we knew she was pissed about this. But we also knew that, whether it struck a nerve with her or not, we were okay with what we were doing.

"Mom, Persia's right," Paris stated. "It's true."

Our mother threw her hand up over her mouth, shocked that we were open about it. She stared at us, long and hard. It was almost as if she would have preferred we'd denied it. "Why in the world?"

"Because all three of us..." Porsha tried to explain, pointing at Paris and me, "...have been in relationships with guys who have either cheated on us, or tried to, so we decided to take matters into our own hands by allowing any man we become involved with to have more than one woman—the three of us."

"And on top of it," I added, grinning, "he gets to experience some of the greatest, freakiest sex he'll ever experience in his lifetime."

I'll never forget the look on her face when I told her that shit. It looked like she was on the brink of a heart attack. All the color in her honey- brown complexion drained from her face. She was flabbergasted. She shook her head in disbelief. "So, let me get this right. My three daughters," she glared at us, "like fucking the same men. Is that what the hell I hear y'all saying to me?" We nodded. "Ohmygod, I can't believe I'm hearing this shit." In melodramatic fashion, she clutched her chest, shaking her head. "Oh, so I guess y'all down between each other's legs licking each other, too, huh? Just doing all kind of sinful shit."

We frowned. "Ugggh," we said in unison. "We share our men, Mom. That's it. We're not lesbians and we aren't licking each other."

"And we always use condoms," Paris added like that would make a difference.

"Besides…" I walked over to where my sisters were sitting. I stood behind them, placing one hand on each of their shoulders. "You always told us to never fight over anything, and to share everything."

She looked at me incredulously. "I taught you girls to share material things, to share your secrets, and your fears, *not* share your goddamn men. I want this nastiness to stop, today. You hear?" Although the question was directed at all three of us, she stared at me, knowing I was the culprit behind it all. And she was right. I was. It took some coaxing—okay, and a little bullying— but not much since we had been known to play pranks with our boyfriends and friends in high school—to get Paris and Porsha to consider it. But, they are my sisters, and we're all cut from the same freaky cloth, so I knew once they experienced it, there'd be no turning back.

I kept my eyes locked on hers. "We're not stopping. You may not like what we're doing, and that's fine. But, we're grown. And you can't tell us what to do, or who we should be doing it with."

She slammed her hand down on the table. "What do you mean, you're not stopping? Paris? Porsha? What do y'all have to say about this?"

"Persia's right, Mom," Paris meekly said. "Sorry. But we enjoy it. And we don't wanna stop."

"It's not like we're hurting anyone," Porsha added. "What we do in the privacy of our own bedrooms is really no one else's business."

"Well, it becomes everyone else's business when you flaunt your nasty ways in public," she snapped. "Do you girls have any idea how embarrassing this is? I done cussed your aunts out, and now I gotta go back and apologize to them for being right."

"Mother, really," I said, rolling my eyes up in my head. "Why would you really care what anyone said, especially Aunt Lucky and Aunt Fanny? It's not like they don't have dirt of their own to worry about. At the end of the day, we're still your daughters."

"Yeah, who are sharing and *fucking* each other's men. And nothing any of you have said has made any damn sense as to why you would want to stoop to some nasty shit like that? I can't believe y'all out there carrying on like a bunch of hot-ass hoes."

Paris's mouth popped open in shock. "Mom, we're not hoes. We're uninhibited, and we like experiencing new things."

"It's nasty," Mother said, rapidly shaking her head and turning her lips up in disgust, "and sinful."

I forced a laugh, knowing there was nothing funny about what

I was going to say to her. "And what do you call a woman who knows her man is cheating on her, but continues baking and cooking and cleaning and sexing him up, knowing that the first chance he gets, he's going to sneak his ass across town to the next woman? What do you call that?"

She huffed. "Stupid. That's what it is. And watch your mouth."

I rolled my eyes. "And what do you call a woman who is crying and begging for her man to stop running out on her every time she catches him cheating on her, but still keeps taking him back? What do you call that same woman who will leave her kids alone in the middle of the night while she goes out looking for her man all over town?"

She looked at me, perplexed. I could tell she was cautiously treading to see where I was going with this. "I don't know," she said, getting agitated. "Desperate."

"No, Mom, it's *you*," I said, glaring at her. Contempt dripped from my voice. She had a look of shock on her face when I said that. "You were that woman for as long as I can remember. Do you think we were that naïve to not know that Daddy was out cheating on you? You really thought we never overheard the hushed arguments, or your whispered phone conversations to Aunt Lucky and them? Do you not think we saw you crying over him? Well, we did."

"You don't know what the hell you're talking about," she snapped defensively. "Your father was a good man, and a good provider."

"There you go, justifying. Yeah, he was a good father. And, yeah, he was a good provider. But he was also a damn good cheater with a good and stupid and desperate wife who"—I jabbed a finger in the air at her—"flitted around this house pretending every-thing was alright, playing Suzy-Goddamn-Homemaker while Daddy was out fuc—"

Before I could get the rest of my words out, she lunged toward me and slapped me, causing me to see stars. Porsha's and Paris's eyes popped open. "Don't you ever," she said through clenched teeth, "talk to me like that, again!"

I could see the hurt and embarrassment in her eyes. I had struck open an unhealed wound. She fought back tears. In that very moment, I knew that in our mother's anguish she saw the enemy—me, my sisters, and any other woman who shares another woman's man. For her, we were the home-wreckers, even though we tried explaining to her that we weren't sharing a man who was already attached to another woman. To her, it made no difference. It was all in the same.

I sigh, shaking that night out of my head as I reach into my bag and pull out my BlackBerry Torch, then scroll down to turn the ringer back on. I have thirteen emails, three text messages, and two missed calls.

Against my better judgment, I return my mother's call, first. "Hey, Mom," I say the minute she answers, pulling out the latest issue of *Vogue* from my desk drawer. I start flipping through the pages.

"Hey," she says, sounding out of breath. "I tried calling you girls earlier, but didn't get any answer." I smirk, knowing she called Paris first—since she's her favorite, then Porsha. And, when she couldn't get a hold of either of them, she called me.

"We were out," I tell her, purposefully leaving out that we were out having breakfast. I sit back in my chair, knowing she already knows, anyway. "Is everything okay?"

"Of course it is."

"Ohhhhkay, so why are you calling *me?*"

She lets out a loud, frustrated sigh in my ear. "Persia, I don't know why you must always be so goddamn—excuse my French, snotty."

"Oh, I'm sorry," I say sarcastically. "What were you calling for?"

She huffs. "To see if you and your sisters were RSVPing for Pasha's wedding."

Pasha is my mother's first cousin, and technically my second cousin. Pasha's grandmother is my mother's aunt, and my great-aunt. She's considered a success story in our family. Having lost both of her parents to murder, she's the owner of one of the hottest hair salons in the Tri-State area. And, quiet as it's kept, engaged to one of the biggest dope slingers in the game. He's been home from prison for close to two years and word has it, he's still up to his same old shit. I guess bad habits don't die easy. The Feds are hot on his ass, but somehow he keeps slipping through their fingers. You'd think after doing four years in prison, he'd learned his lesson. Oh, well. Not my business, nor my headache.

"I don't know," I tell her.

"You know your Aunt Harriett would love to see you and your sisters. She always says you girls don't even call her."

Mmmph, I think, rolling my eyes. *That's because her ass is always trying to get us to sit in church, or starts spewing scriptures.* "The invitation didn't say anything about us being able to bring a date, so maybe not."

"It's nothing personal," she calmly states. "With the baby and that gigantic house they recently bought down there by the shore, they've had to downsize the guest list..."

Yeah, from one-hundred-and-seventy to a hundred guests, I think. Word has it that she and her fiancé, Jasper, purchased an eighty-seven-hundred square foot mini-mansion on three acres of sprawling property. It's where the entire wedding celebration will be. I pull the white and red embossed invitation from out of my top desk drawer, then stare at it:

IN THE CELEBRATION OF LOVE...
MRS. HARRIET ALLEN
REQUESTS THE HONOR OF YOUR PRESENCE AT THE MARRIAGE OF
HER GRANDDAUGHTER
Pasha Alona Allen
TO
Jasper Edwin Tyler
ON SATURDAY, THE TWENTY-SEVENTH OF AUGUST
TWO THOUSAND AND ELEVEN
AT FIVE O'CLOCK IN THE EVENING

She sighs. "...It seems like everyone else's daughters are getting married, except for my own." She sounds disappointed. I toss the invitation back into my drawer, rolling my eyes up in my head, again.

"She's marrying a damn convict and drug-dealer, for crying out loud!" I snap in my head. I keep my thoughts to myself. Decide to fuck with her instead. "Well, don't worry, Mom. We're waiting for that right man to come along to sweep us off our feet, a man who will honor and obey us, handle our ravenous sexual appetites, and submit to our freaky whims."

"Ugh! For the love of God," she says, disgust dripping from her tone. "I know the three of you aren't entertaining no nasty shit like that?"

"Why not, Mother? It's no secret we sleep with the same men. And we're raw-dogging it and sharing each other's spit every chance we get.""

She lets out a disgusted grunt. "Persia, who in the hell are you talking to like that? Have you forgotten who the fuck I am to you? I want to know if you girls have even considered what would happen if the three of you end up pregnant by the same man, and you have the audacity to want to make smart-ass comments."

"Of course we have," I taunt, grinning. "We'll give you beautiful grandbabies who'll be cousins and half-siblings all in one." The line goes dead. "Love you, too, Mother," I say, laughing.

Paris
CHAPTER FOUR

"Paradise Boutique, this is Paris speaking. How can I help you?"

"Hi, yes," the woman on the other end says. "I, um…was in your consignment shop a few days ago…"

"We're not a consignment shop, ma'am," I inform her, slightly annoyed that I have to keep telling people this. "Nothing in our boutique is secondhand. And most of our merchandise is one-of-a-kind exclusives."

Geesh. This shit never ends. I've worked hard to build up my boutique's reputation as one of the premier shopping experiences in the Tri-State area, and I'll be damned if I'm going to let anyone refer to it as a damn consignment shop. After graduating from college and several jobs later, I realized that working a traditional nine-to-five was not something I could successfully do, so I decided that opening my own business was the most practical thing to do, for me.

After college, I landed a job as an assistant buyer for Bloomingdale's on Fifty-ninth Street in New York. Although I loved my job, I realized after six months of being there that it wasn't something I wanted to do for someone else for any long period of time. I worked there for two-and-a-half years while going back to school to get a degree in Fashion Merchandising at FIT—Fashion Institute of Technology, for those of you who might not know, then did an internship at a major fashion house for a year.

Two years later, with savings and a small business loan, I opened Paradise Boutique—a chic, upscale clothing and handbag store in Montclair, New Jersey that specializes in one-of-a-kind fashion by new and up-and-coming designers, as well as, high-end designer handbags. Then two years after I opened its doors, Persia and Porsha bought into the business, and have become partners. Persia maintains and manages the website and does all of our marketing, while Porsha handles the bookkeeping, utilizing their degrees in marketing and accounting, respectively. And thanks to them, Paradise Boutique has become one of the hottest boutiques around.

"Oh, well, excuse me," the woman says, bringing my attention back to her. "I thought it was one of those high-end consignment shops…" *Well, you thought wrong.* I purse my lips. "Anyway, you had a lovely oval beaded clutch there and I'm hoping you still have it."

My ears perk up, and my tone immediately changes. "Oh, yessss, you're talking about the Judith Leiber piece. Yes, we still have it. It's an absolutely stunning bag."

"Yes, it is. I have a wedding to go to in a few months, and it would go wonderful with my dress."

Dress? This clutch is for an evening gown. I imagine her wearing some church-type getup instead of a chic gown, or flowing cocktail dress. *She's about to fuck up this purse wearing some dumb shit.* "Oh, I'm sure it will. It's not only eye-catching; it makes an elegant statement."

"And what's the cost for such a statement?"

"It's on sale for nineteen-hundred-and-ninety-five dollars." I walk over to the glass case and unlock it, then pull the crystal and beaded bag out, locking the case back. "If you'd like, I can hold it for you for twenty-four hours."

"*Nineteen hundred dollars*, for a bag? Oooh, that's a bit pricey. Would you consider coming down on the price a pinch?"

I blink, frowning. *What the fuck kind of store does this bitch think I'm running? I just told her ass this isn't a consignment shop, and it isn't some damn flea market where you can haggle down prices.* "Unfortunately not," I tell her flatly, immediately unlocking the glass case and putting the bag back. "The price is firm. But, if you'd like an evening bag that is a little more inexpensive we have a gorgeous pleated satin clutch." She asks if I can describe it to her. "It has a sleek design of alternating crisp and softly ruffled gold satin stripes with a Swarovski crystal closure. It also comes with a chain strap tucked inside. It's definitely a gorgeous piece."

She grunts. Tells me she doesn't think it will go well with her dress. "And how much is that bag?"

"It's on sale for four-hundred-and-thirty dollars."

She coughs. Repeats what I've said. "Well, do you have anything a little cheaper than that?"

I pull in my bottom lip. Try to catch myself from going off. "No, we don't."

She huffs. "In this economy, those kinda prices for a purse is a bit ridiculous. Some people are barely making ends meet."

Then why the fuck are you calling here? I hear myself ask in my head. "I hear your concern, ma'am. But, that's why they have Marshalls and TJ Maxx to cater to those same people. They offer designer wear at discount prices for people who have to *pinch* their dollars. This is a boutique; not a bargain basement store. Those who can afford the prices will gladly buy. And those who can't, won't. Is there anything else I can help you with today?"

"I don't think I like your tone," she says defensively. "And I don't imagine you getting much business with that kind of attitude. I wanna speak to the owner, if you don't mind."

I smile. "I sure don't. You're speaking to her. And as I said, this is a high-end boutique, with high-end fashion at high-end prices, ma'am. No disrespect. But customers who come through these doors…are already prepared…to spend…top dollar for our merchandise. You can either afford it, or you can't."

I hear a man's voice in the background saying something to her. I can't make out what he's saying, but he's asking her a bunch of questions, then the sound gets muffled as if she's covering the mouthpiece. I hang up. Two minutes later, the phone rings again. It's her, again. "I believe we were disconnected."

I know hanging up on a potential customer is definitely not a good look for business, but I don't have the patience to go back and forth with a customer on a purchase. Either you're going to buy it, or you're not. It's simple as that. I'm not in the business of begging or twisting someone's wrists to get a sale. "Ummm, yes, we were," I lie. "I accidentally hit the receiver." Of course I wanted to say, "No, we weren't, bitch. I hung up on ya cheap ass!" But me being the diplomat that I am, I would never be that blatantly rude. But Persia would. And what I thought is exactly what she would have told her.

She grunts. "Mmmph."

I shift the phone from one ear to the other. "But, I am surprised you called back since you seemed to take issue with our store's prices, and my tone. I figured you weren't interested in buying anything."

"Well, after hearing those outrageous prices, I wasn't. And you're right. I didn't like your snotty tone. But my son just told me that he'll buy the purse of my choice for my birthday, since it's in a few days. And, because I really want the one I saw in your shop, I'm going to make an exception to patronize your store. So I'll let all that slickness slide this time..." I blink. *Oh this bitch really wants to see the other side of me.* "I'll take the beaded clutch. Be a dear and hold it for me? My son will be down there in an hour or so to pick it up."

"And what name would you like me to hold it under?"

"You can put it in his name," she says curtly. "His name is Desmond."

"Okay, I'll have it right here for him; all boxed and ready to go." She hangs up in my ear. *Rude bitch!*

Before I can go back over to the case to pull the clutch out to place it behind the counter, the phone rings, again, as two women walk through the door. I answer the phone, eyeing them.

"Paradise Boutique, how can I help you?"

"Did you get my message?" my mother asks, sounding a bit annoyed that I haven't returned her call. The truth is I wasn't in the mood this morning to have to listen to her whining or complaining about things that neither of us can change. And I'm really not in the mood now.

"Yes, I did," I tell her as another customer walks through the door. I take her in, then shift my eyes back to the two women over in the corner going through a sale rack.

"Well, why didn't you call me back?"

I frown. Take a deep breath. "Mom, I planned on calling you later today when I had time to talk. Is there something urgent going on?"

She huffs. "No, there's nothing urgent. I just thought it was strange that I called all three of my daughters, and the only who returned my call was *Persia*. And she couldn't wait to let me know how none of you like being around me. Is that true?"

I sigh. "Mom, please. Let's not do this now."

"So, it is true."

"Mom, don't put words in my mouth. I didn't say that."

"You don't have to. The three of you call your father almost every day, and I'm lucky if I get a call at least once a week without me being the one to initiate it."

I decide to graciously bow out of this conversation before it turns sour by quickly changing the subject. "Mom, we love you, okay? Now, tell me. How are you?"

Surprisingly, in the blink of an eye, she lets it go—*for now*. "I'm good. Your father and I are going down to Atlantic City for the weekend."

"Oh, that should be nice. When are y'all going?"

"Friday afternoon." I ask her where they'll be staying. "The Borgata," she tells me, excitedly. "We'll be back on Sunday evening."

"Nice. Well, have fun and win lots of money," I say, trying not to sound like I'm rushing her off the phone. But I am! "Mom, can I call you later? It's getting busy here." I keep my eyes locked on the customers.

"Hold on. Before you go I want to know if you and your sisters received your invitations to Pasha's wedding?"

I shake my head, wondering why she's asking *me* what she's already asked Persia, like she's going to get a different answer or something. "Mom, not to be rude, but I'm sure you've already ask Persia this? So why are you asking me the same question?"

She ignores the question as she always does. "Are you all going?"

"I don't know. I really haven't had time to discuss it with Persia and Porsha, yet. Why?"

"Because I'd like for us all to be seated at the same table, that's why. It's been a long time since we've all been out together at a family event."

"Well, it's not a big deal if we aren't at the same table as you and Daddy. I'm sure Pasha will sit us with some of our other cousins who aren't being allowed to bring dates."

"It's not personal."

"I didn't say it was. And I don't feel that it is. I'm only making a statement."

"Well, make sure you don't forget to RSVP."

Mmmph, the last time we RSVP'd to Pasha's wedding it ended up getting cancelled because she had been *allegedly* kidnapped by a bunch of thugs as she was walking to her car coming out of the mall. They beat her senseless, then dumped her in a park. Thank God that early morning jogger found her when she did. There's no telling what else might have happened to her. The crazy thing about that whole situation was that Pasha wouldn't cooperate with the police investigation, which we all thought was kind of strange. But, whatever! Her life, her reasons. She kept saying she couldn't remember anything, or that she just wanted to put the whole ordeal behind her. And she refused to talk about it with her own grandmother, or even Felecia, who she's very close to. It was all very bizarre. Persia, with her overactive imagination, seems to think there's a whole lot more to the story than meets the eye. But, I guess no one will ever know what really happened now. I'm just glad she's alright. After the murders of her mother and father, the last thing Pasha's grandmother needed was another tragedy.

It dawns on me that I haven't spoken to her in months; that I haven't even had a chance to see the baby since his birth. We may not be as close as we once were, but we still have love for each other. I decide to give her a call one day this week to meet for lunch, or maybe I'll stop down at the shop and drop off an early birthday gift for her son since he'll be turning one soon.

"The wedding isn't until August. It's the end of March, Mom. We still have time to RSVP." Why she sent out her invitations so early is beyond me, but what do I care? Not my wedding.

"I know, but still. I want to make sure you girls are going to be there. Your Aunt Harriet really wants to see y'all."

"Okay. Like I said, I haven't really had a chance to look at the invitation, yet. But I'm sure we'll most likely be there. If not, we'll send a gift."

"Well—"

"Mom, look, I gotta go. I'll call you later."

"Okay, then. Talk to you later. Love you."

"I love you, too." I hang up, walking over to the case to get the clutch, then putting it behind the counter. I go back over to help two of the four women in the store with picking out scarves and some accessories. When they've finished selecting their items, they follow me back to the register. I ring up their purchases separately, charging their respective credit cards, then hand them both copies of their receipts.

As I'm handing them their shopping bags, the door opens. And in walks a tall, beautiful dark-skinned man wearing designer shades, looking like he stepped off the cover of a magazine. He fills the store with his masculinity and the crisp, intoxicating scent of his cologne. My pussy immediately tingles, alerting me that this man is fuckable on the spot.

I eye him as he makes his way over to the counter. I smile at him. "Hi, welcome to Paradise Boutique. Can I help you find something?"

"Nah," he says in his thick accent. *It's not a New York accent*, I think, trying to figure out where he's from. *And it's not Caribbean.*

And it's definitely not a Southern drawl. Mmmm. "I'm here to pick up some kind of pocketbook for my moms."

Connecticut, I bet. "Oh, yes, you mean the clutch," I say, allowing my eyes to travel the length of his sexy-ass body. I can tell he's hiding a chiseled, rock-hard chest and abs underneath his Ed Hardy thermal. The two customers leaving the shop admire him as well. *Mmmph, mmmph…I'd like to fuck him real quick in the back.* I pull the purse from out of the storage drawer. "You must be Desmond."

He nods. "Yeah, that's me."

"How will you be paying for this?" I ask, hoping he says with a credit card so that I can request to see his ID. There's something about him that has sparked my curiosity. And he hasn't even said more than twenty words to me. I stare into his intense brown eyes when I ask this, then gaze at his juicy lips. My clit starts to throb.

"Cash," he says, dashing any hopes of learning where he lives without flat-out asking him. I watch as he pulls out a thick knot of bills. "How much?" I tell him the price, ringing up his purchase. He peels twenty one-hundred dollar bills from his roll, then hands them to me. "Don't worry about the change, beautiful."

Beautiful? *Is this fine motherfucker flirting with me?*

Girl, get over yourself. He's only being friendly. He probably calls every woman he comes into contact with that. I tilt my head, take him in as I hand him his change, insisting he take it. "That's kind of you, but I'd prefer you…"

"How much is the brown bag?" one of the women who walked in earlier asks as she walks up to the counter.

"Oh, that bag's fifteen-hundred dollars."

"Whew, that's alright. What about the smaller bag?" I tell her it's six-hundred. She decides she wants it; asks if I accept American Express. I tell her we do. Then bring my focus back to the hunk of chocolate in front of me as I wrap the clutch and slide it into its silk bag, then put it in a box along with his five dollars. Girl-friend asks me another question about another bag and right now I wish her ass would walk up out of here, or shut the fuck up.

"Give me a sec. I'll be right over to get it out of the case for you as soon as I finish up with this customer."

The dark-chocolate man standing in front of me grins at me. There's something alluringly sexy in his crooked grin that makes me want to forget I'm a lady, and fuck him right up on top of this counter for all to see. For a fleeting moment, I forget I am in my store and imagine him making love to my cunt and my clit and my erect nipples with his tongue. Imagine feeding him my juices, riding his dick, then sucking him off until he shoots his hot load down into my throat. I imagine all of this, forgetting I have other customers in the store. I blink back the images. Bring my focus back to the mystery man in front of me. He is staring at me. I look directly into his eyes and a shiver passes through me.

I frown, raising my brow. "What. Why are you looking at me like that? Is there something wrong?"

He shakes his head, pulling a card out of the holder. He studies it. "Nah, I'm chillin', takin' everything in. So, you own this spot?"

I nod, putting the box into a shopping bag, then handing it to him. "Yes, I do. How'd you know that?"

"Call it a hunch." He grins, eyeing me. "My moms had some real choice words for you, but I'ma have'ta tell her you're noth-ing like she said."

I laugh. "What, she said I was a real bitch on the phone?"

He laughs with me. "Yeah, sumthin' like that."

I shrug, removing a strand of hair from my face. I place it behind my ear. "I can be when it's called for."

He rests his forearms on the counter, then leans in toward me. "Well, between you and me, I love my moms to death, but she has a way of bringin' it out of the best of 'em. Don't tell her I told you that."

I smile. "I bet she does. Don't worry. Your secret is safe with me."

He smiles back at me. "Oh, word? What else you like to keep safe?"

I knew it! This nigga is flirting with me.

"I don't kiss and tell," I flirt back, tilting my head and running my fingers through my hair.

"I like the sound of that."

Our eyes stay locked on each other's. There's definitely chemistry between the two of us. I can tell he feels it, too. But, before I allow myself to get caught up in the moment, reality sets in that I am running a business; not a pick-up spot. I shift my body language, and become all business again. "Well, thanks for shopping at Paradise Boutique. We appreciate your business. I hope your mother enjoys her purchase."

He catches the hint, smiling. "I'm sure she will. Look, I'ma let you get back to handlin' ya business. I'll be back through to check out the rest of your *goods*." He says this with innuendo dripping from his lips.

I smile, flirtatiously. "And I'll be here when you do."

"Cool-cool. You got a name, beautiful?"

I grab the keys to the glass case, then walk from around the counter. "If you happen to come back through, I'll tell you what it is then. If not"—I shrug—"you'll never know."

He grins. "Oh, aiight, I see how you doin' it." He glances down at the card in his hand. "It's all good, though. I'll just call you Paradise."

I smile. "Well then, welcome to Paradise; where all of your desires are fulfilled."

He laughs. "Damn, I like the sound of that."

"I'm sure you do."

"I'll definitely be back to check for ya real name."

"We'll see," I say, glancing over my shoulder. "You know where to find me. Again, thanks for shopping at Paradise."

His smile widens. "No doubt."

I watch as he walks toward the door, imagining him naked and sweaty, his dick buried deep in my pussy. For some reason, I decide not to mention him to Persia and Porsha. *Shit, there's nothing to tell*, I think, walking over to unlock the handbag case, knowing if opportunity presents itself, I am going to sample what his fine-ass has to offer, and if it's good, I'll fuck the skin off his dick!

"I want to take you home and fuck the shit out of you," I whisper into the ear of the deliciously dark stallion seated to the left of me. It's Saturday night and Paris, Porsha and I are at the Key Club in Newark—a restaurant, bar and lounge—popping and swinging our hips to DJ Qua's live broadcast as he spins the house mixes and makes the party rock. Paris and Porsha are somewhere on the dance floor sweating it out. Dark Stallion and I are at the bar continuing our off-and-on flirting. We'd danced a few times throughout the night and I had the pleasure of rubbing up against his body some, pressing my ass up against the center of his crotch; just enough to awaken his loins. And we've exchanged a few pleasantries in between. Never one to sweat a man, I've kept my eye on him for most of the night from afar. Watched how he flirted with his eyes and body, on and off the dance floor. I've seen how he moves on the dance floor, now I want to *feel* how he moves in the sheets. We've locked eyes every so often, flashing quick smiles, a slight nod, even a wink. Yet, neither of us has made a move. Still, I've patiently lied in wait, waiting for the right time to strike, like now—when he's at the bar, sweaty and alone, tossing back his sixth Remy Martin on ice. And now that time is winding down, it's time to strike. And go in for the kill. He chokes on his drink, coughing. "Oooh, Daddy, don't get all choked up on my account. You okay?"

"Yeah," he says, covering his mouth as he coughs again. "You caught me off-guard." What else is new? Most men can't handle a sexually dominant woman. They either get scared off, start to feel inadequate, or both. He lets out a nervous laugh. "I see you get right to the point."

"I'm a grown woman," I tell him, eyeing him seductively. I pause, drinking the remainder of my ten-dollar drink. "I don't have time for games. I know what I want, and I go after it."

"I like that in a woman," he offers, taking another sip of his drink. "Now what is it you want again?" He grins.

I tilt my head. "You heard me the first time."

"Yeah, I did. But I wanna hear it again."

I lean into his ear. Repeat myself, slowly. "I. Want. To. Fuck. You." I step back, waiting for his response.

"You have a man?"

I slowly shake my head. "Nope. And I'm not looking for one."

He grins, nodding his head. "I hear that. So tell me. What exactly are you looking for?"

"Besides a hard dick," I tell him, leaning in to him to minimize who else hears the conversation, "a man who can keep up with me. I'm a real freak, Daddy. I love to suck, swallow, lick balls and eat a man's ass, and be fucked all night. And, right now, I want some hard black dick in my life. Is that you?"

He grins, locking his gaze onto my perky tits. He tells me it could be him as he takes the rest of me in. I position myself so that he can see the meaty hump of my ass. I place a hand up on my hip, profiling. His smile widens as he opens and closes his legs. I glance down at his lap, then discreetly scoot over closer to him and cut my eyes around the bar area. I am glad we are sitting on the far end of the bar, and the music is loud enough to drown out what we're saying, but not so loud that I need to scream in his ear for him to hear me. When I am certain no one will notice what I am about to do, I slide my hand between his legs. I feel for his dick over the fabric of his pants. Knead it when I do. It's not as thick as I'd like it to be. But it's long and extra hard. He finishes his drink, tossing it back in one big gulp. "I wanna feel this long dick in the back of my throat."

"Oh, word? You think you can handle that?"

"The question is do you think *you* can handle it?"

He smiles. "Don't let the reserved, preppy look fool you," he says, raising his glass to the bartender when he catches his eye. "I'm a real freak, too, baby; down for whatever," he tells me, eyeing me.

"Uh-oh, I've heard that before," I say teasingly. He tells me he aims to please a woman as long as she's willing to return the favor. I discreetly continue stroking his dick. He tells me I've gotten him horny. I tell him I stay horny. "Mmmm, is that so? What do you like to get into with a woman? What do you fantasize about?"

"I love sloppily eating pussy while I'm getting my big dick slobbered on. I dig women who squirt, swallow cum, or allow me to creampie them." *Oooh, this nasty nigga likes going in raw,* I think, as my lips curve upward into wicked grin. A wave of heat courses through me at the thought of him pumping his cream into my hot pussy, then eating it out as I squeeze it out into his mouth. "Just some things I either would like or do like to do. I'm also into masturbating while I'm being watched, and mutual masturbation. And I dig toys, props and role play."

My grin widens. "Then tonight's your lucky night." He tells me he also has a thing for a woman with big nipples, a woman who loves sucking dick, loves to come. "So do you wanna come home with me? Or maybe go back to your place, then get down to the business of pleasing each other?" The bartender walks over to our side of the bar. Dark Stallion tells him to refill his drink, asks me what I'd like. I tell him three Big Apples, one of their specialty drinks—a mixture of Grey Goose, a splash of Sour with a sliced green apple. I tell him I'll pay for this 'round. He gives me a confused look.

"Nah, I got this, baby. But, uh, you're gonna drink *three* of them? Whew, I guess you're no lightweight."

"No, these are for..."

"Girl, there you are," Porsha says, walking up to us as if on cue. Dark Stallion looks at her, then me. "Yes, we're related," she says to him, smiling. "And you are?"

"In heaven," he says, smiling. "Whew, twins. The two of you are beauties."

"And we're good in bed, too," I tell him seductively, licking my lips. I keep my hand on his dick. I squeeze for emphasis. "But we're not twins."

He tilts his head, taking in the both of us. "You're not. Damn, y'all look so much alike. The two of you are some real beauties."

I grin, then lean into his ear. "And we have some real good pussy, too."

"So what you saying? The two of you wanna get it in with me?"

I shake my head, eyeing Paris as she is walking over from the other side of the club. "No, the *three* of us do."

"Three of you?"

"Yes," I say as Paris approaches us. "The three"—I point at Paris, Porsha and myself—"of us."

Paris huffs. "Ugh, I've been looking for the two of..." She pauses, looking over at Dark Stallion. He's staring at the three of us in awe. She smiles at him.

"Ohhhhh, shit..."

"That's right, triplets," I say, rubbing and squeezing his dick. "And, tonight, you're about to get triple the pleasure. That's unless you don't think you can handle all three of us."

He rubs his chin. "I've had threesomes, and I've done a few trains in my day. But, I've never been approached by a beautiful woman to fuck her and her sisters, triplets at that."

Porsha smiles. "Don't be scurred. We'll go easy on you."

He laughs. "Nah, I think I can handle it." He looks at me as I'm massaging his hard dick. "What you think?"

"I think you are nice, hard and *more* than ready."

The bartender returns with our drinks. Paris, Porsha and I lift our glasses, greedily eyeing the fresh catch I've reeled in for the night. Dark Stallion has no idea what he's about to experience. The three of us smile at him, then to ourselves, as he raises his glass, licking his lips.

"To triple pleasure."

"To triple pleasure," the three of us say in unison, clicking our glasses to his. "And three times the fun!"

Passion
CHAPTER SIX

"Fuck me," Persia moans desperately in Dark Stallion's ear. "Oooooh, yes, fuck me hard!" She digs her nails into his hairy ass.

I am kissing the back of his neck, his shoulders, running my tongue along the seam of his muscular back. His salty skin excites my tongue. He is pounding Persia's cunt, long and hard while watching Pleasure…I mean, Paris, roll her mini-vibrator over her clit, then slip it into her pussy. Legs wide open. Her beautiful cunt lips glisten, beckoning sweet kisses from Dark Stallion's thick, full lips.

"You like looking at my sister's pretty, brown pussy?" I ask him, nibbling on his ear, his neck, trailing my fingertips along the muscles of his back. I take in his hairy ass as he pumps his long licorice stick into Persia, scraping the bottom of her well. I want to suck him off, want to taste his cream-coated cock slathered by my sister's cunt juices.

He grunts. "Aaaaah, shit, y'all some sexy bitches…"

"Oh my pussy's so wet," Paris moans, pinching her left nipple and pulling in her bottom lip as she lets go of her vibrator. Its end pokes out of her slit, buzzing away as she pushes a vibrating butt plug into her asshole. "Aaaaaah…oooooooooh…"

Dark Stallion remains transfixed on the sight before him. Paris gives him a show of seduction, enticing him, teasing him as she pleases herself. He twists and snaps his hips into Persia. She lets out a piercing moan. "That's right, fuck her," I urge, slipping two fingers into my own cunt. It greedily sucks them in, knuckles deep. "Fuck her deep..."

"Yeah, fuck her good, you sexy motherfucker," Paris says. "You wanna see my pussy squirt?"

"Aaah, shit yeah," he groans, twisting his face up. Sweat drips from his face onto Persia.

"Is that dick good, Sis?" Paris asks, eyeing him. "Is he making that pussy feel good?"

"Aaaah, yes...oooooh, yes...this dick is so good?"

"Put your fingers in my pussy," I say, climbing up on the bed beside them. I am on all fours, looking over my shoulder at him. Dark Stallion reaches over, slides two fingers in and finger-fucks me until my juices drip down his hand. "Feed my sister my juices," I tell him. He removes his fingers from my sticky center, then offers them to Persia. She sucks them. I can tell he is on the brink of erupting. The act itself—him feeding Persia my pussy juice—causes him to grunt. His breath escapes in trembling gasps. His eyes are rolling up in his head. "Nooooo, don't you come, yet. Pull your dick out and let me taste my sister's pussy."

"Aaah, shit, y'all some freaky-ass babes," he says, pulling his dick out. Persia shifts her body from beneath him so that I can slide underneath him. I take his condom-wrapped cock into my mouth, sucking off Persia's juices before pulling the condom off and taking his dick raw into my throat while cupping his balls. I suck him deep for several minutes, then switch with Persia. Dark Stallion rolls over on his back as Persia opens her mouth and runs the tip of his bulbous head against her tongue. He moans. She moans. Paris moans.

"Ohhhhhh, I coming," she says, thrashing about. Her body trembles. She squirts a stream of warm juices.

"Ooooh, yeah," I moan, watching as her juices continue spurting out, "Look at that nice, wet pussy. I am lying on the opposite side of him. Persia is on the right side, I am on his left. "You made my sister's pussy skeet," I whisper, kissing him on his lips. His fingers strum my clit in rapid motion, causing my hips to buck. He moans. I moan. "You like how she's sucking your dick?"

"Aaaah, yeah…fuck…y'all some real freaks, baby." Paris crawls over to us, then squats up over Dark Stallion's face. He looks up at her sweetness as she lowers it down onto his lips.

"Eat my pussy," she says to him, running her hands through her hair. It is messy and wild, like the three of us. I watch as his tongue and mouth pleasures her. Watch as Persia's mouth and tongue pleasures him. She effortless deep-throats him, her lips pressed against the base of his shaft, her nose in his pubic hair. He moans, burying his fingers deep into my own smoldering snatch.

"Oh, yes…finger my pussy, daddy…ohhhhh, ohhhhh, ohhhhh…"

He is slurping.

Persia is slurping.

He pinches his nipple with his free hand, moaning, grunting and groaning. I watch as Persia pulls his dick from out of her throat. It is coated with spit; wet and slippery. She sticks her tongue out, then licks the shaft in flat, long strokes.

Paris comes again, squirting and moaning. She soaks his face and mouth. He tries to gulp up as much as he can in between his own moans. Persia sucks the head of his dick, lovingly, then more forcefully, stroking his shaft in simultaneous motion. Head and hands in sync, coaxing a nut out of it.

"Aaaa, fuck…you a real greedy, dick-suckin' freak, aren't you? You ready to catch this nut?"

"Mmmm," she moans, noddin' her head. "MmmhmmMmmm-hmmmm…"

I reach over and grab her by the back of the neck, pushing her down on his cock. "Go all the way down on it." She gags. Extends her tongue, then buries him back into her throat.

"That's right, girl, work his dick over," Paris says, cheering her on.

"Aaaah, fuck…"

"Go 'head, Sis," I root, pinching his left nipple. Paris is hovering over him, licking the right nipple. Persia's loud moans are muffled by a mouthful of hard dick.

"Aaaah, shit, I'm gettin' ready to come…uhhhh…"

Paris and I scurry toward his throbbing cock, slipping a hand between our legs, humping our horny pussies down on them as we eagerly wag our tongues for our hot creamy treat. Dark Stallion has a hand on both of our asses, slapping them.

Persia rapidly strokes his cock, slipping a finger into his ass while Paris and I flick our tongues around his head. My cunt tightens in anticipation. He lets out a loud grunt then, in an instant, shoots out thick, creamy cum. The three of us take turns sucking his dick. Paris and I lick the sides of his shaft, while Persia sucks his balls. The three of us twirl our tongues all around his dick and balls, then lick up his nut before shifting our bodies and offering him our tongues. He kisses all three of us.

He closes his eyes, smiling. "Daaaaaamn, that was good."

"Oh, nooooo," we say in unison.

"The party's just getting started," Persia adds.

He pops his eyes open in shock. "Y'all wanna go another round?"

"Of course we do," Persia tells him. "We never get tired of fucking." Paris and I lick our lips. "You want pussy or ass? What you want first, Daddy?"

He grins. "All the above," he says, shaking his head, grinning. "But, I'm gonna need a minute to rest."

Persia gets up off the bed, walking into the bathroom. "There is no time for rest," Paris whispers into his ear as I take his dick back into my mouth. "Our pussies need attention now."

Persia comes back over to the bed and hands him two pills. He looks at her, confused. "It's Viagra. Take two; it'll keep your cock hard until we are done fucking you."

"Oh, damn," he says, lifting up on his forearm. He takes the pills. "Y'all don't mess around, huh? I probably only need one of these," he says, swallowing one and handing her the other. I am slowly milking his dick back to life with my mouth, lips, and tongue.

She grins, reaching for another condom from off the night-stand. "I told you I wanted to fuck the shit out of you." I remove my mouth when he is rigid and ready. My pussy constricts as Persia rolls the condom down on his dick. "And *we* plan on fucking you nonstop." I climb up over him, lift my hips, while Persia guides his dick into the back of my slit. I moan as I inch down on him. Persia slaps my ass. "Now, ride this nigga down into the mattress."

A few nights later, we're in our media room down in the basement, drinking Moscato and listening to CDs. Tyrese's "On Top of Me" is playing low in the background. Persia is stretched out on one end of the leather sofa, Paris is sitting on the opposite end with her feet propped up on the leather cocktail ottoman, and I am sitting on the floor Indian-style, facing them. When we're not working, traveling, or running errands, this is what we like to do. Sit and chill—listen to music and get caught up.

"Damn, I'd love to have Tyrese on top of me right about now," Persia says, swaying to the music. She starts singing her own version of the lyrics. "Boy, I want youuuu on top...of...me...I got what ya dick needs...climb on up...on top of me...ride this pussy, nigga..."

Paris laughs. "Girl, shut that howling up. You're making my ears bleed with all that screeching and shit."

She sucks her teeth. "Whatever. You're such a hater."

"Hate on this," Paris says, tossing two throw pillows at her. She ducks, swatting them away.

"You think Tyrese has a big dick?" I ask.

"Who cares?" Persia states, twisting her lips up. "That man can have a dick the size of a half-bitten Snickers bar as far as I'm concerned. As long as he eats pussy like a champion and is loaded with hot, gooey nuts, he can still get it."

"Mmmm," I practically purr, taking a sip of my drink. "I'll give it to him. He's sexy as hell. But, he doesn't look like he can bring it in the sheets."

Persia gives me an incredulous look. "Are you serious? He doesn't look like he can bring it? Oh, that nigga's bringing it and then some. Trust and believe."

"Girl, fuck the sheets," Paris snaps. "He can be as stiff as a corpse for all I care. I'll ride down on that nigga's face and fuck the shit out of his tongue, okay?"

I laugh.

"Ummm, speaking of big dick," Persia says, grinning. "Damon wants to see us. He's coming to town for some kind of training next week. I told y'all we'd be hearing from his freaky-ass again."

Damon's this stocky, brown-skinned IT manager from Boston we fuck from time-to-time when he's in town on business. He's a bit nerdy, but a whole lot of freaky. And, although his dick game is on point, he's someone I don't particularly enjoy freaking with. But, Paris and Persia do. So I'll indulge him.

Paris smiles. "Whew, that nigga has one big, juicy dick."

"Mmmmph," I grunt, twisting my lips up. I glance over at Persia.

"Oh, girl, please," she says, taking a sip from her drink, "grunt if you want. Taking Damon's ass makes my pussy extra wet. I love it when he backs that tight, muscled-ass up on my rubber dick. He fucks so much better after *he's* been fucked down real good."

Paris laughs and coughs, almost choking on her drink. "Girl, your ass is stupid. But, uh, that nigga takes dick almost better than you."

"And I enjoy giving it to him," Persia says, laughing with her.

"I'm sorry," I say, frowning at the both of them. "But I can't stand watching all that hard-bodied man let you fuck him in his ass with a strap-on like that. It's sinful and plain ole nasty."

"Nasty hell," Persia scoffs. "There's nothing nasty about a man wanting ass play."

I blink. "Ass play, my ass. Ass play is licking and fingering his hole, massaging his prostrate, not ramming a dick deep in it. No, what that nigga does is...ugh." I shake my head, deciding to let it go. This is one of those situations she and I will never see eye-to-eye on. "Forget it. This is one thing you and I will have to agree to disagree on."

"Answer me this," she says, sitting up in her seat. "Does it get your pussy nice and hot watching me bust his ass out the frame?"

Now, believe me when I tell you, I consider myself extremely liberal and open-minded. But, uh...there's something suspect about a man always wanting a dick up in his ass. I don't care if it is attached to a woman. I feel a man wanting to be fucked in the ass—*all* the time, is trying to tell you something. Now, don't get me wrong. Like I said, I'm all for massaging a man's P-spot—with a finger, even a mini-vibrator, while he's getting his dick sucked or fucking one of us. But, uh, strapping up and running a big-ass dick in his ass is a bit too extra for me. I don't care what you say. A man wanting anything more than two-to-three inches inserted into his ass is very suspect to me. He either fantasizes about being with another man, or the nigga is an undercover, closeted case, if you ask me. But, hey, it's his ass, his desires. So what I care?

"No," I state, shaking my head. "It disgusts me. Watching Paris play in her pussy while I suck the skin off his big-ass dick is what gets me off." I glance over at Paris. "Speaking of which. When's the last time you sucked his dick?"

"Girl, you know I've never sucked his dick. I might have licked around his balls a few times or tongued him in the ass to get him ready for Persia. But I've always left the dick sucking to you."

"Mmmph. Well, I think it's time you wet him up, too." I laugh. "I'm almost embarrassed to say this, but I can't even front. That dick does taste damn good."

"And tell the truth," Persia says, eyeing me over the rim of her glass, "isn't the nut creamier when his ass is stuffed with a dildo?"

Paris and I crack the hell up. "Now you reaching, boo. I ain't saying all that. Anyway, Paris you need to wrap them made-for-dick-sucking lips around his and taste for yourself."

"No, thank you. I'll leave that all for you. I'd rather watch."

I laugh. "Oh, please. Drop down on your knees and join in. We all know you one dick-sucking ho on the low."

"Oh, hooker, I know you're not talking," she says, eyeing me and laughing, "the way you like slurping down a hot nut. You got some nerve. Your ass is the East Coast dick-gulping champion."

I laugh. "Yeah, I like to pop a few back every now and then. Your point?"

"The point is we're three fly, freaky bitches," Persia interjects, raising her drink, "turning niggas out like there's no tomorrow." We raise our drinks, clink our glasses.

"To this goody-goody," I say.

"Dipped in crack, rolled in heroin," Persia adds.

Paris jumps up from her seat, starts patting her crotch area, shaking and jerking her body. Paris is a lot more fun when she's tossed back a few drinks. "Got the niggas strung out, aching for another hit. Wishing for another injection of this hot pussy juice."

Persia and I laugh as she drops down, bounces and rocks on her heels, holding her glass up in the air, not spilling a drop of her drink.

Persia waves her on. "Girl, your ass is a damn mess. If Mom were a fly on the wall she'd lose her damn mind. Speaking of her, she called me today and wants to know if we're going to Pasha's wedding in August."

"I know," Paris and I say at the same time. "She called us, too."

"I figured she did. What'd y'all tell her?"

"Probably the same thing you did," I say, taking a sip of my drink. "I told her we hadn't really talked about it. I mean she already knows we don't do anything without discussing it with each other, first."

"I told her practically the same thing," Paris mentions.

"I went down to the salon the other day to see Pasha," Persia says, pouring another drink. "But she wasn't in. Ghetto-ass Felecia was there, though, wearing this real cute blunt-cut, burgundy wig."

"Popping her gum as usual, right?" Paris asks, reaching for the bottle, then filling her goblet to the rim. Felecia is also a cousin of ours.

My BlackBerry pings, letting me know I have a new text message. I pick it up off the coffee table, glancing at the screen. It's a text message from Irwin, six-three, two-hundred pounds of milk chocolate man meat with an extra-thick, curved, eight-inch dick that hits every angle of the pussy. He hits the spot every time.

I grin, reading his text message. "Guess who hit me up wanting to know if he can come through for a little role-playing?" I ask, glancing up from the screen. I don't wait for them to ask. "Irwin."

"Do tell," Paris states, walking back over to the sofa and plopping down. "Oooh, he has some good dick, too."

"What kind of role-play does he have in mind this time?" Persia wants to know.

"He wants us to pretend we're strippers so he can make it rain on us."

"And then what?"

"And then he wants to fuck the shit out of all three of us."

"Well, shit. Tell him to bring his ass on," Persia says, spreading her legs. "Let that nigga know we got all the pussy he needs to make it rain."

I laugh, texting him back what she said. A minute later, he texts back: AND I HAVE ALL THE DICK Y'ALL NEED. LET'S MAKE IT HAPPEN. I'LL BE IN TOWN 1ST WEEK IN MAY.

I tell them what he says, texting him back to let him know we'll be more than happy to make it happen. I toss my phone up on the sofa. "So what we gonna do about Pasha's wedding? Y'all want to go, or send her a gift instead?"

"It doesn't really matter to me," Paris says, waving her hand dismissively. "But it would be nice to see all the family together."

I agree, nodding. "True. Mom says Aunt Harriett is always asking about us."

Paris shakes her head, laughing. "Yeah, I know. Probably so she can try to get us up in church with her so the pastor can lay hands on us. I can hear her now, telling the congregation that she has three heathen nieces in need of prayer."

"Oh, please," Persia says, sucking her teeth. "The only one she needs to get hands laid on is Pasha's ass. I don't care what anyone says, Pasha got some shit with her, too. *Okay?* Hell, she's marrying a damn drug dealer, for God's sake." She pauses, pursing her lips. "You know. We need to call Felecia and invite her out for dinner so we can pump her gossiping-ass up with drinks, then get her to spill the dirt. You know she always has her nosey-ass posted up on Facebook and BlackPlanet, so I know she knows something."

I laugh. "Yeah, you're probably right." I reach for my phone. "I'm gonna text her right now."

"Tell her we can either meet up for drinks and dinner, or she can come here."

"No, tell her to come here," Paris suggests. "That way we can talk more freely."

Persia agrees. "Good point." She pours herself another drink. The three of us get lost in Eric Roberson's vibe the minute his song "Dealing" starts playing. I lay my head back and close my eyes. I'm not sure where Persia and Paris mentally slip off to, but I imagine candles lit and my pussy being eaten.

Pain

CHAPTER EIGHT

"Come kiss my pussy," I say in a throaty whisper, spreading open my legs. From soft gentle kisses to deep, tongue-probing French-kissing, I love the feel of a man's tongue all up on it and in it. Damon walks over to me, kneels down between my legs and does what he is told, using his mouth and tongue to stimulate all the sensitive areas of my pussy and clit, circling his tongue all over and around it. We are in the Fuck 'Em Down room, decorated in red and black. This is our anything goes room. There is a 4-Point Sling Stand in the far left corner of the room, and a doggy-style sex machine—which can fuck you in the ass or pussy, with a waist bar in the right corner. Over on the other side of the room is a black leather sex swing.

Damon lays his tongue flat against my clit, then flaps it up and down, dragging it along the front and back of my sticky slit. I moan. "Mmmmm, yeah...just like that...Ohhhh, yesssssss...eat my pussy, you nasty fuck...mmmph...you like having a mouthful of pussy?"

He grunts, nodding his head. He tries to talk with his mouth full, but his words come out garbled. I playfully smack him. "Don't talk. Eat. Lick. And stick. Uhhhhhhh...oooooooh..." He sticks his tongue deep into my hole, then jabs it. My pussy grabs at his tongue, pulls it in deeper.

"You ready for Mommy to fuck you deep in that hairy ass?"

He grunts.

"Yeah, I know you want Mommy to take that sweet, manly ass. I'm gonna fuck you real good; okay, baby?"

He nods his head, grunting and groaning while keeping his mouth clamped over my pussy, his tongue expertly zig-zagging all around it. Hearing what I am going to do to him causes him to increase his suction on my pussy. He is turned on by the idea of being penetrated. A sexual taboo he secretly yearns.

Being able to fuck him (or any man) into submission moistens my pussy. From mild to wild, my cunt drips with delicious anticipation as I lure him into forbidden, sexual bliss. Naked and vulnerable, it excites me to be in control of his fantasies; to be the orchestrator of his deepest, darkest desires. To introduce him to a sexual side of himself he never knew existed; an unchartered, unexplored world of deliciously sweet pain.

I am not a sadomasochist. I am not a Dominatrix. I am Pain. Not because I enjoy inflicting intense physical pain. It is the pain of the unknown caused by edging a man to an orgasm, then denying him release; it is the torture of him not knowing when he will be allowed to release that brings him the greatest pain. And it is in that anguish that causes my pussy to swell and erupt into a gushing waterfall. Denial of release while being teased and tickled can be excruciating torture.

When I go into character, pretending to be what I am not, most of my encounters with men are mostly sensual. Although there are a few who insist, beg, for intense pain. And I happily oblige. But, even then, like tonight...I have my limits.

I do not always allow them to fuck me. Nor do they always expect to. But I will *fuck* them. Lovingly or rough and dirty, men have been fucking women—in more ways than one, since the beginning of time. So violating a man stimulates me. Forcing him to suck my big strap-on, having him bend over and spread open his cheeks so that I can stretch open his tight, virgin ass with my rubber cock excites me. He can whine and whimper and plead for mercy. But there is none. He will get what he so willingly has asked for, and then…when I have torn his asshole out the frame, I will—if I am feeling generous—invite him into the folds of my wet lips and soothingly fuck him, give him the illusion that he is still the powerful man he has always thought himself to be. But when I look into his eyes, he knows and I know that the *real* power lies in me. The power to possess his dick, the power to control his pleasures, the power to grab him by the balls and bring him to his knees with one swift yank all placed in my hands. Yes, I am the commander of his sexual fate.

What man would turn down the opportunity to fuck a beautiful woman, knowing he could have her in anyway his heart desired? Knowing that the possibilities were endless? Not many. So imagine that same man having the chance of fucking three beautiful women—triplets with voracious sexual appetites, at the same time. Imagine him having the good fortune of having access to all the pussy his dick and mouth craves. And, with my sisters and me, he can.

However, unlike Porsha and Paris—who both like slow, sweet, seductive sex, sometimes…hell, *most* times, I like it rough and dirty. Shit, sometimes a woman simply wants to be *fucked*—deep, hard and fast; just long, hot, sweaty, ass-slapping, pussy-pounding sex. That's me. Porsha and Paris can have all of that sensual, romantic, love making, mushy shit. Give me a good, old-fashioned pussy beat down! Fuck me until my pussy swells and bruises and aches. Choke the shit out of me, yank and pull my hair, call me *bitch*, *whore*, and *slut*—in the bedroom, that is. Toss me around the room; bite me on the ass. Give it to me kinky, nasty and freaky…shit!

"Enough of eating my pussy," I say, pushing his head away from my treasure. "Go and prepare yourself for what you've come here for." He gets up and I tell him to kiss me. To feed me his cum-slickened tongue. Allow me to savor my juices from off his lips. He does, and when I have sucked his tongue clean, I dismiss him.

He goes into the bathroom to rinse, flush, and shower—an absolute must for any sex or anal play. While he's in the bathroom, I slip my hand down between my legs. Close my eyes. And play with my clit. I graze it lightly with the tip of my finger at first, then flick it. Tonight, I want to fuck and be fucked. And if Damon can withstand tonight's session without cumming all over himself before he is allowed to, he will be invited into my deep pussy, and urged to fuck me long and hard. If not, he will be sent on his way with a well-fucked ass, aching and pulsing.

Paris and Porsha walk into the room, naked. I pull my fingers from my cunt, slipping them into my mouth. *Mmmmm, my pussy tastes so good!*

"Where is he?" Porsha asks, sitting on the opposite side of the king-size bed.

"In the shower," I say, glancing over at the wall clock. "He should be coming out any minute."

"Good," she says, leaning back on a set of pillows. "Because I'm ready to get this show on the road. I can barely stomach seeing all that man getting fucked. It hurts my heart. Why can't he be a regular nigga who only loves his dick getting sucked and eating and fucking pussy without wanting to be fucked, too?"

"Ugh, get over it," I say. "You concern yourself about sucking his dick, and let me worry about his ass getting fucked."

"And I want this shit to be over with," Paris says, running her fingers through her hair. "I feel a damn headache coming on."

I roll my eyes and laugh. "Girl, whatever. You play your position and leave everything else to me and Porsha."

"Oh, goodie," she says sarcastically. "The greatest highlight of the evening will be watching Porsha gobble up his big cock."

Ugh, she's such a bitch sometimes. I watch her position herself down on her knees in front of the sex machine, lying over the waist bar. Her ass is hoisted up in the air, ready for penetration. With a stroke speed of zero to one-hundred-and-thirty strokes per minute she will be fucked mechanically, deep and slow at first, then in rapid strokes.

Damon will get on all fours and eat Porsha's pussy, then she will shift her body and position herself underneath him and suck his dick while I fuck him in his ass with my strap-on. He will keep his eyes fixed on Paris and watch her being banged in strong, steady motion. This is what he's asked for. This is what we shall give him.

Damon walks back into the room, naked. Beads of water cling to his sculpted chest, then slowly glide down his chocolate skin. His dick swings as he walks toward the bed. The three of us lick our lips at the sight of his beautiful body.

Porsha immediately goes into script. "Oooooh, I can't wait to taste that beautiful dick." She says this grinning, rubbing her hands together, ready to feast on his meat. Because the truth of the matter is—whether he likes it in the ass or not, the mother-fucker has one helluva dick.

He grins back, glancing over at Porsha, then Paris. "I've been thinking about this all day. Thoughts of the three of you keep me horny."

Damon gets off on being dominated by women. And he loves ass play. Something most women frown upon. But not us. Well, not Paris and me. We welcome it. Encourage it. Allow a man to experience prostrate pleasure, however he wants.

Porsha walks over to him. "You want Pain, Passion and Pleasure to please you?"

"Yes, baby, in every way possible."

"Then tonight is your lucky night." She kisses him lightly on the lips, then drops down in front of him. She licks his cock from tip to root, then back up again. His dick jerks against her tongue.

"Oh, shit," he moans, planting his hands on his narrow hips and tossing his head back. His eyes close to half-slits as he pulls in his bottom lip. "Suck that dick, baby."

I walk over to the unlocked closet with all of its customized shelves and drawers and pull out a dildo-ball gag—a leather ball gag with a black, thick, six-inch, rubber dildo attached to it. I decide to have him to use his mouth to literally fuck Porsha. He will control how he uses the dildo on her. But I will keep him from talking, pleading, for me to stop grinding into his guts. I decide there is no need for him to say shit. He will only be able to grunt and groan, but no words shall be spoken. Not at first, anyway.

As I strap the gag around Damon's mouth, Paris backs her ass up into the ribbed dildo attached to the thrust arm. Using the remote, she turns it on and it slowly pushes into her pussy and begins to slow stroke herself. It doesn't take long before she is rocking back and forth in sync to its thrusts, moaning.

Porsha lies on her back, legs spread apart, bent at the knees and plays with her clit. She gets herself slick and ready. Damon positions himself between her legs, then starts probing her pussy with the gag. She arches her back, grabbing him by the head. His beautifully muscled ass sticks out. I kiss and nibble on each cheek while he works Porsha's cunt over.

Drool gathers around the corners of my mouth from seeing his tight hole pucker. I stick my tongue in it, then lick it a few times before spitting in it. I don't know what it is about licking a man's ass, but…I love, love, love it!

It dawns on me that I've forgotten the lube. I walk back over to the closet and grab the Anal Balm, then remember Damon isn't a beginner and he doesn't need anything to numb his hole. I reach for the Pjur Body Glide instead; one of my favorites because it's nice and thick and very slick and never dries. Tonight, his ass will need all the lubricant it can get. He will be ass-fucked to no end. Then when I am done, I will straddle his cock and give him this sweet pussy as reward for submitting himself to me; for allowing me to capture every part of who he is as a man. I will not make him feel any less of a man than he was before he grabbed his ankles and allowed me to fuck him.

"Get that ass up in the air…" I slap his ass. Repeat myself. "…Get that ass up in the air like I told you…" He assumes the position, then arches his back. I smile, catching Porsha rolling her eyes. Paris moans. "Pull open that hairy ass." He reaches around and spreads his muscular ass cheeks, buries his face deeper in between Porsha's hips.

I grab my dildo at the base and beat it across his hole. He moans. "Yeah, you want me to fuck you, don't you? You little nasty motherfucker." I reach underneath him, grab his balls and squeeze them.

He moans.

"Oooooooh, shiiiiiit," Paris moans, "watching y'all has me so fucking horny."

I rub the shaft of the dildo across his hole. "You wanna grab Mommy's dick with that tight ass of yours?"

He nods. I press the tip to his hole, then slowly push in. He grunts; his head rapidly moving about between Porsha's thighs. She moans. The more I inch into him, the deeper he pushes his gag into Porsha. The more aggressive he gets with her pussy, the louder she moans. For someone who takes issue with a man getting fucked, she seems to be enjoying everything he's doing to her. As she always does. I glance over at Paris. Give her a look with my eyes, gesturing for her to look at Porsha's horny ass. She grins.

"Does...it...feel good, Passion?" she asks in between her own moans.

"Mmmm, ohhhh, yesssss..." Porsha coos. "Ooooh, he has my pussy on fire. I wanna feel his dick in me."

"You want him to fuck you with that fat, juicy dick?" Paris taunts, winding her hips and backing her ass up on the sex machine in back of her.

"You wanna fuck Passion?" I ask Damon. "You wanna feel how hot you got my sister's pussy?"

He grunts again, nodding his head. I reach under him. Feel how hard his dick is. Feel how sticky and wet it is from the pre-cum that oozes from its tip. My mouth waters with thoughts of licking it clean.

I have his ass pulled open as I remove the dildo. His hole is gaping. I smile. Tell him to keep probing Porsha's cunt with the gag as I force his legs wider apart, then slide my head beneath him and take his dick into my mouth. His nectar is sweet. I lap at the head of his dick, then swirl my tongue over it, then slide back from underneath of him when I have gotten the last drop. I walk over to the closet to get a condom from the large assortment we have and return with a Durex Love condom. Not only is it thin and very easy to roll on, it's long enough to handle all of his eight inches comfortably.

I hand him the condom, then remove the gag, tossing it across the room. He tears the wrapper open, pulls out the condom, then rolls it on. He grabs Porsha by the hips and pulls her down closer toward the edge of the bed. I step back as he pushes her legs back over her shoulders and eats her pussy a few more times, before he works his dick into her. He strokes her in deep, rapid thrusts for a few minutes, then pulls out.

I pinch and slap at my nipples. The stinging excites me. I look over at Paris. Her eyes are shut tight. She is so caught up in her mechanical fucking that she is no longer paying us any attention.

"Get on ya knees, baby," Damon tells Porsha. "I wanna hit this wet pussy from the back."

She rolls over, gets on all fours, then reaches around and pulls open her ass. Her pussy lips poke out, pouty, wet, and full. He enters her.

"Ohhhhhh, yes…ohhhhh, shit the dick feels so good… mmmm…"

Patiently, I wait until he gets into a nice groove, rocking Porsha's back out, then sidle up behind him. I lean into his ear. Nibble on his lobe. "You ready for Pain to fuck you, Daddy?"

"Ah, shit yeah…" He says, slapping Porsha on the ass. "Arch that back, baby. Ain't no need to run from this dick."

She cranes her neck. "Ain't nobody running from shit, nigga. Fuck me…oooh…aahh, shitgotdamnmuthafuck…"

"Yeah, baby, take that dick…mmmm, nice wet pussy…"

I slip my middle finger into his ass, finger him slowly, then slide my index finger in. His hole is still slippery and loose from earlier. I slide back in.

"Whose ass is this?" I ask.

"Uhhh, fuck…" he grunts, lustfully gazing over his shoulder at me. I repeat the question, this time alternately slapping each cheek while grinding into him. "Oh, shit…yours, baby."

"You want a *real* dick in you?" I ask, baiting him. Although I don't believe he does, one can never be so sure; especially if you let Porsha tell it. She is so damn stuck on believing any man wanting ass play is gay, or on the down low. Paris's eyes pop open. Persia snaps her neck in his direction, waiting and watching. His response, his body language will confirm her suspicions, or shoot them down.

He frowns, furrows his brows. "Fuck no. You know I don't get down with no shit like that."

I smile, pulling him into me by his neck, then lightly kiss him on the lips. I slip my tongue into his mouth, then pull back. I stroke him. He strokes Porsha. He moans. She moans.

"What's my name?" I ask him.

"Mmmph...Pleasure."

"No, nigga, wrong sister. What's..."—I slam my rubber dick in him; grind my hips into his—"my..."—I pull it out, leaving only the head in, tip-drilling him—"name?"

My pussy is leaking.

He grunts.

Porsha grunts.

Paris grunts.

I stretch and pull open his ass cheeks as far as they'll go. Watch my dildo glide in and out. Watch his tight hole slurp it in. I am so turned on by the sight. Oh how I love a man who submits every inch of himself to me. Sweat drips from my face, drops onto his back. I reach up under him, grab at his balls, then yank them. "What's my name, nigga?"

"Pain," he finally says, arching his back and clutching and clawing the sheets. "Aaaah, fuck, baby...ohhhh shit, baby...uhhh... you're hitting that spot." I continue my pace, deep stroking him. He bucks his hips into Porsha. I buck mine into him. Then pull my—well, not mine, but you know what I mean—dick out to the head, tip drill him again, then plunge back into his loosened man hole. He chants over and over how I'm hitting his spot. Porsha chants how he's hitting hers. The two of them are feeling the pressure building; his prostrate to her G-spot. I continue my pace. He continues his. I count my strokes. He counts his. I switch my rhythm. He switches his. He is focused on fucking the shit out of Porsha. I am determined to fuck the shit out of him.

Persia cranes her neck, looks back at him and me. A mixture of delightful pleasure and disgust etched on her face. She hates herself for loving this scene. "Aaaah, shit...oooh, the dick is good... beat my pussy up..."

I cut my eyes over at Paris who is now wide-eyed, looking up at us with her mouth slightly parted. She licks her lips.

"Tear...his...ass...up," she encourages in between groans of pleasure. She is clearly in her own zone. She has sped up the thrusts and the machine's arm is power-fucking her so fast it almost looks like steam is coming from out of her pussy. "Fuck... her...good, Damon...ooooh..."

She gasps as the machine's fucking-arm slams in and out of her. Her head thrashes from side to side. Her eyes flutter and roll back in her head. Her body shakes.

Damon grabs Porsha's hips, speeds his thrusts. "Oh shit...I wanna nut...oh fuuuuck...I feel it coming..."

"Nooooo," Porsha whines. "I wanna suck your dick first, then let you nut all over my face."

He pulls his dick out of her. I slowly pull the dildo out of him. We're all sweating and panting. He yanks the condom off as Porsha quickly hangs her head over the side of the bed. Damon stands over her and feeds her his cock. He leans forward, plays with her clit while I pull open his cheeks and slide back in. I grind my hips into him. He grinds his hips into Porsha's face. She has his dick all the way down in her throat, reaching up and massaging his balls. She lightly squeezes them.

"Ohhhh…shiiiit…ohhh fuck…"

"You like this dick in you?" I ask him, knowingly. But I ask anyway because I like hearing the answer. I slap him on his ass again. He grunts, pulls his cock out of Porsha's throat. She reaches between her legs and plays with herself. Damon's tongue hangs outta the side of his mouth. He is panting like a puppy in heat. I pull out again, slowly rotate my hips and slide back in. Repeat the process three more times, then slam back into him. Slow grind. Tip drill. Slam. Slow grind. Tip drill. Slam.

Damon shudders; grunts again. "Uh…uh…uh…aaaaah…ooooh, fuuuck…"

Two minutes later, without hands, lips, or tongue on his cock, he shoots his nut over Porsha's head; his cum splattering all over her stomach and titties. He smears his creamy dick over her lips. I watch on as she licks the head, then slips him deep into her mouth, sucking him back to life.

"Hello, Paradise Boutique?" I answer, folding a multicolored pile of designer tees.

"Wassup, Paradise? Can a brotha finally get your name?" the familiar voice asks. Against my will, I smile at the sound of his deep, sexy voice. "Or do I have to keep coming in droppin' paper?"

"Sir, who's speaking?" I ask, suppressing a giggle.

"Oh, here we go wit' this. I'm the tall, dark, handsome bruh who came in and copped two expensive-ass pocketbooks for my moms. Don't front like you don't remember me, ma."

"Mmmm, I don't recall any man with that description coming in here," I tease. "And we don't call them pocketbooks. They're handbags and clutches."

"Yeah, aiiiight, Paradise. Let you tell it. But, let me come through and refresh ya memory." The shop's door opens. I crane my neck over my shoulder to see who is walking in and almost drop the phone.

"Oh, you," I say, laughing.

He chuckles. "Yeah, okay. You remember me now?" He's casually dressed in a pair of designer jeans and a short-sleeved red Polo shirt with its large white emblem. He has a matching red Yankees-fitted with white lettering pulled down over his eyes. His hood swagger is making my pussy overheat.

"Well, yeah," I say nonchalantly, walking back over to the counter.

"Now I do. But you made a mistake and described yourself as handsome."*But your ass is F-I-N-E!* "That was a bit ambitious, don't you think?" I try to keep a straight face.

He laughs. "Yo, you got jokes, I see. Yeah, aiight. It's all good. I'll be ambitious."

I smirk. "And so you should. And, what's your name again?"

"Desmond. But, my peeps call me Dez. And yours?"

I grin. "I never told you my name, remember?"

He laughs. "Oh, damn. Right-right. So you gonna give it to me, or am I gonna have to keep comin' through until you do?"

I smile, flirtatiously. "I guess you'll have to keep *com*ing through."

"Yeah, aiight. I like the sound of that." He tells me is going to keep calling me Paradise until I tell him my name. The way he says it makes my pussy purr. *Lord, give me strength not to fuck this man right here in the middle of this store. Flush these whorish thoughts from my nasty-ass mind.* I smile to myself as he leans over onto the counter, his forearms resting on top, staring at me. "So what's good, *Paradise?* What you like to do for fun?"

I like to fuck! I eye him back. Take his presence in. Imagine him having a long, black dick—thick and veiny with a huge mush-room-head. Subconsciously, I slowly lick my lips, imagining they're his dick. My mouth *and* pussy start to water. I shake my lusty thoughts out of my head. "Why, is this an interview?"

He smiles. "Could be."

The phone rings as three customers walk in. "Saved by the bell," I say, grinning. I answer. It's a woman calling to see if we carry used Louis Vuitton bags. I tell her no. Tell her to call a consignment shop. She tells me that's what she thought this was. I hang up, shaking my head. I excuse myself, then walk over to where the three women are. I can feel his eyes on me, studying the sway of my hips, counting the number of times my ass bounces as I make my way over to them. I glance over my shoulder, catching him. He grins. I playfully roll my eyes. He watches as I help each woman select her items. Waits as I ring up their individual purchases, then smiles at me as they walk out the door.

"Now back to our conversation," he says, glancing at his watch. "Let's go chill somewhere. Grab a bite to eat and get better acquainted."

"And how do I know you won't take me somewhere and try to have your way with me?" I tease. Flirting with this man seems so natural. There's something about him that I find…intriguing. Yeah, that's it. He's piqued my curiosity. I want to see him naked and stretched out.

He laughs. "Baby, I'd never do anything you don't want me to. But, for now, I'm only interested in feeding you."

I admit. I'm starved. But, I'm not sure if my hunger pangs are for food or for this delicious hunk of man standing in front of me. *They're for both, bitch! Feed us!*

"I like the sound of that. Where would you like to go?"

He shrugs. "It's whatever. You tell me."

The store phone rings, again. I tell him to give me a minute as I pick up. It's Persia. "Paradise Boutique," I answer out of habit. I take my key and lock the register.

"You wanna meet up for lunch?"

"Well," I say, looking over at Mr. Sexy. He winks at me. "I have plans already."

"Plans with whom?" she asks, being her usual nosey self.

I cover the mouthpiece of the phone. "Give me one second, and I'll be ready to go."

"It's cool," he says. "I'll wait on you for as long as you need me to." Innuendo drips from his tone. I smile, placing the phone back up to my ear.

"Hello? Are you still there?"

"Yeah, I'm here," I say, walking to the back office.

"Well, I asked who you had plans with, then it sounded muffled."

"I was with a customer," I tell her, unlocking the safe, then placing the register key in. "Anyway, to answer your question, Miss Nosey-Ass, I'm meeting a business acquaintance out for lunch." The lie quickly rolls off my tongue without much thought. *She doesn't need to know anything about him*, I think, going into the bathroom to freshen up. Yes, I'm a grown woman capable of doing whatever I want, with whomever I want. Yet, as close as we are, I still feel the need to keep some things—like the sexy nigga waiting on me, from Persia—at least, for a while. I tell her my lunch date is with a young designer interested in having some of his one-of-a-kind designs in our boutique. She wants to know more. Wants to know where we're going to eat. I tell her I am unsure. That's the only truth to this whole conversation. I glance at the time. It's twelve-thirty. I tell her I have to get going. Tell her we'll talk when I get home tonight. Two minutes later, we hang up and I am walking back out to the front of the store with my handbag and keys.

He's standing in the same spot, waiting. He smiles when he sees me.

"Sorry about that. It was my sister."

"Ah, you good, ma. It's your world. I'm just tryna fit in."

I flash him a wide smile, pulling my shades down over my eyes. "Would you like for me to drive?" I ask as I place the BE BACK IN AN HOUR sign in the window on the door.

"Nah, baby, you wit' me. I got this. The only thing you gotta do is tell me where you wanna go." He disarms the alarm to his truck, then opens the door for me. He waits until I slide in, then shuts it. I'm impressed with his gentlemanly ways. I fasten my seatbelt. He climbs into the driver's side, turning the ignition. "It's me and you now, *Paradise*. Let's go eat." He pulls off.

I smile, resting my head back. "Yes, let's eat." *And the first chance I get I'm gonna be eating the nut out of that dick!*

"I've been meaning to ask you. How'd your meeting go the other day?" Persia asks Paris, taking a sip from her wineglass. We're having one of our usual nightcaps, unwinding from our day. Tonight's wine of choice is Belondrade y Lurton Rueda, a delicious Spanish white wine. Dwele is playing low in the background.

Paris makes a face, giving her a confused look. "What meeting?"

"Uh, hellllllllooooo. The meeting you had with some hot new designer who wants to sell some of his designs at the store."

She laughs. "Ohhh, that meeting. Girl, it went really well. I like really him."

"Okay, now I'm feeling left out," I say, tucking a leg underneath me. I take a sip of my wine, smacking my lips. "Mmmph, I can drink this all night." I am sitting on the sofa next to Paris. Persia is sitting in the chair across from us.

"I know," Paris agrees. "We'll end up being a bunch of drunken winos, messing with this bottle."

I laugh.

"Uh, excuse you," Persia says, laughing with me. "Speak for yourself. Now finish telling us about this designer."

Paris takes a large gulp of wine. "There's not much to tell. He's fresh out of F.I.T. with his MFA. And his designs are definitely edgy."

"Well, all I wanna know is," I say, hoisting my glass up. "Is he fuckable? Or is he a Tutti Frutti?"

She laughs. "Girl, I don't know. I wasn't looking at him like that."

I roll my eyes. "Girlfriend, you don't have to be looking at him like that. But you can still tell if he's someone we can slide down on the dick with, or if he's someone we'll be buying heels with."

She keeps laughing. "Girl, I'm not messing with you."

"Well, then. On another note," Persia says, abruptly changing the subject, "my pussy's twitching for some dick. Y'all feel like fucking tonight?" It's been almost a week since our sexapade with Damon. And like usual, Pesia has tossed back three glasses of wine and is ready for another round of dick.

Paris and I both say, "Sure."

"Who do you have in mind?" I ask, taking another slow sip from my glass. Aside from Damon, I wonder how many other men secretly seek *ass play* with women. And how many openly admit it.

"How about we invite Emerson over for some pussy? It's been a while since we've worked him over. Hopefully it'll prove my suspicions of him wrong." She picks up her cell and dials his number. When he doesn't answer, she leaves a message. "Hey, baby, it's Persia. There are three hot, horny, pussies here wanting to get fucked good tonight. Come through and feed us that big dick." She disconnects, then texts him. "If he doesn't call or text back in fifteen minutes or so, or isn't ringing this doorbell in thirty minutes, his number gets deleted."

"Mmmm, that's too bad," I say, closing my eyes and imagining sucking on his dick again. That nigga has some of the best dick cream I've tasted. I lick my lips. "I can sure use another round of that nut."

Paris laughs, knowingly. "I second that emotion."

An hour and a half goes by, we are on our second bottle of wine, and Emerson still hasn't called back. Nor has he responded to Persia's text.

"Mmmph," I grunt, glancing at my watch, "looks like we won't be hearing from Emerson tonight."

Paris agrees. "It sure looks that way, doesn't it? Come to think of it, this makes it the second time he's done this."

"No, try his third," Persia states, reaching for her cell. "Delete, delete, delete. His ass is officially cut from the team."

Paris and I watch her walk out of the room. I close my eyes when Will's "Full Course Meal" from his Sex Tape mix starts playing. And that's exactly what Emerson had. An entrée of perky tits, juicy asses and hot, wet pussies he could have any time he wanted. But, obviously it wasn't enough. Surprisingly, I'm disappointed. And I'm not exactly sure why. From the beginning, although I haven't been able to put my finger on it, I've always felt like there was something different about Emerson. Anytime he was fucking me, or I was sucking his dick, he always wanted to look into my eyes. He always kissed me longer than he would Persia or Paris. It always felt like he wanted to make love to *me*, not fuck me like he'd fuck my sisters. I never said anything, but I noticed it. I wonder if they noticed it, too. Then again, they could probably not care less.

"Greedy niggas always fuck up a good thing," I say, shaking my head.

"They sure do," Paris agrees, taking a sip from her wineglass. "But all well-traveled roads must eventually come to an end. And his has run its course straight into a dead end, good dick and all."

I nod, thoughtfully, but don't say anything. Truth is, I'm going to miss fucking him. He isn't only a good pussy eater with good dick. He knows how to be a passionate lover. I think. Remember the first time we fucked him.

We had him strapped to the bed, blindfolded and naked. His wrists and ankles tightly cinched in padded cuffs. Arms and legs stretched out wide. The thought of him wanting to be helpless and completely at our mercy, made my pussy pulsate, made it clench with need. A warm, sticky wetness seeped between my thighs from anticipation.

I grazed my lips over his skin, placing soft kisses along the curve of his neck, his shoulders, along the center of his chest while Persia lowered the smoothly waxed lips of her cunt to his mouth, then leaned forward on her arms as he nuzzled his nose into her hot, dripping pussy and suckled on her creamy essence.

His thick, rigid cock bounced freely. It's tip, leaking precum.

I licked my lips, catching the drool that gathered in the corners of my mouth as I took his scorching hot dick into my hand and stroked it, then slipped it into my hungry mouth. Paris watched from across the room. Her pussy splayed open by teasing fingers.

We taunted him, teased him; edged him to the brink of an orgasm. Each of us alternated feeding him our pussies, challenging him to use his senses to figure out which one of us mounted his face, his cock, next. We ground our hips against him, allowed him to savor the heat before lifting up, then switching positions. His mouth full of pussy, he moaned in pleasure. Groaned from the unexpected, twisted and jolted until he erupted spurts of hot, flowing lava.

"...I'm going to call that little sexy waiter from the Je's..."

I shift in my seat. Persia's voice slices into my thoughts. I look up and bring my attention back to her. She has her cell pressed up against her ear, holding the receipt he wrote his number on between her fingers.

Paris's eyes light up. "Girl, are you serious? Leave that boy alone."

"Leave him *alone*, hell. Let him answer and bring his ass over here. He's gonna go from manchild to man with three clicks of this pussy." She pats her crotch. "Then get turned the fuck out."

Paris shakes her head. "Persia, you know like I do that he is nowhere near ready for us."

"You don't know that. But, ready or not, that little mother-fucker was sexy as hell and looked like he had some good dick. And I want some of it, damn it. Now are you hookers with me?"

"Ooh, ooh, ooh," I say, raising my hand. "I am."

"Well, count me out of this one," Paris says as she takes a slow slip of her drink. Sometimes she can be such a party pooper. "I don't want anything to do with robbing that young boy of his innocence. But I'll sit back and watch the two of you turn him out."

Persia waves her on. "Girl, hush. There isn't anything inno-cent about his ass; trust me. You saw how he looked at us when... hello, is this Royce? Hey, baby boy, it's Persia. You waited on my sisters and me a few weeks ago...yes, the sexy- ass triplets...I see you remember..." She gives me and Paris one of those "see I told you" half-nods.

"This bitch is crazy," I say, laughing. She waves me on.

"Look...what are you doing now? Oh, really. Well, are you up for some wet, juicy pussy? Yes, now..."

Paris shakes her head. "Pour me another drink," she says to me, holding her glass out. "I can tell I'm gonna need to be lit the hell up for what y'all about to do to that poor boy."

I laugh. "Don't blame it on the alcohol, boo. If he comes through, he's coming as a willing participant."

"...Oh, and remember, you'll be fucking all three of us. So make sure you bring enough condoms for more than one round...

ohhhh, we shall see, big boy...Well, you just make sure you bring us a clean, hard dick." She gives him the address, then hangs up.

She grins, filling her glass with more wine. "Well, y'all freaky bitches, looks like we're about to get us some young, tender cock tonight."

"Hooker, what's this 'you'll be fucking all three of us' shit? I told you I wasn't fucking him so why'd you tell him that?"

"Because I know you'll be changing your mind the minute you see his naked ass stretched out on the bed."

Paris rolls her eyes. "Whatever."

I glance at my watch. It's almost eleven. "I guess I better go upstairs and wash my pussy out," I say, getting up and tossing the remainder of my drink back.

Paris gets up as well, laughing. "Yeah, please do. The last time your cat started leaking it smelled like rotted fish juice."

I laugh with her. "Heifer, please. That was the two-week old nut crusted up around your lips you kept picking at."

"Porsha, sweetie, kiss my ass." We are both laughing as we make our way out of the room, leaving Persia to finish off her drink while we get ready for our fuck of the night.

Passion

CHAPTER ELEVEN

His mocha skin atop Persia, Royce stretches her with his width, taps the bottom of her well with his length. I silently laugh to myself as her eyes roll up in the back of her head. As she squirms and arches her back, I am fully aware that the joke is now on her. He is surprisingly more endowed than any of us anticipated. Eleven-and-a-half inches of thick, curved, uncut cock. And this young stud is amazingly skilled at delivering every inch of it with deliberate purpose. I watch the deep dimples of his muscled ass as it tightens with each thrust.

He's nothing like the shy, awkward-acting guy who waited on us a few weeks ago. This is a young man who is used to servicing pussy, used to delivering the dick with precision. I wonder how many other women have foolishly mistaken and assumed he couldn't handle them because he was young.

"Ooooh…aaah…yes, fuck meeeee with that big-ass dick, baaaaaaby," Persia coos.

"Fuck her, lil' daddy," I encourage, slipping two fingers into my slit, then stirring my insides before pulling them out and sucking on them. Watching him serve Persia the dick relentlessly has my pussy sizzling. My juices bubble out of my slit and coat my fingers with hot, sticky nectar. I feel compelled to walk over and bite his ass cheeks and feed him my sweetness. "Bust her pussy open, baby."

I get up and walk over toward them, pushing my fingers back into my pussy. I keep them buried deep inside of me, scoop out my cream, then slip my fingers into his mouth. He lovingly sucks them, then presses his lips to Persia's and offers her his tongue. She kisses him back, sucks on his tongue.

"Damn, pull open ya pussy, baby, and play with that shit," he says to Paris, looking over at her. She is lying on the other side of the king-size bed, facing them. Her legs spread wide. Her clit and swollen cunt lips beckoning his mouth, his tongue. "Let me see that shit skeet."

"Is this what you wanna see?" Paris asks him, pulling open her pussy and revealing her pinkness. I am not a lesbian, nor do I desire to be one. But, seeing her perfectly shaped pussy pulled open, slick and ready, causes a bolt of sparks to shoot to my clit. I pinch my nipples, and let out a soft moan.

Persia arches beneath him, and her moans turn to gasps. She gulps in air, continues to roll her eyes up in the back of her head, then lifts her legs and digs her heels into his ass, pulling him deeper into her. Her nails dig into his back; sink into his skin. Royce starts to ride her faster as the heat in his balls begins to rise. His grunts and rapid thrusts are indications that he is ready to erupt.

She opens her eyes and warns, "Don't you nut, yet."

He slows his pace, then in one swift motion he rolls over onto his back with Persia now on top of him, his dick still buried deep inside of her. She rides him like the freak she is. Fast, frantic and nasty.

He grunts.

"You like this pussy?"

He grunts again.

I am surprised when Paris—who said she wanted no part of this young stallion's sex, crawls over to them and tells Royce to eat her pussy. She leans in and kisses him, slips her tongue into his mouth, then straddles his face and rides his tongue. His hands pull open her ass, giving him full access to her creamy cunt. His mouth moves over her clit, swift and eager, he drags the flat of his tongue over it, causing Paris to toss her head back and let out a moan.

I watch as he assaults her clit with swift licks and flicks, as he buries two fingers into her slit, stroking and coaxing a nut out of her. My own pussy begins to ache for release. Persia's greedy ass is hogging the dick, forgetting that I am still waiting for my turn. The steady slap of their fucking, and his slurping, has me on the edge of an orgasm. My own fingers find my clit and strum until I cum again. But I am not satisfied. I *need*, *want*, to feel the stretch of his young cock, too.

"Bitch," I hiss low in her ear, "stop hogging the nigga's dick and let me get a ride. Damn."

She sucks her teeth, rolls her eyes and continues riding him several more strokes before reluctantly lifting up off of him. His XL Magnum-covered cock is coated with her cream. She takes it into her mouth and sucks her juices off of it before allowing me access. I mount him. Slowly ride the tip of his dick. Allow myself time to accommodate his girth. In unhurried strokes, he lets me maneuver his dick into me, one inch at a time, until I have all of him inside of me. It hurts so damn good that my pussy nuts four times all over it. I believe his eleven-and-a-half-inch is the most dick any of us has taken. Ten inches, check. Nine inches, double-check. Eight inches, check. And we've even fucked less than seven inches. But, this nigga's dick is a whole new experience.

"Oooooooh, shiiiit, this dick is so damn big...you stretching this tight pussy wide open, baby..."

He thrusts upward, grabbing onto my hips. "Yeah, baby, give me that tight pussy…"

I moan.

I need a distraction, something, to help take my mind off the sweet burning being caused by the stretch of his dick. I moan with pleasure as he tears into my pussy. I lean forward, let my titties sweep across his chest and kiss him. Greedily tongue him down. He locks his arms around my waist and begins bouncing my ass up and down on his dick.

"Aaaaaah, shit, you got some nice wet pussy…"

Of course I do. "You feel how wet you got this pussy? The deeper you fuck it, the wetter it gets. You like fucking this good pussy?" I ask, riding down on his dick. My pussy is now juicy and loose and able to handle to his long, thick, hard dick. "You like how this pussy's grabbing your dick?"

He grabs me by the ass, thrusts his hips and dick up into me. "Uh, fuck…"

"Fuck him good, girl," Paris says, rubbing her clit, then sliding two fingers into her pussy. She pulls them out, then slides them into Royce's mouth. He sucks on them, slides his tongue in between each finger. "You like how my pussy tastes?"

"Hell, yeah…oooooh, shit…uh, fuck…"

I run my fingers along his smooth, muscular chest. My mouth finds his shoulder and neck and begins to suck and bite.

"Fuck the shit outta her," Persia urges, pinching and twisting her nipples. "Dig her guts out. Fuck her hard and deep 'til she begs you to stop. Fuck her 'til her pussy swells up…"

I want to tell her to shut the hell up; that she's really going a bit overboard. But I am lost in his rhythm. He rapidly pounds up into my wetness.

I nut, again. Coat his cock with cream.

Then somehow he lifts me up and starts fucking me standing. He is much stronger, much more agile, and virile, than any of us anticipated. He slows his thrusts, stirs his dick inside of me, brushing against my walls. Mmmm, it feels so damn good!

"Ohhh, yes...fuck me," I whisper, begging seductively. His curved cock hits my spot, boomerangs around my pussy, causing a rush of waves to wash over me.

Persia is now standing in back of him, kissing his back, kneading his shoulders. She slowly lowers herself, leaving a trail of kisses along his spine. Tells him she wants to taste him. That she wants to eat his sweaty ass. If I weren't being fucked so good I'd laugh at her nasty, ass-eating self. Tell her she's always somewhere trying to tongue out some man's hole. But the dick is feeling too damn delicious to comment. She pulls open his ass, loses her tongue in him.

He gasps. "Oh, shit...uhhhh, fuck...aaaaah..."

I can tell this is a new experience for him. One he'll never forget. "You like how she's tonguing your ass?" I whisper, gazing into his eyes.

He grunts. "Yeah...uhhh...oh shit..."

His legs start to wobble. She has him on the brink of exploding.

"Don't nut, yet," Paris says, sauntering over to us. Her hand lost between her thighs. "Not until I feel you inside of me. Not until you fuck me deep."

I toss my head back, glance back and smirk at her. "Yeah, you better come and get some of this young buck's dick...uhhh... uhhh...ooooooh, its soooooo fucking big..."

He shovels his dick in and out of me a few more times. "Mmmmm...mmm...nice tight pussy...ohhh, shit..."

He pulls his dick out. Lets me down, abandons my poor pussy; leaves it empty and stretched and lonely. It aches and weeps and is throbbing with desire. I want more. Persia watches as he pulls Paris into his arms. I can tell by the look in her eyes, keenly aware, that her pussy, too, yearns for more cock. We both look on. Watch as he tongues Paris down. Presses his body into hers, then enters her standing. She moans as he pulls her legs upward, holding her up in the air and pistons his dick balls deep. She yelps and gasps, determined to endure the sweet pain he is giving her.

Persia and I are both in awe when she lowers her head and body backward and reaches toward the floor with her hands. "Harder," she instructs him. "Fuck me deep...uhhh...oooh...Pound my pussy...uhhh, yesssssss...faster..."

Sweat dripping from his face, he fucks her harder, faster, more determined, until her eyes roll in the back of her head. He grips her waist tighter, then starts swinging her around in a circle, pounding his dick into her. He spins and fucks her, mercilessly, until they are both dizzy.

A part of me is jealous that I am not the one leaning backward and reaching for the floor, being swung around as if I'm on an imaginary merry-go-round with a pussy full of cock. He walks and fucks her backward toward the bed, then lowers himself down on it so that Paris is now straddling him.

"Yo, somebody come give me some pussy to eat," he says, leaning back on the bed and looking over at Persia and me. I practically sprint over to him, almost knocking Persia out of the way, and leap onto his face. The minute his tongue brushes against my clit, I am coming again. On his tongue, his lips, his chin. My juices splash out of me. This is how worked up he has gotten me.

I fuck his face, smother him with my pussy, rocking back and forth over his mouth and tongue until I am moaning and groaning and I am weak. Reluctantly, I finally get up and trade places with Persia. She mounts his face, rides down on his mouth. But I know she wants what I want: more of his dick. And I tell Paris so. Yet, she keeps galloping up and down on him, acting as if she hasn't heard me. *This cock whore is ignoring me*, I think, tapping her on the shoulder.

She gives me a disgusted look and keeps riding his dick. And it is obvious she has no plans of stopping until she gets hers.

"That's right, lil' daddy," Persia says, grabbing her titties. "Tongue my pussy." She twirls her tongue around her left nipple, then her right. "Oooh, yeah...you ready for this nut?" Royce grunts as he continues working her hole with his lips, mouth, tongue and fingers. "Here it comes, baby...open wide, catch it in your mouth...uhhhhh..."

She comes hard, slumping forward as Royce continues sucking her juices.

I walk behind Paris, count the number of strokes she's taking and enjoying, waiting. Up. Down. Up. Down. Five, six, seven, eight. As soon as she lifts up for the ninth time, I lift her ass up in the air, causing Royce's cock to pop out of her pussy. She topples over.

"Ohmygod," she says, rolling off the bed. "Bitch, I can't believe you just tossed me off of him like that."

I shrug. "I asked you nicely to switch, boo. My pussy needs to be stuffed, too."

I take Paris in, and burst out laughing. Her eyes are wide, her face is sweaty, and her hair is disheveled. She's shocked, but can't help but laugh, too. Persia looks over her shoulder to see what the commotions all about. Before you know it the four of us are laughing.

"Yo, you wildin' for real, ma," Royce says, shaking his head at me. "No need to go knockin' ya peeps off the cock. I got enough dick to go around and more than enough nut for all of you. It's all good."

Paris pulls her hair from out of her face, still laughing. "Oh, I see how we playing this now. Every chick for herself."

I reach up under me and press the head of Royce's dick into me. "Basically," I say, slowly maneuvering an inch at a time in me. "Now...uhh...go play...mmmm...with ya'self...ohhh, shit... while...I feed...mmmm...my pussy."

Persia huffs, "Ohmygod. Will you hookers get it together, please? Y'all are really tryna fuck up my nut."

"Good," Paris says, pushing her over onto her side, then hopping up on Royce's face, facing me. "It's every woman for herself. Isn't that right, Porsha?" She cuts her eyes at me.

Royce continues laughing. "Yo, hol'up y'all..." He holds Paris up with botho hands by her ass, then shifts his face from underneath her slit, moving from beneath her. He lifts me up off his dick, then stands. "I told you, ain't no need to fight over the dick. I got you. Now let me handle this my way so I can break all three of you sexy babes off with some of this good-good."

Persia, Paris and I look at each other, smirking. We decide to let him take control. Let him *handle* us as he sees fit. He tells the three of us to get up on the edge of the bed on our knees side-by-side and arch our backs. We do.

"Aiiight, get them asses up in the air so I can give you what you want." He slaps our asses, then—as if on an assembly line—jabs his cock into the back of each of our pussies a few times, before grabbing us by the waist and fucking us, one by one, deep and hard. We moan and groan and throw our asses back up on his dick, handling every inch of him.

Persia moans. "Uh...ooooh...Let...us...uh...mmmm...know when you're ready to nut." She cranes her neck to look at him as he digs her back out. "Yeah, baby...mmmm...fuck me with that long black dick."

And that's exactly what he does to the three of us until he's ready to nut. He pulls out of me. "Oh, shit...oh, shit...I'm getting ready to cum..." We quickly hop off the bed, our holes wet and sore and happily fucked, and turn to face him, getting down on our knees. He rapidly strokes his dick in front of us, slapping it up against our faces, across our lips, every so often. "Where y'all want it?"

"In my mouth," I say, opening my mouth and licking my lips.

"Give it to me on my face," Persia says.

"Mine, too," Paris adds.

"I'm a heavy shooter," he warns, stroking the upper part of his shaft. Every so often his hand glides over the head. He grunts and growls and howls, gives us the impression he is about to splash a bucket of hot creamy cum all over us. We anxiously wait. Tongues wagging, we beg for it. Rubbing our pussies with one hand and tweaking our nipples with the other, we moan for it.

He grunts louder. "Uhhhh...aaaaah, shiiiiiit...Mmmmmm, fuck..."

I am the first one he stands in front of, his dick hovering over my face. I hold my head back and open my mouth wide, bracing myself for a mouthful of nut, as he jerks himself. My mouth begins to water in anticipation. "Ssssssh, aaaah...here it comes..."

He thrusts his hips, and squeezes out a teenie-tiny drop of cream that slow drips into my mouth. Paris and Persia look over at me, me at them. They are surely thinking what I am: Motherfucker, all that dick and that's it?! Heavy shooter, my ass! All you got for me is a stingy ass droplet of cum?

I frown. Well, pout 'cause I am disappointed *and* pissed. I catch Persia with her head down holding back a snicker as he shifts over to Paris, still jerking and grunting. She offers him her face, smirking.

"Yeah, baby, give me that big nut," she says teasingly. I roll my eyes up in my head. He moans, bucking his hips. This time he spurts out a thick wad that sticks to the side of her face. I am annoyed that I got gypped. That she got the nut that should have been shot into my mouth instead of being wasted on her face.

He now moves over to Persia. She looks up at him, reaches for his balls and gently kneads them. I'm sure not expecting him to shoot no more than what he's already served. "C'mon, lil daddy, show me what you got. Give me that hot nut right in my face." She lifts her head and closes her eyes, waiting.

"Uhhhhh, shiiiiiiit...fuck..." he takes a step back, aims his dick at the front of her face and—to all of our surprise—literally blasts out a long stream of cum that splashes all over her face. His dick becomes a shooting cum cannon, coating her up with a white sticky paste.

Paris and I stare at Persia, at him, bewildered and amazed at the amount of cum that has just gushed out of his cock. Persia's whole face is drenched in nut. It dangles from her lashes, nose and hair; sticks to her lips. She tries to wipe it from out of her eyes with her fingers. But it smears. She licks his custard from her lips.

Royce walks back over to the bed, leans back on his right forearm, still stroking himself. "Who's ready for some more of this dick?"

The three of us are still down on our knees, with our mouths open, speechless.

CHAPTER TWELVE

"I got your message."

I narrow my eyes, glancing at the clock. It's 10:15 in the morning. *Is this motherfucker serious?* "Emerson, are you for real? That was two damn days ago."

"My bad. I woulda hit you up sooner if I could have. But I was tied up for a few days on some last-minute-type shit."

"And you have a cell phone, no?"

"Yeah, and?"

I blink. "*And* you couldn't use it?"

"I couldn't get any service where I was."

"Oh really? So where were you, vacation?"

"Nah, doing some demolition work up in the Poconos."

Yeah, beating up some bitch's pussy. Demolition, my ass! The only walls he was tearing down were attached to a uterus. Interesting thing is he's not our man so I don't really care where he was. But I do care that his ass is sleeping with someone else other than my sisters and me. "Mmmm."

This nigga must really think I'm some damn fool. My sisters and I have been fucking him for eight months straight. And anytime I've called or texted him, he's always been Johnny-on-the-damn-spot up until the last three weeks or so. I guess he doesn't think I've noticed how it takes him much longer to get back to me. Or the fact that all of sudden he hasn't been able to stay the night after we've fucked him down. I swear. Some men are so fucking stupid when it comes to women. Just because we don't always mention shit we see doesn't mean we aren't paying attention, and aren't noticing what's going on around us. Sometimes we're sitting back waiting for his ass to slip up. Other times, we're pretending to not notice to keep him believing we're as dick-dumb as he already thinks we are.

I decide to fuck with him. "So are you coming through?"

"Uh, nah. I'm good."

"You good?"

"Yeah," he repeats.

Mmmph...since when this nigga start turning down pussy?

Since he started fucking some other bitch, that's when.

"I'm feelin' someone. And I need to fall back, plain and simple, until I can figure out how I'ma handle it."

"Well, do you. Fall back, lean back. Take it as far back as you need to. But make sure you delete our numbers, okay."

He sighs. "Yo, whatever. It's not that serious."

"Well, good. But before we hang up, answer me this: how long have you been dealing with this chick you're *feelin'*, as you say?"

"Yo, not that I owe you any explanation 'cause you gonna think what you want. But, we're not dealing. I've been feelin' her for about four or five months now."

"You were fucking her while you were fucking us?"

"Yeah, something like that."

"Interesting. And why didn't you tell us you were fucking someone else? You know our rule."

"Yo, hold up," he says, sounding annoyed. "If I'm single doing me, and we're getting it in with no-strings attached, what the fuck does it matter who else I'm giving this dick to? I'm not committed to anyone, and I don't have to answer to anyone; especially to you. So you need to check ya'self for real."

"You're right," I say, swiveling my chair from side to side. "You don't have to answer to me. Nor am I asking you to. And you can definitely fuck whomever you want, so do you. But what you're not gonna do is fuck me, my sisters, and some other bitch, too. Sorry, wrong answer. I told you when we first started wetting your dick that we don't share dick outside of our circle. And you said you were cool with that."

"And I was until shit got complicated."

"Complicated for who? Never mind. Do me a favor and delete our numbers."

He laughs. "Yo, you sound like you pissed that I'm feelin' someone. And that someone ain't *you*."

I let out a sarcastic laugh. "Ha, don't flatter yourself."

"You know what; you funny as hell. Sharing dick is sharing dick, no matter who you're sharing it with. And I'm sure I'm not the only dick y'all riding. But for you to think a muhfucka can't fuck someone else outside of you and ya sisters is nutty as hell. But, it's all good. I'ma delete ya digits. No problem, baby. I'm out."

Click. Oh, no the fuck he didn't, I think, staring at the phone. "Hello? Hello? That nigga really hung up on me." My first thought is to call him back and curse him out, but then I decide he isn't worth the energy. I pick up my cell and call Paris.

"Hey," she says as soon as she picks up.

"Guess who had the nerve to finally call?"

She laughs. "Emerson. So is he seeing someone?"

"Girl, he's been fucking some bitch he claims he's feeling." I replay the phone conversation to her.

"Wow."

"Yup, wow is right. And that's why he's cut."

"I liked him."

"Girl, fuck him."

"Mmmm, oh well," she says, changing the subject. "Listen, before I forget. I'm meeting Mom for lunch today."

"Have fun," I say, sarcastically.

She laughs. "Gee, thanks. Since you and Porsha seem to be too busy for her, I get to have her all to myself."

I grunt. "So basically she did what she does best. Made you feel guilty." She laughs with me. Tells me that sometimes she feels bad for our mother; that she wishes the three of us had a better relationship with her. I roll my eyes up in my head. "Well, unfortunately, you know that's not going to happen with her and me. You might be able to get Porsha to get on that bandwagon, but I got off a long time ago."

She sighs. "I know, but still…she's our mother. And she really does love us."

"Yeah, well. She can love me from a distance."

"Mmmm," she says thoughtfully. She pauses. "So he's really out?"

"Who?"

She sucks her teeth. "Emerson, who else?"

"Girlfriend, what part of the conversation did you not hear?"

She sucks her teeth. "Persia, don't *you* get disconnected, okay? I'm only asking you a question."

"And I thought we were done with the conversation."

"We were. But now I'm back on it."

"I *told* you what he said. And I told him to do him. So he's tossed out like last week's trash."

"Mmmph. That's too bad. The sex was good."

"Whatever. What that nigga *had* was good. Good pussy, good brain, and nonstop fucking. But, that wasn't enough."

"True. But don't you think…and let me finish before you start spazzing out...that maybe—in this case—you might be overre-acting? I mean. Up until the last few times Emerson has always been reliable and consistent when it came to serving up the dick. So, okay, he left us hanging a few times; big deal. It's not like that stopped us from getting dick from someone else."

I groan. "*And*, your point?"

"The *point* is he's not our man..."

"Uh, ohhhhkaaay, tell me something I don't already know."

"And it's not like we were dating him exclusively. We fuck whoever we want, whenever we want. So why couldn't he?"

I roll my eyes. "Ohmygod, why are you acting like you're trying to keep the man around? We don't share a motherfucker outside of our circle, period."

"Well, if he's feeling this chick, then good for him. Obviously he needs more," she says.

I raise my brow. "What, more pussy? More head? Please. He had, not one, not two, but three bad-ass women sexing his ass up and down. You know like I do we served up that nigga lovely."

"True. But maybe he's one of those men who wants to be connected to someone. You know. Maybe be in a committed, monogamous relationship. Not treated like he's a piece of meat; only good for fucking."

I frown. *Well, he was.* "And what gives you that impression? Were the two of you having sideline conversations Porsha and I don't know about? 'Cause the way you're talking, I'm starting to look at you sideways."

She sighs loudly in my ear. "Persia, whatever! You can look at me sideways all you want. The fact of the matter is he's a grown-ass man. And at the end of the day he was never obligated to us. So who or *what* he does with his dick on his own time isn't any of our concern."

"The hell if it isn't. We told him the rules from the beginning. And he said he was cool with them."

"No, *you* told him the rules. Porsha and I went along with them."

"Oh, and you don't now?"

"I didn't say that. But what I am saying is that maybe Emerson changed his mind."

I twist my lips. "Then his ass should have made sure we got the memo."

"Listen, girlfriend, take down all that stank in your tone. If he's dismissed, he's dismissed. No biggie. All I'm saying is maybe he needed more than pussy, more than having his dick sucked and ass licked; more than what we were willing to give him. I mean, every man isn't only about getting his freak on with a bunch of women. Some men really want only one woman to be his freak. Not two and three. Maybe we were substitutes until he found what he was really looking for."

"Mmmph. Maybe we were. Anyway, enough talk about him. He's old news. What do you think about Royce becoming a regular?"

"Uhhhhhh, let me see. Huge dick, gaping pussy…uh, no thanks! He had *too* much dick for me. But if you and Porsha want him, then have at it. I'll watch from the sidelines."

I suck my teeth, laughing. "Hooker, please. Not the way you were riding down on it. You handled that shit like a real pro. Then your greedy ass didn't wanna get up off of it, or did you forget that part?"

The thought of that night with Royce causes my clit to twitch. That young motherfucker tore our pussies up; gave us two rounds of dick, then was grabbing at his dick for a third go 'round. We had to soak for almost two days. I press my legs together, pinching back the memory.

After we finished fucking Royce that night, he explained how he can typically nut three or four times back to back, and that the first two nuts are usually small amounts of cum. Then he had the nerve to laugh and say he should have warned us that the third or fourth nut is a gusher. I wanted to say, "Uh, nigga, you think?"

She laughs with me. "Look who's talking. You were trying to hog the dick more than Porsha and me. Shit, I'll admit. That dick was good. And his ass knew how to serve it."

"Mmmph, yes he did. And that's exactly why I think we should add him to our list of fuck buddies."

"Girl, please. Your nasty ass just wants some more of that thick cream up on your face." She laughs. "You should have seen your face when he hosed you down. Ohmygod. It was priceless. And can you imagine if he would have shot all that cum into Porsha's mouth? She would have chocked to death."

I join in her laughter. "Or die trying to swallow it all."

"I can see it now all over the news. 'Local freak found with her throat sealed shut by a heavy white, cream-like substance over-flowing out of her mouth. Cause of death: a nut overdose.' And let's not even get on you. 'Authorities say there was a second freak found blind at the scene. No further information is available at this time.'"

"Girl, you know you ain't got no damn sense, right? But, I'll say this. My face glowed for two days afterwards."

She keeps laughing. "Yeah, you were glowing alright. Like one big ass cream puff. A mess, I tell you."

I chuckle. "Well, I'd love to fuck him again. And I know Porsha's game."

"Hmmph, well if we're gonna have him around for awhile, then I'd suggest we each invest in a pair of goggles and don our swim caps 'cause there's no way I want him gushing his nut all up in my face, trying to blind me. Glowing skin or not, no thank you."

I laugh. "Girl, I can't lie. He shocked the shit out of me. I was totally caught off-guard. When I saw him drip that little bit of cream out for Porsha, then that little dab of a nut on your face, I figured he'd be serving me the same shit. "

Paris is laughing hysterical. "He had your face smothered in nut. Whew, I am so glad that wasn't me. If he's gonna be a regular, I know to be first in line."

"Hahaha, well, you go right ahead. I'm quite alright being last."

"I bet you are."

"So are you down or not?

"Down with what?" she asks.

I shake my head, sighing. Paris can sometimes come off being so damn ditsy. "Uh, earth to Paris, down with Royce. Geesh, keep up with the conversation."

She laughs. "Persia, kiss my ass, okay? How about you keep up with the conversation. I already told you I'm not interested in letting him stretch my pussy out. But if you and Porsha want to do him, then fuck and be merry. I'll watch."

"Yeah, yeah, yeah. The next time he's lying on his back with his dick rock-hard, let's see how long it takes before your pussy is begging to be *stretched*."

"Yeah, we'll see. Won't we?" She and I go back and forth reminiscing over our night with Royce a few minutes more, then disconnect.

The rest of the morning I update the boutique's website, go through emails, reply to Facebook messages, and return phone calls to potential clients. Running my own web design company for the last three years has been not only very lucrative, it's also been rewarding. Though my bachelor's degree is in marketing, my love is now in graphic design. And I owe it to Paris.

Designing the website for Paradise Boutique was the start of me realizing where my true talents lie. After all the rave reviews she had gotten about the design of her website and the numerous email requests for design quotes I'd gotten, I knew then I had found my calling. And from that came the birth of Sleek Media Designs where I provide premier web design and development, e-commerce, and Internet marketing solutions.

I get up from desk, walking over to the window. I see Porsha pulling up in the driveway. She parks her convertible 650i behind my Jag, then gets out. For some reason, my phone conversation with Emerson pops in my head. *Mmmph, I'ma make sure Paris and Porsha know to delete his number, too. Talking about he ain't feeling me. Nigga, please!*

CHAPTER THIRTEEN

As I'm driving down Bloomfield Avenue, heading to Union to meet my mother for lunch at the HUCK Finn diner, I find myself thinking about my phone conversation with Persia the other day and her attitude toward our mother. The last thing I want is to be sucked into Persia's contempt for her. To distract myself, I slide Marsha Ambrosius' *Late Nights, Early Mornings* album into the CD player. I press the CD changer until I get to track 6. When "Lose Myself" starts playing, I sing along, turning off J.F. Kennedy Drive onto the Garden State Parkway. I bear off exit 140, pay the toll and head down Morris Avenue. I spot the diner on the right side, turning on my signal to turn into the parking lot.

Once I find a parking spot and park, I take off my Versace shades, flipping down my visor. I slide open the mirror, making sure my hair is still in place. I run my fingers through my curls, deciding to pin it up. I rummage through my bag, pulling out a crystal encrusted hairpin, then flip my hair up into a twist ponytail. I slide my shades back over my eyes, then step out of my car, hoping my mother and I can get through our meal without incident.

She's already seated when I walk through the door. Lips pursed, her face tight, she glances at her watch the minute she sees me. I sigh. "Hello, Mother," I say, greeting her with a forced smile as I lean in and kiss her on the cheek.

"Fashionably late as usual," she starts in. "But if I were your father, you would have been here way before me. I don't know why you girls treat me so indifferently."

I give her an incredulous look. "Really, Mom? Are you serious? I'm five minutes late. Geesh. I haven't even sat down good and you're already picking. Can we, for once, spend the day without you starting up?" I hear Persia's voice in my head. *That woman's unbearable.* "All I want to do is enjoy a nice peaceful lunch with you. Do you think you can handle that without ruining it?"

She puts her hands up in mock surrender. "Fine. I'm only stating the obvious. Not looking to get into a fight with you."

I raise a brow, feeling myself already getting frustrated. "Then don't."

My cell vibrates. I pick it up and see that I have a text from Persia. I bet she's already getting on your nerves. hahahaha

I text back. whatever!

A few moments later she replies back with a smiley face. "So are you gonna fiddle with that phone all day?" I apologize to her. Tell her it was Persia; that she told me to tell her that she sends her love. Yeah, we both know it's a lie. I smile. She gives me a look of disbelief, grunting. "Really? I find that hard to believe."

"Mom, contrary to your feelings, Persia does think about you. We all do."

"Well, they have a strange way of showing it; more so Persia than Porsha. At least Porsha will call me. Not as much as you do, but it's still a whole lot more than what Persia does. That girl acts like I've done something to her when all I ever did was cater to you girls."

I sigh, fully aware that this will turn into a drawn-out laundry list of all the wonderful things she's done for us, the opportunities she's afforded us—the private schools, summer camp, ballet and piano lessons, trips abroad, paying for our college tuitions, blah, blah, blah. The list never ends. "Mom, listen...I don't want to talk about that. We're very much aware of everything you've ever done for us. And we're appreciative. Why you insist on reminding us every chance you get is beyond me."

I hear Persia's voice, again. *She does it because she wants us to keep kissing her ass. She wants us to feel obligated to her.*

"Well, it seems like you girls sometimes forget all of the sacrifices your father and I had to make to ensure the three of you wanted for nothing."

I bite down on my bottom lip, pulling in a deep breath. My phone buzzes, again. She stares at it, waits to see if I'm going to pick it up, raising her brow. I turn it off, then toss it in my bag. "There. Now, how have you been?"

She opens her mouth to say something when the waitress comes over to take our orders. She orders the breakfast special. And I order their Greek salad. She watches the waitress walk off, then tells me that she's doing well. I am mindful to not ask her anything about my father; especially knowing she realizes we talk to him every day. I ask her if she's done anything new to the house since we've last been there. She tells me no. Tells me money's been tight. Then, in the next breath, says she's looking to buy a new Benz—the S-class series. I don't say a word. She stops talking when the waitress returns to the table to fill our glasses with water. She asks her to bring us some lemons, then waits for her to walk off again.

"I wanted to put in a new kitchen floor and buy some new appliances, but your father said there's nothing wrong with what we have. I swear, that man can be so tight when it comes to spending money. He is so cheap. All he wants to do is save. I ask him what he's saving for; it's not like we can take it with us if something happens to us. I want to spend my money. What's the point of leaving my hard-earned money behind for someone else to spend up? I told your father there's no sense of leaving any of it with you girls. Y'all have gotten enough out of us over the years. I told him we sent y'all to private schools, paid for your college educations and made sure none of you had to be stuck with student loan bills. So we've done all we need to be doing. I want to enjoy my money while I'm alive. Not leave it for some-one else to mess over."

I stare at her, then blink. She's oblivious to what's come out of her mouth. I am so glad Persia isn't here right now. This situa-tion would definitely turn ugly real fast. I take a deep breath. Say a silent prayer that I can get through this lunch without incident. "So, what else is new?"

"Zena's husband done left her. The shit—excuse my French, done hit the fan over there."

"Oh really?" I ask, trying to seem disinterested in wanting to know the details. But inside I'm dying to hear every juicy morsel. And knowing my mother, she is going to deliver the gossip whether I ask for it or not.

"Mmm-hmm...he waited for her to leave for work, then packed his things and moved out. He left his wedding band on the kitchen counter with a note." She shakes her head. "I told..." She pauses when the waitress returns to the table with our food. "...Oh, can you bring me a cup of coffee, please?"

"Sure, no problem," the waitress says. She looks at me. "Can I bring you a cup as well?" I tell her no. Ask her to bring me a glass of cranberry juice instead. "I'll be right back with it."

"...And I'm not one bit surprised by it, either. I told Lucky he was going to end up leaving her. We all knew that last child of hers wasn't his. He just didn't know it. Well, maybe he knew it but didn't want to accept it. The truth hurts. And the truth was staring him right smack in the face for ten years every time he looked at that little boy. Bless his heart. And he's the innocent one in all of this mess. I don't know what's wrong with these nasty-ass women these days…"

I'm surprised when she takes a break from her incessant chatter and starts eating her food before it gets cold. She scoops a forkful of home fries into her mouth, carefully chewing, then swallowing. I pick over my salad. The waitress returns with her coffee and my juice, then leaves us alone.

"Well, what happened?" I finally ask, picking out an olive and eating it. "How'd Aaron find out?"

She wipes her mouth with her napkin. "Well, from what I've gathered from talking to Fanny, who sometimes gets things all twisted around, is that he came home from work a few weeks ago and, out of the blue, asked her if Aaron, Junior was his."

"Wow. I'm sure that must have caught her by surprise. What did she tell him?"

"What do you think she told him? She lied right through her raggedy-ass mouth; excuse my French. Then the messy heifer had the nerve to call her mother crying, saying he accused her of cheating on him while he was overseas when all she's ever done is be a good wife and mother to his children. And that after all these years he wanted a paternity test because he didn't trust her. I told your Aunt Lucky I knew y'all were hot in the ass. But that Zena…mmmph, she has nothing on you girls. That girl can light hell on fire with the flames coming from out of her tail. Even as a girl, she was always somewhere prancing her behind up in some man's face. Anyway…so, of course, Fanny, with her meddling-ass, excuse my French, gets on the phone and calls him up acting a certified fool. She told me she cursed him out something terrible, for the old and new. Told him her daughter was the best thing that ever happened to him and that she would never do some nasty shit like that. Mmmph, I told her 'never say never' 'cause I wouldn't have never thought in a million years that my own daughters were out there doing the shit that they're doing, but they are. So don't ever say what your child won't do 'cause mine are doing every nasty thing under the sun with God knows how many men."

I blink. I am literally speechless, listening to her right now.

"Unbelievable," I finally say, referring more so to her comments about my sisters and me than anything else.

She grunts. "Mmmph. No, what's unbelievable is her naming that little bright-faced boy after him like that. Aaron, Junior. Mmmph. You tell me how that can be? That man is as dark as soot—ooh, but he has some beautiful skin and gorgeous hair. Anyway, and she's about as brown as a tree and her trifling-ass—excuse my French, trying to pass some half-white looking child off as his. She had no business doing no nasty shit like that. Of course, Fanny is pissed that I said what I said about it. I mean, shit—excuse my French, it's not like Lucky and I wasn't saying it behind her back. Now it's all out in the open…"

I feel a headache slowly making its way to the front of my forehead. I take a gulp of juice, slowly breathing through my nose. I press on. "I'm sure she didn't like that."

"I'm sure she didn't. But she'll get over it. Like I said, these trifling-ass women out here sleeping around with all these men, then getting pregnant like it's nobody's business makes no damn sense. Not even knowing who the damn fathers are." She sighs, eyeing me. "I hope you and your sisters are not stupid enough to be screwing all those men without using protection, exchanging all those bodily fluids like that is just nasty."

I huff, dropping my fork in my plate. I sit back in my chair and eye her back. "Mom, what does Zena's situation have to do with who *we* sleep with? I mean, really. We're not the ones married. And we're not the ones who slept with someone else and got pregnant on our husband. So what is the point you're trying to get at here? Because obviously I've missed it."

She picks up her coffee cup, eyeing me over its rim before she takes a sip. She takes a slow, deliberate sip, then sits her cup on its saucer. "The point is I'm glad it's not the three of you being the topic of discussion for once. Fanny loves throwing dirt up on everyone else, but now she has her own pile to shovel through."

I've had enough. I abruptly get up from my seat, digging through my bag. "Where are you going?"

I toss a twenty up on the table. "I'm outta here. I am so freakin' done with you right now."

She looks around the diner. "What are you talking about?"

"I'm talking about this...you," I say, jabbing my finger through the air. "I've had enough of your holier-than-thou bullshit for one day."

She gives me an appalled look. "Paris, what in the world has gotten into you? You're acting just like your sister, Persia—rude, using that tone of voice with me. And then you're cursing at me. That is so not like you. We're sitting here having a peaceful conversation."

"No, there has been nothing *peaceful* about this whole conversation. For the last thirty-five minutes I've been sitting here listening to *you* not only insult me and my sisters, but confirm how you sit around with your busybody, gossiping-ass sisters and talk about us, and any-and-every body else in the damn family."

"Will you sit down," she says through clutched teeth. "You're making a scene."

"No, I will not sit down. And I don't give a damn about making a scene. Every chance you get, you have to get a damn dig in. You can't ever simply have a conversation without finding some kind of way to make some sort of snide comment about our lifestyle. Well, get over it," I snap, raising my voice. I am so pissed right now that I'm trembling. I've never spoken to her like this, but today I have had enough. "Yes, Mother, we sleep with the same men. How many times must we keep going over this? Yes, you think it's nasty. So what? Who gives a shit?! It's our life! We're fine with it and if you can't be, then leave us the hell alone."

She slams her hand down on the table, visibly shocked by my outburst. "How dare—"

I put my hand up to stop her. "Don't. I'm sick of it. How dare *you* sit here and offend my sisters and me and act as if it's okay? I am so disgusted with you right now."

"*You're* disgusted with *me?*" she asks indignantly, raising her voice. She catches herself, glancing around the diner to make sure she hasn't drawn any more unwanted attention. She lowers her voice; speaks through clenched teeth. "How do you think I feel? My daughters out here doing all kinds of nasty shit—excuse my French, with all kinds of men, *together*. How do you think that makes me feel?"

"Newsflash, Mother: Who we suck and who we *fuck* is none of your damn business."

She gasps. "You mean to tell me you'll stand here and disrespect and curse me like this. Persia, yes; Porsha, maybe. But, you…" She shakes her head. "Never would I think you'd stoop to this and let your sisters turn you against me."

I scoff. "Ugh, this has nothing to do with Persia or Paris. This is about you, and your attitude toward us. And the ugly shit you allow to come out of your mouth. I sat here and tried to overlook the mess you were saying about not leaving us money, about what you've done for us, about who we sleep with, about how we embarrass you. Get a grip, Mother! You and your damn sisters are pathetic. Now go back and gossip about that."

By the time I'm done saying all this, I am on the verge of tears. But I will not give her the satisfaction of seeing me break down. Not today. I strut off, leaving her sitting at the table with her jaw dropped open.

By the time I finally get home, I am emotionally exhausted. The only thing I want to do is crawl up in my bed. "Damn, that was a long lunch," Persia says the minute she sees me walking through the house. "How was it with the ole Wicked One?"

I grunt. "Ugh, I don't have the energy to get into it right now." I drop my bag on the floor and remove my shades, tossing them up on the table. "Right now the only thing I want to do is listen to some music, soak in the tub, and take me a nice long nap."

She shakes her head, taking me in. She walks over and wraps her arms around me, giving me a hug, then lets me go. I walk toward the stairs.

As I climb the stairs, I hear her saying, "Poor thing. I keep telling y'all that woman is hateful."

Persia
CHAPTER FOURTEEN

I t's almost seven o'clock in the evening when I finally decide to go upstairs and check in on Paris. She's been up holed up in her room long enough. I've given her enough time and space to sulk; now it's time to snap her out of it. When she came home this afternoon with her eyes all swollen and red, I knew that she must have finally gone off on our mother for, once again, saying something slick. Crying is Paris's M.O. after she's gone off on someone.

Even growing up, she was always the most sensitive out of the three of us; always wanting to please everyone; always wanting everyone to get along; always wanting to be sure everything was in its proper place. Whereas Porsha and I were always very vocal about our feelings, she kept hers bottled inside. Then when it got too much for her, she'd go off. And afterwards, feel bad about it. Although she's more outspoken now than she's ever been, she still has a ways to go. I'm telling you. It took everything in me not to call our mother to see exactly what in the hell had come out of her mouth *this* time. I wanted to scream on her. But I didn't.

With four crystal tumblers filled to the rim on a tray, I tap on Paris's door, trying not to spill any of our drink—Remy Martin XO with a light splash of Coke. *Two stiff drinks apiece should do the trick*, I think as I approach her door. Normally, we simply barge into each other's rooms, not caring what we might walk in on. There have been plenty of times when we've walked in and caught one of us with either our fingers or a toy of some sort shoved deep in our pussies. But since my hands are full I decide to tap on the door with my foot.

It takes her a minute to finally swing open the door. She has a towel wrapped around her body, and one wrapped around her hair. "Since when you start knocking on doors?" she asks as she pops her hips back into her bathroom.

"Well, if you slowed your behind down, hooch, you'd see that I come with a tray of drinks. And I didn't knock, I kicked."

She sticks her head out of the door. "Whatever. I needed that drink earlier today after the fiasco down at the diner with Mom. But, now is good, too."

"Yes, it is," I say, walking into her bathroom, handing her a glass. She takes a sip.

"Ohhhh, yes...this is good. It's exactly what the doctor ordered."

"Shuga," I say, smacking my lips together, flipping the lid to the toilet down and taking a seat. "Let's cut to the chase. I'm dying to know what popped off between the two of you 'cause when you walked up in here, you looked wrecked."

"Girl..." she pauses, gulping back half of her drink. "Whew, that hit the spot." She removes her towel from around her head and starts blotting her hair. She takes another sip of her drink.

I huff, impatiently. "Hooker, will you tell me what the hell happened between you and Mom today? You've kept me in the dark long enough. Now spill it, damn you!"

She laughs. "Okay, okay...calm down. No need to get all indignant. I get to the restaurant and before I can even get in my

seat good, she started up. I was literally no more than five minutes late and she was ready to pounce." She replays the whole
ordeal back to me. And when she's done I'm practically laughing,
wishing I could have been a fly on the wall to see her going off.
"Ohmygod, why are you laughing? I don't see anything funny
about this shit."

"Girl, the idea of you turning out the diner and Mom sitting
there slack-jawed is absolutely priceless! I bet she wanted to get
up and slap you sideways for talking to her like that. *And* you
cursed her. Oh, yeah. She wanted to give you a beat down right
there on the spot."

"I'm sure she did. But she stayed in her seat. But I could tell
she was fuming. Still, I didn't care one bit. She took it too far this
time."

"Oh, well," I say, watching her comb out her hair. "She got
what she deserved. She'll get over it; and if she doesn't, so the
fuck what? I don't know why you're surprised. I mean, when has
she not come out of her face sideways?"

"I know, but still. I shouldn't have spoken to her like that. And
definitely not out in public like that."

I roll my eyes. "Oh, please. She's always somewhere running
her damn mouth. She's the one who cranked it up. She wasn't
concerned about what she was saying to you, so why should you
care?"

"It still doesn't make it right," she says, combing conditioner
through her hair. "I'm gonna call her to apologize for allowing
her to take me there."

I buck my eyes at her. "And why in the hell would you do that?
After she carried on the way she did?"

"Because it's the right thing to do. I've never spoken to her like
that. No matter what she's ever said, I've always bitten my tongue."

"Well, I'm sorry. She needed that tongue-lashing. Trust me. It's been long overdue."

She shakes her head. "It wasn't right. I owe her an apology."

"Mmmph, you're good, boo. But do you."

She takes another sip from her drink. "Umm, I don't mean to bust your bubble," she says, walking out of the bathroom. I follow behind her. "But everyone isn't as mean and nasty as you."

"Excuse you?" I ask, feigning insult. "I beg your pardon. I am far from either of those things."

She rolls her eyes up in her head, dramatically, putting her hand up. "Girl, talk to the hand. Save that mess for someone who doesn't know you. I've seen you in action, sweetie. Okay?"

"Then you know I only bring it when it is called for," I state, inching my way up on her bed. I'm on one end of the bed, and she's on the other side. Both of us have our backs up against the headboard with pillows propped up behind us. "And you know like I do that over the years that woman has said and done some of the craziest shit."

"Well, that woman happens to be our mother and she still deserves some respect."

I lift my glass up to her. Then take a sip, before saying, "Well, you keep on respecting her then. In my book, you get what you give. And she's done nothing to get much respect from me."

She shakes her head, cutting her eyes at me. I can tell she's thinking something, but doesn't say what it is. Instead, she raises her glass at me. The two of us sip our drinks in silence. Then somehow we end up talking about our childhood, reminiscing over some of the things we witnessed our mother saying and doing whenever she suspected our father was cheating on her. Why I even initiated the conversation about our father's philandering ways is beyond me, but I do.

"Do you remember the time Mom baked those goodies and drove them over to Miss Janie's, all pretty and sweet as she pleased, pretending that she didn't know that she and Daddy were fucking?"

Miss Janie and our mother used to sponsor bus trips down to Atlantic City twice a year as a fundraiser for their church. The two of them had become good friends over the years, and travel buddies up until our mother caught her coming out of the same motel room as our father. But instead of jumping out of her car to confront them, yelling and screaming and fighting, she continued like she had no clue. I remember overhearing—because I was always somewhere ear-hustling—her phone conversation with Aunt Lucky, saying, "Oh, trust me. I had that bitch up in my house, eating my food, smiling up in my face and all the while she's fucking my husband. Oh, no…I'ma fix that bitch real good. You right I should beat her ass. I don't know why these hoes got to try me. I try to live a good, clean life. Try to do right. And here come these heathen-ass can't-get-a-man-of-their-own bitches trying to disrupt my home. But, no, I'm not going to stoop that low and bang her in her head. I know she crossed the line…oh, don't worry. I'm gonna deal with him, too. But, first, I need to tend to that, bitch…"

The night before their bus trip, she baked a big batch of double-chocolate chip cookies and fudge brownies, adding in a whole box of laxatives. Then she drove them over to her house. They sat and laughed and talked for a while, then our mother got in her car and drove back home. The next day they were all on the bus on their way down to AC when Miss Janie's stomach started bubbling.

"Ohmygod, yes," Paris says, laughing. "And the poor woman ended up shitting on herself that day because someone else was taking forever to get out of the bathroom. And they couldn't turn the bus around because they were already halfway there."

"And then Mom had the nerve to get up and slap her face."

"After she told Aunt Fanny and them that she wasn't going to get on that bus and act a fool."

Paris and I are hysterically laughing. "Miss Janie had the shits for two days after that."

"I know, right," Paris says, wiping tears from her eyes. "Ohmygod, we have no business laughing at that woman like this."

"And then Aunt Fanny said she had heard that Miss Janie's asshole was enflamed and on fire for almost a week from all the wiping she had to do."

We keep laughing.

"Mom was so wrong for that," Paris says.

"Yes, she was," I agree. "But, that goes to show you just how messy she could be. And she's still messy."

"Oh, so this is where the party is," Porsha says, standing in the middle of the doorway with her hands up on her hips. She is still in her skirt and heels. "You heifers up in here cackling and sipping on yak while I'm out slaving over tax forms. This shit ain't right."

"Oh, hush," I say, grabbing a pillow from off of Paris's bed and tossing it at her. She catches it, throwing it back at me. "How was work?"

"Oh, it was fabulous," she says, smiling. *Is that a twinkle I see in her eyes?* "I made about twenty-eight hundred dollars today. And I had a delightful working lunch with a potential client."

I raise my brow, smirking. "It must have been some lunch 'cause, girlfriend, you have that just-got-fucked-good glow."

She lets out a laugh, shifting her eyes. "Oh, please. I wish. I'm feeling good; that's all. Anyway, what were y'all in here cackling about? I could hear the two of you all the way downstairs."

"We were laughing at the time Mom gave Miss Janie the shits for two days."

Porsha laughs. "Ohmygod, no. That was some funny mess. Why'd you have to bring that up? I felt so bad for her."

"I don't know why," I say, waving her on. "Miss Janie was messy, too. She knows she was dead wrong for smiling up in Mom's face like that, knowing damn well she was sucking Daddy's cock every chance she got. I'm sorry. She crossed the line doing that. I would've given her the shits, too." Porsha and Paris continue laughing. "I remember overhearing Mom on the phone, saying, 'Every time she wipes her ass, she'll think about how she shitted on me by fucking my husband.'"

The three of us are practically clutching our sides from laughing so hard at the thought. Suddenly, Porsha stops laughing and looks at Paris, then me. "Wait a minute..." she twirls a finger in the air. "Bedroom. Drinks. *And* you had lunch with Mom earlier today." She squints, looking at me. "And you're up here making her laugh. What in the hell did Mom say now?"

"How 'bout you get outta them clothes first; fix yourself a drink...better yet, bring up the bottle," I say, gulping back the rest of my drink. "Then come sit with us so you can get the scoop, boo."

It doesn't take long before the mood shifts and the three of us are all comfy sprawled out on top of Paris's king-size bed, listening to Paris paraphrase everything she told me earlier. Porsha looks stunned. "Damn, I don't even know what to say about all of that."

"What can you say? I mean, really. Not a damn thing," I say, feeling myself becoming agitated all over again. "That's how she feels, then that's how she feels. We make our own money; pay our own bills. And own our own shit. We don't ask her for a damn thing. So she doesn't have to leave us a motherfucking thing. I'm telling y'all, that *bitch* is crazy."

Porsha and Paris gasp. "Ohmygod, I can't believe you called her a *bitch*," Porsha says, covering her mouth in shock.

"Persia, you done gone too far now," Paris says. "You didn't have to call her that."

I roll my eyes. "Please. Believe it. That's how I feel. At least I didn't say it to her face. Not that I won't if she ever brings it to me like that."

"You go right ahead," Porsha says. "And you're gonna end up with more than your face slapped, again."

"Rightfully so," Paris agrees. "You remember what happened the last time you called her that. I thought she was going to kill you for sure, if Daddy hadn't come home when he did."

Porsha winces, then cracks up laughing. "Oooh, I felt that ass whooping myself." I suck my teeth at Paris for bringing that horrible night up. I was fourteen. And, as usual, our mother and I were arguing over me not being allowed to go outside because I didn't do my chores. One word led to another and before I knew it, I had called her a *bitch*. Although I had mumbled it under my breath, she had heard it plain as day.

"Excuse me? What did you just call me?"

"You heard what I said," I snapped with a hand up on my hip. Yes, I thought I was grown. Then I repeated it. The words rolled off my tongue as smooth as cream. The next thing I remember is being down on the floor with her on top of me, beating me like a chick from the projects. Suburbia went out the window, and the hood came in. She fought me like I was her worst enemy. And I tried to fight her back. However, she was much stronger than I anticipated. So I did the only thing a girl could do in that situation. I bit her. And that only made her more furious. I remember Paris and Porsha screaming for her to get off of me, yelling that she was going to kill me. She probably would have if our father hadn't come in when he did. When he finally pried us apart, I had a busted lip, two black eyes, and my nose was bleeding. She had a long scratch across her neck and she was bleeding from where I bit her. I had to stay home from school for almost two weeks until my face healed. But the two of us couldn't be left alone together.

"And you got to go with Daddy on the road," Porsha says, shaking her head. "Ohmygod, Paris and I were so mad at you for getting to go across country with him."

Paris laughs. "Well, it was that, or you ending up riding in the back of a hearse 'cause Mom really wanted to kill you."

I grunt. "Well, I'm sad to announce this, but this time I would beat her down, mother or not. I'm a grown-ass woman, now. And I have had it with her." They both look at me like I'm crazy, or drunk. "Don't look at me like that. I mean it. I will toss her up if she ever tries it."

Porsha pats my leg, laughing. "Persia, sweetie, I think you're okay. Mom practically avoids you at all costs. She realizes you're a little nutty, boo."

"And so she should."

Paris tilts her head. "Bitch, you don't need anything else to drink tonight. Calling Mom out her name like that was messy."

"*She's* messy," I say. "She always has been. But she tries to act like she's not. And she has the nerve to disrespect us. So she deserves to be disrespected. But, let's drop this shit. I don't wanna talk about her anymore. We need to snap you outta this funk, girlfriend. And I know exactly what will do it."

She smirks, knowingly. "And what's that?"

"Some good-ass dick," Porsha and I say in unison. The three of us laugh, giving each other high-fives.

"I'm gonna call Calvin. I almost forgot he sent me that message on Facebook the other day saying he'd love to see us. He's in town visiting his mother for the next week or so. So, no time like the present to get reacquainted with his freaky-ass. Y'all game?"

"Count me in," Porsha says, pouring herself another drink.

Paris shrugs. "I guess."

"Oh snap out of it, girl. Don't let that woman pull your spirits down. You cursed her out real good; now let it go. I'm telling you, she'll say or do something else soon enough and you'll be glad you told her ass off when you did." I stand up. "Now finish up these drinks and get ya mind right while I go call Calvin. We're gonna get our fuck on, then send him on his way. I'll tell him to get here within the hour if he can."

I walk out, leaving the two of them sitting on the bed, pouring drinks, laughing and talking about the other fights Mom and I had growing up. Some of them funny; others real nasty, like the time I tossed a hot cup of coffee into her lap. Or the time I started throwing dishes at her for trying to make me rewash dishes that weren't even dirty. I fucked that kitchen up.

I hear Porsha say, "I thought the two of them would end up killing each other for sure."

Paris laughs. "Persia's ass was crazy."

"Shit, what you mean 'was'?" Porsha questions, laughing with her. "She still is."

"I heard that," I yell out, laughing along with them. Yes, I was definitely the wild child out of the three of us. And yes, I was the one our mother had to watch out for. And I still am.

Bound and blindfolded, I brush my lips against his lobe, whisper in his ear. "Are you gonna submit fully and completely to me?"

He nods his head. "Yes, my beautiful mistress." Although he knows I am *not* a real mistress—nor have any intentions of ever being one, I enjoy pretending that I am. And he likes pretending that I am, too.

At six-two, two-hundred-and-ten pounds, Calvin is a dark-chocolate delight with his lean, toned, muscular body and deliciously fat, Hershey-colored cock. As masculine and aggressive and rugged as he is, it amazes me how he transforms into a submissive man-toy behind closed doors. It is his acceptance into his role that has me creaming in my panties.

I smile, reaching into a bag of ice and pulling out a miniature cube, then gliding it over his left nipple. "Good 'cause tonight you're in for the time of your life." He shivers. "Too cold for you?"

He shakes his head. "No, Mistress Pain."

I slowly swirl the melting ice over and around his nipple while pinching the other one. His body shudders, briefly. I'm sure in response to the painfully chilling reality that the unknown and unexpected will follow.

I reach for the surgical tape, ripping off a strip with my teeth, then tape the ice to his left nipple. He flinches. I do the same to his right nipple. He flinches again, and his hard dick bounces up and down in response.

Porsha comes into the room, naked. Her silky skin shimmers from the glow of the candles flickering around the room. Without speaking a word, she looks at me and nods, then drops down in front of Calvin and wraps her mouth around his dick. She sucks him slowly at first, then picks up the pace, causing slurping and popping sounds to emit from her mouth. Calvin moans. The ice is slowly melting. Cold streaks of water are running down his chest.

Five minutes into Porsha's head service, I signal for her to stop, then instruct Calvin to lift up in his seat. I squeeze out a glob of Platinum wet, then spread it in and around his asshole. His hole puckers.

"Yeah, you want me to finger-fuck that tight, little hole, don't you?"

He nods. "Yes, my lovely mistress. I submit to you. Your commands are my wish. Anything you demand of me, I seek to please you."

Porsha rolls her eyes up in her head. I stick my tongue out at her, and she gives me the finger. I slip a finger into his ass. He tenses. His hole grips my finger, attempts to push it out. "Relax," I tell him, pushing my finger back in. Slowly, he relaxes and loosens up and allows me to finger him. His dick springs up and down. It is clearly an act he enjoys. I work a second finger in.

"Aaah, shit," he moans.

"You like that?"

"Mmmhmm...oh, shit..."

I smile. "I'm so glad you said that," I say, pulling my fingers out, then unlocking his left hand. I reach into the bag for another piece of ice and place it in his hand. "I want you to put this cube of ice into your ass." He hesitates. "Did you not understand me?"

"Yes...Mistress." Reluctance clings to his words.

"Do you not wish to please me?"

He nods. "Yes."

I slap his ass. "Yes, what?"

"Yes, my mistress."

"Much better. Don't have me remind you of your place. Did you not say my command is your wish?"

"Yes, my mistress."

"Then do as you are told and you shall be rewarded." He leans forward, squatting as if he's about to take a shit, then reaches back and attempts to stick the cube into his ass. Its coldness causes him to flinch. I get impatient and slap the ice out of his hand. "You must want your mistress to get angry, don't you?"

"No, Mistress Pain."

I hand him another piece of ice. "Then try it again. And now you'll have to put three cubes in instead of one for taking too damn long." He finally pushes it in. He grunts. "That's a good slave boy." I hand him another piece. Porsha looks at me, mouth agape, shaking her head. I ignore her look of shock. "Now put this piece in."

His body jerks. And my patience is running low. "Hurry the hell up before I add two more cubes on top of the three." The thought of having five ice cubes stuffed in his ass seems to motivate him to hurry this shit up. When he pushes the second cube in, I hand him the last one. He pushes it in, grunting. I tell him to sit down. "I know it's cold, but the fire in that hot ass of yours will melt it soon enough." I cuff his hand again. He squirms in his seat. Porsha snickers, popping an ice cube into her mouth, then dropping back down in front of him, taking his dick back into her mouth.

He yelps, squirms in his seat. "Aaaah, shit...oh fuck..."

I yank off the tape from his nipples, taking a piece of ice in both of my hands, then leaning over him and pressing the ice up against his nipples.

He shivers and jerks. "Aaaah...Ohhh...oooooooooh...ahhhh, fuck!"

"You like that, don't you?"

"Yes...aaaaah...aaaah, fuck...ohhhhh, shit!"

I glide the ice cubes in circular motion over his nipples, zigzag across his chest, then up along the sides of his neck before tossing the ice in an empty cup. I allow my cold, wet fingers, to trace his shoulders, then travel back down his chest. I pinch his nipples. "You like how Passion's sucking your dick?"

"Yes...uhh...oh, yes...fuck..."

He squirms in his seat. My pussy begins to quiver and drip at the thought of him having a sweet and excruciating ass freeze. I lean into his ear. "Ooooh, my pussy's so wet. Clench your ass muscles around that ice." His body shudders in pleasure, again. There's a distinct difference between a shudder of pleasure and one of discomfort. He tosses his head back and loudly moans. The combination of ice melting out of his ass and causing a puddle in his seat and the melting ice out of Porsha's mouth dripping down his cock, Calvin is experiencing a delicious agony until she abruptly stops sucking his dick, standing up. She walks over to the wooden table and retrieves a condom. She tears open the wrapper, then walks back over and rolls it down onto his aching cock. Porsha is ready to offer him her cunt. And his hard, eager dick is ready to take it. With her back to him, she reaches underneath her and positions the head of his cock at the mouth of her pussy, then sits down on it, slowly rocking her hips, accepting him into bliss.

"Aaah, shiiiiit…"

"You like Passion's hot pussy?"

"Oh, fuck, yesssss!"

She lets out a moan.

"Is that dick good, Passion?"

"Oooh, yes," she moans, leaning forward and grabbing her ankles. She bounces her ass up and down on him, causing it to clap around his cock.

I pinch my nipples. "Oooh, fuck him good, Sis."

He leans his head back, his mouth parted. I bring my nipple to his lips and he takes it into his warm mouth and sucks it. A string of pleasure threads its way down my spine and around my clit.

I step out of my panties, then stuff them into his hungry mouth. "You like how my panties taste?" He nods and grunts. "Good. Chew my pussy juices off them. And when you finish, I'll feed you this wet pussy. Would you like that?"

He nods, moaning and grunting. I remove his blindfold. Allow him to see. Allow him to watch Porsha's rhythmic movements up and down on his dick. I unlock his hands. Free them so they can roam her body. He caresses her skin, glides his hands along the curve of her hips, then grips her waist. He stretches his legs out and greets Porsha's pussy with hard, deep thrusts.

She greets him back.

"You like that pussy?" I whisper in his ear, pulling my panties out of his mouth with one hand, and pinching his nipple with the other.

"Oh, shiiiit, yeah…it's some good-ass pussy."

"Fuck her good, then. Show me how good that pussy feels to you."

He piston-fucks Porsha until the both of them are sweating and panting and moaning.

Watching the two of them fuck has my cunt slick with my juices. I reach over and grab my mini-vibrator from the tray, turn it on high, and slide it over my clit, then dip it into my slit.

Paris finally walks in and Porsha lifts up off his dick; allows her to straddle him. Calvin watches excitedly. Yet, no words are spoken. He knows he is to speak when spoken to.

She breathes warmly on his ear and tickles his earlobe with her tongue. "Watching from the other room has gotten me soooo horny for your cock." She reaches in back of her, strokes his dick. "Mmmm, your dick is so hot and heavy. I can't wait to feel it deep in my tight ass." She nips at his ear. "Put your dick in my ass, baby."

Porsha and I both blink, then glance from her to each other, stunned at what we've just heard. Calvin's eyes light up. He is surprised as well. "You want my dick in your ass?"

She coos in his ear. "Yes, baby. My fat…tight…hot…juicy *ass*. What, you don't want to feel my tight ass wrapped around your dick?"

"No, I mean, yes. You can have my dick anywhere you want it."

And so she does. He fucks her. She fucks him back. He gives her all of him. She gives him all of her. They are both panting and sweating. She is moaning. He is moaning.

Porsha and I watch, fondling our clits, pussies and tits. In sync, the three of us bring ourselves to orgasm, then Paris lifts up off Calvin's dick, pulls off his condom, then steps back.

Disappointment and confusion paint his face, but quickly disappears when Porsha takes his meaty dick into her mouth. Pushing her own limits, she takes him all the way down in her throat, then pulls out and caresses it with the tip of her tongue, running it from the base to its swollen head and swirling it around. She makes a loud, purposeful, gulping sound as she takes him back into her warm mouth, pushing the head of his dick to the back of her throat.

Calvin lets out a moan.

I urge her. Encourage her to suck the life out of him. "Go 'head, girl; suck that nigga's dick. Milk the nut up outta him."

She is slurping and slobbering and stroking every inch of him. Bobbing up and down, fingering her pussy as she does. Calvin's breathing changes and she glances up at him, knowingly. We all know. He is ready to explode. But he knows he can't unless I give him permission. His pleading eyes shift in my direction. He is close to the edge; afraid she is going to make him cum before I allow it.

"Don't you nut, yet," I warn, pinching and twisting his nipples.

"Aaaah, fuck! Uhhhhh...ooooh, shit...Gotdamn it!"

If Porsha didn't have a mouthful of dick, I'd think she was smirking at me, at him, for the deliberate torture.

"Beg for that nut."

"Uhhhhh...uhhhhhh...pleeeeeeease...oooh...oooooooh...uh, fuck, fuck, fuck...pleeeeaaaaaaaaaaaase, baby...I can't...uhhh... hold it..."

"You wanna cum all in her pretty mouth?"

"Uhh....oooooh, fuck...aaaah, shiiiiiit...Yesssssssssss, can I cum? She's fuckin' killin' me...aaaaaaah, fuck...aaaaaah fuck....aaa-aaaaah..."

I give him permission to release.

He grunts, and comes hard; his nut filling Porsha's mouth. He doesn't give her a chance to swallow before he is coming again, causing its overflow to spill out on her chin and down on her breasts. She looks up at him, swallows, wipes her chin and chest with her fingers and sucks them clean. Then takes his dick back into her mouth and sucks him clean. When she's finished, she stands up, rests the palms of her hands on his knees and slides her tongue into his mouth. He sucks her tongue and probes her mouth for remnants of his sweet, salty nut. Then, as if on cue, she and Paris walk out of the room, leaving the two of us alone. They will watch the rest of the show in another room.

Calvin gazes at me lustfully, knowing he is not done, yet. That he must be able to scratch my libidinous itch, and deliver another round of pussy pounding dick before he leaves.

A devious smirk forms on his lips. He realizes the tables will now turn. My pussy throbs at this knowing. My clit aches with anticipation as he gets up and walks over to me. Lust flares in his eyes. There's an animalistic hunger in them that excites me. With one hand, he grabs me by the throat. With the other, he slaps up my titties. The stings shoot through my body like bolts of electricity, zapping my clit.

He pushes my legs apart, cuts through me, running the blade of his hand up the inside of my thighs. He cups my pussy. I stifle a moan. "I'm going to fuck the shit out of you."

"Yeah, nigga, fuck my slutty pussy."

His dick springs alive.

"Fuck me like the whore you want me to be. Fuck me like the dick-sucking, cum-loving bitch I am."

His dick jerks, violently.

He loops his hand through my hair, yanks my head back, and looks me in the eyes. "Whose whore are you?"

"Yours," I tell him. He leans in, and kisses me on the mouth. I open it to him. His tongue is hot; it fills my mouth. My cunt explodes as he sinks to his knees and buries his face between my legs. My cum drips down my legs as he drags a finger along the length of my slit. He alternates between flicking my clit with his tongue and thumb while moving his fingers deep inside me. I lift one leg and drape it over his shoulder, giving him full access. He does not accept it. Instead, he gets up and spins me around, pushing me up against the wall.

"Don't...fucking move," he warns. I hear the familiar sound of a condom wrapper being ripped open. It doesn't take long before he is pressed up against my ass, grinding; his covered cock slicing into its crack.

My pussy whimpers. I whimper. I have a yearning to feel his cock inside of me. Craving him buried deep into the warmth of my wetness; wanting to cum hard and heavy and loud. "Fuck me," I demand, beg, with pleading eyes. He is doing this to me; taking my control from me. And I am letting him.

I push back against him.

He bites down on my neck.

I moan. Push back against him, again. "Fuck me."

"Not yet," he tells me. "You're my whore. I'll fuck you when I'm good and ready." I thrust my bottom lip forward into a pout. Defiantly, I stand up on the tips of my toes and try to ease myself onto his dick. He yanks me by my hair. "Oh, you want this dick, hunh? You think you can just take it; don't you, whore?" He wedges his knee against my thigh and forces my legs open wider. He jabs the head of his cock into my opening. "Is this what you want?"

I let out a moan. My hips jut, slowly winding to capture all of him. "Yes. Fuck me."

He jabs the mouth of my pussy, again, then pulls out. "Where you want it?"

I am shaking with desire. "In my pussy, in my ass. I don't care. Wherever you want to put it; just *FUCK* meeeeeeee." He steps away from me, tells me not to move. I glance over my shoulder, watch him as he walks over to the tray on the table. Watch him as he digs his hand into the plastic bag and scoops out a handful of half-melted ice.

"One good turn deserves another," he says, walking back over to me with ice water dripping through his fingers. My body tenses in anticipation. He cups my right titty and shoves his cock into my pussy, hard—pushes it in all the way until I cry out; pain and pleasure escaping from the back of my throat. I press my ass into him, spread my legs. I want him. Oh how I want him! "I'm going to fuck you until you pass out, whore," he says in my ear; his words harsh and raspy. He pulls out, yanks me by my hair, pulling me away from the wall. "Bend over."

I bend over.

He slaps my ass, hard. Slaps it again. Sharp stings pulsate to my clit. "Pull open your ass."

I pull it open. And he rams his dick into the back of my pussy, pushing what's left of the dripping ice into my asshole. He is rough and determined. I squirm and yelp.

"Don't run now," he says, stuffing my ass. "Take what you give." I let out a load moan. My heated pussy gets hotter as the ice freezes and numbs the walls in my ass. The contrasting sensations drive me over the edge.

"Oh yes...uhhhhh...fuuuuuccccck me..."

Like a wild animal, I grunt and growl and greedily gulp his dick in with my pussy, winding and pumping my hips. I reach in back of me. Pull him into me by the back of his thighs. Dig my nails into his flesh.

He hits my spot; he can feel it. I can feel it: an orgasm swelling. He continues pounding me, fucking me deep and hard and fast. I am losing myself to his rapid thrusts, losing myself to his sweet, merciless fucking. My body shakes. My knees wobble. And I come hard, wet, dripping; coating his cock, soaking his balls, my thighs, the floor.

T he minute I walk through the door, I realize that I have no business being here. That being here could become potentially problematic—for whom, I'm not sure. But that is what I was feeling when Emerson called me this morning and asked me to meet him at the Sheraton for a *late* lunch. "I only wanna talk" is what he said to me.

"We can talk over the phone," I shot back, replaying Persia's conversation she said she'd had with him. She asked Paris and me to ignore his calls, and delete his number. Paris said she would. I was silently reluctant, but agreed to as well. A part of me did want to see him, shit...*and* fuck him again, too. Still, I resisted, fought to keep him at bay; partly out of loyalty to Persia for wanting to dismiss him, even though I wasn't ready to. And I don't think Paris wanted to either. Then again, it probably didn't matter to her one way or another. She usually just goes with the flow. But, I wanted to keep him around a little longer. Shit, I like...uh, *liked* him. There was something different about him. Oh, well. Anyway, the three of us have a pact. Whatever men we each bring into our space, if we say they have to go, then we each respect it. And out they go. And we never, ever, go behind the other's backs to see them, again; no matter what, especially when he isn't someone one of us has brought into our circle ourselves.

That's what we agreed upon. Well, that's what Persia suggested we do. And, thus far, that's what we've done. So hearing Emerson telling me he wanted to see me, *today*. That what he had to say was not something he wanted to say over the phone had sparked my curiosity, to say the least. Still, my allegiance to the pact forced me to push out, "I can't."

He sighed. "Yo, don't give me that. You can do whatever you want. What, you scared of Persia finding out or something?"

I frowned. "I'm a grown-ass woman," I snapped with attitude. "I do what I want, when I want. Persia is my sister. Not my keeper."

"I can't tell."

"Think what you like," I retorted.

"Well, then, let's talk."

"I'm listening."

"Porsha, c'mon. You've known me for over seven months. Have I ever called you asking to see you alone?"

I thought about his question for a moment. *Mmmm. Now that I sit here and think about it, he's never called me; only texted.* "No, I can't say that you have."

"Exactly. So all I'm asking for is an hour of your time. That's it. Is that too much to ask?"

"Why can't you take no for an answer, and leave it at that?"

"Why should I?"

"Look, Persia told us all about the chick you *feeling*, so what we need to talk about?"

"Listen. I don't wanna get into this over the phone. I'ma be at the Sheraton over on Frontage Road at two. I wanna talk. That's all I'm asking. At least hear me out. I'll be there until three o'clock. If you don't show up, then I won't bother you again. Don't let me down."

"I'm not coming." I told him flat out. And at the time those words left my mouth, I meant them. Yet, here I am—sitting across from his sexy-ass at The Bar, sipping on my second drink two weeks after his phone conversation with Persia, staring into his dreamy eyes like I don't have a care in the world.

"Sooooo," I ask, eyeing him over the rim of my drink. "What's so urgent that you needed to say it to me in person instead of telling me over the phone?"

He smiles, eyeing me back. "I wanted to see you."

I frown. "You already said that."

He leans forward, touches my hand with two gentle strokes of his fingers. "I've missed you."

I tilt my head. "You've missed...*me?* Oh really?" I question, skepticism dripping from my tone.

He strokes my hand again. His touch feels good. "Yeah, I've missed *you*."

I pull my hand away from his. "Since when, Em?"

"Porsha, I've always dug you." I raise a brow. "No bullshit."

He tells me that I'm the chick he's been feeling. That he realized he was catching feelings for me four months ago, but had tried to ignore them; tried to push them aside. Tells me how, after nights of fucking my sisters and me, he would go home and lie in bed, thinking about me. Trying to figure out how he got so caught up in me. I sit here and stare at this fine-ass man as he shares this with me. As he tells me how much he thinks about me; how he had to distance himself from the three of us because it was becoming more difficult for him to sex the three of us and not feel uncomfortable. That for the last two months, anytime he was with us, he'd try hard to block out Persia and Paris and keep his focus on me. My kiss, my touch, the way I felt when he was inside of me. I almost fall out of my seat when he tells me he felt a connection to me the first time we kissed.

"I know you felt it, too," he says, licking his lips with the tip of his tongue.

I narrow my eyes, trying to figure out how he knew that I had also felt it. There was something in that first kiss. The minute his lips had touched mine, then his tongue danced its way into my mouth, I felt myself get weak at the knees as a surge of something much greater than lust washed over me. But I dismissed the feeling. Well, made an earnest attempt to. But anytime he kissed me, that weak-at-the-knees kind of feeling would come over me, again. So most times I would avoid kissing him.

"Maybe I did; maybe I didn't. At this point it doesn't really matter. What does your girl have to say about all of this?"

"What? Have you not heard anything I've said? There is no *girl*."

The way he emphasizes girl causes an alarm to go off in my head. I blink. *Ohmygod. I've sucked this nigga's dick raw.*

Yeah, but Persia's licked all up in his ass. She would have definitely put him on blast if she suspected he liked tossing his ass up.

But he likes it licked.

So what? That doesn't mean he's into other men. Besides, he's never asked to be plugged or fingered, so maybe not.

Yeah, but that doesn't mean...

Ugh! Don't tell me this nigga has been fudge-packing another nigga in his ass, instead.

Girl, stop! The way he slings that dick up in a pussy, there's no way.

"Are you bisexual?" I ask, trying to shake these racing—okay, paranoid—thoughts out of my head. I keep my eyes on him, gauging his response.

He frowns, matching my stare. "*What?* Why would you ask me some crazy shit like that?"

"Well, the way you said 'there is no *girl*' as if you were telling me in an underhanded kind of way that there *is* someone else, but it isn't a female."

"No, what I am telling you is that there is *no one* else; period. I mean, yeah, I was talking to someone for a minute. It wasn't anything serious. I thought she would help keep my mind off you. But, it didn't. It only made me think of you more. Don't know how many times I was tempted to say, 'fuck it' and let things stay the way they were just so I could keep seeing you. But, I couldn't. That shit was killing me."

"So there's no other chick?"

"No. No one."

"Hmm. Well, you still haven't answered the question."

"What question is that?"

"Are you bisexual? I mean, if you are, it's okay with me. Wait a minute. No, the hell it wouldn't be. I'd be pissed the hell off at you for not telling us up front. But I still want to know. So are you or not?"

He shakes his head, smirking. His body language, his eyes... nothing shifts in a way that heightens my concern. "I'm from far that. Trust me. Never have; never will. I don't knock anyone else's flow. But that ain't mine. There ain't shit a nigga can do for me, aiight. So relax."

I silently sigh, relieved. "Were you really in the Poconos doing construction or were you up there laid up with some broad?"

He keeps his eyes locked on mine. "Both."

"So, is it *me* you miss, or the idea of still *fucking* me and my sisters?"

"I guess you're still not hearing me. Or listening to a word I've said. Are you?"

"I heard you. So you're telling me you didn't enjoy my sisters and me tag-teaming the dick?"

He laughs. "Oh, wow…so that's what y'all were doing, *tag-teaming* the dick?"

I laugh, too. "Don't sit here and try to act like you don't know. And you loved every minute of it."

"Yeah, aiight; true-true. I'm not gonna front. Fucking the three of you was like…wow. How many cats get to fuck three fine-ass women, sisters no less, at the same time? And then for y'all to be triplets, identical at that." He shakes his head, smiling. "We had some good times."

"Yeah," I say, finally pulling my hand back, "we did. And now you've been cut from the team."

"Hold up. I wasn't cut from jack. I told Persia I wasn't beat anymore." I raise a brow. Tell him that's not what she said. "Listen, I don't care what she said. I'm telling you what I told her."

"Okay. And what did you tell her?"

"That I'm feeling someone. And I couldn't keep fucking the three of y'all. Listen…" He pauses. I take a slow sip from my drink, waiting. "I ain't gonna lie. Yeah, I miss that pussy. The three of y'all together are beasts. But I already told you. I *miss* you the most." I laugh. "Yo, why you laughing? I'm—"

I put my hand up to stop him. "Em, don't. You call me out the blue telling me all this. Let's be honest here. My sisters and I are mirror images. When you look at one of us, you see all three of us, okay. So…how are you only missing me?"

"Yeah, true. The three of you are sexy as fuck. I can't front. But, you know like I do that the three of you are very different, too. At first glance, you all definitely seem to be alike in every way. But if someone is around the three of you long enough they'll notice that as much as the three of you are very much similar, y'all are equally different. Persia's all dominate and controlling. Paris comes off like she's reserved and innocent. And, then…"

He smiles. "There's you—a mixture of the two. And you're the sexiest, to me. Bottom line, I'm not interested in being back in *their* beds."

"Then what *are* you interested in?"

"*You*," he says, resting his forearms up on the table. "I thought it was obvious. I guess not. So let me make it clear. The only woman I'm interested in is *you*. The only woman's bed I wanna be in is *yours*." I blink. Then stare at him. *This nigga must be high.* "Why you looking at me like you think I'm bugging or something? Like I told you, I started pulling away purposefully. Not because I'm out here getting pussy somewhere else. I know what I want. And I know who I want it with."

"And what's that, Em? What is it you want?"

"I wanna spend time with you, *alone*. No Persia barking orders, cracking whips 'n shit. No Paris watching us, playing in her pussy. I wanna take you away for the weekend. Make love to *you* on a beach somewhere."

"So you just want pussy?" I ask, feeling myself starting to become aroused. I press my legs together.

"Yo, I want more than your pussy. I can get that anytime. Shit, I was getting it with you and your sisters, remember?"

I roll my eyes. "Whatever."

"Roll them pretty eyes all you want. Bottom line is: I want you. I don't care about who you and your sisters have slept with together. Or how many cats you've let knock it down solo. I wanna spend time with *you*. I wanna make love to *you*. I wanna fuck *you*. Maybe I'm fucked up for wanting that. But, it is what it is. And that's how I feel. I wanna chill and do nothing at all, with you. It's all good. We don't even have to fuck, if that's what you want. I'd be cool with that, too. Like I told you, there is no other chick I'm seeing *or* fucking. I've had you on the brain hard for a minute. You have my nose wide open, Porsha. I wanna see where it goes. If it doesn't work out, then cool. At least I gave it my best and that's as real as it gets. We can take it slow, or we can speed race it. It's whatever. I'll let you decide how we proceed."

Wow. I sit back in my chair, speechless. I sweep my bang across my forehead, pulling its end behind my ear. This is all too much for me to digest. "Give me a minute to process this."

He sits back in his chair. Gives me space, allows me a moment to contemplate.

Don't even think about going there with him.

I'm not.

Then why are you sitting here entertaining the idea?

I'm not. I'm simply mulling over everything he's told me. No harm in that.

Bitch, lies! Who you kidding? This damn man has your pussy steaming right now. Fuck him for old time's sake. No one has to know.

I keep my eyes on him as he reaches over and takes my hand in his. In spite of my smile, there's an awkward silence, filled with a thick sexual tension between the two of us that I'm trying my damndest to ignore. But there's no denying it. And the fact is, I want dick!

Don't do it. You know the rules.

Fuck rules. Rules are made to be broken.

How you think Persia will feel when she finds out? She'll be pissed.

Oh, please. What's there to be pissed about? Emerson was never her man. He was our *fuck toy.*

"So, what's up?" he asks, slicing into the one-sided conversation going on in my head. "What you thinking about?"

You! "Em, I've heard everything you've said. And I'm still trying to wrap my mind around most of it. I mean, the fact that you're sitting here telling me you have feelings for me is one thing. And the fact that you were fucking my sisters and me is another. I don't think I can go there with you. Actually, I know I can't."

He glances down at his watch, then around the room. It's slowly starting to get busy in here. I glance down at my watch and see why. It's going on quarter to four. "Look, how about we go somewhere else to finish talking about this."

I tilt my head, eyeing him. "Like where?"

He grins. "I got us a room."

I'm not sure why I'm not surprised by what he's said. Not that I expected to hear this. But now that I have, I'm of two minds. One is saying stay. The other is saying get the hell up and run.

To fuck him or not to fuck him.

That is the question.

The answer comes quick the minute he stands up. "Let's go."

"I feel awful about how I spoke to you at the diner," I say to my mother, deciding it was time to make amends. It's been three weeks since that incident and this is the first time that I've spoken to her. "I'm really sorry for my behavior."

"Well, you should be," she says. I sigh, realizing she's not going to make this an easy process. "I've never tolerated disrespect from you girls. I raised you better than that. That behavior was so unlike *you.*"

"I know, Mother," I say apologetically. "I feel really bad about it."

She grunts. "Mmmph. You ought to. Then it takes you *three* weeks to come to your senses and realize your wrongdoing?" *My wrongdoing? What about yours?* I remind myself that this call isn't about her. It's about me. I apologize again. Tell her how bad I feel. "Well, you should. You don't know how bad I wanted to get up and slap you into yesterday, but I wasn't going to act a fool up in there. I figured you were doing a good job of that on your own. And don't think I didn't tell your father how you carried on. All we were doing was having a simple conversation and, out of nowhere, you went wild. You spoke to me like I was some bitch—excuse my French, out on the streets."

I cringe at her using the word, *bitch*. That is so not like her. I've only heard her use that word when she was referring to one of our father's numerous mistresses. "What you did was uncalled for," she continues. "You were really trying to take me to the streets and have me go ghetto on you. I had to really catch myself from beating your ass."

I roll my eyes. Once again, she takes no responsibility for her mouth. She doesn't even realize what she says. Or maybe she does and doesn't care. Persia's voice creeps up in my head. *I don't know why you waste your time. I keep telling you that woman is unbearable.* I take a deep breath. Decide to give her another dose of truth. *Don't even waste your breath.* "Mom, do you even care that you have three daughters who practically avoid you? Don't you want to have a better relationship with us?

She huffs. "Of course I do. What kind of damn foolish question is that?"

I shake my head, accepting that this conversation is going to go nowhere real fast. "Mom, you're right. It was a foolish question. Whatever was I thinking? Like I said, I only called to apologize to you; that's it. Not for you to try to make me feel worse than I've already been feeling for disrespecting you the way I did. You either accept it or you don't. But I'm not going to get into it with you again."

"The way you spoke to me hurt me deep."

"Ohmygod, Mother. Don't." My sisters and I call her *Mother* when she's gotten under our skin. Well, Porsha, being Porsha, calls her that whether or not she's grated on her last nerve.

"Don't, what?"

"Don't play victim. We *both* know you're *not* the victim here."

"Paris, I don't know what I did wrong."

I take a deep breath. "You didn't *do* anything wrong. It's what you said, that was totally out of line." I kindly replay the conversation back to her.

"Are you serious?" she asks incredulously. "I was speaking honestly. And you take offense to that."

"Mom, you know what. I'm gonna let you go. You call me when you understand that some of what comes out of your mouth is hurtful; maybe not to Persia, or even to Porsha. But it hurts *me*. And you simply brush it off like it's okay. Well, it's not. I want nothing more than to have a better relationship with you, one where I'm not walking on eggshells wondering when you're going to say something thoughtless or callous. But I'm not going to allow you to say disrespectful and hurtful things to me, or about me or my sisters. Mother or not, I'm not going to stand for it any longer. You're my mother. I love you. But sometimes I don't like you. And I don't think you like yourself. How could you?"

Surprisingly, she's quiet—too quiet if you ask me. I pause. Ask her if she's still on the line. "I'm here," she says, curtly. For some reason I get the sense that Daddy has spoken to her. That perhaps he's put his foot down with her.

"Well, have you heard a word I've said?"

"Oh, I've heard you loud and clear. You think I'm a horrible mother. That nothing I've done has been right."

Oh, for the love of God! Here we go with this victim shit again. I sigh. "If that's what you've heard, then shame on you."

"You basically want me to walk around pretending that I'm happy about how you and your sisters are living. Well, I'm sorry, I won't. And I can't."

"And you've sadly missed the whole point. You don't have to be happy about anything we do. I'm not asking you to be. All I'm asking is for you to be mindful about what you say, and how you say it. I don't think that's much to ask for. We barely come around you, now. Persia barely speaks to you. And Paris tolerates you with a long-handled spoon. And if you keep it up, I'm gonna cut you off next. Is that what you want?"

I massage my temples, fighting back a headache.

She lets out an annoyed sigh. I can tell, trying to bite her tongue.

"Of course it's not. But I'm the parent here. Not you, Persia or Porsha. And I will not tolerate being disrespected by any of you."

"Then try respecting us. Try treating us like grown women, not little girls who have no clue about the world around us. We are beautiful, educated, successful women, thanks to you and Daddy. So you should be proud of our accomplishments, instead of always criticizing us."

"I *am* proud of you girls. I just don't like what the three of you are doing with your lives."

"Mom, bottom line: it's none of your business. So, leave it alone."

"Fine. From now on, my mouth is shut."

"Good," I say, glancing at my watch. *Thirty minutes going around in circles with her. This makes no sense.* "Allow us to be your daughters; not your enemies." She tells me she only wants what's best for us. That she worries we'll end up getting hurt. I want to tell her so badly that no one can hurt us as much as she has. But I don't. I don't have the heart to tell her this. "Mom, I know you do. But you go about it all wrong."

"Well, it's obvious we're getting nothing accomplished with this phone conversation."

"That's because you're not open to hearing anything," I tell her, glancing at the time again. "Look I have to get going. I'll call you one day next week, okay?"

We exchange a few more words before I tell her that I love her, then say our goodbyes. I immediately call Porsha. She picks up on the sixth ring. "Hey, girl, I just got off the phone with Mom."

She clucks her tongue. "Mmmph. Let me guess. She found a way to put it all on you, right?"

"She tried, but I didn't let her."

"Good for you. So how did you end things with her?"

"I apologized and she accepted."

"Mmm," is all she says, pausing. I can tell she wants to say more, but she doesn't. "So, is it busy at the boutique today?"

"It's Monday," I remind her. "The store is closed."

She laughs. "Oh, that's right. Girl, my mind is all over the place. I have so many clients scheduled this month I don't know if I'm coming or going."

"That's a good thing," I say. "That means business is keeping you busy."

"It's a great thing. Trust me. Thank God for Uncle Sam, and all of his taxes. You won't ever hear me complaining. But I need to get out of here for a few hours. Play hooky for the rest of the day. What are you doing?"

"Not a damn thing," I say, staring at my reflection in the mirror.

"How about we drive to Short Hills and hit the mall? I need to pick up something cute to wear this weekend?" I ask her what she has planned.

"Angel's flying in for the weekend."

"Oh, okay. How's that nut doing?"

She laughs. "Nuttier as ever, but that's still my girl."

Angel's her best friend since junior high school. And she's the thorn in Persia's side. For some reason, Persia has never liked her. I believe it has to do with the fact that the two of them are very close; almost like sisters. Although Persia will deny it, I think she's jealous of Angel and feels threatened by their relationship. Why is beyond me since the three of us—though we've had our share of cat fights and misunderstandings like any other siblings—we love each other dearly and are extremely close. Come to think of it, Persia has always been overprotective of Paris and me, even when there was no reason to be. And she has always seemed to have a problem with anyone who she thinks might get in the middle of our relationship.

"Some things never change," I say, chuckling.

"They sure don't," she agrees. "I can't wait to see my sistergirl. We are gonna cut up something terrible." I smile, knowingly. "Anyway, I need to find something fierce to wear."

"What time do you wanna go?"

"Right now. Something Gucci and cute is calling my name."

I laugh. "Come to think about it, it's calling mine, too."

"Good, then. It's settled. I'll swing by to pick you up and we'll be on our way. See if Persia wants to go."

"Uh, it's you and me, boo," I say, walking into my closet to find something to wear. "Persia's out somewhere reeling in a new customer."

"Good for her. We'll pick her up something *cute*."

"See you when you get here," I say before hanging up. I glance out the window, looking at the sky, deciding today's a nice day to wear a denim wrap dress and a sexy pair of heels. I hop in the shower, wash myself good, then hop out. Wrapping a towel around me, I strut out into my bedroom with beads of water still rolling down my skin to answer my ringing cell. Glancing at the screen, I frown, not familiar with the number. "Hello?"

"Hey, cuz. Long time, no hear."

"Gaaaaaaaaaarrett," I scream into the phone, excited to hear his voice. "How's my favorite cousin doing? Where the hell have you been, man? I haven't talked to you in ages?"

"I know, cuz. I'm real sorry for not staying in touch. Things were real hectic for a minute. But, I'm good. How've you been? You've been in my thoughts, babe."

"And you've been in mine," I say, applying lotion to my legs. "I'm fabulous, boo; still fly and sexy as ever. You know how I do it."

He laughs. "I wouldn't expect anything less. How are Persia and Paris?" I tell him they're good. He wants to know how my parents are doing. My father and his father are brothers. Although Garrett's a few years older than us, growing up we spent a lot of time together; especially during the summers. He was like the son our father never had, and the big brother we dreamed of. "Dad's doing wonderful. Mom, well…you know her. She's still mom. Still fussing about something every chance she gets."

He chuckles, knowingly. "That's good. Tell them I asked about them."

"I sure will." I ask him how his parents are doing. He tells me well. Tells me they're thinking about moving to Florida to get away from the brutal Jersey winters we've been having and all of these high-ass taxes. I tell him I definitely understand.

"How's business treating you, Miss Big Time Boutique owner?"

"Believe it or not, it's been good this year. It was a little scary the first two years, with the economy being all crazy. But, surprisingly, things have picked up and I can keep the bills paid."

"That's definitely a blessing," he says. "I always knew you'd be successful."

"Awww, thanks," I say, sliding into a purple thong. "It's definitely a blessing." I toss the matching bra back into the drawer, deciding to let my titties bounce freely. "Listen, enough about me. I wanna hear all about you and *your* blessings. What in the world have you been up to? Daddy told me you had a baby."

"Thanks. Yeah, I have a son. His name's Garrison. He's almost a year old, and into everything. But that's my little man."

"And why don't I have any pictures of him?" I ask, feigning hurt. "I thought I was your favorite cousin."

He laughs. "You are, babe. Charge it to my head; not my heart. Bianca handles all that kinda stuff."

"Oooooh, Biiiiiiiaaaaaanca…Do tell, now. So she's your baby momma."

He laughs. "She's actually more than my baby momma; she's my fiancée."

"*Fiancée?* Oh nooooo. You didn't clear this with me," I tease, walking into the bathroom to comb out my wrap. "I need to meet homegirl, ASAP."

"Most definitely," he says, sounding really happy. "You might have seen her before."

"Oh really? Is she from our old neighborhood?" He tells me no. Tells me her family is from Plainfield, but she's lived in Maplewood for over ten years. He mentions that she gets her hair done down at Nappy No More—Pasha's hair salon. "Really? I haven't been there in a while. But you're probably right. I might've seen her there before. Speaking of which, did you hear Pasha's getting married?"

"Yeah, I know. Bianca got an invitation. So, it looks like we'll be seeing you there."

"They're friends like that? Oh, wow. That's great, then. I can't wait to see you and to meet her as well." I glance at the time. *Porsha should be almost here*, I think, slipping into a pair of Jimmy Choos. "So when are the two of you tying the knot? I want details. And don't hold anything back. How'd y'all meet? What's she's like? How long y'all been together? I want it all, boo. I wanna know from start to finish what you've been up to and who this woman is that's kept my favorite cousin from staying in touch with me."

He laughs. Tells me they've been dating for almost two years; that they're getting married in October. That that was one of the reasons he was calling. He needed our address. Tells me he expects to see us there, celebrating his big day. "Oh, trust me. I wouldn't miss it for the world. Now tell me all about *you*."

He tells me that he's finally obtained his master's degree in

Criminal Justice from John Jay College in New York, and is up for a promotion at his job with the New Jersey State Police. I smile. As a kid, he was always helping someone, saving someone (or something), or trying to protect them. Garrett was like a Superhero—always looking for the good in people, somewhere trying to save the day. So it was no surprise to me when he went into law enforcement. He tells me that he and his fiancée, Bianca, met through her brother who he's close friends with and who's also a State Trooper. That their relationship started out as a causal thing, but evolved into more. Tells me she avoided him like the plague. That she wanted no parts of him outside of sex. That she had ended things between them when he pressed her for more. But he wouldn't give up. Tells me he had to have her. And, then when he learned she was pregnant with his child, he knew there was no turning back. States getting her pregnant wasn't planned; that she initially planned to keep it from him and have an abortion. But something changed her mind. And he's glad. He states he asked her to marry him right after her trip to Egypt. But she refused. Then he asked her again after their son was born, and she said yes. He tells me they hadn't set a date until recently. The way he's talking, the pride and joy beaming from of his tone, he sounds like a man who is truly in love.

"Wow, congratulations," I say, smiling. "You sound really happy. She must be a really special woman."

"Thanks, cuz. She is. And I am happy, very. She's a good woman, Paris, and a great mother to our son. I can't wait for you to meet her." I tell him I'm looking forward to it. I hear Porsha coming through the door. I reach for the bottle of Joy by Jean Patou from my perfume shelf, dabbing a little—because at five hundred dollars a bottle, that's all you need—behind my ears, then on my wrists. I rub it in. Inhale in its peachy and leafy green scent. *Delicious!*

"What about you? Seeing anyone special?" I tell him no. Tell him that work keeps me too busy; that I don't have time for anyone special. "You're too beautiful not to. You have to make time for love, babe. Life is too short not to allow someone special into your life."

"Well, before that happens," I tell him as a glide a coat of Berry Bling lipstick across my lips, "He's going to have to find *me*, first." I pop my lips together, pleased with my succulence. *Way to go, CoverGirl! The Queen Collection never lets me down.* "And right at this moment, it doesn't look like that's going to happen anytime soon." He tells me he wants to introduce me to one of his boys, a state trooper. That he thinks I'd like him. I laugh. "Uhh, no thank you. The last time I let you fix me up with someone he was cross-eyed and had a serious overbite. He looked like something from out of *Star Wars*."

He laughs. "But he was a nice guy."

"And he was ugly."

He keeps laughing. "And he really dug you."

"Mmmph, I wouldn't know."

"That's because you didn't give him a chance," he says, still laughing.

"I'm so glad you find that funny."

"I'm sorry, babe. You crack me up; still witty as ever. I wish you woulda gave him a chance. He looks nothing like that now."

"I couldn't. It hurt my eyes looking at him...."

"Hooker, why aren't you ready?" Porsha snaps, walking into my bedroom. "You know I'm tryna get my shop on and you up in here bullshitting. Let's go." I tell her I am ready. Let her know who I'm on the phone with. She grabs the phone from me, practically snatching my ear along with it. "Ohmygod, Garrett, how the hell have you been?...No, it's Porsha..."

While the two of them are talking, I open my Valentino hand-bag, dumping everything out onto my bed. I decide to change bags, placing everything into a denim, crinkled leather Prada bag.

Porsha cuts her eye over at my bag, squinting. Fact is it's hers. I've simply claimed it as mine. I ignore her stare… "Ohmygod, you're getting married? When? Congratulations…Boy, now you know we'll be there with bells on. Wouldn't miss it for the world… okay…well, when are we gonna meet her?…Oh really? Oh, then we'll see her there…cool. I look forward to meeting her…I will… Promise…Okay…Love you, too." She presses the END button, then hands me back my phone. "Bitch," she snaps, pointing at her handbag. "I was looking for *that*."

I laugh, grabbing my shades and walking out the bedroom. "Oh, girl, get over it. You couldn't have been looking *too* hard. I've had it for the last six months."

"Whatever," she snaps, following behind me. "I'm gonna start locking my shit up. That'll keep your thieving ass outta my closets."

I slip my sunglasses on the minute I step outside. "Yeah, right; picture that. How you gonna lock me out of anything when, nine times outta ten, I'll end up being the one with the spare key?"

She laughs, disarming her car. "Hooker, get in."

I slip into the passenger seat of her convertible Jag, fastening my seatbelt, laughing at her as she speeds around the circular driveway, like a nut, toward our destination.

"There are three types of niggas, okay," Angel says, eyeing me over the rim of her chocolate martini. She's in town from California for the weekend and we're playing catch-up. Friends since freshman year of high school, Angel's the one person outside of my sisters I trust, and share almost everything with. Being that she now lives in L.A., we only see each other four times a year. She flies out every April for her mother's birthday, and, again, during the Thanksgiving holiday. Then the other two times I fly out there. Tonight we're at Jacksonville Restaurant & Lounge—a cozy spot for the grown and sexy—in Paterson. The atmosphere, scrumptious food, and live band make this a great spot to mix and mingle. Tonight is their Friday night Open Mic series, and of course she convinced me to meet her here so she can tear the spot up. Why she doesn't get serious about her vocals and get into the studio is beyond me—the girl can blow, but she enjoys performing at open mics instead, and will serve them every time.

I sway a bit to the band's rendition of Sade's "I'm A Soldier of Love." "Oooh, this is my shit," I say, snapping my fingers. "I can't wait to see her ass in June."

"Bitch, are you listening to me?" she snaps, feigning annoyance that I've slipped from the conversation; no matter how brief the moment.

I laugh. "Girl, I heard you. Now go 'head and finish what you were saying."

She shoots me a look, tucking a curl of hair behind her right ear. The one-carat diamond stud in her lobe twinkles. "Are you sure? 'Cause I can wait until the song is over if you'd like."

I roll my eyes, waving her on. "Girl, go on and break down the types of men for me. I'm all ears."

"Like I was saying, there are three types of niggas. The first type is the nigga who fucks real good. He typically likes to fuck fast, hard, and deep. He'll dick you down rough and dirty and beat the pussy up all night long. *And* have you stealing your momma's social security check to pay his bills...." I laugh. "Girl, I'm serious. Them the type of niggas you gotta fuck in small doses to keep ya ass from becoming strung out. 'Cause if not, he'll have you kicking off your heels and getting real ghetto wanting to throw bricks through windows and shit when he doesn't return your calls...."

I laugh, shaking my head. "Girl, I can't...I just can't. You are killing me right now."

"I'm telling you. He'll have ya ass hiding behind bushes with a can of mace waiting to bring it to a chick's face."

"Where in the world did you come up with this mess?"

She sips her drink, then pops her lips. "While I was on my flight here, I started thinking about all the men I've dated and dumped. Then the idea sorta evolved from that."

I smile.

Angel has always had a very overactive imagination, along with an extremely high sex drive, which is probably why she has a hard time keeping men. Her mind is always going a mile-a-minute, and she tries to fuck every man she's with to death. In all the years I've known her, she's been with more men than I can keep up with. She's been married once—a marriage that only lasted for six months before she left him, engaged three more times after that, and has never stayed in a relationship longer than two years. And she's only thirty-one. Her explanation is, "I'm easily bored with men."

"Oh Lawd," I tease. "You and your imagination. I'm scared to hear the rest."

"Whatever. Are you gonna let me finish or not?"

I raise my glass. "Carry on." I take a sip of my drink, giving her my undivided attention. "I'm dying to hear what that mind of yours has conjured up."

"Mmmph…Annnnnyway. The second type is the nigga who makes love real good. This is the nigga who seduces you into a trance-like state. He likes to grind up in the pussy. He knows how to wind his hips slow and deep. He gives you the dick real sexy-like. He listens to your body, explores every inch of it with his lips, mouth, tongue and hands, then dicks you down with intense, passionate strokes. He makes love to your mind, body, and soul. Making sure he gets up in every nook and cranny of your inner being. He's gonna make sure you get yours before he gets his. This nigga aims to please you. And he makes sure you feel loved—even if he really doesn't. And he makes you feel like you're the only woman in his life, even when you're not. Then when he's done serving you, he avoids your calls, and ignores your pleas for more of that good dick. He'll have you blowing up his phone like a mad woman. Or have you somewhere crouched down low in a corner wringing your damn hands, or curled up in a corner crying."

I shake my head. "Hilarious."

She takes another sip of her drink. "I'm telling you some good shit, girl."

"And the third type?" I ask, picking up my Lemondrop martini. I lick the sugary rim, then take a slow sip.

She leans in, props her forearms up on the table and clasps her hands together. "Girl, the third type is the nigga who knows how to do both. Whew, his ass is double trouble, okay. He'll have you wanting to make a mold out of his dick just so you can carry it around in your purse to pull out and use at your discretion."

I wave her on. "Girl, your ass is crazy."

"Crazy hell," she says, chuckling. She pauses, to sip her drink. "Girl, I'm telling you. This is the type of nigga you'll wake up and find yourself either locked in a padded room over, or sitting up in a jail cell 'cause you done blacked out and sliced the nigga's dick off. Then went out and stabbed up every bitch who you *thought* he might have been fucking. This is the nigga who'll make ya ass nutty for sure. And he's definitely the one you need to try to stay away from if you know ya ass is already unstable."

Angel has me laughing hysterically. It's a good thing I don't have on any eyeliner. Otherwise I'd have black streaks running down my face from laughing so hard, looking like a damn clown. "Okay, so answer me this," I say, pausing to collect myself while dabbing my eyes with a napkin. "What do you call a man who wants you to do all the work while he just lays there like he's king of the jungle?" I ask the question already knowing the answer—well, my answer: He's a selfish motherfucker! But I'm curious to hear her spin on it.

"Oh, you're talking about Mister King Ding-a-Ling, the one who thinks his dick's been wrapped in gold and his balls dipped in honey. Girl, that's an easy one. That's the kinda motherfucker who'll have you running out searching for new dick real quick."

"Okay," I say, snapping my fingers. I hoist my glass up in the air. She does the same. "Poof, poof...gone." We clink our glasses. "Lazy-dick motherfucker."

She scrunches her face, shaking her head as if in thought. "Mmmph. A lazy-dick nigga is the worst kind, if you ask me. And why does it *always* have to be them big-dicked motherfuckers wanting to lay back?" I tell her I don't always think it's hung niggas. She waves me on. "Girlfriend, you need to go back and rewind the tapes, okay. Trust me. Sit back and watch the show. Now I'm not saying all. But, it's typically them niggas who have more dick than they know what to do with doing that dumb shit. You know like I do that the little dick motherfuckers don't mind putting in extra work. Shit, they're the ones who usually feel like they have something to prove to you so they'll try to fuck and suck your pussy all night long in order to make up for what they lack in the dick department."

The waitress comes over to us carrying a tray with two drinks on it. "These are from the gentleman at the bar," she says, pointing toward the bar area. Angel and I look over in his direction. He nods at us, raising his drink. We do the same.

"He looks like he might be fine as hell," Angel says to me. "But the light's not bright enough over there to know for sure."

I laugh. "Girl, enjoy the damn drink. Who cares what his ass looks like?"

She bucks her eyes. "Shit, I do. I might wanna get me some dick tonight." I laugh at her ass. *Mmmm, he does look like he can get it*, I think, cutting my eyes in his direction on the sly. She jumps. "Oh, shit. They're getting ready to start open mic."

The emcee introduces the band, then opens the floor to those who wish to perform. I ask her what song she's going to sing. She tells me she's going to serve them Alicia Keys' "Lesson Learned." I smile, knowing she's going to bring the crowd to their feet. I take a sip from drink, and wait for the show to begin.

The first performer does her rendition of Beyoncé's "Halo." And I must say she kills it. Right after her a tall, sexy, thuggish brown-skinned man with cornrows takes the floor and sings that old school joint "'Cause I Love You" by Lenny Williams. Whew, the way he holds those notes starts to make my pussy pulsate. I close my eyes and take in his voice, imagining him singing this in my ear, offering me up some thug passion. Then just when I think it can't get any better and my pussy can't get any hotter, the next performer is the same guy who sent over drinks to Angel and me. And he's not only sexy, he's *very* fuckable. He has an exotic look about him, like he might be mixed. He takes the mic and sings Eric Benet's "Sometimes I Cry." He sings it with such a beautiful passion that everything in me starts to melt. I close my eyes and sway, imagining him standing in front of me butt-naked, singing this as I am down on my knees sucking his dick. By the time he finishes the last note, I feel my pussy pulling in my thong. Every woman in here is waving their hands up in the air. Some are jumping up out of their chairs, cheering him on.

As the waitress brings me over another drink, Angel is taking the mic. The minute she belts out the first note, I spot Mr. Sometimes I Cry walking in my direction. I catch his eye as he approaches my table. I smile. Decide to not let him get away without saying something to him. "You can sing to me anytime. You really killed it."

He smiles back at me. "Thanks. Glad you enjoyed it. I 'preciate that. I was on my way back to the bar and saw you sitting over here by yourself so I decided to come over and holla at you. You mind if I sit?"

Hell no, I don't mind if your sexy-ass sits, I say in my head. I extend him the chair. "Sure. I'd like that." He glances over toward Angel, who is belting out one note after another.

"Yo, your girl can blow."

I smile. "Yes, she can." *Not that I've paid attention. But, I'd damn sure like to blow you.* Dirty thoughts of crawling under the table and caressing his cock with my lips and tongue start invading my mind. I press my legs together. "So what motivated you to sing that particular song?" He looks away for a moment, then brings his attention back to me. Tells me he had lost someone special in his life and although it's been two years since her death, it still hurts. And sometimes he cries over the loss.

For some reason I feel endeared to him. Without thinking, I reach over and place my hand over his. "I'm so sorry to hear that. What happened to her?" He tells me she was serving in the military. That she was killed over in Iraq. I can see the love and hurt in his eyes as he tells me this. "Oh, wow," I say, feeling myself getting choked up. "So sorry to hear that."

"Thanks," he says, placing his other hand over mine. "I'm good, though."

I get tingly all over. "Ohmygod, you have some soft hands for a man."

He laughs. "I hear that a lot."

"I'm sure you do," I say coyly. "I bet you give great massages, too."

He grins. "Yeah, I can do a lil' sumthin'. So, is it aiiight if I buy you another drink?"

I glance over at Angel when I hear the thunderous applause. "How about I get this round, and you get the next?"

"Cool." He flags over the waitress, motions for another round. "I'm Faruq, by the way." I tell him mine. He nods his head, approvingly. "Nice name. I saw you when you and your girl walked in and was hoping I'd get a chance to holla at you."

"Well, I'm glad the opportunity presented itself." I lean forward in my seat. "So, Faruq…I like that, by the way. Are you Muslim?" He tells me his family is, but that he doesn't follow its doctrine. That he's originally from Egypt, but has lived in the States since he was ten; that his name means one who distinguishes truth from falsehood.

"Oh, wow, interesting. I've always wanted to visit Egypt. It looks like it's a beautiful place." He tells me it is; suggests that I visit. That he thinks I'd love it there. "Maybe when I go, you'll come along to be my tour guide."

He smiles. "Oh, cool. I'd like that." After a few stops along the way from patrons telling her how great she sounded, Angel finally makes it back over to the table as the waitress returns with our drinks. Since Faruq's back is toward her, he doesn't see her raising her brow at me and mouthing, *"Bitch."*

I smile. "Faruq, this is my girl, Angel. Angel, Faruq." She comes around and faces him.

He stands up and extends his hand. "Nice meeting you."

She takes him in, extending her hand. "Likewise," she says, allowing her hand to linger in his a little longer than she should. He's the first to let go. She takes a seat next to me, then pinches me under the table. I flinch.

"Oww."

"You alright, boo?" she asks, feigning concern. I ignore her, taking a sip of my drink.

"Yo, you have a beautiful voice."

She grins, tilting her head. "Oh, you heard me sing?" She cuts her eyes over at me. "'Cause I know this one here didn't hear a word of it with you being such a beautiful distraction. But, thanks. You definitely have it going on yourself."

His smile widens, revealing one dimple in his left cheek. I find myself even more turned on. He thanks her for the compliments.

I laugh. "You know me so well. But you do have a beautiful voice."

She playfully rolls her eyes up in her head. "Whatever. Tell me anything. Annnnyway…Faraad, right?"

He laughs. "Nah, Faruq."

"Oh, Farooook, okay. My bad. Soooo, let's get down to the

nitty-gritty. Who you here with? Are you straight, gay, bi or one of them down-low niggas?"

He laughs at her bluntness. "I see you go in real hard."

I shake my head, placing a hand over my face. "Ohmygod, I don't believe you."

She shrugs. "What? I'm only asking. Well, are you?"

He continues laughing. "Nah, it's all good. Do you, ma. But to answer your questions, I'm here solo. That's how I like to move. And I'm all hetero-man, baby. The only thing swinging low on me is my..." My mouth starts to water as he stops himself. *Oh nooooooooooooooo, don't stop now! Say it, damn it! Saaaay it! Let me hear how low ya dick swings.* "...Let me stop," he continues, chuckling. "Tonight, I'm being a gentleman."

"Oh, don't stop on my account," she teases, twirling a lock of hair. *Oh, this messy hooker is really gonna try 'n make a move on him right in my damn face, knowing he was sitting here talking to me, first.* I decide to bow out gracefully, guzzling down the rest of my drink, then getting up from my seat. Okay, so I'm a little annoyed at her ass. I'll get over it.

"I'll be back. I'm going to the ladies room." He gets up and watches me walk off, then sits back down. As soon as I get into the bathroom, I pull out my phone and check my messages. I have two voice messages, and six text messages. I check my voice messages first, then respond to my text messages. My mother wants to know if I want to drive out to the outlets with her one day next week. Emerson calls. He wants to know if I can squeeze him in to do his taxes. I smile. *Yeah, right. Taxes, my ass*, I think, saving the message. *He wants some more pussy.* Five minutes later, I return to the table and Faruq is nowhere in sight. A part of me is disappointed. "Please don't tell me you chased that fine-ass man away." I am standing with my hands on my hips, squinting at her.

"Oh, relax," she says, waving me on. "He went to the bathroom. I thought you fell in, you were gone so damn long." Of course she's being sarcastic. I let it go over my head, asking her if she was able to weave her web around Faruq. "Girl, I was trying. Trust me. But he flat out told me he was interested in *you*. The whole time you were gone, he kept drilling me about you."

I'm surprised. Well, not really. I mean, why wouldn't he be? But I'm shocked that he told her that. Angel doesn't always do well with rejection. "Oh, and what did you have to say to him?" She tells me she told him she hoped he was enough man for me because I was a whole lot of woman. She gets up from her seat, gathering her bag. "Where are you off to?"

"Girl, I'm ready to blow this joint. It's getting late, and I have to get up early in the morning." I laugh. "What's so funny?"

I shake my head, deciding to keep my comments to myself. But the truth of the matter is, since she couldn't sink her claws into him, now she's ready to go. If the shoe were on the other foot, she'd be trying to shut the place down. "Oh, nothing."

"Are you coming?" she asks as Faruq returns to the table. He stands next to me. Tall and sturdy, towering over me. "Never mind. I already know the answer." I laugh as we hug. I tell her to travel safe and to text me the minute she walks through the door so that I know she made it home. "Don't worry. I will." She looks up at Faruq, extending her hand and smiling. "It was nice meeting you."

"Likewise," he says.

"Now let me see your driver's license," she snaps, eyeing him up and down. "In case you turn out to be a nut-case and try any slick shit on my girl, I need to know who I need to hunt down." He laughs. She raises her brow with one hand on her hip, holding her other hand out. "I'm serious." I shake my head, smiling. He pulls out his wallet and shows her his license. She makes a mental note of his full name and address, then hands it back to him. "Now, y'all have a good night. Don't do anything I wouldn't do." She tosses a wink my way, then flounces toward the door. Her ass bounces in her skirt with each step.

Faruq turns his attention back to me. "Your girl is a real piece of work."

I smile. "That she is."

"I hope you're not leaving, too." I tell him I had planned to but was willing to stay a little longer. "Cool, 'cause I'd like to get you know you better."

And I'd like to fuck you. I smile wider, staring him up and down. *Damn, he's tall.* "Well, I'll stay under two conditions."

He seductively eyes me. "What's that?"

"You buy me another drink. And you dump the gentleman act. I'm not interested in being treated like a lady tonight."

"Oh, is that right?" he questions, sounding caught off-guard. "Well, tell me how you wanna be treated, baby. And you got it."

"I like the sound of that. Let's sit, order drinks and I'll tell you exactly how I want to be treated tonight." He waits for me to sit, then he takes the seat next to me. I lean into him, whisper in his ear. "I'm into role-play. And tonight I want you to treat me like your pretty little slut. You think you can handle that, big daddy?"

He grins. "Let's do this then."

"How tall are you?" He tells me he's six-five, two-hundred-and-twenty-five pounds and I begin to drool, soaking in every inch of him. I wonder how big his dick is. He reads my thoughts.

This time he leans into me and whispers, "And I have a nine-inch cut dick that loves to nut."

And I have a fat, wet pussy that loves to get fucked. I smile, eyeing him lustfully. "I like the sound of that. You're definitely my kind of man."

He grins, rubbing his chin. "Is that right?"

I allow my eyes to roam over his thick neck and broad shoulders down to his muscled triceps and biceps. Talking to this nigga is making my pussy wetter by the minute. Inhaling his cologne, a bolt of electricity seemingly shoots through my clit. My sign, my cue: I need to get fucked. No explanation needed. FUCK me; that's it. I drop my eyes down to his crotch, then discreetly slip my hand into his lap. I let my gaze and hand linger long enough to let him know what I'm most interested in.

He doesn't stop me. His erection begins to stir in his pants. "You like what you feel?" he asks, grinning.

"I sure do. And I wanna *feel* it, too; *every* inch of it deep in my slutty pussy." His cock is now rock hard. I whisper in his ear again. "You don't know me. And I don't know you. But I wanna fuck. Will you take me somewhere and fuck me good?"

He nods. "Baby, as fine as you are, I'll take you wherever you wanna go and fuck you with this hard-ass dick." I massage the head of his dick. "Oh, shit, damn..."

"Let's get out of here."

"I thought you wanted another drink."

"Fuck a drink," I say, squeezing him over his pants. "I want dick. I'll drink you instead."

He laughs. "A woman who knows what she wants. I like. And there's a lot of me to drink, baby. Believe that. But, uh...I can't get up just yet." He looks down in his lap. "You've awakened The Beast. And he's hungry." I laugh, removing my hand. "Give me a minute to put him back to sleep."

"You go on and put him back to sleep. But, be clear. Tonight he's gonna get fed like he's never been fed before." I get up and toss a fifty down on the table. "Meet me outside when you get *him* calmed down."

Passion
CHAPTER NINETEEN

O ooh, *I'ma about to get me some Egyptian ding-a-ling. And I'ma fuck him straight back to the Motherland.* I laugh to myself, thinking about Angel's summation of the types of men there are. I wonder which type he is, then decide it doesn't really matter. *If he's a lazy dick nigga, it's fine by me. I have no problem getting on top and doing all the work.* After all, I propositioned him. *Then again,* I think, glancing up at the sky. I stretch out my arms up over my head. *Please let this man be a good fuck.*

Persia and Paris would have a field day with this fine-ass man, I muse, watching as he struts out of the restaurant walking toward me. But, tonight, he's mine—all six-feet-five inches of him. I don't care where we go. I just want to fuck. I glance at my watch, taking in his in his stride—cool and confident. For some reason, Emerson pops into my head. I blink the image away, bringing this Egyptian prince into view.

"Take me somewhere cheesy and fuck me good," I tell him as he walks up on me. I'm parked on the street, but he's parked over in the parking lot not too far from here. I pull him into me. He leans down and offers me his lips. We kiss. His tongue slips into my mouth, my tongue twirls around his, and I feel my juices slowly seeping out of me. After several more tongue-probing seconds, I push back from him. Tell him sluts don't kiss.

He grins. "Oh, right-right. So, tell me. What does a slut do?"

I look up and down the street, taking him by the hand and pulling him to the side of the building. "They suck dick outside," I tell him as I drop down, reaching for his zipper. I unzip his pants, then fish out The Beast. It has already begun to thicken. I kiss the tip, then swirl my tongue around and over it before placing it into the warmth of my mouth. I lather it with spit, then suck it to its full capacity. Suck him until he's teetering on the edge of an orgasm. I look up at him. Tell him to talk dirty to me.

"Oh, shit...damn. . ." He takes his big hands, holds the sides of my head like a basketball, then thrusts his cock in and out of my mouth. "Yeah, swallow that dick; slutty bitch...oh, fuck..." The harder he pushes, the deeper I swallow. Sucking his dick outside in pitch darkness on the side of a building has my insides overheating. Loud gurgling sounds emit from the back of my throat. Saliva splashes from out of my mouth, drips down to my chin where it clings, then drops to the ground. "Motherfuck...mm-mmph...oh, shit...ya slutty throat is so fucking good. Damn, baby...you a good dick-sucking bitch..." I respond with a moan, gulping him in. "Aaaah shit...I'm gettin' ready to cum..."

In my head, I'm thinking, *well, damn. I just started sucking ya shit five minutes ago and you already bucking 'n shouting about you nutting.* "Yeah, that's it baby. Make that big dick skeet...give me that sweet cream, boo."

It doesn't take long—four minutes, to be exact—for him to announce that he's ready to nut. I grab his balls and gently tug at them, causing him to jerk. "Ohhhhhhh, fuuuuuuck...aaaah... aaaah...shiiiiiiit..."

I stand up, licking my lips as I dig inside my purse for my wipes. *I hope nutting like that isn't this nigga's M.O.* I hand him a packet, then open one for myself. "I hope you don't think this party's over," I say, grabbing him by his sticky dick. I gently yank it.

He smiles. "I damn sure hope not. I'm just getting started."

"Good. 'Cause I have two more holes to be filled." I strut off, heading back to my car with him following behind me.

Fifteen minutes later, we are holed up in a cheap, smutty, run-down motel in downtown Paterson. The room is small. It's scent stale. The smell of smoke and sweaty fucking lingers in the air, clings to the walls. Perfect for a night of hot, slutty fucking!

As soon as we're in the room, we're clawing at one another, practically ripping each other's clothes off. By the time he kicks off his shoes, I've already taken his cock into my mouth, sucking him for the second time. I work my way up and down on it. Bob my head back and forth, fingering my pussy in sync to sucking him. I pull his dick out of my mouth, spitting all over it, then jerking it while sucking on his balls before taking him back into my throat. His hands are running through my hair. Without even knowing him, I know enough to know he is about to cum again. *Oooh, this nigga nuts quick*, I think, gazing up at him with my big brown eyes. *All of this dick and the nigga can't hold his nut.* I work his shaft with my hands as I bob my head back and forth. Slurp, gulp, slurp…slurp, gulp, slurp…*All I know is if this mother-fucker can't get it up again I'ma be hot!*

He lets out a moan. "Ohhh shit, ohhh shit…hol'up, hol'up… you about to make me nut, baby…I don't wanna cum, yet…" He takes hold of my hair and gently pulls me off of him. "You have me so motherfuckin' horny…I wanna eat that fat ass…"

"Oooooh, I want your tongue all in it. Then I want you to eat my sweet, black slutty pussy. You wanna eat my wet pussy?"

"Yeah, baby…"

"You want me to be your slutty whore tonight?"

"Yeah, baby," he says, bending me over, then dropping down on his knees. "I wanna taste all of you. Ya ass, ya pussy..." He pulls open my ass and buries his face in it, gliding his tongue along my crack, then over my hole.

"Mmmm...aaah, yes...you like how that slutty ass tastes?"

He moans, nodding his head as his tongue caresses its opening, then wiggles its way inside. I moan. Tell him to spit in my ass. He does. And this only makes me hornier. I tell him to bite it. Slap it. He does. I crane my neck, look at him. "Ooooh, yessssss, you wanna fuck me deep in my slutty ass?"

He tells me he does. Tells me he wants to fuck me all night. *Nigga, please. Not if you're gonna be nutting all quick and shit.* I tell him to put on a condom. Tell him my ass is aching for his cock.

"I don't have any on me," he says, grinding himself into my ass. The furnace in my pussy goes down by ten degrees. *Oh no the hell this nigga doesn't think he's about to go in me raw*, I think, shifting my ass away from his cock. I tell him where he can find one inside my bag. *Now what if I really* was *a slut?* I shake the looming notion that he'd still fuck me out of my head, concentrating on feeling his wrapped dick in me.

I'm so wet and slick and ready when he finally finds the condom and rolls it on. He positions himself behind me, pulling open my ass. "I want you to fuck my pussy, first," I tell him, arching my back and reaching up underneath me. I take his dick in my hand and guide him to my slippery opening. The head of his dick enters me and I lift my hips up to greet him. "Oh, yes...slam that big cock in me."

He smashes into me, hips frantically banging up against my ass, causing me to jerk forward. "Where the fuck you going? Don't run from this dick, slut..." He slaps me on the ass. "Nasty 'lil bitch..."

"Oh, yessssssss...fuck me, motherfucker...talk that nasty shit..."

"Uhhh, shit...slutty pussy feels so motherfuckin' good..."

Faruq slows his pace, begins to fuck me in slow, deep strokes. With each thrust, my pussy grabs at his dick; his pulsing cock beating against the mounting surge inside me. I writher and wiggle beneath him, moan loud and wild. "You all up in this slutty pussy, motherfucker...ohhhh, yes...fuck me...you want me to be your little slut?"

His hands coil through my hair. Yanking my head back, he pulls my locks like reins on a horse and rides my ass rapidly. "Uhhhh, you got some good-ass pussy...you ready for this dick in that ass?"

Giddy up, motherfucker, I think, moaning. "Yeah, nigga...fuck my pussy...stretch it open, uuhhhh, yessssss...you 'bout to make my pussy nut..." He tells me to roll over on my back, then hoists my legs up over his shoulders, then slips himself back into me and pounds me; his balls slapping up against my asshole. "Uhh... choke me motherfucker..." His hand finds its way to my throat. He presses. "Harder...uhhh, yessss...ooooohhh...aaah, yeah... choke me...mmmm, mmm...fuck me...aaaah...aaaah...yeah, yeah...choke me harder, motherfucker..." He tightens his grip, practically shutting off my airway. I feel myself getting light-headed. This only intensifies my orgasm. He rapidly bangs in and out of me until my walls shake and I explode all over his cock.

He leans in, breathes warmly on my ear, then tickles my earlobe with his wet tongue. "Daaaaamn, baby...this pussy...aaaah, shit...so wet..."

I coo in his ear. "You ready to fuck my fat, juicy, slutty ass? It's real tight for you, too, baby. It's nice and hot, and hungry for some dick. You wanna fuck me deep in it?"

Within minutes, my legs are bent at the knees and pushed up

over my head. His tongue finds my hole, puckering in anticipation. He swirls his tongue around it, causing me to grip the sheets as he works my asshole and slides two fingers into my slippery slit. He uses his thumb to tease my clit while he licks his way up and down my crack. He pushes his tongue into my ass. I moan. Urge him to put his dick in; to fuck me—*now!*

"You have any lube?" he asks, rubbing my entrance with the head of his cock.

"No," I say, reaching down and splaying open my pussy so he can see its pink flesh. "Sluts don't use lube. Use your spit." He spits into his hand, smears it around my hole, then presses the tip of his dick at my opening. He slowly works himself in. I whimper as the head pops into my ass. "Oh, yes...work that dick in..."

"Uhhh...shiiiiiit..."

I moan breathlessly. "You like how this slutty ass feels wrapped around your cock?"

"Ohhhhh, fuck...yeah, baby..."

"You wanna bust your big dick all up in my guts?" He moans loudly, fucking me full-throttle, like a conductor on a runaway train. "That's right, nigga...fuck me in my ass...fuck my slutty hole open..." The bed is rocking back and forth, its headboard smacking up against the wall. He stretches my ass in long, deep, rapid strokes. He grunts, rolls his eyes up in his head, then shudders.

I turn my head and glance over at the clock. I blink, blink again. *Eight minutes?! That's it! All this sweating and grunting for eight motherfucking minutes?* My pussy was just starting to heat up good. I inhale, then slowly exhale. "Did you cum?" I ask the obvious, hoping not. He nods, tells me that talking dirty to him; telling him to fuck me deep in my ass got him overly excited. That it was so hot and tight. That he's never fucked a woman in her ass before; that the feeling took him over the edge. I breathe in, breathe out. Take inventory of the situation before deciding whether or not I should put on my clothes and storm up out of here—pissed the fuck off, and still horny. Okay. He's fine, check. Nice body, check. Nice, juicy lips, check. Thick dick, check. Feels good in the pussy, check. Ass eater, check. Has personality, check. Willing to role-play, check. Has potential to be good in bed, check.

He lifts up on his arms, his soft dick slipping out of me. He looks me in the eyes. "Damn, that was real good." I stare at him. He pecks me on the mouth. I blink. I can't say I'm disgusted. But, I'm definitely disappointed. And I'm dissatisfied with his endurance. *It's a good thing I test drove this nigga, first, instead of bringing him home to Persia and Paris. Shit, he can barely last with me alone. Imagine the three of us. We'd have him coming in less than two minutes. And Persia would lose her fucking mind.*

"Hey, you alright?" he asks, stroking the side of my face. He's lying beside me propped up on his elbow. I take him in. *Damn, he's fine! Yeah, but the nigga can't hold his nut?* Beautiful copper-colored skin that looks as if it's been slow baked in the sun, curly black hair, hazel eyes, and thick nose. He looks Mediterranean. "What you thinking about?"

I really don't want this night to end without getting what I came here for. "A good fuck!" Persia would say, "Fuck, it. Ditch the dick." Paris would say, "Let's help him maximize the experience."

I smile, reaching for his sticky, condom-wrapped dick. It is flooded with nut. My mouth starts to water, wanting to slurp every drop of it out. If I knew him better, I would. I feel myself getting the shakes. "I'm thinking about sucking on this dick." He grins. "I really hope you can get it up again." It is a plea disguised as a request. I pull off the condom, careful not to spill its contents.

He shifts his body, lying on his back. "Oh, I definitely think The Beast can rise to the occasion." I lick my lips. Stroke him, slowly. Within seconds, his dick springs back alive. He folds his arms in back of his head. "See. It's all yours, baby."

I position myself between his legs, taking his cum-stained dick in both hands. I lick its underside, then each side in slow, wet tongue strokes. I glance up at him. He's looking down at me, his bottom lip pulled in.

"Do you know anything about Kegels?"

He nods, looking at me with confusion on his face. "Yeah, they're the exercises women use to keep their pussy tight." I take his cock into my mouth. Swallow down to the base, lapping at his balls every so often, then pull it out. I swallow in the scent of my ass and the salty remnants of his nut. I clean his dick with my mouth, lips, and tongue. "Aaah, shit…"

"You ever tried them?" I ask in between sucks, slurps and gulps.

He opens his eyes. Looks confused. "Tried what?"

"Kegel exercises?" He tells me no. Tells me he thought they were only for women. I spit on his dick, stroking it as I explain to him how men can also benefit from them. I put in plain words what he needs to do. Let him know I came here to be fucked. Not by a damn bunny rabbit, but by an African warrior. I tell him I want a pussy slayer. Not a damn minute-man. "And we're not leaving here until you deliver."

Surprisingly, he doesn't get offended. "Daaaaamn, it's like that?"

I give him a blank stare, then tilt my head, raising a brow. "Oh, trust me. It's *exactly* like that. You will not…" I pause, licking his dick all over, then stop. "…not fuck me the way I need to be fucked. No, tonight, buddy, I wanna be *fucked* rough and dirty. But, not quick."

He glances at the clock, then down at his hard dick, then back into my eyes. "I have nowhere else to be."

"Good," I say, cupping his balls in one hand and jerking his dick with the other, "'cause I had no intentions of letting you leave. Now let me show you how it's done."

I inform him he is not to nut until I say he can. Instruct him to close his eyes and focus on his body, on the sensations. Tell him to let me know when he feels himself about to explode. I make him repeat back what I've said. When he does word for word, I take him back into my mouth and suck him, stopping him along the way, edging him.

"Uhhhh...uhhhh...ohhhh shit..."

"Relax," I coax, slowing my hand strokes. "We have all night." I get up, walk over to my bag and pull out another condom.

He catches his breath. "Damn, baby, you're a beast in the sheets; fucking insatiable."

I climb back in bed. "And I'm not leaving here unsatisfied." I roll the condom onto his dick, then straddle him. I lean forward, place my right nipple up to his lips, then guide him inside me. "Now let me show you how I need to be fucked."

"Hi, Daddy," I say into the phone, smiling. "How are you, handsome?" Hearing his voice always puts a smile on my face. The one thing I love about him is the fact that no matter what he did in the streets, no matter how many times he fucked other women he never slighted me, or my sisters. And he never treated us any less special. All three of us were his "little beauties" as he called us. He still does to this day. I remember being a little girl and every Saturday he'd take us out to breakfast, leaving our mother home. He'd tell her that was *his* time with his girls. Then he'd take us shopping. And we'd get back to the house loaded down with shopping bags, filled mostly with toys and dolls we didn't need or would play with only once because we had so many to begin with. That didn't matter to him. Seeing smiles on our faces was all he cared about.

From school plays, track meets and dance recitals, he made it his business to be there to cheer us on when he wasn't on the road. And when he and our mother drove my sisters and me down to D.C. the summer of our freshman year at Howard, he broke down and cried. His baby girls were growing up. I remember overhearing our mother one time on the phone, when I was like fifteen—telling one of my aunts how she felt like he cared more about us than he did her. "He treats *them* better than he does me," she had said. "And I'm the one who's *supposed* to be his wife!" I heard the resentment in her voice. Sometimes saw it in her eyes. Oh, well. That's not my issue.

He chuckles. "I'm good, beautiful. How's my baby girl doing?"

"I'm doing wonderful now that I'm talking to my favorite man in the whole world," I tell him, picking up the crystal picture frame of him flanked by my sisters and me. I hold it in my hand, staring at it as we talk. My smile stays painted on my face. "Are you working today?" He tells me he is, but will be off all of next week and wants to take all of us to a show and dinner in the city. "Awww, Daddy, we would love that. Have you spoken to Paris and Porsha?"

"No. You're the first one I called."

I sit the picture frame back on my desk. "Okay, well, hold on and let me get Paris and Porsha on the line."

"Okay, baby girl." I place him on hold, then call Paris. She picks up on the fourth ring. I tell her I have Daddy on the line, then click over, bringing her in on the call.

"Hi, Daaaaddy," she coos into the phone. "How you feeling today?"

"I'm fine, baby girl. How are you?"

"I'm great. You just made my morning."

In my mind's eye, I can see him smiling. "Aww, shucks. You girls sure know how to pull at ya old man's heart strings." She tells the both of us to hold on while she calls Porsha. A minute later the three of us are on the phone with him acting as if we haven't spoken to him in weeks, when in fact it's only been since yesterday. He tells them what he told me about taking us into the city.

Porsha and Paris excitedly say in unison, "I can't wait."

"Say when," Porsha adds. "And we're there."

"Is Mom coming?" Paris asks.

"No, this is our night." *Good*, I think, silently sighing. *The last thing we need is her ruining the night with her bullshit.* "I told your mother I had a date with three beautiful young women." I smile. Ask what she said when he told her that. "She said, 'Well, have fun.'"

"Wow, I'm surprised she didn't start fussing about wanting to go," Paris states, knowing how much she likes going into the city. And, sadly, how much she loathes him having time alone with us.

"Well, she's gonna be in Vegas," he informs us.

"*Vegas?*" the three of us ask, surprised.

"Yeah, your Aunt Fanny has a timeshare out there, so they're all going out there for a week."

"She didn't mention anything about going away when I met her for lunch a few weeks ago," Paris says. "And I've spoken to her on the phone regularly since then."

That's because she was too busy being her messy self, stirring shit up with you. Of course I keep this to myself. Between you and me, I'm still surprised Paris went off on her the way she says she did. That's so unlike her. But, of course, Paris being Paris, she did in fact call her to apologize. And our mother, in true fashion, made her feel guiltier than she already did. I'm sorry, mother or not, she needs to learn boundaries. And she needs to learn when to keep her comments to herself.

"This is one of them last-minute trips," Daddy explains. I laugh to myself, realizing he's taking his vacation while she's on hers. Porsha asks who is all going to Vegas. "Well, let's see. It's gonna be Lucky, Fanny, your mother, and I think Penny is flying out." He chuckles. "I overheard your mother on the phone saying something about Penny saying she wouldn't be able to stomach more than three days with all of them sitting around talking about everybody so she'd fly out toward the end of the week. That way she can miss most of the gossip."

We laugh, knowingly. "I can only imagine what Mom had to say when she said that." He laughs, telling us he heard her say she needs to keep her prissy, uptight-ass home then.

"Sounds exactly like her," Porsha says, still laughing. "I can see them now, making faces and giving Aunt Penny the finger when she isn't looking." We crack up with laughter, knowing exactly how messy Lucky and Fanny can be after tossing back a few drinks. We start reminiscing about the time they had all been drinking at Fanny's fiftieth birthday bash and one of them had said something that wasn't to Aunt Penny's liking so she picked up Fanny's birthday cake while our mother was lighting the candles and smashed it into Fanny's face. The two of them got to fist-fighting, swinging each other all around the ballroom. It took my father and four uncles to pry them two apart. Aunt Fanny's titties were hanging out of her fancy party dress and she had cake and frosting all over her face. It was a hot mess! They didn't speak for months after that.

"Let's hope and pray they all get along and don't end up tearing Vegas up while they're out there." We all agree. We talk and laugh a few minutes more before finalizing our plans to spend the day with our father. We decide to go into the city on Wednesday. Paris says she'll close the boutique early that day. And Porsha and I indicate we will clear our schedules for the whole day to ensure nothing comes up to keep us from spending time with him.

"Your old man loves you beauties."

"Aww, Daddy," we coo in unison. "We love you, too."

"Talk to y'all tomorrow," he says. We give him kisses through the phone, then wait for him to disconnect.

"Can you imagine the four of them in Vegas together without getting into it about something?" I ask, laughing.

Paris laughs with me. "Not with booze around; that's for sure."

"The only one any of them have an issue with is Aunt Penny 'cause she doesn't entertain their messiness," Porsha states.

"Oh, don't get it twisted," I say. "You know Lucky and Fanny go at it, too."

Porsha agrees. "Yeah, true. But not as much as they do with Aunt Penny. They act like they can't stand her sometimes."

Paris laughs. "Girl, it's the other way around. You know Aunt Penny isn't having it."

"Promise me," I say, getting up from my desk and walking out into the hallway to go downstairs to the kitchen, "we don't end up like them when we get their age; talking about any-and-every-body, minding everyone else's business but our own. And fist-fighting each other."

"Oh, puhleeze; shoot me and put me outta my misery now," Porsha says, laughing. "Listen, y'all, if I didn't live with you hookers, I'd stay on the phone with you all day, cackling. But I have appointments up the ass today, so I gotta get cracking. I'll see y'all tonight."

"Ohhhh, noooo, Miss Lady," I say. "Wait one minute. Don't think I didn't notice you tiptoeing in at five in the morning with your hair tossed all over your head. And I *know* you weren't bumping pussies with Angel, either. "

She laughs. "I wasn't tiptoeing. I was limping. If you'd been paying close attention, you would've seen I had one shoe on and one off. And, no I wasn't laid up with Angel. What the hell you doing spying on me any-damn-way? Ya nosey-ass shoulda been in bed asleep."

"Hooker, I wasn't spying on you. I happened to be looking out of my window when you pulled into the driveway."

"Mmmhmmm, lies. Tell me anything. But to answer your question, Miss Nosey Ass, I was out test driving some dick."

"And the outcome?" I ask.

"Yes, do tell," Paris chimes in.

Porsha sucks her teeth. "Look, I gotta go. My appointment is here. You hookers can get the scoop when I get home to—"

"Well, damn," I say, cutting her off. "Don't leave us hanging. At least let us know if he tore the pussy up. Geesh."

"Let's just say, 'I think I can, I think I can.' His fine-ass was The Little Engine That Could."

Paris and I laugh. "Oh, Lord. This sounds like something we should discuss over drinks tonight."

"*Exactly*. Now, leave me the hell alone so I can make my money. Talk to y'all heifers later."

"See you tonight," Paris and I say in unison. She hangs up.

"Her ass is a mess," I say, thinking about her comment. I laugh. "I'm dying to hear all about her night out with the Little Engine That Could."

"Girl, I can only imagine. He either had a little dick or…"

"He nutted quick," I finish for her, laughing.

She joins in my laughter, adding, "Or both."

I gasp. "Girl, that's grounds for a Man Down call."

She continues laughing. "Pull the trigger; lay his ass down."

"Exactly. Leave his ass butt-naked, sprawled out in the middle of the bed for all to see."

She adds, "With a note attached to his forehead, saying, 'Had to shoot him down for having a little-ass dick and for coming too quick.'"

We crack up. "Ohmygod, girl, you know we we're going to hell, right?"

"I know," she says, still laughing. "Ohmygod, I can't. We're dead-wrong. I'm so sorry. Forgive me, Father."

"Well, he's dead wrong for tryna fuck somebody with his little piggy dick."

"Girl, we need to stop. We haven't heard what Porsha has to say about him, yet, and here we are dragging the poor man for having a little wee-wee. And that might not even be the case."

I laugh. "And don't forget, for being a Johnny-cum-quick motherfucker, too."

"Yeah, that too."

"Well, it's one or the other," I say, sliding my mouse around on the mousepad to bring my computer back to life. I check work emails. There are several inquiries for web services. I decide to respond back later. I click open the box for my Yahoo account. "And we'll hear all about it tonight over mojitos."

She smacks her lips. "Mmmmm, that sounds refreshing. Look, let me get off this phone. It's starting to get busy up in here."

"Yeah, I have some work orders to tie up today. I'll see you when you get home."

"Are we ordering in?" she asks.

"Umm, I don't know. That's up to y'all."

"Well, shit. You're the one who gets to work from home. The least you can do is have us a hot meal ready when we step through the door." I laugh, telling her I have a hot meal for her alright. "It's called, kiss my ass, sweetie."

She laughs. "Right back at you, boo." We talk a few minutes more, then hang up.

As I'm scrolling through my personal emails, my cell dings alerting me that I have a text message. I reach for my phone and read the message. It's from Donte—a half-Latin, half-Brazilian hunk of man we used to mess around with a few years ago. Asses, mouths and cunts, we kept his thick, uncut cock fucked, sucked and drained to the damn bone until we found out he was married with a very pregnant wife at home. Word has it she finally left him about a year ago because of his incessant cheating. Good for her!

HEY. ITZ BEEN A LONG X. I'M A FREE MAN NOW. AND READY TO RECONNECT. CAN'T STOP THINKIN BOUT ALL THE FREAKY SHIT WE USED TO GET INTO. I WANNA EAT YOU AND YA SISTRS HOT ASSES AND PUSSY JUICES. WANNA GIVE U MULTIPLE ORGASMS. I MISS HAVN MY FACE BURIED BTWN THEM THIGHS AND MY TONGUE LICKIN THEM SOAKN WET PUSSIES. MY DICK STAYS HARD. HMU

I shake my head, deleting the text. *Nigga, please. You might miss these pussies, but these pussies don't miss your clown-ass.* As I'm reading a few emails, another text comes through. It's from Royce. YO, WATS UP? WHEN WE GONNA CHILL AGAIN? HMU

I text back. WHEN U WANT 2?

Tonight, he replies back. I tell him tonight isn't good; that I'll let him know when the three of us are ready for him again. We go back and forth with text messages for a while before it turns into hot, steamy sexting. I'm talking dirty to him. He's talking dirty back. And before I know it, I've invited him over for an early afternoon romp, a quickie between the two of us. HURRY UP SO I CAN FUCK THAT BIG DICK

IM LEAVN WORK NOW. IMA HAVTA SHOWER WHEN I GET 2 UR SPOT

NO PRBLM, I text back, reminding him that it'll be only him and me. WE CAN WASH EACH OTHER, THEN DRY EACH OTHER OFF WITH R TONGUES

DAMN. SOUNDS GOOD TO ME

U GOT MY PUSSY REAL WET

LOL, AIIGHT. I'M GOOD WIT DAT ...MY DICK'S MAD HARD 2

I WANT U TO EAT MY PUSSY THEN FUCK ME DEEP

Girl, you know you need to leave this young boy alone.

I GOT U MA

Oh, I'm counting on it.

I'll stop messing with him after I finish fucking him a few more times.

I smile, rushing around to finish up some last-minute work before Royce gets here to break my back in. Images of his long, hard dick swirl through my head, causing my nipples to harden. Subconsciously, I pinch them. *Oooh, I'm gonna fuck him good!*

Pain

CHAPTER TWENTY-ONE

I throw my arms around his neck, nip at his bottom lip, lick his neck, pinch his nipples until they sprout up like little round chocolate dots, then push him back onto the bed. I stroke his cock, caress his balls. My pussy drips as he gets long, thick and rock-hard. "Mmmm, this big-ass dick..." I lick it, kiss its tip, then slide the head into my wet mouth.

Royce moans. "Ohhh, shit...yeah, suck that dick, ma..." He runs his fingers through my hair, palms the back of my head, forcing his dick to push past my tonsils. Its thickness plugs my airway. I concentrate; stay focused on the task. I feel myself about to gag. I swallow. Extend my tongue; breathe through my nose. Tears gather in my eyes as I suck his dick with a determined purpose, to swallow as much of him as I can. I grab his balls, juggling them in my hands, gently kneading them. When my vision starts to blur, I remove his dick from my throat, come up for air.

I'ma fuck you all day, little daddy," I say, catching my breath while shifting my body so that he has access to my pussy. I tell him to slide his fingers into my wetness. Tell him to fuck me knuckles deep. He loses one finger, two, then three, into my pussy. "Yeah, little daddy, let me nut on them fingers...oh, yessss..." I glance over my shoulder. "You feel how wet that pussy is? You wanna put this big dick up in this pussy? You wanna beat it up?"

He grins. His eyes are slits of lust. His dick bounces. "Damn, ma, you real nasty. Hell yeah...I've been thinkin' about fuckin' you and ya sisters all week."

"Well, now you get to fuck one of us...all day. Take your fingers out of my pussy and lick 'em." I watch as he sucks on his fingers, savors my juices. I twist my body so that he can share his fingers with me. When I've finished cleaning his fingers, I straddle his face. Clamp my thighs around his head. Offer him my slick cunt. "Open my ass and make love to my pussy with your mouth and tongue." His tongue flicks across my slit as I take his dick back into my mouth. I moan as I suck and stroke him. His mouth finds my clit. I moan louder. I suck him harder, faster. Cause him to buck his hips. His toes stretch open, then close. His legs extend, then bend at the knees. I suck him with a hunger that makes him grunt.

"Oh fuck...gotdamn, ma, you suck dick good..."

His fingers, his mouth, his tongue, work my pussy and clit. I rotate my hips, grind on his face. Then coat his lips and tongue with a sweet, sticky cream.

Three minutes later, I have a Magnum rolled down on his dick and I'm straddling him. My back faces him as I ease him into my pussy. I want him watching my ass bounce and shake up on his thick, juicy cock. Want him to see how his big dick gets lost inside of me. I lean forward, brace myself on his shins and rump shake up and down the length of him.

"I'ma fuck you deep and dirty, little nigga...uhhh..." I rapidly jack his cock with my cunt muscles. "You like how this wet pussy feels?" I ask, glancing over my shoulder at him. His eyes are rolled up in his head.

He grunts. "Shit yeah..."

I smile, knowingly. *Of course you do.* I'm a champion dick rider. Fucking a nigga's dick is about rhythm and technique. You have to put your back into it. Hips and pelvis and contractions have to be in sync. You have to know exactly how and when to grab the dick. Milk the head, rotate the hips, slow wind down to the base, then pop and clap your ass cheeks together.

I slowly twist my body around, bouncing my ass up and down and around on his cock until I'm facing him. I squat into a frog position. Pressing my chest to his, I let my ass and hips do the work. He reaches for me. I grab him by the wrists, pin his hands up over his head down onto the bed.

"You want me to nut all over this big-ass dick? Ooooooh, this dick feels good...Bang up into my pussy..."

I nibble on his neck, nip at his earlobe.

"Oh, shit...damn, ma...aaah fuck..."

I whisper in his ear. Tell him how much I love the dick. Tell him how hot he has my pussy. Let him know how horny I am. Inch by excruciating inch, I fuck myself on his dick. Rhythmically rock and roll my hips, my pussy clutching his shaft. I tease the dick. Lift up, fuck half of his dick, then lift up to the head, using my muscles to milk it. I glide my pussy up and down on him, taking him in about a third of the way, rotating my hips. I lift up again, this time riding only the tip, still rotating my hips. Royce attempts to thrust his cock in me. He wants more dick in. I grind all the way down to the base. "Is this what you want, little daddy?"

He grunts in response. I can tell he's at his breaking point. I have pushed him to the edge. "Stop teasin' me, ma. Give me that pussy...I wanna fuck..."

I let go of his wrists. Allow him to grip my hips as he thrusts his hips upward, his dick stabbing at my pussy. I grunt and smile and murmur in delight. The delicious pain causes tiny waves of orgasms to splash up against his cock. I press my lips to his. My scent still lingers on his mouth, his tongue. I suck. Push my tongue deep into his mouth. We kiss. Devour each other until we are both moaning.

"Mmmmm...you wanna be my little boy toy, huh? You wanna keep fucking this pussy?"

I match his thrusts. Fuck him while he fucks me. He shoves himself deep inside me. A mixture of pleasure and lust are in his half-closed eyes. He has given in to ecstasy, has allowed uninhibited desire to take its course.

"Yessssssssssssssss...oh fuuuuuuuuck..." He bucks his hips. "I'm cumming...I'm cuuuuuuuuuuuuuuuummmmmming...aaaaaah, fuck!" I ride him, gallop hard and fast and cum along with him, staring into his glazed eyes. I collapse on his chest, panting. "Damn, that was good," he says, running his hands along the small of my back. He kisses the side of my head. His dick is still hard. "I want some more."

I glance up at him, smiling. I watch him intently as he removes his overflowing condom, reaches on the nightstand for another, then rolls it down on his sticky dick. I roll over on my stomach, tuck my knees under, rise up on my hands, arching my back. My hot pussy is still throbbing from my orgasm. Still oozing out love cream. He eases up behind me, places the head of his dick at my opening, then slowly enters. I gasp. Inch by mesmerizing inch, he fills me, stretches me. A low whimper escapes the back of my throat as my pussy contracts around his cock. We rock together, enjoying the sensations. He fucks me with slow, steady strokes. I reach for my clit, pressing my fingers up against it. It is sensitive and swollen. Instantly, I'm moaning loudly and coming.

"Fuck me...oooooh, fuck me..." I demand, throwing my ass up

on his dick. He grabs my hips, bangs deep into me; fucks me hard. I swing my hair from side to side, clutching the sheets. I'm coming and coming and coming. "Aaaah, yesss, beat my pussy up…that's right, fuck me good…"

"Damn, ma, you so wet…That's right…keep nuttin' on my dick…oh shiiiiit…you feel so fuckin' good…."

He slaps my ass.

"Oh, yes…slap that shit harder…"

He slaps it until it stings, then pulls out until only his swollen head is nestled between my pussy lips. He teases my slit, urges me to grab at it before sliding into me once more. He's thoughtfully taking his time, stroking my walls—gently…too gently. I want him to fuck me, to lose control and bang my pussy inside out. "No, fuuuuuuck me…" I insist. "I want it rough and hard and fast…fuck me…" I raise my ass to him, brace my elbows on the bed as he grips my hips tighter and fucks me roughly. "Slap my ass some more, nigga…" *Smack, smack, smack!* "Harder." *Whap!* "Harder." *Whap! Whap! Whap!*

"Uh, fuck…yeah, keep grabbin' that dick, baby. You handlin' this big dick, ma…"

"Oooooh give it to me…ooooooooh, that's right. Fuck me… aaaah…fuck me, baby…Mmmm…right there…right there. Oh, yes, oh yes…make my pussy nut…there you go. Oh, yeah, oh yeah, oh yeah…right there…mmmm, harder…"

His breathing changes and I know he's ready to explode. I'm panting. He's panting. He tells me he's ready to come. I push back into him as hard as he's thrusting in me. I give, as good as I'm getting.

I gasp. "Give me that good nut, little daddy…oooooh, ooo-oooh, ooooooh…c'mon, c'mon…give me that nut…Bust it all in my pussy…."

He moans as he comes. I moan as I come with him. I drop to the bed and he collapses on top of me. His warm breath tickles my ear as we both struggle to steady our breathing.

"Damn, that was some bomb-ass sex." He rolls over onto his back, arms thrown over his head, toned legs spread wide, condom-wrapped dick smothered in cum. He turns his head toward me with a satisfied smile, brushing sweaty hair from out of my face. "Whew. You a real beast, ma."

I return the smile. Peck him on his lips, then reach for his cock. Fucking this young boy is amazing. His rock-hard cock, his stamina, his lean-muscled body make up for his age. "And I'm just getting started," I state, slowly rolling the condom up. It's filled to capacity with his man milk. I reach for the hand towel on my nightstand, fold the condom inside of it, then place his wet dick between my titties and titty fuck him while licking and flicking my tongue over the head of his dick.

"Aaaah, shit..." Within moments, he's coming again. This time he coats my tits, drenches them with his cum. I cup them in my hand. Stare at him as I smear his nut into my skin, licking what clings onto my nipples. With his eyes glazed, he pulls in his bottom lip. "You a real freak, ma. I wanna fuck some more..."

"Oh you haven't seen anything, yet," I tell him, smiling. "The day's just getting started."

He grins. "Then get up on this dick and show me what you got." He reaches for me. Pulls me into him, then kisses me. This time it's a long, tongue-probing, passionate kiss. And before long I'm rolling another XL magnum down onto his hard dick, easing him back into my greedy pussy.

I'm in the back of the boutique in my office, standing in six-inch stilettos with my skirt hiked up over my hips, thong pulled to the side, my fingers probing my horny pussy. There has been a fire blazing between my thighs since early this morning, one that I tried to extinguish with my bullet and glass dildo. But to no avail, the flames keep spreading. I need dick. I need to be fucked. But, today, I want my own man. One I don't have to share. One I can keep out of the clutches of Persia and Porsha, for at least this very minute.

My phone buzzes. Alerts me I have a new text. *Ugh, fucking great*, I think, glancing over at it. I start to ignore it, but decide against it. I quickly stop what I'm doing and go over, licking my fingers. I pick up my phone. Porsha has sent me a text. *Irwin wants to cum thru 2morrow nite. You have any plans? Persia's free to play.☺ R u?* I smile, knowing she has no idea how fucking horny I am. That my fingers were buried in my pussy just seconds ago. I text her back: *Yes!!!! And tell him to cum ready to fuck all night.* I turn my phone off, tossing it over on the chair. *No more distractions until I get this nut. Now, where was I?* I slide my left hand back between my legs. And continue where I left off, strumming my clit with my fingers. My right hand cups my left breast, pinches my nipple.

"Mmmmm…"

The boutique's door is locked. A sign "Out to Lunch" hangs from the window so that I can have this moment to myself—without interruptions. Tuesdays are always slow so today is a perfect day for playing in my pussy without disruptions. Yiruma's CD *First Love* is playing in the background. Its sexy instrumentals are perfect for lovemaking. If only I had someone to make love to. For some reason, I consider calling Emerson behind Persia and Porsha's backs. Think about making love to him; only once, then sending him on his way. But the thought quickly fades.

Closing my eyes, I hump my hand. Allow my mind's eye to conjure up fantasies of big hands kneading my breasts…a wet mouth clinging to my clit…eager cock pummeling in and out of my hot pussy doggy-style, my gushy cunt splashing its juices with each stroke—deep and determined.

I imagine my chocolate knight with his boxers at his ankles; his engorged cock—with its bulbous head—rigid and ready, bobbing up and down as he whispers dirty things to me; promises of how he'll fuck me into a delicious trance; his breath hot against my ear.

I plop up on the edge of my desk. Reach for my Utopia Rabbit vibrator—a sleek silicone vibrator that twists and vibrates at seven different speeds; turn it on low speed. Then gasp the minute its tip touches my swollen clit. I shut my eyes tighter, massaging my clit with the vibrator. Over and over, I stroke myself, bringing myself closer to an orgasm. A soft whimper escapes me. I scoot further back on the desk, spread my legs wider, one leg propped up on the desk, then slide the tip of the vibrator into my wet pussy. I push it as far as it will go inside of me, imagining it is a probing finger, a hungry tongue, an eager cock, pulsing deep inside of me.

"Ohhh, yes…fuck me…aaah…mmmm…my pussy needs you… you gonna keep fucking me with this good dick?"

Yeah, baby, anytime you want it. This dick is yours…

"Mmmm…ooooooooh…it feels sooooooo good…you like how this pussy feels?"

My imaginary lover wraps my hair around his hand, yanks my head, looking into my eyes he tells me how much he loves my smooth, shaven pussy. Tells me how wet it is. How hot it is. How good it feels wrapped around his dick. I plunge my vibrator in and out of me. Allow my juices to splash out. My body begins to shudder as its vibrations caress my G-spot.

I'm now lying all the way back on my desk. My imaginary lover hovers over me, pressing my knees back toward my shoulders, then pushes his hot, hard cock into me—and fucks me until I scream.

My pussy makes sucking and popping sounds, grabbing at my vibrator as I jab it in and out of me. "Ohhhhhhgod, yesssssss… feed my pussy with that big-ass dick…uhhhhhhh…uhhhhhh… fuuuuck—"

"Oh, shit, daaaaaaamn…my bad…"

Legs up, slit pulled open by fingers and vibrator, a puddle of pussy juice on my desk, everything around me comes to a screeching halt. My eyes pop open. My mouth drops open. It takes a minute to register that the voice I just heard isn't the one in my head. That there's a man—not just any man, but a fine, sexy-ass motherfucker—standing in the doorway, licking his lips with a crooked grin plastered on his face, staring at *me*.

"Don't stop on my account," he says, leaning up against the doorframe with his arms folded. "I was really starting to enjoy the view."

I jump up, skirt bunched up around my hips, shirt unbuttoned, titties exposed. "Ohmygod, what the fuck are you doing in here?!" I yell, dropping my vibrator and quickly trying to cover myself. With one hand over my chest, I snatch the remote to the stereo off the file cabinet, shutting it off. I'm completely shocked, embarrassed, and too muthafucking through! "How in the hell did you get in here?"

A grin locks on his face as he tries hard to keep his eyes from roaming from my erect nipples to my bare hips. I attempt to pull my skirt down over my bare ass. I want to slap that damn smirk off his beautiful chocolate face. "I walked in."

"No, you didn't," I snap, grabbing my cell off the sofa. "You broke in my damn store and tried to rob me. I'm calling the police…"

He walks up on me, grabbing me by the arm. "Yo hold up. Now you reachin'. Stop the theatrics and listen to me. Like I said, I walked in. The door was unlocked. What the fuck I wanna break in ya spot for when I was just up in this muhfucka a few weeks ago and dropped almost two grand for a damn bag for my moms?"

Well, he has a point. "Well, you should—"

He cuts me off. "Well', nothin'. I stood at the register and waited for you. I even called out for you. But I guess you were, uh, caught up in the…music." He rubs his chin. "And from the looks of things, looks like you were really in a zone." He starts laughing and this only pisses me off.

"I don't see shit funny. And get your damn hand off of me. You're trespassing. *And* you assaulted me by putting your damn hands on me."

He laughs harder. *This nigga is crazy*, I think, frowning. *I just threatened to call the police on his ass and he's standing here laughing.* "I didn't barge in on you, beautiful. And I'm not trespassing. And

I damn sure haven't assaulted you. Once, twice, three times, the door wasn't locked and I walked in. The only thing I'm tryna do is stop you from makin' a damn fool outta ya'self." He shakes his head, letting my arm go. "Yo, you wanna call the cops, then do you." He takes a seat. "I'll be right here waitin' on 'em."

I storm out of the office to assess the situation. I scan the store. Everything looks to be in order. Then I go over to the door and turn the knob. It opens. There are no signs of tampering with the lock or forced entry. Now I really feel like shit for accusing him of breaking in when I didn't even lock the damn door. I thought I had. *You fucking idiot! How could you be so damn stupid?* I shake my head, locking it. I tuck my blouse into my skirt, then zip it, smoothing out the fabric, then walk back into the office to face him.

I stare at him, raise a brow. *Whew, this man is fine as hell.* But I'm still mad. Mad at myself for being so careless and getting caught like that. And mad at him for being so goddamn fine, and me not being able to have him in between my legs finishing off what he disrupted. *Or can I?*

He smirks. "Did you call 'em?"

"No, I didn't." He asks why, smirking. "Because there's no need to."

"Hmmm, isn't that sumthin'? So, it wasn't the dark, handsome cat with the sexy-swag who did it after all, huh?"

I roll my eyes. "Okay, whatever, smart-ass. You still had no business walking back here. This is an unauthorized area."

He laughs. "Yo, beautiful...admit it. You fucked up, babe. But, it's all good 'cause ya screw up turned out to be my blessing." I suck my teeth. "Next time you in here tryna get ya finger swerve on, you might wanna double-check to make sure you have the door locked. So now you owe me an apology, don't you think?"

I huff, sweeping my bang across my forehead. "Didn't you see the sign in the window?" I ask, ignoring him as I stomp into my private bathroom, slamming the door on him. I lock it.

"Yeah, I saw it as I was turning the doorknob to come in," he says on the other side of the door.

"And you *still* walked in, knowing no one was in?" I stare at myself in the mirror as I wash my hands. *Fuck, fuck, fuck! How the hell did you not lock the damn door? What if someone else had walked up in here? See, that's what your horny ass gets.*

"Someone was here," he says, laughing. "And she was mad busy tryna get it in."

Shit! "Hahaha, hell. So glad you find this amusing." *Way to go, bitch! You have definitely given this motherfucker something to talk about with his boys.* "Well, you still had no business walking up in here like that."

He keeps laughing. "Shit, I'm glad I walked in when I did. I might've missed the show. It's not often a man walks up on a sexy-ass chick getting herself off."

Oh, so he thinks I'm sexy. I wonder how long his ass was standing there watching me. For some twisted reason, the idea that he'd been standing there watching my mini-sex performance the whole time causes excitement to rush to my clit. I shake the thought from my head, sucking my teeth. "Okay, so you caught me with my hands in my pussy; big deal. Don't act like you haven't seen my pussy before."

He chuckles. "Yeah, true. And a pretty pussy it is."

I stare at my reflection in the mirror, grinning. *Whew, this nigga is gonna be a problem. If I don't cut him off soon.* "Mmmph. Flattery will get you nowhere."

He laughs. "C'mon, ma, don't be like that. You know what it is. You should be glad I walked up on you instead of some other muhfucka."

"Mmmph."

He laughs again. "Don't worry, baby. Your secret's safe with me. Like everything else we've been doin'."

I swing the bathroom door open. He's now leaning back up against the doorframe. "Darrin, right?" I ask, teasingly.

He grins, playing along. "Nah, wrong cat. It's Desmond; Dez for short. Don't act like you don't know."

"Okay, Dez for short. Why are you here?"

He licks his lips, slow and sexy like. "I made a special trip down here to see you. You know. Maybe take you out to lunch, again. But, uh, I ended up getting something much more exciting."

His masculine scent mixed with his cologne swirls all around the room. I quickly glance at his crotch and notice a thick, meaty lump in his designer sweats. My clit pulses. My mouth starts to drool. *Bitch, get a grip on yourself.* I swiftly move around the office, wiping off my desk with a lemon-scented bacterial wipe.

I feel his eyes on me as I try to avoid looking at him. My pussy muscles clench.

Oh, go ahead and fuck him, then send him on his way. You know you want to.

I stop what I'm doing. Place a hand up on my hip. "Um, why are you standing there grinning at me?"

He points at the floor. "You forgot to pick up ya *lil'* toy." The way he says little sounds as if he's implying he has something much bigger for me to play with. I walk around the desk and quickly scoop down and pick it up. I go back into the bathroom and wash it off, glancing at my reflection in the mirror.

Ohmymotherfuckinggod, being around this sexy motherfucker makes my pussy wet.

Then fuck him!

But what if he's married or in a relationship?

Hooker, it's a little too late to be concerned about that now, considering you already fucked him twice.

Ugh, Paris, stop this shit! Other than his name, you don't know shit about his ass.

And that's what makes fucking him more exciting.

"So, am I gonna get that apology or what?" he asks, slicing into my thoughts. "All a brotha wanted to do is get at this sexy ass store owner who won't give me her name, but let's me eat her pussy, and now she tryna hem a muhfucka up wit' bogus charges." He laughs. "That's real fucked up."

I take a deep sigh, trying not to smile. "I apologize," I say, sticking my head out of the doorway.

He smiles at me. "What are you apologizin' for?" I look at him as if he's two screws from crazy. "Yo, I'm sayin'. I wanna make sure you know what you're apologizin' for."

I suck my teeth. "I apologize for accusing you of breaking in, then threatening to call the police on you."

He walks up on me. I try not to take him in. Try not to stare at the lump in his pants. But it's too late. My wet pussy senses his presence. My nipples swell. "And what else?"

I frown, placing my across my shoulder to block his view of my erect nipples poking through my blouse. "What do you mean, 'and what else'?' There's nothing else to apologize to you about."

"Oh, yeah it is," he says, pulling in his bottom lip.

"And what's that?" I ask, inhaling his scent. He reeks of masculinity. My pussy lips start to quiver.

You can let me fuck you with this fat black dick, I hear him say in my head. I blink, stepping back when he steps up in my space. "You can apologize for stoppin' what you were doin' and leavin' a muhfucka hangin'."

It's motherfucking on now, girl. I glance up at the ceiling, silently thanking the heavens for this chocolate hunk appearing in my doorway, then bring my attention back to him. *I'ma fuck this man real good*, I think, smiling.

"Oh, so you think I left you hanging, huh?"

He nods. "Yeah, you did." He takes another step toward me. This time I don't move. In my heels, he still hovers over me. I like that. I look up at him. "But I gotta way you can make it up to me."

"Oh, really? Do tell," I say coyly. He tells me I can start by giving him my real name. Tells me he wants my number and to take me out to dinner tonight. *Fuck a dinner*, I think, grinning. *Give me the dick!* I glance at my watch. It's eleven-thirty. Since customers don't usually start coming through until about one or so on Tuesdays, I decide to take opportunity by the balls, and seize the moment. "Well, that's nice and all. But, I tell you what. I have an even better way to make it up to you."

"Oh word? I like the sound of that already. So what's good?"

"Give me one sec while I use the bathroom," I say, stepping back into the bathroom, then slowly closing the door while keeping my eyes on him. I lick my lips and shut the door.

He laughs. "Oh, aiight. I see how you doin' it. So am I gonna get your name or what?"

Oh, don't worry. You're about to get more than my name. I step out of my skirt, unbutton my blouse, then take it off, hanging it on back of the door. I take in my reflection, standing here in my red La Perla sheer lace chemise. "Yes, you're about to *get* my name. "But, before you do, I need to know one thing."

"What's that?"

"You have a woman? Or someone you seeing on a regular?" I hold my breath, waiting.

"Nah, why?"

I let out a sigh of relief, stepping out of my thong. "Good," I say, grabbing my vibrator, then slowly opening the door. "Now let me finally introduce myself to you." He's no longer in front of the door. I walk out into the office and find him sitting on the sofa, fiddling with his cell. I stand in the middle of the room, waiting, until he looks up.

His eyes pop open. "Oh, shit. Gotdaaaaaaaamn!"

I slowly saunter over to him. Allow my hips to jut out at him with each step. "My name is Pleasure..."

Pleasure

CHAPTER TWENTY-THREE

"So you wanna watch me play in this pussy?" I ask in a low, sweet whisper as I lean back on the desk, lift up my legs and spread open my lips.

Desmond revels in the view, grabbing at his cock and grinning. "Hell yeah." He squeezes his dick, then strokes it. "Fuck."

My fingers strum along the folds of my lips, slithering along my slit. My juices start to stir. I allow him to see and hear the swishy sloshing sounds my pussy makes as my fingers get lost in its wetness. My excitement intensifies with the knowing that this fine, mysterious hunk of man gazing at me while I finger myself is a complete stranger. "Mmmmm...ooooh...you like looking at this tight pussy?" I pull it open, offering him a better view. I spread my legs wider. Allow my pussy lips, pouty and full, to poke out a little more. Allow him to see all of me—the core of who I am—ready and wet and hot.

He licks his lips. "Damn, that's a pretty pussy, baby."

"Mmmm...and it's so wet. Pull out your dick. Let me see it." He fishes it out from out of his sweats. It's already erect and eager. I moan, pulling in my bottom lip. "Oooh, look at that dick...nice and thick...mmmm...stroke it for me, daddy..."

I watch as he spits in his hand, then slowly glides his hand up and down the length of it. His eyes lock on my glistening pussy. "Is this what you want? You wanna see this dick get hard?"

"Ooooh, yes," I coo, turning on my Rabbit, then laying it on my clit. "Let me see how big it gets…" I dip the vibrator inside of me. Let its vibrations echo along the walls of my pussy as I watch him lift his hips up from off the sofa and inch his sweats and boxer briefs down over his hips. They are now draped around his ankles as he sits back with his legs gaped over. His perfectly shaped balls look like two chocolate Easter eggs—hanging low, waiting to be scooped up. I swallow back my wanting to roll my tongue around them, my yearning to place them into my drooling mouth. "Ooooh, yeah…stroke that dick… mmm…let me see you play with them beautiful balls…"

I keep my eyes trained on his hand. Count the strokes. Memorize the rhythm. Then play them back in my head, matching his movements with my own; my fingers rapidly dancing over the hood of my excitement. My clit, my cunt, my ass…are on fire. Flames of lust shoot out everywhere.

"Aaaah, fuck…you got my dick hard as hell. I wanna feel that wet pussy around this dick…you got some good pussy, baby."

"It sure is…it's real good. Nice and wet…"

"Damn, I wanna fuck…"

He walks up on me. Dick in hand, he dips at the knees. I tell him to step back.

"You can only look, not touch," I warn, pulling my fingers from off my clit, then sliding them into my mouth. I make love to them with my mouth and tongue, savoring my creamy center. His eyes roam my nakedness, trail over my body, admiring my curves, the rise and fall of my breasts. I let go of my Rabbit, clench it with my muscles to free my hands as I cup my breasts and squeeze them together. I lick my nipples—one at a time. Then dip my hand back between my thighs, pulling out my vibrator, then swirling it around my clit before sliding it back in.

I pull it out again. Let him see the mouth of my pussy open and close.

"Let me taste that pussy, baby…" I remove the vibrator. Slip my fingers in. Dig deep. Moan. Scoop out two fingers of sweetness. Then offer it to him. I watch as he waddles his way toward me. Midway, he stops and kicks his pants and his underwear off, leaving them in middle of the floor. He is up on me, licking his lips. Then leans into me as I reach up and press my fingers to his lips, coating them with my sticky cream, then slipping them into his mouth. His mouth is hot. His tongue wet. I finger-fuck his mouth, slow and deliberate, as he devours my essence. When he is done, I slip my fingers into my own mouth, and lick all over them.

"Damn, you got some good pussy juice…Let me eat that shit."

"Suck my titties." My request comes out as a command. Once he heeds, I remind him that he must keep his hands on his cock. I urge him to continue stroking it. I glance down at it. I can see a string of nectar leaking from the slit of its swollen head. "You want me to wrap these pretty lips around your dick and suck it, don't you?"

He grunts, swirling his tongue around my nipples. "Yeah, baby…" He lightly grazes my nipple with his teeth, then tugs it with his teeth. I flinch. Tell him I don't like my nipples rough-housed.

"Lips and tongue," I tell him. "Suckle them; not bite them."

"My bad," he says, glancing up at me. "I got carried away. You have me so fuckin' horny." He finds a gentle groove with his lips and tongue, teasing my nipples to an aching hardness that forces a moan to escape from the back of my throat.

My fingers, my vibrator, vie for my pussy's warm, wet snugness.

"Why you fuckin' with me? I wanna get up in that pussy, ma."

"You can taste me; that's it." I scoot off the desk, leaving small puddles of cunt juice behind as I turn around and spread open my legs, then pull open my ass cheeks. I tell him to eat my pussy from the back. Remind him to not touch; to keep his hand on his dick, stroking it until it releases. Desmond kisses and nibbles all over my ass, before pressing his face in between my cheeks. His nose hits my asshole as he flicks his tongue across the back of my pussy. I push back against his face, slowly shake my hips side-to-side, ass-clapping his face. "Oh, yessssss...eat that pussy...you still stroking that fat dick for me?" He grunts, reaching up to grab my hips. I slap his hands down. "Don't touch. Eat..."

The store phone starts ringing. I count the number of rings before the call rolls over into voice mail. It rings again. Desmond pulls his tongue out of me, leaving my pussy vacant.

"You wanna get that? It could be important."

This is important! Whoever it is will have to call back. I glance back at him over my shoulder. He has a glazed smirk on his face. "No...put your tongue back in my pussy." Without further words, he eats me out until my body shakes and I cream on his tongue.

When he is done gulping down my juices, he gets up off his knees, licking his lips. His meaty dick curved to the left. "Damn, girl, your pussy's right. You so muthafuckin' fine...fuck all this jerkin' off shit...Let me hit that pussy..."

He walks over and picks up his underwear and sweats and tosses them up on the sofa. He turns to face me. I'm now sitting up on the edge of desk. My legs spread open. Pussy still ablaze, I beckon him to come closer to me.

I wrap my leg around his waist, draw him in. He gazes into my eyes. I match his lustful stare, reaching out for his hot cock. I stroke it. Then, without words, without permission, he finds my mouth with his and kisses me. I'm taken by surprise. But I don't resist. I give into temptation. Give into desire. And allow his tongue to find mine. Before long, his hands are grasping tightly onto my hips, his fingers deep into my ass. I've let go of his swollen dick, wrapping my arms around his neck. My fingers get lost in the deep spin of his waves. I've gotten caught up in the moment. Have tossed rationale and reasoning out of the window. Dare myself to play Russian roulette. I feel him, this stranger, dark-chocolate flesh, sculpted and molded around layers of muscle, pressing his way into me—his dark brown cock sliding between my thighs; its tip inching its way into paradise.

I close my eyes, toss my head back. Allow the bullet to spin into the chamber. "I wanna feel my dick inside of you."

Click.

The head of his dick pushes past resistance.

Click.

I hoist up my hips, arch my back. Give in to reckless abandon.

Click.

More dick slides in, stretching out apprehension.

Click.

"Ohhh, shit…you feel so good…aaah…this pussy's so wet…"

Click.

My head starts to spin. My heart leaps in my chest. My body weakens. I am blindfolded, tiptoeing on the edge of a cliff, dancing along the edges of danger. The well in me rises and swells. I'm too caught up now. There's no turning back.

Click.

He's all the way inside of me now. "You feel so good," he pants. "I can get lost in this pussy all day…"

I want to push him off. But I don't want this feeling to stop. He uses his dick with skill, hitting my spot; just so. "Don't cum in me," I push out, a thread of panic stitching through my voice.

"Aaaaah, shit," he groans against my ear. "I got you, ma… oooohhh, fuck…muthafuckin' pussy's so good."

"Uhhhh…oh yes, fuck me…"

He lifts me up off my desk and pounds himself in me, deep strokes jabbing away. I lock my arms around his neck and match his thrusts. His dick stabs at my spot. My pussy muscles violently contract. I'm screaming. He's grunting and groaning.

"Oh, shit's this pussy's fiiiiyah…oh fuck…"

A wave of burning heat whips through my wet basin. And, before long, my cunt cries out, spewing hot, boiling juices. I cum, coating his dick and squirting streams of steamy pleasure, knowing that after today nothing will ever be the same.

"So what did you do all day, Miss Works-from-Home?" I ask, taking a chilled glass from the tray, then filling it to the rim. Persia has made a pitcher of mojitos. She lifts the frosty glass to her lips and takes a sip. She waits patiently for me to get situated as I set the glass pitcher back on the tray, then settle into my seat with drink in hand.

"Besides fucking Royce today," she says matter-of-factly, tucking a leg beneath her. "Not a damn thing. But I don't wanna talk about that right now. I wanna hear all about this little choo-choo train that you went off and fucked all night long."

I laugh. "Oh no, Miss Hooch. Not so fast, boo. I wanna hear all about you having that fine-ass young boy all to yourself. You fuck him here?"

She grins. "I sure did. And he fucked me like there was no tomorrow. I'm telling you, Porsha, that young nigga knows how to use that big dick. He has my pussy still humming."

"Oooh, I'm so mad at you," I say, feigning a pout. Although the truth is my own pussy still throbs from my encounter with Emerson today. I can still feel him inside of me, pounding away. I swallow back the thoughts of my afternoon romp. There's a part of me that feels guilty for sneaking off and seeing him. My sisters and I have never kept secrets from each other. And I feel bad. But then there's that other part of me that is excited by the idea of getting caught by one of them fucking him. I'm sure, at some point, I'll tell them all about Emerson and me. But, for now, the Sheraton—for the last three weeks —has become our secret meeting place. And fucking him behind my sisters' backs has become my newest guilty pleasure.

"So where we really going with this?" Emerson had asked, pulling me into his arms after forty-five minutes of dicking me down into the mattress. My head was on his chest. "At some point, I want more than this…us sneaking around in hotel rooms and shit. I'm gonna want you to be my woman."

I looked up at him. "I don't know where this is going, Em. I haven't thought that far ahead. Right now, I'm living in the moment. You told me you'd let me choose how things moved with us, so you're going to have to let me figure it all out."

"I did say that. And I meant it. I don't want to put any pressure on you, Porsha. But all I want to know is if we're moving in the same direction. I told you how I feel about you. I've laid every-thing out on the table for you."

"I know you have," I acknowledged, playing with the strands of hairs around his nipples. I wet the tip of my finger with spit, then swirl it over his nipple. It hardens. "And I appreciate that. I'm not sure what I want. I do enjoy being with you. And I'm not going to deny the connection I feel to you when were together. But it's complicated for me."

He lifted up, resting on his forearms. "It's only complicated because you want it to be."

"You know my lifestyle," I reminded him, referring to my sexual activities.

"Yeah, I do. And I told you that has nothing to do with me. But is it something you can at some point let go of?"

"If I were in a committed relationship, of course I could." He eyes me, questioningly. "I'm not a cheater, if that's what you're thinking."

"Neither am I. But that's not what I was asking."

"And I answered. Yes, I can. Right now, I'm single. So I fuck who I want."

"And so you should. It's your body. I'm not questioning that. I'm asking about you and me."

"Em, you know how we met—through Persia. I'm not sure if I can allow myself to get emotionally involved with a man who's fucked my sisters. Sharing a man who I have no emotions to is one thing. And having feelings for one who I *know* I've been sharing with my sisters is another. I don't know if I—"

He leaned in and kissed me, cutting me off. When he finally pulls back, I'm breathless. "I'm not asking you to do anything you're not comfortable with. But, let's be honest here. I can't help how we met. And I can't help that I've gotten it in with you and your sisters. That was something the three of you wanted. And I was more than cool with giving it to you. But, at the same time, I can't help it that I caught feelings for *you*. It wasn't planned, it happened. So should I be penalized for that? Should you have to walk away from something that could possibly be good for the both of us? I mean, tell me something, Porsha. I need to know if I'm playing myself." I opened my mouth to speak. He stopped me. "Before you say anything, be honest. Based on what you know about me, am I the kind of man you could see yourself with?"

I thought about it. He didn't have any children. He'd never been married. He had two sisters and was very close to his mother; his father died when he was twelve. He was a hard-worker. He saved his money and had good credit. He was driven and ambitious. He was thoughtful. And damn good in bed.

I smiled, reaching between his legs and cupping his balls, then stroking his dick.

"Yes," I answered, honestly. "But—"

He kissed me again. "No 'buts.' I need you to give me some hope, baby."

I stared into Emerson's brown eyes and, for the first time since I've known him, I saw something I hadn't notice before. I saw the soul of a man who wanted to love...*me*.

"...Don't be mad," Persia says, bringing me back to the conversation. "It wasn't planned."

"How come you didn't wait for me?" I ask, knowing damn well I would've been in no position to fuck that horse-dicked buck. She tells me it was in the middle of the day. That he had texted her wanting to see all three of us, but things got really heated between the two of them so she decided to fuck him solo.

"Girl, he had my pussy so wet. There's no way I was gonna be able to wait until later on when y'all got home. I wanted that dick, right then and there. And, girl, did he deliver."

I smirk. "I'm sure he did. And did he smother that face of yours with more of that beauty cream again 'cause you need a ton of it with ya ugly ass?"

She laughs, giving me the finger. "Fuck you. You're uglier than me, hooker."

I laugh with her. "Yeah, you wish."

"Whatever. And no, he didn't smother my face in his nut. I learned my lesson. I did let him bust that first nut on my face because I knew it wasn't going to be that much. But, the other two..." She shakes her head. "...No thank you, boo. I let him coat my titties and stomach with it."

I smack my lips. "And what did you do with all that creamy milk?"

"Uh, what do you think I did with it? I sucked it off my titties, then scooped the rest of it off my stomach and ate it."

I toss back my drink, swallowing down lust and envy. "Ooooh, you nasty, bitch."

She laughs. "Don't hate me, boo. You know I like to share."

"Whatever. You need to give me his number so I can have on-call access to his sexy ass, too." I say this not certain if that's what I really want. Since I've started seeing Emerson behind Persia and Paris's backs, I've been giving thought to scaling back on fucking some of these niggas. Not that he's pressured me into doing so. But I have to wonder if all of these wonderful distractions will make it difficult for me to consider giving Emerson a chance. I'm still not sure if that's even what I want. Persia reaches for her cell, then rattles off his number. "Wait, hooker," I say, getting up, laughing. "I don't have my phone down here. Let me get a pen and write it down." I walk over to the credenza, opening a drawer, then pulling out a pen and pad. She repeats the number. I write it down, then fold the paper and slip it into my bra.

She laughs. "You a damn mess."

"Please. I gotta keep this number close by until I can get it programmed into my phone. Anyway…now, that we got that outta the way. Where is Paris?"

She shrugs. "Your guess is…" The chirping alarm alerts us that she's opened the door. "Well, there she is." She yells for her to hurry up and get downstairs so I can tell them all about my night with Faruq. She picks up her phone, calling Paris. "And you might want to get you a chilled glass from out of the freezer and bring two down for me and Porsha…*whaaaat*ever, hooker…yeah, yeah, yeah…blah, blah, blah…and hurry up." She disconnects the call. "Well, all I want to know is was he fine?"

I nod. "Fine ain't even the word to describe his ass. That man was *fucking* beautiful. His body was on point. He had these gorgeous hazel eyes. He kissed good, ate pussy good..."

"But?"

I laugh. "You'll have to wait until Paris gets down here."

She rolls her eyes.

It takes Paris almost ten minutes before she finally saunters her way into the room. She's taken her clothes off and is now in her panties and a Howard U tank top. "Well, it's about damn time," Persia huffs, feigning annoyance. "This heifer here wouldn't tell me about her night with the mystery man she fucked last Friday until you got down here. Now hurry up and pour your drink, then sit the hell down so I can get the juice."

Paris gives her the finger. "Ugh, bite me. This hooker is so damn bossy."

I agree. "Always has been, always will be. You know some things will never change."

Persia laughs. "Whatever." Paris pours herself a drink, then takes a seat next to me on the sofa. "Okay, lights, camera, let's rock and roll. And don't leave a damn thing out. I want to hear every detail." I laugh. Then for the next twenty minutes, I dish them the 4-1-1 on the Little Engine That Could.

"Girl, nooooooooooooo...say it ain't so?" Persia cackles. "All that nigga could serve you is fifteen minutes of dick?"

"Well, twenty-five minutes, as long as I didn't talk too dirty."

"Mmmph," Persia grunts. "That shit is sinful."

Paris laughs. "Persia, your ass is a mess. Good sex doesn't have to always be a long, drawn-out event. Everyone doesn't need to have their pussies pounded for more than an hour."

Persia clucks her tongue. "Says who? I don't know about you, but—other than the times when I'm in the mood for a fifteen-minute quickie—I'm not completely satisfied unless my pussy's being fed at least forty minutes of dick. Anything less than that leaves me with a very wet, angry pussy."

Paris and I laugh at her. "So now I understand the world crisis," I tease, shaking my head. "It's full of angry, wet pussies. Mmmm, I wonder what Obama can do about that."

She chuckles. "You can joke if you want. But I'm serious."

"Oh, I know you are," I tell her, knowing her appetite for sex has always been insatiable. Even as a teenager, Persia was fucking long before Paris and me. Sure, we had boyfriends or guys we liked. And, yes, we bumped and grinded—and even sucked a little dick from time to time. But we weren't *fucking*. Persia, on the other hand, was a real hot box and had already sexed seven different boys by the time she was a freshman in high school, two of them being Paris and my boyfriends. Don't ask. It's a whole other story for another time.

Persia grunts. "I know, different strokes for different folks, blah, blah, blah. But this sister here needs to be long stroked for more than fifteen minutes." She makes a face as if she's inhaled something dead. "Who in the hell fucks and doesn't talk dirty these days?"

I shrug. "I don't know. All I know is the brotha was fine as fuck, had a gorgeous body, a nice damn dick, and could hit it right as long as you kept your mouth shut. But the minute you opened your mouth and started spewing out filth"—I snap my fingers—"he was through."

Persia gives me a disgusted look. "Mmmph. I need me another drink." She refills her glass. "So after all that coaching, he still couldn't last long?"

"He tried," I say in his defense. I almost feel bad for talking about him like this. After all, I did enjoy myself with him...well, sort of. "I'm telling you, he's a really nice guy and he has the potential to be damn good in the sheets."

"Well, for someone else," Paris states, taking a sip from her glass. "He might already be."

Persia dismisses the thought with a wave of her hand. "I'm glad you didn't bring him here; that's for sure. If he could barely handle you, there's no way he could ever handle the three of us."

I nod, knowingly. "Trust me. When he came in six minutes—from getting head, I realized then I couldn't bring him here."

Paris shakes her head. "Believe it or not, if a man can't hold out longer than you'd like, he can still satisfy you. We have to learn to be more realistic in terms of what a man is capable of bringing to the table, sexually speaking. And talk to them openly and honestly about what it is we need from them in the sheets."

"So I'm supposed to accept a man who nuts quick, and be okay with it?" Persia asks, raising a brow. "Is that what you're telling me?"

"I'm not saying you should be okay with it. But you should be okay with not making him feel less than a man. And you should be okay with encouraging him, and showing him how to do better. Look at Porsha. Instead of walking out on him, or embarrassing him, she showed him what she wanted. And he was open to trying to deliver what she asked for."

Persia rolls her eyes. "Okay, Oprah. And he still came up short, or should I say, in his case, came too quick."

"Yeah, but he tried. And that was only a one-night stand. Imagine if he was someone you wanted to invest some time in. There's no telling what would happen with a little patience and understanding."

Persia shakes her head. "You can have that. I'm not interested in teaching no man nut control. Sorry."

"Well, nut control or not," Paris continues, "between foreplay and the actual act itself, the whole experience can be stretched out to an hour or more, and still be extremely enjoyable for both."

Persia agrees. "That's true. Still…"

My cell dings. I reach for it off the coffee table, leaving Paris and Persia to continue their discussion. I have a text message from Emerson. WAS THINKN ABT U. HMU WHEN U CAN

I text him back. Tell him how sweet and thoughtful that was.

I WANNA C U 2NITE. It doesn't take long before I forget Persia and Paris are in the room and Emerson and I get caught up in texting each other back and forth.

Me: ME 2

Em: CUM C ME

Me: 2NITE?

Em: YUP

Me: CAN'T

Em: CAN'T OR WON'T

Me: WON'T

Em: ☹

Me: LOL

Em: I WANNA HOLD U. NO SEX

Me: YEAH RIGHT

Em: ☺ I PROMISE. I JUST WANNA LIE NAKED WIT U, AND HOLD U

Me: I HAVE TO GET UP EARLY

Em: STAY THE NIGHT

I blink, surprised that he is extending an invitation for me to come to his place; to stay the night. I can't remember the last time I slept at a man's place, let alone stayed the night. The thought of waking up in his arms entices me.

Em: THEN I CAN MAKE LUV 2 U B4 U LV 4 WORK

I smile.

"….Ummm, excuse us. Hello…"

I look up from my phone. Paris and Persia are staring at me. "What? Did y'all say something to me?"

"What, or should I say *who*, are you over there smiling about?" Persia asks.

"Oh nothing. Some silly text message," I tell her as I text Emerson back, asking him for his address. I get up and stretch. "Listen, hookers. I'm going out for a bit."

"Must be some text," Persia says, eyeing me.

I gulp down the rest of my drink.

Paris smirks, a hint of mischief in her eyes, as if she has a secret of her own. "Have fun."

"Don't wait up," I say over my shoulder, walking out of the room.

Passion

CHAPTER TWENTY-FIVE

Tank's "Amazing" is playing in the background. The candles are lit. The mood is sexy. I slowly slip off my sheer robe. Allow it to slide off my shoulders, then fall to the floor. I'm standing in the middle of Emerson's bedroom in a pair of red four-inch Christian Louboutin sandals. I run my hands seductively over the curves of my hips, up to my breasts, up my neck, then through my hair. I slowly twirl my body in a slow, seductive circle. With my back facing him, I glance at him over my left shoulder, stick my tongue out of the corner of my mouth, then bend over and grab my ankles. My ass cheeks peek out from under the hem of my negligee.

"Damn, baby…you gotta fat ass."

I grin. *Of course I do, nigga*, I think, slowly turning back around to face him. I have no business fucking him. Have no business sneaking off to be with him. But his dick is good. So very good! "You wanna fuck me in it?" I ask, spreading it open to give him a closer peek.

My hands journey back up and down my body until they reach their destination, until searching, eager fingers find their mark, wet and sticky—between my thighs. I press on my clitoris, swirl my two fingers over my love button, emitting a low moan. Emerson's hand snakes down to his ever-growing erection as he watches me intently. He sits on the edge of the bed, hard dick in hand, as I slowly inch my way toward him. The thought of taking him into my mouth and pressing my nose into the thick patch of pubic hair that surrounds the base of his swollen dick causes my clit's pulse to quicken.

"C'mon, Porsha, baby…"

"It's Passion," I correct, parting my legs. "You want Passion to wrap this wet pussy around your dick?"

He squeezes his dick, rapidly strokes it, then stops. "Hell yeah. This hard-ass dick needs that shit."

"Oh, yeah? How bad does that dick want it, baby?"

"Bad," he says, spitting in his hand, then jacking his dick. He twirls his hand over its thick-mushroom head. "Real bad, baby… mmmm…you have no idea how bad I want you…"

I pull open my slippery hole. "Is this what you want?"

"Yeah, baby," he says in a throaty whisper. He bites down on his bottom lip.

I slide my middle finger in. And fuck myself. I let out a low moan. "Ooooh…you want this pussy?"

He leans back on his right forearm, stoking his dick with his left hand. "Stop fuckin' with me, baby. You know I do. Let me eat that sweet pussy, then make love to it…"

I nut on my finger, keeping my eyes locked on Emerson's hard, heavy dick. I slide another finger in, scoop my pussy cream out, then walk over to him and feed him my juices. He takes both of my fingers into his mouth, slowly sucks, then licks.

He reaches for me, but I back away, twirling slowly to the music. I dip down low, slowly pop my hips, then lean forward and shimmy my way toward him. He reaches for me again. I plant a heeled foot up on the bed between his legs and gyrate my hips, allow him to run his hands up my silky thighs. He slinks his hand up toward my ass, nuzzles his face between my thighs, inhaling my sweet musky scent. My pussy is wet. I allow him to kiss it, lick it, then push him backward on the bed, stepping out of his grasp.

"Why you fuckin' wit' me, girl?"

I stifle a smile as I slip down the straps of my negligee, then sliding it down my body. Emerson watches intently; his lips curl into a grin.

When Trey Songz's "Red Lipstick" starts to play, I reach for him. "Dance with me," I say, grabbing him by the wrists. He gives me a confused look. I repeat myself, pulling him up. His rigid cock greets me as he steps into me, wrapping me in his arms. I move to the music and he follows my lead. Hip to hip, skin to skin, our naked bodies blend and melt into one. I close my eyes and breathe him in, fill my nostrils with his strength and masculinity. His hands glide up and down my body, finally resting on my ass where they stay through most of the song. Panting, we both get lost in the music.

He squeezes my ass; grinds deep in me. "Damn, what the fuck you tryna do to me?"

"Sssh," I say, looking up at him, pressing a finger to my lips. "Just dance."

Three songs later, Emerson and I are still grinding in the middle of his floor, no words being said. His arms feel so good wrapped around me. His hard body feels good against mine. I don't want this feeling to end.

Then don't let it.

I have to.

Then what the fuck are you doing here?

Living in the moment.

Mmmph, if you say so. And exactly where are you going with this?

I don't know.

Bitch, you can't lead this man on.

I'm not. We're simply two consenting adults enjoying each other's company.

This man wants more from you. He has feelings for you. He's a good man.

I know he is.

Then what the fuck do you want from him?

I don't know.

What are your feelings toward him?

I don't know…

I glance up at Emerson; he's gazing at me. Catching me off-guard, his mouth opens and he's kissing me, loving me with his mouth—thick, luscious lips pressing against mine, pulling in my bottom lip. I'm scrambling for footing before I slip and fall into his web; his tongue weaving its way deep into my mouth. Slowly, without much resistance, I've become entangled in a maze of passion.

"Why are we still dancing?" he finally asks, coming up for air.

My breath catches in my throat. "Because it feels good." He asks if this is what I want to do all night; stand here, grinding and teasing him. He presses his dick into me for emphasis.

"No," I gasp.

"Good," he says, scooping me up in his arms, then laying me down on the bed. He kisses my stomach, then trails his kisses up to my breasts, my nipples, then back down to my navel. "I'm gonna make love to you tonight."

I flash him a breathless smile, spreading open my legs as he rolls on a condom. He glides his dick back and forth over my slit, slaps it up against my clit, then slides into me. I grab him by the ass. Pull him in deep, inviting him into a night of passion.

Like a hot knife, his rhythmic thrusts slice into the center of my pussy, melting my sugary walls. And, before long, I'm coating every inch of his cock with a hot, sticky paste. He reaches a hand underneath me, strokes my titties, then runs his fingers down my body toward the front of my pussy. He seeks my clit, rubbing it with two fingertips. His circling fingers and the stroking of his dick morphs my swelling river into a roaring ocean of hot, foamy waves of orgasms, each wave crashing against my inner walls and splashing up against his dick. I'm drowning him in my wetness. I clutch his shaft, milk the length of him with each stroke, sending him into trembling moans of candy-coated joy.

"Ohhh, shit…aaah…oh Passion…aaah, fuck, baby…Your pussy's so fuckin' good."

"Is it as good as my sisters'?" I ask him this, knowing I'm putting him on the spot. The truth is I already know the answer: all three of us have good pussy. Damn good pussy. I only want to see how he responds.

He grunts, slows his thrusts. "Your pussy is better." He looks me in the eyes when he says this. He cups my ass, pulls me in, burying his dick deep. "Oh, shit…much better."

"Lose your dick in me," I whisper to him, gliding my fingertips along his spine, until my hands rests on his firm ass. I squeeze his cheeks, pulling him deeper into me. I look in his piercing brown eyes; connect with his troubled soul. Tonight, whatever his issues might be, they don't exist; they don't matter.

As he moves his body, I move mine. Our hands, our bodies, our lips, our tongues are dancing to the same music. Our grunts and moans are in beat to our rhythm.

"Fuck me…" I whisper. Squeezing my ass in his hands, he pounds his dick into my warm, eager cunt. I moan as he plunges his way in, moving slowly at first, then faster.

I glance up at the mirror-covered ceiling at our lusty liaison. I smile at the sweaty reflection of his muscled back, my legs wrapped around his waist, as I greedily meet his thrusts.

His breathing becomes ragged. I grab his dick; clench my muscles around it. Urge him to release his seed and unload deep in me.

Our bodies intertwine. Our lips lock and dance as we thrust and crash into each other; hips grinding and bucking. Sweat dripping. He grunts and groans; fucks and sucks and holds onto me, hoping to stretch out the night for as long as he can. He's a desperate, horny lover, needing, wanting our connection to go on forever. But the reality is, it can't. And it won't. Lord knows, I can't let it.

"Hi, Mom," I say, answering my cell. "How was your trip to Vegas?"

"It was good. Of course, your Aunt Penny and Lucky almost got into it, again. The two of them are like oil and water. They really don't mix. But other than that, it was great. We saw the Temptations perform and had the seafood buffet at Rios. That was really nice. The food was delicious. Then, of course, we saw the water show at the Bellagio. And one night we went to see some kind of sex show at that hotel New York, New York."

"A sex show?" I asked surprised. "*You?* Were there naked bodies and people actually having sex?"

"Oh, heavens no," she says, chuckling. "Now you know I wouldn't be in for none of that nastiness. It wasn't really a sex show. It was erotic." I ask her what the name of it was. She says she can't recall. Tells me it started with a Zee.

I smile, shaking my head. "Zumanity?"

"Yeah, that's it. Whew, they were some kinda freaks up in there. I told Fanny I could see you, Persia and Porsha up there doing all that na—"

"Mom," I interrupt before she can finish. "Don't. I'm enjoying the conversation; let's not spoil it."

"Well, what did I do now?"

I catch myself from letting out an exasperated sigh. "Nothing, Mom; let's move on. So what do I owe the pleasure of this call?"

"I wanted to tell you that I love you. And that I thought about what you said the last time we spoke. And I want you to know that I heard you. And I've heard your father and your Aunt Penny." She pauses. "I'm going to do better. Of course, Lucky and Fanny think I should be raising holy hell at how you girls treat me. They think it's—"

"Mother," I snap, feeling myself starting to get annoyed. "What's wrong with you? You say something nice, then you turn around and piss all over it with craziness."

"Paris, what in the world did I say that was so crazy? I'm simply telling you that I heard you. And that I'm going to do better. I want a relationship with my daughters. All three of you."

I let out a sigh of relief. *There's hope after all.* "Thank you. That's all I want is for us to be able to get along and spend time together."

"Me, too. So let's put what has happened behind us." I tell her I'd like that. "Let's spend the day together, you and me."

I frown. "What about Porsha and Persia? I thought you said you wanted to have a relationship with *all* three of us."

"I do. I'm hoping to do something with each of you, separately." I decide to stay optimistic, knowing she'll have a better chance of dancing with the devil than she will at getting Persia to go anywhere alone with her. I tell her I'm sure they'd like that. Tell her I'd really like spending the day somewhere with her. I ask her what she'd like to do. "Let's drive out to Woodbury Common," she says. "I want a new pocketbook. And, hopefully, I can find a wedding gift for Pasha, too." Although driving for an hour to a shopping outlet isn't exactly what I'd hoped for, I see it as her way of extending an olive branch. So I graciously accept her offering.

"I'd like that. When do you want to go?" She tells me toward the end of next month. "Okay, that sounds good. I'm looking forward to it. Thanks, Mom."

"For what?"

"For trying."

"Well, despite what you girls think, I do love you. And I'm always going to be your mother. And I'm always going to have my opinions."

I take a deep breath. "Mom—"

"But, I'm going to *try* to keep them to myself."

I smile. "That's all we ask," I say as two customers walk into the boutique. "Mom, I have to go. Thanks for calling. Give Daddy a hug for me, and you enjoy the rest of your day."

"I will. You enjoy yours as well."

As soon as I hang up, the phone rings again. I answer on the third ring. "Paradise Boutique, how can I help you?"

"You can help me by going away with me," the deep, baritone voice says.

I smile. "And why should I do that?"

He laughs. "'Cause I can't stop thinkin' 'bout ya sexy ass. You've become my love drug."

I laugh as well. "Oh, okay, Raheem DeVaughn. What you gonna do now, sing?"

He keeps laughing. "Yo, if that's what it's gonna take to get a yes, then hell yeah." He starts singing.

"Oh, nooooooo," I say, laughing. "Please don't."

"Am I gonna get a yes?"

"Let me think about it."

"Yo, you killin' me, ma. You got me sprung."

"Oh, please," I say, laughing. "You don't even know me. And you probably say that to all the girls."

"Nah, I ain't that dude. I keep shit a hunnid, ma. I don't *know* you, know you, but what I know so far, I'm diggin'. And I wanna get to know you better. But, I tell you what. We can hold off on going away—for now, if you come chill wit' me down in Atlantic City for the night."

"I'm flattered," I say, smiling. "But—"

"No 'but', ma. So wassup? Spend one day wit' me, and let's see what happens. If you ain't feelin' me after that...cool. We part ways and go on 'bout our business."

"How 'bout you part my cunt lips with your tongue," I hear myself saying, feeling a rush of heat searing through me as I replay our night together. Blood rushes to my clit. I close my eyes. Feel his fingers on the curve of my hips, pulling my pussy deeper into his mouth, burying his tongue in between my soft, sticky folds. I'm horny. And I want to fuck him again.

"I tell you what. Come lick my pussy."

He laughs. "Yo, you wildin', ma."

"I'm not laughing," I tell him low and sexy. "I don't have on any panties."

"Yo, don't tease me, ma," he says in a throaty whisper.

I smile. There is definitely a lot of sexual chemistry between the two of us. But more than that, I really am starting to like him. "I'm not. Does it sound like I'm teasing? I wanna feel your tongue. Don't you wanna taste this pussy, again?"

"Hell, yeah I do. I wanna get all up in that shit. You got my dick hard as steel right now."

I moan. "Mmmm...I like the sound of that. The store closes at six. Bring me that hard-ass dick, and that long tongue."

"I'll be there at five-fifty-nine."

"I'll be waiting," I say before disconnecting.

CHAPTER TWENTY-SEVEN

I'm naked standing in front of my mirror, staring at my reflection. Jaguar Wright's "Do Your Worst" is playing on my Bose stereo. I sway a bit as I oil my body. *Do your worst...but damn it...make sure it's your best...*I grab the remote from off the dresser and raise the volume. I part my thighs, massaging my clit. I work myself up to an orgasm, then stop when I feel myself on the brink of coming. I walk into the bathroom to retrieve my bottle of Wet, then squirt some all over my Luna Pleasure Beads. I slip the weighted balls into my pussy, then slide on a pair of black spandex shorts and a matching tank top. While I'm out getting my two-mile run on, I'll be working my pussy muscles out as well. I love the feeling of those tiny vibrations rippling through my pussy as my feet hit the pavement. My walls milk these balls, trying to keep them from slipping out. Thirty minutes a day and this pussy stays extra tight.

I step into my Nikes, humming along to Jaguar as she sings the shit out of this song. *I don't understand...how I can I tell you what it takes to make me happy...and for some reason whyyyy. . . you only seem to do what makes me crazy....*

Persia walks in, wearing a pair of pink short-shorts and a white tank top. Her dark nipples are showing through her shirt. "You off to the gym?"

"No, the park," I tell her, pulling my hair up into a ponytail. I turn the music down, then walk over and pick up my cell. The flashing red light alerts me that I have new messages or missed calls. "You should run with me," I say as I scroll through my phone. I have four text messages.

"No thanks, boo. I'll save my running for the treadmill downstairs." We have a customized state-of-the-art gym in our basement that we use regularly; still it's nice to get out and run in the breeze.

"Mmmph. Suit yourself. It's a gorgeous day out. You never know who we might *run* into while we're out running in the park. Oh, Irwin sent me a text. He'll be in town this Saturday. He wants to know if we're still on."

"Of course," she says, patting between her legs. "Momma could use a good feeding. Tell him to make sure he pops a Viagra and a Cialis mix so he's extra hard and ready to knock this pussy out the frame."

I laugh, texting him to let him know we're still on. "Girl, you're a damn mess. You're trying to send that man to the ER. You know that shit would have his dick about to explode. Shit, it might break off."

She laughs. "Yeah, hopefully, right into my pussy."

I laugh with her. "Girl, your ass is crazy. Have you talked to Paris today? I tried calling her and sent her a text earlier, but haven't heard back from her."

"No, I haven't spoken to her. Hmmm. Come to think of it, she's been M-I-A lately. Whenever I call or text her, she takes forever to get back to me. That's not like her."

I've noticed it, too, but don't mention it. "Maybe it's been hectic down at the boutique."

"Yeah, but the store closes at six. Sometimes I'll send her text around seven or eight and it takes her almost an hour or more to respond back."

I shrug. She means well, but sometimes Persia forgets we don't have to answer to her. That she's not our mother. "Paris is a big girl. I'm sure she has her reasons for not responding back as quickly as *you'd* like. Fact is, she's a grown woman."

She frowns. "Well, shoot me for caring," she says, sounding offended. "I realize she's grown. And she doesn't have to answer to me. Still, I worry. We're all we've got. We have to always look out for each other."

"And we do. But you don't have to always think the worst when one of us doesn't text or call you *right* back. I don't mean to sound messy, but we have lives outside of you."

She huffs, putting her hands up on her hips. "Oh, and I don't?"

"I didn't say that."

"Well, sounds like you're implying it. I've never said or thought the two of you didn't have a life outside of me. All I'm saying is, I worry; that's it. And having the decency to let someone know you're not coming home is about common courtesy."

And trying to control us, I think, knowing she'll never admit it. I decide I've had enough of this conversation. "Paris and I recognize how much you worry about us. And we appreciate you for that, sis." I walk over and give her a hug. She hugs me back. "I don't wanna fight with you. But I'll beat your ass if need be."

She laughs. "Yeah, right. You wish."

"Well, let me get out of here so I can get to the park. These beads are already working my pussy muscles overtime and I haven't even started my run yet." She laughs, reaching between her legs and pulling at the opening of her shorts. She shows me the string dangling from her slit. I frown, grabbing my iPod. "Ugh! Hooker, TMI."

She laughs. "Oh, but it wasn't too much information for you to tell me about the beads in your pussy."

"But I didn't show you my snatch, did I? Big difference, nasty ass." She follows me out the room, then down the stairs.

"Whatever. It's not like you haven't seen it many times before."

I grab my keys, then walk into the kitchen and grab a bottle of Dasani out of the 'fridge. "Yeah, don't remind me. That ugly thing gives me nightmares. I swear I think it has teeth."

She laughs, playfully swatting at me. "Yeah, right. You wish. I have a pretty pussy, boo. Don't hate."

"Lies," I say, laughing as I head toward the door. "I'll see your freaky ass later."

"Takes a freak to know one, boo," she says, closing the door behind me. I wave her on, dismissively, disarming my car. I slide in, start the engine, then drive off.

An hour and a half later, I'm heading home when my music fades and my cell rings through the speakers. It's Emerson. I grin as I answer. "Hello."

"Hey, beautiful. How you?"

"I'm good. What's up with you?"

"Chillin'; thinking about you."

I smile. "That's sweet of you."

"What you got planned for the day? I was hoping we could catch a movie and grab a bite to eat later on."

I blink. Outside of meeting him a few times at the Sheraton, going out in public isn't something we've done thus far. Fucking him behind closed doors is how I've wanted to keep things between us—for now. At least, until I can figure out what I want. However, I thought keeping this thing between us under wraps is what we both agreed on. "I can't," I tell him. "How about we meet up at your place later on tonight instead?"

He sighs. "Yo, c'mon, Porsha. How long we gonna sneak around? It's been weeks. Don't you think it's time we step this up a notch?"

"Em, you told me we could move at my pace. That you wouldn't pressure me. You do remember saying that, no?"

"Yeah, I said it. But, damn…"

"Look, if you're having second thoughts, then maybe we should stop now before things get too serious."

"Is that what you want?" he asks, sounding frustrated. Truth is, I don't know what I want. The more time I spend with Emerson, the more attracted I am to him. He's a damn good man. *Yeah, and he's fucked my sisters and me.* "Look," he says, not waiting for me to answer the question. "I wanna spend time with you out and about during the day. Not holed up in a hotel or my spot, ordering take out all the time. And not at night. You're a beautiful woman. And I wanna do things with you. Go out. Take day trips into the city, or weekend drives down to the Baltimore Harbor. I wanna chill with you. Damn, is that too much to ask?"

"No," I state, turning into my development.

"Then what's the problem?"

"I'm not ready. I'm still trying to figure things out. Still trying to come to terms with potentially getting involved with a man I've shared with my sisters."

"I told you, I'm cool with it. I mean, it's nothing we can do about it now. It happened. If you're worried that I might wanna get it in with 'em again, don't be. The only woman I'm interested in is you."

I pull into my driveway and park behind Persia's car, turning my engine off. "That's not what I'm worried about."

"Then what is it? Persia? You think she's gonna be pissed that you're giving into your own feelings for a change, and doing something you want to do for yourself?"

I frown. "How dare you? I'll have you know, I run my own life. Persia doesn't control shit, I do." *But she tries*, I think, looking up at the second floor of our home. Persia's curtain moves. She's stepped away from the window. "I'm my own woman. The fact is, Em, I'm not ready; period. Now if that's too much for you to deal with, then let's end this now." I'm not sure if it's the fact that he *knows* I'm concerned about how Persia's going to react to the news that has me so pissed at him right now, or if it's the fact that I *am* letting her control aspects of my life, indirectly.

"C'mon, Porsha, let's not do this. I don't wanna turn this into a fight. All I'm sayin' is sometimes you gotta take some risks. I know what I want. I just want you to know what it is you want, too. All I'm askin' is for you to give us a chance. That's all."

I glance back up at Persia's bedroom window. I see her shadow again. I sigh. "I don't wanna fight with you, either."

"Cool. I tell you what. How 'bout we do this: I have a time-share I need to use the last week in June. How about you fly out to Curacao with me? Let's spend the week together. And see how things go. If you're still not sure about what you wanna do, I'll bow out gracefully and let you do you."

"Em—"

"Before you say no, think about it. In the meantime, I wanna see you tonight. Sounds like you could use a nice, relaxing, full-body massage. Come through and let my hands make love to your body."

I smile. "I'll be there at eight."

"Aiight, see you then."

I disconnect the call, then step out of the car, shutting the door behind me. I activate the alarm, making my way inside the house. As soon as I reach for the handle, the door swings open.

"Girl, I didn't know what was going on. You were sitting out in that car for a long-ass time. Is everything alright? I thought I was going to have to call nine-one-one."

Persia steps back, lets me in. "Everything's fine. I was finishing up a phone call."

"Well," she says, following me up the stairs. "It must've been some call for you to stay out in the car all that time."

"It was," I say, walking into my bedroom, then stepping out of my sneakers.

I feel her eyes burning a hole through me. I turn to face her. Tilt my head. "What?"

She narrows her eyes. "Anything you wanna talk about?"

"Nope," I tell her, removing my workout gear. I walk into my bathroom—naked, turn on the shower, adjust the setting, then step in.

"Well, how was your run?" she asks, walking into the bathroom, leaning up against the sink.

What are you afraid of? Persia? "It was good."

"You sure everything's okay? You seem kind of distant."

Sometimes you gotta take risks. "Everything's fine. I'm tired. That run wore me out. I'm going to take a long nap when I get finished in here." *You're a beautiful woman...I know what I want...* I toss my head back, let the water beat against my face and neck. Pretend Persia is no longer leaning up against the sink, staring at me. I close my eyes. *Let my hands make love to your body...*

When I'm finished with my shower, I step out into my room, wrapping a towel around me. Persia's lying across my bed, waiting. "You wanna order in later? Or go out and grab something to eat?"

I fish my phone out of my bag. "Ummm, not tonight." I text: I'LL BE THERE @ 6

"I have plans," I tell her, slipping on a pair of silk boxer shorts.

I let my titties bounce free, pull back my comforter, slipping in between my 1500-count Egyptian cotton sheets.

I fake a yawn. Right now, I want to be alone. *All I'm askin' is for you to give us a chance.*

"Okay, girl. Well, I'll let you get some rest," Persia says, getting off my bed and walking toward the door. "We'll talk later."

"Okay," I say, pulling the covers up over my head. *The only woman I'm interested in is you.* I close my eyes, drifting off to sleep.

Passion
CHAPTER TWENTY-EIGHT

Emerson pulls his dick out of my smoldering cunt, slaps my clit with it, then slowly slides it back in—deep. He thrusts a few times, grinds his pelvis against mine, then pulls out again, beating his dick against my clit and slit. I moan. Hoist my hips up in an exchange, my pussy for his dick. He taunts me. Slips the head back in, slowly whines it in. Tip fucks me, then pulls it out. He has my hands pinned back on the bed. I jut my hips upward.

"Damn, baby...you're so beautiful..." He stares into my eyes. His intense gaze penetrates my soul. He looks into me, raw and naked and vulnerable. He plants gentle kisses all over me—the tip of my nose, my eyelids, my chin, my neck, my breasts. His kisses go on and on, covering every inch of my flesh. "You're so damn beautiful, baby," he says, again, pushing his dick back into my well. I gasp. He slow fucks me for another ten minutes, while tonguing me. Gets my pussy swish-swishing; my juices splattering against his cock, then abandons my mouth. His tongue travels along my skin, flicks along the side of my neck. He kisses my collarbone. His hands cup my ass as he loses his dick inside of me. Tendrils of arousal gather in the pit of my pussy, then burst into colorful orgasms, coiling around my clitoris. I don't know how much more of this man I can take before I fall for him, hard.

"I want you so fuckin' bad, baby...I wanna get lost in this pussy...I wanna own this pussy..." His dick hits my spot and I feel lightheaded.

"Mmmm...oooooooooooh..."

"Open up, baby...let me in..." He hits the bottom of my abyss. "Give me all of this good pussy...give me all of your heart..." His dick swells, brushes against my walls, causing my muscles to constrict and expand. I moan again. "Let me in, baby...Ohh, shit, you feel so good...Let me have you, Porsh..."

"Uhhh...you have me," I say soft and sweet. Not sure if what's come out of my mouth is said in the heat of the moment, or if it's what I mean. He hits my spot again. My eyes roll in the back of my head. "Ohhhhh, Em...mmmm...what are you tryna do to me?"

"Make love to you," he whispers, slipping his tongue in my ear, then nibbling on my lobe again. I shiver. Yet we are in front of his fireplace, sweating and panting. The glow from the fire, its flames dancing about the room, adds to the intense heat emitted between my legs. "I could make love to you forever...I love you, Porsh..."

It is in those three words that my emotions collide. Fear, excitement, lust, and desire all connect, then explode into petals of joy. In my heart, I believe, I feel, I know, Emerson is a good man. He's a man worth loving, and being loved by. Still, we say things in the moment. Things we don't always mean. I won't, can't allow words spoken but not meant, to have value in my life.

I close my eyes, block out the echoing of his words. My eyes snap open when he pulls his dick out of my pussy, leaving it yearning for it back inside of me, deep and thick and full of power. I plead with my eyes. Beg for him to put his dick back where it belongs. He ignores my pleas. Kisses down to my stomach, dips his tongue into my navel, then slides it along my clit. I squirm and wiggle as he eats my pussy, lapping up my hot juices that spurt out onto his tongue. He mounts his mouth over my clit, dipping his tongue into my wetness, rapidly nursing on my clit until I start to shake and buck my hips.

I'm spent. But that doesn't stop him from entering my cum-slick pussy and hitting my bottom all over again. "Ohhhh, shiiiit... you feel you so good, baby..."

"Oooooooh, Em...it's your dick, baby...it's all you, making me feel good..."

He kisses me. Tells me he loves again. I choke back tears.

We become silent, staring into each other's eyes as he strokes my insides. The crackling of the fire becomes the music that guides our rhythm.

"How do you know?" I finally whisper against his lips in between kisses. He keeps his gaze locked on mine, kisses me deeply enough to leave no doubt that what he feels is real; that he is more than sure.

Paris

CHAPTER TWENTY-NINE

I pull back the sheets and stare at Desmond's naked body as he sleeps. My eyes hungrily rove every inch of his sculpted physique, causing my mouth to water. I'm so turned on by the sight of him that I can barely contain my desire to fuck him all over again. My pussy aches, still wet from the last three rounds. But it's hungry for more of him. I scoot down some, then take Desmond's dick in my hand and gently stroke it, placing gentle kisses all over it before licking its head like an ice cream cone. I roll his beautiful dick between my palms, slowly gliding my hands up and down his shaft. I love this strong black dick. Love the way it tastes; the way it feels. Love the way its vein throbs when it's aroused; the way its eye leaks clear, sticky nectar whenever it's excited. He doesn't have as much dick as I envisioned he would with his height and all. But, it's not a disappointment in the least. The man knows how to use what he has. And that's all that matters to me. It's about six-and-three-quarter inches of dark chocolate, brick-hard and thick cock. Damn, did he work this pussy over!

He stirs, but doesn't awake until I am rapidly sucking his hard dick. "Aaah, shit," he moans, opening his eyes. "Damn, baby, you tryna suck the life outta a muhfucka."

I pull his dick out of my mouth long enough to ask, "You got a problem with that?" I wrap my lips back around the head and continue sucking before he can respond.

He laughs. "Hell no, baby. Do you. You got a muhfucka trippin' hard right now."

I smile. And for the next fifteen minutes, I suck and slurp until he's grabbing at the sheets and bucking his hips, nutting down in my throat. I lick him clean, then flop back on the bed beside him. He attempts to steady his breathing, pulling me into his arms. He kisses me on the side of my head. "Damn, you really gotta muhfucka feeling some kinda way; got me all off my square. I'm really diggin' you, ma. I wanna really get to know you. You know, spend some time with you...."

I lay my head on his chest, playing in the patch of hair in the center of his chest. My hand glides over to his nipple, slowly swirl the tips of my fingers over it until it hardens. I am half-listening to him talk, half-listening to his beating heart.

"...no pressure, though...."

The voice inside of my head is telling me to get up and put my clothes on; to tell him getting to know me isn't an option, then walk out the door and never look back.

But he's so damn fine.

And you're into foursomes with your sisters.

He doesn't have to ever know about that part of your life.

But he will! It's only a matter of time.

Then tell him before he hears it from someone else.

He wouldn't understand.

Then let this be the last time you fuck him.

I'm only having fun with him, so he doesn't need to know.

My gut tells me to roll out of his arms. Instead, I lie still. Stay wrapped in his embrace. His muscular body feels so good pressed up against mine. I close my eyes and drift off to sleep, deciding that at this very moment, this is where I *want* to be.

Two hours later I awaken to Desmond watching me. He smiles at me, then kisses me on the tip of my nose. "Yo, anyone ever tell you how mad sexy you are when you sleep?"

I smile back at him, shaking my head. "No, this is the first time I'm hearing it. Thank you."

"No doubt. So what you wanna do the rest of the day?"

I glance over at the digital clock. It reads: 4:18 P.M. I still can't believe that on my day off I snuck down to Atlantic City and have been laid up in a suite at the Borgata with this man since last night. Against my will, I find myself slowly liking him. Find myself thinking about the possibilities of a relationship; maybe not with him, but the idea of having someone special in my life surfaces. Yet, the thought of giving up what my sisters and I share...I sigh. A part of me is okay with giving it up all up for a more traditional life. Then there's that other part of me—the kinky side, that looks forward to sharing every part of a man with my sisters. I enjoy the sexapades. Enjoy the randomness of it all. *Then why the hell are you here?*

I don't know.

Bitch, your ass is confused.

"I don't know," I tell him, shifting my attention back to him. "Maybe go downstairs and try to gamble a bit since I don't know the first thing about gambling. Then grab something to eat. I'm in the mood for sushi."

He grins. "Stick with me, baby. I'll teach you."

I smile. "Oh, is that so?"

"No doubt," he says, kissing me on the tip of my nose. "So you dig sushi?"

"Yup, love it," I say, stretching.

"Oh, word? That's my shit, too. And they have a Japanese spot downstairs. My man told me it's bangin'."

I smile. "Sounds good to me. I can eat sushi every day."

"Oh word?" he says, eyeing me. He kisses me on the lips, pulling back the covers. "So what else can you eat every day?"

"I'm not telling you all of my secrets," I say, licking my lips, glancing under the covers at his cock. I climb out of bed. "A girl has to keep some things to herself."

He laughs, watching as I walk over to the dresser, my bare ass shaking and bouncing. "Yeah, aiight. Damn, you gotta beautiful ass."

"Glad you like it." I pull my phone out of my handbag. I have four text messages. One from Porsha telling me Irwin's going to be in town this weekend.

"Like it? Yo, I love it! You got one of those nice ol' juicy-biscuit booties." I glance over at Desmond, laughing.

"Ohmygod, hilarious."

"Nah, baby. I'm serious. You sexy as fuck."

"You're full of compliments," I say, scrolling through my phone. There's a text from Felecia inviting us to Pasha's bachelorette party the night before her wedding. And there's one text from Persia, wanting to know if I want to order in. "What are you trying to get, some more pussy?"

He laughs. "Nah, I'm tryna get up in your heart." I drop my phone, coughing. "Yo, you aiight?"

"Yeah," I say, patting my chest. "You kind of caught me off-guard with that."

"Yo, don't choke, baby. I'm keepin' shit real. I wanna snatch you up. That's real talk."

I pick up my cell from off the floor. I'm not going to be able to keep this up much longer. At some point, I'll need to make a decision. I'll either need to tell him about my man-sharing escapades or end this rendezvous before it turns into something complicated. Right now, I'm not going to worry about it. "Well, how about we live in the moment and simply enjoy each other's company. Whatever else happens…happens."

"Aiight. That's wassup. So since you wanna be in the moment, put that phone down and come back to bed. I wanna hold you in my arms."

I smile. "Give me a sec. I need to let my sisters know where I'm at." I text Persia, let her know I won't be coming home, then shut off my phone and toss it back in my bag. "There," I say, walking back over to him. He pulls back the covers as I climb into bed. "I'm all yours."

He pulls me into my arms. "Aaaah, yeah. That's what I wanna hear."

Seven o'clock, we're downstairs seated at Izakaya. The ambiance is sensual. The décor contemporary. I've ordered a shrimp, lobster, crab and scallop dish with a side of charred Japanese broccoli, and one baby dragon roll. Desmond's ordered Japanese sea bass and a spicy tuna roll. He orders a two-hundred-and-twenty-dollar bottle of sake.

"So when you gonna hit me with them digits?" he asks, taking a slow sip of his drink.

I sweep my bang across my forehead, smiling. "When I'm ready for you to snatch me up. In the meantime, you know how to reach me. And you know where to find me. So there's no need for you to have any other numbers. Not yet, anyway."

He grins. "Oh, aiiight. That's how you doin' me?"

I eye him over the rim of my ceramic cup. "For now."

"I see your work. I got you, though. It's all good. I'ma just keep comin' down to ya spot until you give in."

I smile, raising my eyebrow. "Hmmm, sounds kind of stalker-ish to me. Don't have me call the cops on you."

He laughs. "Oh, here you go with that again. You stay tryna call the police on a muhfucka. What's gonna be my crime this time?"

"I don't know" I say, teasingly. "I'll think up something real creative."

"Yeah, aiight. You do that. I'll be bailed out before the ink dries, and right back at ya spot. Now what? You not shakin' me that easy, ma. I already told you what it is."

Girl, you better slow this down before it spins out of control. And you find your ass in something you can't get out of. I shrug. "I'll take my chances."

Every so often I find myself stealing glances at him. I can't lie. He's piqued my curiosity. A series of questions are racing through my head. What kind of work does he do? Does he have any children? How many baby mommas does he have? Did he go to college? Does he own his own place? Does he live alone? Is his credit all fucked up?

I ask the questions and learn that he's thirty-one, has no children, and has never been married. That his family's from New Haven, Connecticut, where he still lives; but has an apartment in Jersey that he shares with one of his cousins. That he has three brothers and two sisters; that he's the middle child. He tells me his parents, along with a few other family members, live in Jersey, which is why he's here so much. That he's very family oriented, and spends a lot of time chilling with them.

"Speakin' of which, one of my cousins is gettin' married in a couple of months," he says, taking a swig of his sake. "I'm actually his best man."

I smile. "Nice. I bet you clean up really well, too."

He rubs his chin, grinning. "Yeah, no doubt. I can definitely do a lil sumthin-sumthin."

"I bet you can. You'll have to take pictures so I can see for myself."

"No doubt. I got you. On some real shit, wish I woulda met you sooner. I woulda had you on my arm so you could see firsthand how I get down."

I laugh. "And what makes you think I'd want to be on your arm?"

He grins. "Don't front. I know you diggin' me. And you'd be on my arm, 'cause that's where I'd want you to be. That's real talk, baby."

"Yeah, okay. I'm sure that cockiness has gotten you real far."

"Don't confuse confidence with cockiness, baby. I get what I want."

I eye him over the rim of my drink. "So, what kind of work do you do?"

He takes another sip of his drink. "Is that really important?"

I shrug; slowly shake my head. "No, actually it's not. Forgive me for asking." *I mean, it's not like you tryna marry the nigga.*

"Nah, you good. I don't usually like discussin' what I do for a livin'. Some chicks be on some gold-diggin' type shit, feel me?"

I nod. "I understand. Trust me. I'm far from a gold digger. If you haven't noticed, I do very well for myself."

He takes in the two-carat diamond studs in my earlobes, the tennis bracelet and diamond-encrusted Rolex on my wrist, the two-thousand-dollar handbag. "Yeah, I see how you grind. You'd have a cat goin' broke real quick, tryna get at you. He'll have'ta dig real deep in them pockets."

"That's so not true," I say, feigning insult as I take a slow sip from my drink. "I make my own money and buy whatever I want. Trust me. I don't need a man to buy me anything. And I'm definitely not a gold digger."

"Nah, baby, I wasn't callin' you a gold digger. I'm sayin' *if* I were your man, I'd *want* to buy you shit. You the type of woman I'd wanna spoil."

I smile. "That's so sweet of you."

The rest of the night we eat our meal, laughing and talking and finishing up the bottle of sake. I glance down at my watch. It's already nine-thirty. Desmond pays the check, then grabs my hand and leads the way out the restaurant. We walk around the casino for a while until he decides he wants to gamble. He wants to play *The Amazing Race* game, which is situated next to the *Sex and The City* slot machines. I'm impressed with the graphics. And see why every seat for the game is filled. He takes a seat at the last *Amazing Race* slot machine that's next to the last *Sex and the City* machine. Surprisingly, the woman playing the machine decides to get up. I grab the seat, digging in my purse for my wallet.

"Yo, take this," he says, pulling out a stack of bills and handing me two one-hundred-dollar bills. I tell him no, but he insists. I take the money, thanking him. He reaches over and kisses me on the lips. I'm shocked at his public display of affection, and even more shocked that I allow it. And like it.

"What was that for?"

"For good luck. And for bein' so damn sexy."

"How sweet," I say, sliding the bills into the machine. There are four grids and I have no idea how to play the game so I read the printed instructions. Once I think I have the gist of it down, I decide to play all four grids. After about seven or eight tries, I win a few spins and about forty dollars; nothing to write home about. Thirty minutes later, I'm down to forty-two dollars. "I should cash this out before I lose it all."

He laughs. "Play that shit, baby. It's only money. You win some, you gonna lose some. We're here to have fun."

I shrug. "Say no more," I tell him, accidentally hitting the MAXIMUM BET button. "Oh, shit. I didn't mean to do that."

"Don't sweat it, baby. Like I said, you lose some, you win some."

Next thing I know, bells are going off. "Ohmygod, ohmygod, ohmygod!" I scream, jumping up out of my seat. "I hit the jackpot!"

Persia

CHAPTER THIRTY

"W ell, well, well," I say as Paris sashays her way into our
media room, wearing a wide I'm-happy-as-a-clam-
rolled-in-shit smile on her face. "Look who's finally
decided to come home"—I glance down at my watch—"almost
twenty-nine hours later. Mmmph, must've been some night."

She flops down on the sofa next to me. "Girl, it was. I won
almost fourteen hundred dollars playing a slot machine called
Sex and the City."

"Oh, wow. Congrats, sis. Who'd you go down there with?"

"I went by myself; why?"

I eye her. "Girl, you don't even gamble. Sooooo, what would
possess you to drive way down to Atlantic City?" She shrugs.
Tells me it was a spur-of-the-moment decision. That she felt like
doing something different. "Well, why didn't you ask if Porsha
or I wanted to ride down with you to get our gamble on, too?"
She blinks. Tells me she wanted to go alone. I purse my lips.
"Hmmm. Well, it definitely seems like it was well worth it."

"Oh, trust me, it was. What's the name of this movie you're
watching?" she asks, quickly changing the subject. I tell her it's
The Holiday with Cameron Diaz and Jude Law, a comedy about
two dizzy chicks, depressed and miserable, across the globe with
man drama. One's in love with a man who is getting ready to marry
another woman. And the other finds out the man she's living with

is cheating on her, so they swap homes in each other's countries. "Oh, I heard this is a really good movie."

"So far, it's a cute movie," I say, eyeing her as she pretends to be all caught up in the movie. Truth is the movie isn't that damn comedic in my opinion, although it does have its moments. Still in all, it's like I said: a *cute* chick flick. She laughs, keeping her eyes glued to the screen. I stare at her.

After about two minutes of me burning a hole through her, she decides to peel her eyes from the TV, glancing over at me. "Umm, why are you giving me the eye like that?"

"Hooker, don't sit here and try to act like you're all into this silly movie," I say, snatching a pillow from off the sofa and playfully hitting her with it. "I wanna know who you took your hot ass down to AC with. And don't give me that I went alone shit. I know when you're hiding something."

She laughs. "Ohmygod, Persia. Your ass is too damn funny. There's nothing to hide."

I squint at her. "So, you're telling me you decided to hop in your car and drive waaaaay down to Atlantic City *all* by yourself?"

"Yes," she says, tucking her hair behind her ears. "Why is that so hard to believe? And for the record, it's not *that* far of a drive."

"Whatever. I know you," I tell her. "And your ass didn't go there alone. But if that's your story, then stick to it, boo."

She waves me on. "Sssh, I wanna watch the movie."

I won't lie. I'm a little disappointed with her for not sharing with me who she went down there with. But at some point, she'll tell me. Still, the question remains. Why does she even feel it necessary to keep it from me now? I can't recall a time when she's ever not shared everything with me the moment it happened. *So why now?*

I roll my eyes. "Fine, keep your little secret."

"Where are you going?"

"Don't worry about it," I tell her, heading out the room. "It's a secret."

She laughs. "Whatever, smart-ass."

While I'm upstairs in the kitchen fixing myself a salmon salad, I decide to call Porsha. Her phone goes directly into voicemail. I disconnect, try her office number. There's no answer. *Hmm, that's odd.*

A few minutes later, the house phone rings. I walk over to the counter and pick up the portable phone, glancing at the caller ID. I sigh. "Hello, Mother," I say, going into the refrigerator. I pull out a green pepper, then the sweet relish, spicy mustard and mayo. "Which one of your daughters would you like to speak to? Paris or Porsha?" There's a tinge of sarcasm in my tone. One I'm sure she's picked up on. I grab a red onion out of the pantry closet.

She huffs. "I've called to speak to you."

I blink. "About what?"

"I would like to have lunch one day next week with *all* three of my daughters."

"Ohhhhhhhkay, so why do you need to speak to me about it first?"

"Because it's *you* who seems to have the most problems with me. And it's *you* who seems to have a big influence on your sisters. It's like they seek your approval or permission to have a relationship with me."

I roll my eyes up in my head, opening a can of red salmon. "Mother, I don't have any control over anything Porsha or Paris do. They're both grown women, as I am. If they choose to have a relationship with you, that's on them. I have nothing to do with that."

"Persia, what have I ever done to you for you to be so cold and callous?"

"Mother…" My cell phone rings. I grab it from off the kitchen table. Glance at the screen. It's Royce. "I don't know what you're talking about. But, look, I have another call that I need to take."

"Need or *want* to take?" she asks, sounding offended.

"It's a call I *want* to take…"—I answer my cell—"hold on one minute," I tell him, then continue my conversation with her as I mix my ingredients together.

"So you'd rather take another call than talk to me?"

"Yes. Just plan the day you want to do your little lunch thingy and let Porsha or Paris know. I'll be sure to be there. I gotta go." I hang up, placing my cell up to my ear. "Hey."

"How you, ma?"

I smile. The way he says *ma* tickles me. And I'm going to be honest with you. I find the hint of his Caribbean accent sexy. My pussy twitches. "Reeeeeeeal horny," I tell him, lowering my voice into a sexy purr. "I want some dick."

I almost see him grinning. "Oh, word? So what you wanna get into tonight?"

"Your boxers."

"That's wasssup. Me and you, or are your sisters gonna get it in, too?"

"I'm not sure what they plan on doing. I can ask. But if not, it'll be you and me. You okay with that, little daddy?"

"No doubt, ma."

"You know I shouldn't be fucking with you, right?"

He laughs. "Why you say that?"

"'Cause you young as hell," I tell him, pulling out a box of Triscuits from one of the cabinets.

"And how old are you, ma?"

"Ummm, excuse you. Don't you know you're not supposed to ask a woman her age?"

"Oh, word? Nah, I ain't get that memo." He laughs. "But, uh, I'ma grown-ass man, ma. You already know what it is. Let's see how young you think I am when I put this big-ass dick up in you tonight."

My pussy purrs.

"Mmmmm, I like the sound of that." I glance up at the wall clock. "What time can you be here?"

"It's whatever. You tell me."

"My pussy wants you now," I tell him, scooping salmon onto a plate with eight crackers, then walking over to the kitchen table. My hunger for Royce's thick West Indian dick has spoiled my mood for salmon. I grab my plate, getting up from the table to wrap it up for later. Right now, I want to be fed a long, hard dick. I tell him this. Tell him tonight I'm going to be his horny little bitch. That I'm going to drink his cum. Telling him all this makes my cunt juices seep. I go into the refrigerator and pull out a thick cucumber, washing it at the sink.

"Daaaaaamn, word? I like that shit, ma." His voice dips to husky whisper. "What else you gonna do?"

"I'm gonna suck on daddy's balls...you wanna be my little daddy, baby?"

He grunts. "Yeah, ma. You got my dick hard as hell. Shit. You know I'm on my way, right?"

"That's exactly what I wanna hear," I say, hopping up on the counter. I prop one leg up on the counter, spread my legs. "I want you to fuck me good." I rub my pussy over my boy shorts; pat it a few times. I moan in his ear.

"Damn, ma. What you doin'?"

"Playing in my pussy until you get here. I can't wait to get up on that dick."

"Damn, ma. You got my dick ready to bust outta my drawz."

I pull open the leg of my shorts, then rub the chilled cucumber over my clit. I gasp. "Aaah...are you in your car yet?"

"Yeah, just got in."

I slide the thick vegetable over my hot slit. "Pull that big dick out and stroke it for me while you drive."

"Oh, word?" he asks, sounding surprised. "You tryna get me fucked up on the road, ma."

"What, you've never jerked off and drove before?" He tells me no. Tells me he's never had anyone ask him to. Tells me he's never even had his dick sucked while driving. "Aww, poor baby," I tease, pushing the cold tip of the cucumber into my pussy. I gasp as it enters me. "Uhh...mmmmm...you don't know what you've been missing. Uh...my pussy's soooo wet...pull your dick out."

"Aiight..." I hear him fumbling around. "Damn, I can't believe I'm about to really do this." I instruct him to keep his eyes open and to keep one hand on the steering wheel and the other on his long, fat cock.

I slow fuck myself with the cucumber until my hot juices warm it. "Mmmm...you got that dick out?"

"Yeah, ma. Now what you gonna do to it?"

"I'ma lick up and down your shaft before I take your sweet, black dick into my hot, wet mouth...spitting and slurping and sucking down your dick, making popping sounds with my juicy mouth.... Mmmm...just talking about it has my pussy tingling..." I remove the cucumber, stick it in my mouth and suck all over it. Make a bunch of gushy sounds. "You hear that?"

"Yeah, ma..."

"This is how I'm gonna suck your dick, little daddy." I lift up my hips, slide my shorts over my ass, then kick them off. I lean back and spread my wet, sticky lips, pulling open my juicy hole.

"I wish you could see how wet you got my pussy." I slide the cucumber back in. Fuck myself deeper, faster. "Uhhh...ooooh..."

"You fuckin' that pussy, ma?"

"Oooooh, yeah..."

"What you fuckin' it wit'?"

"A long, fat cucumber...oooh, I wish it was your dick in me instead."

"Damn, ma. Aaaah, fuck...me, too."

"You stroking that dick for me?"

"Aaah...shit, yeah. I wish you could see how hard you got my shit. Finish tellin' me what you gonna do it when I get there."

I grin. Then tell him how I want him to smack my lips with his cock. Tell me to stick my tongue out, then slap his dick on it. How I want him to slide it into my mouth. Then grab the sides of my head and slow grind his dick down into my throat. I tell him I want him to make my pussy cream as his balls hit my chin. Tell him I want him to yank my hair while I titty fuck him, flicking my tongue over the head of his dick.

He moans. "Aah, shit, ma...ohhh, fuck..."

"You wanna slap my titties, nigga? Then reach up under me and play with my pussy, hmm? You gonna let your little bitch eat daddy's ass? Can I run my tongue across your asshole, hunh, daddy?"

"Aaah, shiiiit...I ain't never had my ass licked before, ma."

"You stroking that big-ass dick?"

"Yeah, ma."

"You gonna let me taste your ass, hmm? Licking a man's ass makes my pussy real wet. You want my pussy to get real wet, then you can fuck me deep in it?"

"Damn, ma...I'm gettin' ready to nut...uhhhh, shit..." He tells me he's never had a chick lick his ass before. I tell him all the nasty little things my tongue is going to do to his hole. "Oh, shit…"

"Mmmm, your ass tastes so good, little daddy. You wanna suck on my tongue? You wanna taste your ass while you slide your long, black dick in my pussy?"

I pull the cucumber out, lick off my juices, then slide it back in. Hearing Royce moan and breathing heavy into the phone excites me. I tell him I'm going to fuck him like he's never been fucked before. That he'll never want another young bitch again. That I am going to dominate him, then let him dominate me. Tell him I'm going to chain lock his cock. That he must lick my pussy while I tease his caged cock with a vibrator and if he can prove himself a good pussy licker I will release his dick and allow it to roam freely into the dampness of my deep, steamy pussy. I tell him that I'm going to turn his ass out.

"Aaaaah, shiiiiiiiit…aaaaah, shiiiiiiiiit…you got me nuttin' all over my car…"

I moan. Come, too. Ask him how much longer before he gets here. He tells me he's five minutes away. Tells me he can't wait to fuck me. I smile as we end our call.

"Ohmygod," Paris says, leaning up against the doorframe. "You're one nasty-ass hooker." I hop off the counter, leaving a puddle of my pussy juice.

I shrug. "What?"

"*What?* Hooker, I watched you fuck yourself up on our kitchen counter, that's what?"

I laugh. "How much did you see?" She tells me most of it. "Well, why in the hell did you stand there and watch? Mmmph. And you call me nasty."

"Heifer, I wanted to see how far you were going to take this." She watches me as I lick the cucumber, then go to the sink and wash it off. "Uhhhh, I *know* you're not about to put *that* "—she points at the cucumber in my hand—"back in the refrigerator after you done fucked yourself with it."

I wave her on, opening up the 'fridge. "Girl, please. Do you know how many of these you've eaten after I've fucked myself with them?" I toss it back into the vegetable bin.

She frowns, shaking her head. "Ohmygod, you're so fucking nasty." The doorbell rings. I switch my bare ass to answer it. "Ummm, excuuuuse me. But you've left your pussy juice up there on the counter."

"I know," I tell her over my shoulder. "Royce can lick it up. That's him now at the door."

"Uggggghhh. I don't believe this shit."

I laugh, swinging open the door. Oooh, this young boy is so fine. "Come in," I tell him, stepping back to let him in. "I left you a treat on the counter."

Passion

CHAPTER THIRTY-ONE

Irwin is what we call a strip-club whore. He spends a bulk of his dollars in gentlemen's clubs and seedy strip bars, tricking up his money on lap dances and private-room romps where he's either gotten head, or fingered their pussies. But, he's never actually taken a stripper home with him, or fucked one. We've heard of plenty of men who frequent strip clubs, wanting to take one of the strippers home and fuck them all night. Some do, many others don't. So his dream to be seduced by three sexy strippers doesn't surprise me.

We'll bring his fantasy to life in one of the many rooms we've created down in our finished basement. The Freakum Room is a lounge-like room with a customized stage, bar and private bathroom. The bar is stacked with all types of liquor. There are strobe lights situated throughout the room. And two ceiling-to-stage floor stripper poles are in the middle of the stage. My sisters and I have invested thousands of dollars into each of our fantasy rooms, including this one. The dimly lit room with the music blaring out of the speakers, mirrors lining the walls, and the multi-colored lights swirling around the room give you the illusion of being in a real club. There's a fog machine in the left corner of the room that is on low, slowly fogging up the stage.

Tonight, Persia is playing the role of the doorman and cashier.

I am in the utility room, adjacent to our laundry room, watching everything on the surveillance cameras we have installed throughout the house. I pinch my nipples as Persia frisks Irwin, grabbing at his dick until she feels it harden, then collects his fifty-dollar cover charge and leads him through the house. I keep my eye on them as he follows her down the stairs. He takes a seat as she strips down in front of him, seductively slipping into a barmaid's costume. Tonight, she will serve him drinks, while Paris and I play the slutty strippers.

One foot in front of the other, Persia saunters toward the double doors, knowing Irwin's eyes are locked onto her ass. When they reach the doors to the room, he removes all of his clothes except for his boxers, Timbs, and wife beater. I watch lustfully, reaching between my legs and pinching my clit. Persia opens the doors and leads Irwin into the room. He sits at the bar as Perissia walks behind it, then leans over the bar and says something to her. She grins and nods her head, then drapes a red silk scarf she's found behind the bar around his neck. She grabs a hold of the ends, and pulls him into her, kissing him. I watch as her tongue darts in and out of his mouth. She pushes him back, then climbs up on the bar, turns around with her ass facing him, then squats down on all fours, offering him the back of her pussy.

He leans over the bar and says something to her. She grins and nods her head, then drapes a red silk scarf she's found behind the bar around his neck. She grabs a hold of the ends, and pulls him into her, kissing him. I watch as her tongue darts in and out of his mouth. She pushes him back, then climbs up on the bar, turns around with her ass facing him, then squats down on all fours, offering him the back of her pussy." Irwin pulls open her ass cheeks, then buries his face in. I watch as Persia arches her back and backs up on his tongue. I reach down and lightly pinch my clit, then brush my fingertips over my nipples.

Paris walks out of the bathroom, disrupting my peep show. "Is he here yet?"

"Yeah, Persia has already started serving him snacks at the bar," I say, glancing over at her. She's standing in the middle of the room with her hair pinned up. Her body naked and slick with scented baby oil shimmers in the light. Like Persia's and mine, her body is flawless. I watch as she slips into a metallic-silver bikini-top with matching thong, then shimmies into a white fishnet mini-dress. Then she slides her feet into a pair of eight-inch, metallic thigh-high boots. She stands, balances herself with ease, then struts across the room.

"Whew, I hope I don't snap my ankles, fucking around in these heels tonight."

"Girl, you're fierce in that getup," I say, getting up and slipping into my outfit—a turquoise Lycra one-piece, T-romper and a pair of seven-inch clear sandals with rhinestones. I tie the string in back of my neck, then ask her to tie the other string around my back. "But I probably wouldn't drink if I were you; to be on the safe side."

She chuckles. "You're probably right. One shot is it for me." She stares at me. "Girl, this shit is sexy as hell. When the hell did you buy this lil' number?"

"I ordered it a few months ago, but hadn't felt like wearing it. I had planned on saving it for our next island getaway."

"Yeah, mon, show dem de pum-pum," she jokes, smacking me on the ass.

I laugh, bending over and fastening the straps on my heels. "Your ass is so damn silly. You ready to go out and rock this nigga's cock?"

"Strippers and hoes do it best," she says, laughing. "Let's go make it rain."

I grab the portable microphone, while Paris grabs the floor mat, lube and baby oil from off the table. We go through the laundry room, then open another door that leads us into the Freakum Room where the stage is located. I wait for Paris to place the the mat, lube and oil up on the stage, then step back out of view. I climb the four steps to the stage, then make my presence known.

I turn the microphone on. "Alright, muthafucker, it's time to get this party started. You ready to make it rain up in this biiiiotch?" Irwin hops off the barstool and makes his way over to the stage, barking. His thick dick is already hard, pressing itself up against his underwear. He yells and whistles into the air, clapping his hands. "I said, are you ready to make it rain up in this biiiiotch?!"

"Hell yeah, baby, I'm ready. Gotta hot, hard dick and a handful of money."

"Then let the games begin." I step back as Paris takes the stage. "I bring to you Pleasure." Persia shines the spotlight on her. Irwin continues to catcall and whistle.

Paris goes in character, scans the room as if she's in a real strip club. Hands on hips, legs spread apart, she poses, waits for the music to start. Trina's "Dang A Lang" featuring Lady Saw and Nicki Minaj starts playing. *"Mi have a watch...mi have a chain... mi have a whole heap of money in da bank...mi just want him fi him dang a lang..."*

Paris twirls and wines her hips, sways to the beat, then grabs a hold of the pole and slowly twirls herself around it with one hand. Then slowly coils herself around the pole like a python, hoisting herself up. She slides herself up and down it. Rides it like a hard, uncut dick, bouncing her ass every so often.

"...Dang so damn hood, dang a lang so good...like foot long sub... eat it all if you could..."

I glance over at Persia who is standing on top of the bar, gyrating her hips, and slowly shaking her ass. She drops down low, grabs her ankles, then stands. Her ass sways and jiggles. I watch her getting into character, making love to her body. Irwin snaps his neck from the bar back to the stage, then back to the bar. His dick is aching to be released from his striped boxers. He gulps down his drink, then orders another one, yelling it across the room to Persia. He brings his attention back to Paris.

"Work that shit, ma..." Paris comes to the edge of the stage, drops down and does the butterfly with her hips and thighs— pulling her g-string to the side, giving Irwin a sneak peek at her pussy. He reaches for her, but she scoots back. Teases him, gyrates her hips.

He tosses money up in the air like confetti. Bills float down onto the stage beside her.

Persia saunters toward him—gyrating and shaking her hips, his drink in one hand, and a double-sided dildo in the other. It's my cue that it's time for the real show to pop off.

I turn off the portable mic. Persia is standing behind Irwin, grinding her pussy into his ass with one hand wrapped in front of him grabbing at his cock.

He takes a swig from his drink as Persia's hand travels up over his chest. She pinches his nipples. I pop my hips off the stage toward him. Persia and I sandwich him, grind our bodies into his. Then I drop down in front of him, brushing my face up against his ever-rising erection, then turn around and bend over and bounce my ass up on it.

"Oh fuck, y'all bitches sexy..."

"And we 'bout to fuck the shit outta you," Persia warns him as I yank down his boxers and take his meaty dick into my hands, kissing the tip, then licking the precum. His hard, thick dick points like an arrow, aiming for its target.

When Twista's "Wetter" starts playing, I abruptly stand up, leaving his dick unattended. Persia hands me the dildo and I slowly walk back toward the stage, swaying my hips and stopping every so often to wind them, and jiggle my ass. Once I hit the stage, I press a button and the recess lights over the stage come on, giving our one-man audience a lighted view of the show. Paris seductively removes her clothes, pouring baby oil all over the front of her body. I grab a hold of the pole and start working it watching as Paris rolls the mat out, then sprawls out on it, drizzling baby oil all over her pussy, then playing with it.

"Damn...work that shit, baby..." Irwin says, tossing more money up in the air. Persia's down on her knees with his dick in her mouth while he tries to keep his eyes on Paris finger-fucking herself, and watch my pole action. I seductively wind my body down and around the pole in sync with the music, then slowly step out of my attire, standing only in my heels and nakedness.

I continue my alluring dance routine, watching Paris remove her middle and index fingers from her slit, then suck on them before reaching over for the dildo. The pulse in my clit quickens, causing my juices to seep from my pussy as Paris gets on all fours, then slowly pushes the dildo into the back of her sweetness. My muscles clench in anticipation as I move toward her, eyeing the dildo hanging out from between her glistening lips, reminding me of a tail waiting to be yanked. I inch my way over to her, then drop down on my knees, scooting backward closer toward the tip of the dildo. Back arched, ass up, I reach under me, and slowly guide its head into my wet slit.

Persia gets up off of her knees and pulls Irwin toward the stage by his hard dick, leading him up the stairs. He watches intently as Porsha and I ease both ends of the dildo into our slick holes, pushing and rocking back and forth, causing it to disappear, then reappear. We allow our asses to smack up against the others with quick, steady thrusts. She's moaning. I'm moaning. We fuck ourselves relentlessly, watching as Persia mounts Irwin's condom-covered cock, then slide up and down the length of him. He watches Paris and me as we skillfully gobble up both ends of the jet-black, double-headed dildo, sinking it deep into our sopping wet pussies.

Over an R. Kelly track, Irwin lets out a loud groan, lets his eyes roll up in the back of his head as he grips Persia's hips and matches her rhythm. Thrust for thrust, grunt for grunt, they fuck each other with reckless abandon.

"Ride that nigga's dick, Pain," Paris says.

"Fuck her pussy good, big daddy," I urge, scooting up and allowing the dildo to slip out of me. I turn around and suck my juices off the head, using my hand to continue pushing it in and out of Porsha's slickness. She moans, arches her back; allows me to feed her pussy while I savor my sticky cream. I pull the dildo out, then hand it to her. She sucks, and licks, and enjoys her sweet sauce, then leans back on her forearm and slides it back into her pussy.

I walk over and straddle Irwin's face, then lower my pussy down onto his wet, waiting tongue.

"Oh, baby, it's so good," he moans in between deliciously deep strokes of his tongue. He mounts his mouth over my pussy and sucks on it until my knees give out. I lean forward and brace myself with my arms extended so I don't topple over.

"Yeah, nigga...eat my pussy...oh, yes..."

He starts chanting and moaning. "Mmmmhmmm...mmmm-hmm....yes, yes, yes, yes...uh, uh, uh...mmmmhmmm...oh fuck..."

"You want me to cum all over your cock?" Persia asks, bucking up and down on his dick.

He grunts and groans. "Aaah, fuck yeah, baby...wet that big-ass dick...all up in that good pussy..."

A few minutes later, Persia is moaning, then cumming. She lifts up off his cock, and Paris takes her place, reaching for his dick, then stuffing it into the back of her pussy. He starts power-fucking her. His balls are flapping a mile a minute. Paris is taking it, galloping fast and hard on his dick.

"That's right," I urge, craning my neck to look at her. "Ride his dick, girl. Fuck him good!"

She stops moving her body and squats, allowing Irwin to jack-hammer her pussy. "Yeah, fuck me like that...ohmygod...yes, yes, yes...oh, yeah...mmmhmm...ooooh, his dick's so damn good... Passion, you wanna ride his dick, girl? You wanna feel how big his dick is?"

"Yeah, let me get some of that dick," I say, lifting up off his face and walking around to feed my pussy. Persia now squats over his face, serves him her snatch.

"Oh, yes...mmmm...your tongue feels so good in my pussy... aaaah..."

"Oh, fuck...y'all got some good-ass pussy..."

The three of us alternate from fucking his face to riding his cock, then shifting positions so that he can fuck us doggie-style, ramming and slamming his dick deep into our pussies, moving down the line to serve all three of us equal amounts of the dick, then back up, again. Then we shift to Paris lying on her back with Persia and me lying on either side of her while Irwin is fucking her. Paris has her legs up over his shoulders. He uses his left hand to fuck me with the dildo, and his right hand to finger fuck Persia and play with her clit.

"Oooooh....yes, fuck that pussy, nigga...mmmm..." Persia moans.

"You like how Pleasure's pussy feels on that dick?" I ask, cupping my right titty, then licking the nipple.

"Aaaah, fuck...oh shit...yeah, this some good-ass pussy...uh, uh, uh...y'all got a nigga's head spinning..."

"Fuck us, nigga! Beat the pussy up..." Paris taunts, pinching her nipples. "Make my pussy cry...uhh...mmmm..."

"Aaah, shit...goddamn it...

For the next forty-five minutes, Paris, Persia and I fuck every inch of Irwin until he is literally slurring his words. He wanted to fuck a room full of strippers, and that's exactly what we gave him. Three hot, slutty-ass strippers who we let fuck us in the pussy, ass and throat. Drained and wobbly, he doesn't stumble up out of here until almost three in the morning.

L *ord, puhleeeeeze don't let this day turn into a nightmare*, I think as Paris pulls up to the elegant country house known as the Manor in West Orange. Amidst its hand-carved ice sculptures and ornate flowers, the restaurant is considered one of the best places to dine in this area. And I must agree. It is wonderful. And it's where our mother wanted to meet for Sunday brunch with the three of us; something we haven't done in over a year. And, reluctantly, Persia and I agreed. I suppose this is Mother's peace offering. But right at this moment, I'm anything but peaceful. I'm on pins and needles, hoping she doesn't say or do anything that's going to set Persia off. She's already on edge, anticipating a conflict. And honestly, I believe it's what she wants. A reason to make a scene and curse our mother out. Growing up, that seemed to always be Persia's mission; to do and say things to antagonize her. I'm silently praying that today isn't one of those times.

We've all been quiet for the most part of the ride here. Persia's stared out of the passenger window and I've been texting, well sexting, back and forth with Emerson. He has my pussy sizzling with anticipation for what's to come later today. I can't get enough of him. My pussy, my body, my lips long for his mouth, his tongue, his touch. Thoughts of his hard-body pressed against the softness of mine makes me want to pull out my mini-vibrator, pull my panties to the side and fuck myself right here in the backseat. I press my thighs together. Text him, let him know how wet I am. Let him know how horny I am.

Paris glances at me through her rearview mirror, then cuts her eyes over at Persia, who's in the vanity mirror gliding a coat of lipgloss over her neatly painted lips. "Geesh, girl, you over there acting like we're about to walk into a funeral."

Persia grunts, flipping up the visor, looking over at her. "Mmmph. More like walking into hell."

"It won't be that hot," I say, smiling at the picture he's just sent of his hard dick. He tells me it's all mine.

"Please," Persia says, craning her neck to look at me, "that woman's a dragon and you know it."

Paris waves her hand dismissively. "Whatever. Let's go in and *try* to have a nice time." She opens her door and hands the attendant her keys as we step out of the vehicle. The three attendants blink, then do double-takes as we walk by. The three of us, heeled, bagged and dressed like runway models, flash them smiles, making our way to the door. "Persia, can you at least try to give Mom the benefit of the doubt? Don't go in with a shitty ass attitude, looking for something to go wrong, please."

"Yeah, Persia," I tease. "Don't start pissing on fires that aren't lit, yet."

She huffs, glancing over her shoulder to get a quick look at the young, buffed Italian guy who's standing outside with an older woman waiting on their car. "Fine, but the minute she cranks it up, I'm going to get up and walk out. And if she goes too far, I'm going to embarrass her."

Paris huffs. "Persia, stop being such a bitch; damn. We haven't even gotten to our table and you're already picking a damn fight."

"I'm not looking for a fight. I'm stating a fact. But, whatever. I don't even like this stuffy ass place. I would've preferred Sweet Basil's instead."

"Well, get over it," Paris says as we walk into the restaurant. "It's not always about you."

Our mother is already inside, waiting. She glances at her time-piece when she sees us. It's twelve-twenty five. We have a twelve-thirty seating. "You must've driven," she says to Paris knowingly, as Paris walks over and gives her a kiss on the cheek. "Otherwise…" Paris shoots her a look that keeps her from saying more.

"Hello, Mom" I say, kissing her. She greets me, kissing me back.

"Hello, Mother," Persia says, half-heartedly.

I can tell Mother's taken aback that Persia doesn't give her a kiss as well. Paris squints at her. I raise my brow. And she acquiesces. Mother smiles and says, "The three of you look beautiful."

"Thanks," we say in unison. There's a nervous energy between us, the four of us apprehensive and cautious. Remembering the last time we met for brunch at Galloping Hill in Union and how it ended. Everything was going good up until Mother, being her opinionated self, felt it necessary to remind us of how nasty she thought we were for still sleeping with the same men. Well, that didn't sit well with Persia.

"No, Mother," Persia had said through clenched teeth. "What's nasty is you staying with a man you knew was a whoremonger. So what if he was your husband and our father? You still knew he was shoving his dick in other women. What, were you that damn dick-whipped? Or were you so desperate to hold onto him? You have a lot of damn nerve, always judging us."

Needless to say, Mother was embarrassed. Persia stood up and practically told her to kiss her ass, then spun on her heels and strutted out the door with Paris and I following right behind her.

So today, we try this again, hoping for a better outcome. I bring my attention back to Mother; tell her how lovely she looks. Even Persia agrees. She's wearing a beautiful cream pantsuit with a silk emerald green blouse. Her neck is adorned with the emerald and diamond choker the three of us bought her for her fiftieth birth-day. Her shoulder-length hair is neatly coiffed in a French-roll.

After two rounds of mimosas, Paris, Mother and I are relaxed, having lively banter while we feast on shrimp and lobster. And Persia is sitting here being...shitty. She keeps glancing at her watch like she has someplace better to be and rolling her eyes up in her head anytime Mother opens her mouth to say something. This childish shit is starting to really get on my last nerve. Mother also notices it.

"Persia, so how are things going with you?"

"Fine," she answers curtly.

"How's the web design business going?"

"Good," she answers, shifting in her seat. "Where's Daddy?"

"Your father's home," Mother offers, squinting at her. "Were you—"

I cut her off before she says something to escalate the growing tension between the two of them. I ask her how Aunt Fanny and Lucky are doing. Ask her when's the last time she's spoken to Aunt Harriett. She tells me everyone is doing well. That she spoke to Felecia and Pasha's grandmother a few days ago. How she wants to have all of us attend Sunday service the day after Pasha's wedding.

Paris and I start shaking our heads. "Gotta love her," I say.

Persia grunts, mumbling something under her breath as she pulls out her cell. She starts texting.

Mother stares at us and smiles. "I know we don't always see eye-to-eye, but I'm really glad to have..." Mother looks at Paris and me, then cuts her eyes over at Persia. "...the three of you here with me," Mother says, lifting her flute. "Hopefully this is a good start to a new beginning."

Paris and I raise our glasses. "Hopefully," the two of us say in unison, watching as Persia scoots her chair back and stands up.

"I feel like I'm gonna be sick," she says sarcastically. "I'll be back."

The three of us watch as she walks off to the front of the restaurant. Mother waits until she's out of view, then says in a hushed voice, "I'm done trying with that girl. She could have kept her nasty ass—excuse my French, home. I'm tired of her shit. All she—"

Paris gives her a disappointed look, cutting her off. "Mom, don't. Not today. So far everything's been good between us. Let's not…" She hops up from her seat, holding her stomach with one hand and her mouth with the other. She races toward the bathroom.

I excuse myself, pushing my chair back and getting up from the table. "I need to go check on her." I don't wait for her to respond.

I walk into the bathroom and find Paris in one of the stalls, leaning over the toilet throwing her guts up. I walk in; rub her back. There's a film of sweat on her forehead. "Ohmygod," I say, rushing out of the stall. I grab paper towels and wet them. Go back and place them across her forehead. "Paris, we need to get you to the hospital."

"No, I'll be fine," she says, standing up. She looks pale.

"Sweetie, you don't look good," I say, touching the side of her face. She feels warm.

"I need to lie down," she says, walking over to the sink. She splashes water on her face.

"Girl, I hope it isn't food poisioning," I state, handing her three paper towels.

"No, I don't think that's what it is. You and I had the same thing. I'm coming down with something; that's all."

"C'mon, girl, let's get you out of here."

When we return to the table, Mother is at the table with a concerned look on her face. And Persia is still missing in action. "Is everything alright?" She gets up from her seat. "You don't look well at all."

"I'll be fine," Paris says, grabbing her purse. She apologizes for having to leave. Tells Mother she's going to have me take her home. That she'll call her later. Mother gives her a hug, kisses her on the cheek.

"Don't worry about it. You get home and get some rest."

"Have you seen Persia?" I ask, scanning the room.

Mother tosses her hand in the air, dismissively. Says Persia walked toward the table but turned on her heels when she noticed Paris and I weren't there. "Check the men's room. She's probably up in some man's face as usual." Paris shoots her a look.

I roll my eyes, pulling out my phone to text her. *Bitch, where r u?*

I reach into my clutch and pull out a hundred dollar bill. "Mother, here's money toward the bill." She hands me the money back. Waves the waiter over and tells him to bring the check.

"Brunch is on me. You get your sister home. I'll call later to check on her." She gives me a hug, kisses me on the cheek, then whispers in my ear. "Thanks for coming."

It is in that moment that I realize how much I've missed her. How having a better relationship with our mother is just as important to me as it is to Paris. I smile. Hug her back. "I had a nice time. I'll talk to you later."

Mother closes out the check, then gathers her things as well. Tells us she'll walk out with us. Persia texts back. Says she's with Royce heading home. I huff. "C'mon, let's get out of here."

"Where's Persia?" Paris asks.

"On her way home," I tell her, looping my arm through hers and helping her out of the restaurant. She gives me a confused look. "Don't even ask. I'm so over her ass right now."

A week after brunch with our mother, I'm downstairs in the den with my laptop propped up on my lap catching up on season one of *The Good Wife* online, anxiously awaiting season two, when Persia storms through the room disrupting my moment. I'm still annoyed with her for how she acted, but she's not fazed. Persia only cares about what Persia cares about. Herself, first; Porsha and me, second; and President Obama, third.

She plops down next to me. "I'm so sick of these tea-bagging motherfuckers fucking with Obama. Girl, they need to leave that man alone and let him do his damn job."

I press PAUSE on the screen, and look up from my PC, shaking my head. The way Persia carries on anytime someone says anything negative about Obama, or does anything to undermine him, you'd think she was related to him. She takes the shit way too personal, like it's an attack on her. "Who's fucking with your boy now?"

"Who else, them snake-ass Republicans! They make me fucking sick. They've been fucking with him from day one, and the shit's getting old. Hating-asses. They're a bunch of bigots and shady motherfuckers." She shakes her head. "I swear. This is one fucked-up country. It's no wonder motherfuckers laugh at us. Instead of trying to work as one government, they'd rather tear us down just to be fucking spiteful."

Ohmygod! All I wanna do is watch the rest of The Good Wife. *Not get into a long, drawn-out debate with her ass. I'm so not in the mood for this. Not tonight.*

She leans forward, clutching her stomach. "Ohmygod, I'm gonna be sick. If the Republicans end up back in office, they're gonna fuck us over worse than they already have." h

I laugh. "Girl, hopefully that'll never happen. "But to be on the safe side, we all better be out at them polls to ensure it doesn't. Obama has been catching heat from day one. Everything going wrong in this country is his fault. They fail to see the shit that he's already done since being in office. But, it's not enough. No matter what that man does, there's always going to be someone pointing a finger at him, blaming him for something. As long as he's President, he'll always be under the microscope."

She frowns. *"Why?* Because he's black?"

"No. Because he's a man who isn't taking sides. For him it isn't simply a black thing, or a white thing. It's a people thing. And he's about holding everyone accountable, particularly those in politics and other positions of power."

She grunts. "Mmmph. And you mean to tell me that nothing them haters put him through has anything to do with the fact that he's black?"

I shake my head. "No. Not all of it."

"Yeah, right," she replies indignantly. "You and I both know it's all about race. So don't even try to sugarcoat it. This is a racist country, boo. It's what it was built on. And you know it."

Porsha walks in. "What are y'all in here talking about?"

"President Obama, who else?" I tell her, shaking my head.

She backs out of the room. "Oh, no thank you. I want no part of this conversation. Call me when y'all are done."

I laugh. "Girl, take me with you."

"Mmmph, whatever," Persia snorts at the both of us.

"Where are you going?"

"To fix me a damn drink," she huffs over her shoulder, switching her way out the door. "Talking about this shit has got me hot."

I laugh, pressing the PLAY button and resuming my show. "Well, you might as well fix me one, too, 'cause listening to you is gonna give me the shits if I don't have one."

She laughs. "Well, get over it. I'll be right back with it."

"And don't come back in here with any more of that Obama mess. I don't wanna end up going to bed with a damn headache. I want to catch up on my show, have a drink, and take it down for the night, peacefully."

She flicks her wrist at me. "Whatever."

The doorbell rings. I glance at the time on the lower right corner of my laptop. 8:24 P.M. *I wonder who's coming here this time of night. And I know we're not planning on fucking anyone tonight.* I go back to watching the rest of the show without giving it another thought.

Fifteen minutes later, Porsha comes waltzing back into the room, saying, "Girl, look what the wind blew in." She's carrying a tray with a pitcher of white sangria and four wineglasses on it. I glance up to see what she's talking about.

"Heeeeeeeeeey, Diva," Felecia says, spreading her arms wide open as she struts in the room. I'm surprised to see her. It's taken her almost two months to finally get over here so we can get the gossip.

I slide my laptop over onto the sofa, getting up. "Ohmygod, girl, where in the hell have you been, Cuz? It's been ages." We hug.

"I know," she says, kissing me on the cheek. "It's a damn shame we don't stay in touch. It's so good to see you."

"Yes, it is. Good to see you, too." I give her another big hug, then step back, taking her in. She's stylishly dressed in a denim dress that grazes her knee and a pair of black, four-inch ankle booties. She's wearing a black lace front wig with strawberry blonde highlights. It's bone-straight with baby hair around the edges, and hangs past her shoulders. "Girl, you're looking fierce as ever. And I'm loving the do."

"You know how I do it, boo," she says, flinging her hair over her shoulder. "It's the silky Yaki, girl; got it on sale for three-hundred-and-four dollars."

Porsha cuts her eyes over at me, filling the glasses with wine. I'm sure she's thinking what I'm thinking: *Why the hell is she always wearing wigs?* I don't think I can ever recall a time when she's worn her own hair out. Not even as a teenager. Weaves, wigs and head wraps; that's all we've ever seen. Shit, now I have to wonder if she even has any hair of her own.

"And you're wearing it well," I say. "So how are you? What's new? I've been meaning to get over to the shop but every time I plan on coming down there, I end up getting sidetracked."

"Girl, you know I understand. But, umm, everything is everything. Things down at the salon are good. Pasha's busy with getting ready for her wedding. And as you can see,"—she spreads her arms open—"I'm doing faaaaabulous."

I smile, taking her all in. "So it seems. We really need to do better with staying in touch, though."

"I know," she says, taking a seat on the sofa. I close my laptop, moving it off the sofa and sitting it on the floor, then sit next to her. "It really makes no sense."

"Well, you're here now," Persia says, waltzing in the room. Porsha hands Felecia a drink, then Persia and me.

"Yes, I am," Felecia says lifting her glass. We follow suit. "To us."

"To us," Persia, Porsha and I say in unison, clinking our glasses with hers. And for the next hour we sip and chat it up about little shit. Vacation spots, the boutique, the salon, family, mutual acquaintances, and the upcoming wedding. But, outside of talk about the salon and the upcoming nuptials, she's still very tight-lipped about anything else that has to do with Pasha.

"And I know I'm gonna see y'all at the wedding, right?" Felecia asks, downing the last bit of her wine.

"Oh, yes, we wouldn't miss it for the world. Here, let me top you off," Persia says as she graciously gets up and refills Felecia's glass. A sly smirk curls her lips. We all know Felecia's an undercover lush, so we'll keep her glass filled until her tongue starts to loosen. In the meantime, we keep the conversation light.

"How's Aunt Harriet doing?" Persia asks, settling back in her chair.

"Chile, Nana is Nana; still feisty as ever."

And spewing scriptures I'm sure, I think, smiling.

Porsha asks, "Is she still forcing you and Pasha to go to church with her?"

Felecia laughs. "Girl, you already know. Every chance she gets."

"Some things never change," Persia replies, shaking her head, laughing with her.

"Isn't that the truth? I love Nana dearly. I don't know where I'd be if it weren't for her. I try to spend as much time as I can with her." She takes a sip from her drink, then asks how our parents are doing. I tell her they're doing well; that they'll be celebrating their fortieth wedding anniversary in November. "Wow, forty years. That's amazing. I don't think most couples last longer than four to six years these days."

"Mmmph," Persia grunts, leaning up and setting her glass up on the coffee table. "You better try four to six *months*. You know like I do that most people in relationships are in the *wrong* relationships with the *wrong* people, trying to make it right, doing all the *wrong* shit."

"Giiiiiiiiirl," Felecia says, shaking her head, "you better preach.

I don't understand that kinda shit. I mean, if you're with some-one who you *know* is bringing stress into ya life, why put yourself through all the aggravation? Let that ass go."

Persia replies, "Because misery loves company. And the fear of being alone outweighs the need for peace of mind."

"And common damn sense," Felecia adds.

"Speaking of relationships," Porsha says, reaching for the pitcher of sangria and refilling her glass. "What's up with you and your man, Miss Lady? Y'all still together?" She pours more into mine as well.

"Thanks" I tell her, taking my drink, then shifting back into my seat to get comfortable.

"Chile, Andre and I are doing wonderful. Four years strong, and still counting."

"Wow, four years," I say in between sips of my drink. "Time sure flies."

"Yes, it does," she agrees. "Half the time I don't know where it goes." Persia wants to know when he's going to put a ring on it. "Who knows when that's gonna be? That's on him. Don't get me wrong. I would love to marry Andre. But I don't put any pressure on him. I love him, and I know he loves me, so whether we get married or not isn't gonna change anything. We have a really good relationship."

Hmmm, that's what they all say, I think, pressing my lips to my glass. *Until they find out he's fucked her best friend.* "Well, it definitely sounds like you're in love, girl. I wish you nothing but happiness."

She reaches over and grabs my hand. "Thanks. I truly am." She glances around the room at us. "Now what's going on with you divas? Who y'all loving or should I say *doing*? 'Cause I know how y'all like to get it." She laughs.

"Girl, we're loving life and doing us," Porsha answers for the three of us.

"And if someone worthy comes along in the process," Persia adds. "Then maybe we'll love him, too."

"So in the meantime, y'all just keep sharing men?" Felecia asks, although it feels more like a statement than anything else. She twists her body in my direction. "Triple the fun."

I nod.

"And fun it is," Persia says, raising her glass to her.

Felecia raises hers as well. "I heard that, girl."

"That's right. Three freaks in the sheets are always better than one, okay."

Felecia laughs. "Seems like you all have been freaking men like that for quite a long time."

Porsha laughs. "Yeah, it's been several years off and on; more on than off in the last five, though. And, hey, it works for us."

"Well, shoot, if y'all like it. I love it. Do you. I don't give a damn what people do in the comforts of their own sheets; as long as they ain't doin' my man."

"I know that's right," Persia says.

Felecia continues, "I don't know how y'all do it, sharing men and whatnot. I'm too selfish for that shit. I'd end up wanting to cut a bitch and fight his ass if he gave her more dick than he was giving me. I'm the kind of woman who needs to have my man all to myself." She pauses, taking a sip of her drink. She licks her lips. "Any woman sharing another woman's man has some real fucked-up self-esteem, in my opinion." She quickly realizes what she's said and tries to clean it up. "No disrespect meant to y'all, but that's how I feel. Not that I'm implying I think any of you have low self-esteem."

"Oh, and no disrespect taken, *Hun*," Porsha says, shifting in her seat. I glance over at her, hoping she doesn't curse her out before we find out the filth on Pasha. The two of them have been known to get into some very heated conversations, particularly when Felecia has had one drink too many. She's the type that doesn't care what comes out of her mouth once she's liquored up. "Our self-esteems have always been on high, boo."

"Oh, okay," Felecia says, giving her one of those if-you-say-so looks. "You don't have to convince me. Y'all are truly the exceptions to the rule because most of the chicks I know who fuck around with someone else's man have some deep-rooted issues."

"Well, we don't have that problem," Persia informs her. "My sisters and I have always been very comfortable in our skins. What we do has nothing to do with self-esteem, or some traumatic life experiences. Shit, bagging a man of our own has never been a problem for any of us."

"Exactly," Porsha states. "There's no jealousy between us and no fighting over a man because *we* agree to fuck him on our terms. Not his and definitely no one else's."

Felecia takes it all in, then asks, "So what happens, let's say, when you meet a guy that one of you wants to fuck but the other two doesn't; then what?"

"Then nine times out of ten we won't fuck him," Persia answers for the three of us. "Well, I know I don't. Porsha and Paris can speak for themselves."

"No, you're right," Porsha says, pouring another drink. She refills Felecia's glass, too. "We definitely won't fuck him. No matter how fine he is."

My secret romp with Desmond last week down in Atlantic City immediately pops into my head. Fucking him, again, was exactly what I needed. He made love to every inch of my body, slow and tender. Made sure I got exactly what I asked for. As rough around the edges as he appears, he's a gentle, attentive lover. And, although I still haven't given him my cell number, I'll definitely fuck him again, and again, and again. Strong hands, muscular arms, chiseled chest...yes, Lawd, I'll fuck him down. Whew, he had my pussy singing.

"Umm, what are you sitting over there smiling about?" Porsha asks, eyeing me. All three of them have their eyes glued on me.

"Yes, do share," Felecia says, twisting her body in my direction.

I shake my head. "I was sitting here thinking about some of our encounters over the years," I lie, smiling wider.

Persia sits up in her seat, fanning herself. "Girrrrrl, and we definitely have some stories to tell. Mmmph."

"Ooooh, I bet y'all do," she says, laughing. "'Cause y'all some real freaky bitches."

We all laugh. Persia starts telling Felecia about one of our sexapades. The time we fucked a NFL football player while vacationing on Saint Lucia. We were staying at the Windjammer Landing Villa Beach Resort, where he was staying as well for a wedding he was attending. Six-six, two hundred forty pounds of solid man muscle. When Porsha walked back up into our villa with him in tow—bare-chested, wearing a pair of swim trunks and Louis Vuitton flip-flops, my pussy immediately moistened. And I knew Persia's did as well, the way she started twisting in her seat. We had been on the island for over a week without any dick or suitable prospects and we had been getting antsy. So when Porsha walked in with him we knew we'd hit the jackpot. We encircled him, then pounced on him like starved lioness, devouring every inch of him. Porsha and Persia sucked his dick while I sucked on his balls. Then we alternated sitting on his face, grinding down on his tongue, anticipating getting fucked with his thick seven-and-a-half inches. But, unbeknownst to us, pussy wasn't what he had in mind. He wanted ass. That was his fetish. That was his desire. And that's what we gave him. Deep and fast, we rode down on his cock, keeping his mouth stuffed with titties and pussy until he had us squirting out of our cunts and asses. We fucked him two days in a row, and would've fucked him for the rest of our stay there had he not come out of his face asking us to eat each other's pussies.

Felecia grimaces. "Ugh, no, he didn't ask y'all to do some perverted shit like that. And that nasty motherfucker couldn't see that y'all were sisters?"

"Yes the hell he did," Persia responds. "And his ass was dead serious, too."

Porsha chimes in. "Girl, he was really trying to take it over the edge with that shit. Then he kept pressing the issue when we told him we didn't get down like that."

"He even offered to pay us," I add, shaking my head.

Felecia's eyes pop open. "Oh, wow…how much?" She asks this as if the amount would've made a difference. I tell her ten grand. "Ten thousand dollars? And all y'all had to do is eat each other out? That's a lot of money to turn down."

I blink, then frown. *Bitch, you must be sick!*

"No thank you, boo," Porsha says, "There's not enough money in this world for something like that to go down."

Felecia eyes her, then cuts her eyes over at me and Persia. "Hmmm…now back to these sexapades. Y'all have never licked and lapped on each other, or wanted to?"

Persia and I shake our heads in unison. "Ugh. Never."

"I love my sisters," Porsha adds, getting up from her seat. "But I don't love them enough to ever have them finger, face, or tongue-fuck me. And I'm sure they feel the same way." Persia and I concur. She grabs the pitcher. "I'm gonna go refill this."

"Oooh, wait," Felecia says, extending her arm and opening and closing her hand like she's trying to grab for something in the air. "Let me get some of that fruit that's down on the bottom.

That's where the real treat is." Porsha takes her glass and scoops out a few pieces of mango, melon, and strawberries, then hands it back to her.

"Anyone else?" Porsha asks Persia and me. We shake our heads. "I'll be right back, then." She walks off, leaving the three of us to continue where we've left off. Felecia wants to know if we've ever been with other women.

"Oh no, baby," Persia informs her. "I'm all about the dick. The only clit I wanna feel is my own. There's nothing another woman can do for me except tell me where the next shoe sale is, okay." She swirls her finger inside her drink, then pulls it out and sucks it. "Fuck what you heard. Dick does the body real good."

I have nothing to add so I twirl my glass between my fingers, then take a sip. My mind floats back to Desmond. His face, his mesmerizing eyes, his sculpted body, his delicious dick, and the way he spooned in back of me and held me in his arms . . .

And then...I wonder if *he's* somewhere thinking about *me*.

How could he not be? I fed him my cunt, creamed in his mouth, sucked his sweet, salty nut out of his dick, then we fucked...hot, sweaty, toe-curling fucking until we cried out, clinging onto the waves of pleasure.

"Well, like I said," Felecia goes on, still stuck on talking about our romps with men. "I really don't know how y'all do it. What happens if one of you start catching feelings for one of the guys y'all fucking? Or if he catches feelings for one of you?"

"Hmmm, good question," I say. "I guess we'd have to cross that bridge when we got to it. But if it did happen, where one of us started feeling some kind of way toward a man, I don't believe any one of us would pursue it further; especially knowing that he'd been fucking all three of us."

"Well, what if he wanted to be in a relationship with the three of you?"

I shrug. "Unless he could afford to take care of us, I don't see something like that ever working. Then there'd be the issue of kids. I don't know if we'd want to put them through all that. Kids can be real cruel and the last thing I'd want is to have my child being teased and taunted about having cousins who are also their half-brothers and sisters. That would be a mess."

"Girl, you ain't never lied about that," Felecia states, making a face.

"Besides, our mother would take to the grave for sure." I laugh, glancing over at Paris. She's sitting over there, looking like she's lost in thought. I lean up and snap my fingers over in her direction. "Earth to Paris...where are you, girl?"

"Huh, what did you say?"

Felecia laughs. "Damn, girl, you were real deep in thought. You wanna share?"

"Chile," Paris says, shifting her eyes, "it's been a long night and this wine has me zoning." She sips the rest of her drink. "Now what were y'all saying about someone having kids with the same man? I only heard bits and pieces of the story."

I eye her.

She eyes me back. "What?"

"Annnyway," I say, turning back to Felecia, "changing the subject. Do you think you've ever shared Andre with another woman?" I cross my legs, wait for her answer.

She picks another melon from out of her glass and bites into it. "Mmm, this is good." She dabs at the corners of her mouth with her napkin. "*Not* that I know of. And hopefully I'll never have to. I mean, I can't say what he will or won't do 'cause shit happens."

I toss back the rest of my drink, then sit my empty glass down on the table. "Girl, please. Shit does not *just* happen. It happens because we want it to, okay, whether it's planned or unexpected."

"Well, true," Felecia agrees, holding her glass out for more wine when Porsha walks back into the room with a fresh pitcher full. "All I'm saying is a man's gonna do what a man's gonna do; especially if he thinks he can get away with it. I'd rather not find out about it."

"Well, has he ever shared *you* with someone else?" Porsha asks, eyeing her, as she fills her glass.

I smile, watching as she guzzles down her drink. Now this is the lush we know and love. *Yeah, boo, go on and get ya drink on so we can pump ya ass for dirt.* She wipes the corner of her mouth with her thumb. "Are you asking me if I've ever cheated on him?"

What the fuck you think? I tilt my head. "Well, have you?"

"Ohmygod," she says, covering her face. "I can't believe I'm sitting here getting ready to tell y'all this…"

I suck my teeth. "Oh, girl, please. Your secret's safe with us."

"Oh, I know it is. So to answer your question, *yes*, I did. Only once, though."

"Ooooh, girl, you nasty tramp," Porsha teases. "How long ago was that?"

"It was like in the beginning of our relationship. You know, when I wasn't sure where things were going with us." Paris asks her if Andre knows about it. "Oh, helllll no. He would lose his damn mind if he found out about that shit. No, thank you. I'm taking that shit to my grave. He won't ever beat my ass behind no shit like that."

"So who was this man and where'd you fuck him?" I inquire.

"I met him in Jamaica, fucked him in Jamaica, and left him in Jamaica. Never to be seen again." She tells us it was during one of her weekend getaways with Pasha. I ask her if she felt bad about cheating on her man. She shakes her head. "You know what. Not really. Like I said, it happened when Andre and I were still new into the relationship. But I definitely wouldn't do that shit now." She asks us if we've ever cheated in a relationship. Porsha and Paris tell her no.

I skirt around the question by saying, "All cheating ever does is hurt the ones being cheated on. And it requires too much work and telling too many lies."

"Yes, it does," Felecia says, tossing back the remainder of her drink. Porsha starts filling her glass before she gets a chance to sit it down on the coffee table good. I hold back a snicker. "Ooh, girl, thanks." She takes another sip. "This is deeeelicious. This is my first time having the white sangria. Did you make this?"

Porsha shakes her head. "No, Persia did."

"Girl, you did your thing," Felecia says, lifting her glass toward me. "Cheers to you, boo." I smile, raising my glass as well. "I could drink this all night."

Yeah, 'cause ya ass is a lush. "Thanks. I'm glad you're enjoying it. Drink up, we have plenty more." Porsha and Paris smile, patiently waiting along with me for the drinks to finally kick in.

"So tell me," Felecia says, gulping down the rest of her drink. *Okay, this is glass number four; when the hell is she gonna get loose,* I think, eyeing Paris on the sly. I mean really. It's going on almost nine-thirty and this hooker is still talking like she's been sipping on water all night. *Yeah, Aunt Fanny was right. She's definitely an alcoholic.* "When's the last time any of you had your own man? I mean, one none of you fucked together." I silently inhale a deep breath. This is not what the hell we invited her ass here for. We tell her it's been a long while.

"Speaking of Jamaica," Porsha says, quickly changing the subject. "Did you hear Zane is having some kind of freak-fuck-fest there next week? Word has it she's rented out a whole resort for the event. And Mr. Marcus himself is gonna be one of the featured guests."

Felecia perks up in her seat excitedly. "Ohmygod, when?"

"I think it's like May twelfth to the fifteenth or something like that."

Felecia pulls out her BlackBerry and starts scrolling through it. "Shit, I musta missed that memo. And I'm usually up on all the happenings. Mmmph. I love me some damn Zane; the two of us are friends in my head."

"She's too over-the-top for me," Paris says. "I mean, some of that stuff she writes about is soooo damn nasty."

"Girl, please," Felecia says, fanning herself. "The nastier the better. I've freaked Andre's ass plenty of nights to some of her shit; especially after a night of watching her *Zane's Sex Chronicles* on Cinemax. Whew, it was one sexy-ass show. I'm so mad she's not doing another season. But, anyway…this Jamaica thing sounds like it's gonna be off the damn hook. I swear I wish I could go. Anything that freaky-ass Zane does is gonna be top-notch."

"Well, maybe you and Andre should go," Porsha says. "From what I've heard, she still has a few rooms available." She says Andre would never go for it. That he's real reserved when it comes to stuff like that. "Well, then, you should take Pasha. It could be her last getaway as a single woman before she goes down the aisle in a few months."

"I don't know," she says thoughtfully. "Pasha's real different now that she's had the baby and all. She's not gonna want to leave him. And Jasper is definitely not gonna let her ass go off to some Zane event. Not without him."

I smile, glancing over at Porsha. I wink at her on the sly. "So, how is Pasha, *really?* We haven't seen or spoke to her since she's had the baby. And every time I come down to the shop she's never there."

Felecia twists in her seat. Porsha reaches over to fill her glass. *Drink number five.* "Girl, y'all know how to keep the drinks flowin'; just how I like it. Keep a bitch's glass full, okay." She takes a long sip. Finally, her eyes are starting to get that glassy look that lets us know she's feeling nice. We laugh. "But, umm, Pasha's good," she continues, not sounding too convincing.

"Are you sure?" I question, raising a brow. "I mean, after all she's been through…you know, with being kidnapped *and*…" I pause for effect, shaking my head. "…beaten. I can't even imagine what that must've been like for her."

"Girl, none of us can. It was horrible. She wouldn't let any of us come up to see her in the hospital. Not even Nana. It tore her up."

"Ohmygod," Persia says, clutching her chest. "I'm sure it did. But, I'm surprised she didn't want you there. Y'all have always been very close."

Felecia looks off. "Yeah, I didn't understand that. But, I respected her wishes. Jasper was by her side every day and kept me informed of her progress." She guzzles back the rest of her drink, then reaches over for the pitcher. This time she pours her own troubles. Paris wants to know if Pasha had been raped. I ask where they found her since all we knew was that she was found in a park badly beaten. Persia asks if she's been in any counseling for it.

Felecia shakes her head. "No, she doesn't think she needs it. She won't even talk about it. It's crazy. It's like it never happened. If you bring up, she immediately shuts down."

"I'm sure she does," Paris says sympathetically. "It was a traumatic experience."

Felecia takes a sip from her drink. "Yeah, it really was. All she worried about was losing her baby. Her only focus was putting the whole ordeal behind her and carrying her baby to full-term."

"Where was she found again?" I ask. She tells me Branch Brook Park in Newark. "Did they ever find the person behind it?"

She slowly shakes her head, then takes another sip of her drink. "She refused to cooperate."

I raise my brow, cutting an eye over at Porsha and Paris. "That's strange, don't you think? Why wouldn't she want the police to get whoever was responsible for kidnapping and beating her off the streets?"

Felecia shrugs. "Your guess is as good as mine. It's like she's protecting whoever did it."

"Maybe she does know," I say with raised brow.

"Mmmm," Porsha says, pursing her lips. "Or she's trying to keep something from coming out."

Felecia glances around the room at the three of us. "I don't even wanna go there. She swore she didn't know who the men were."

"*Men?*" Paris asks, cupping her hand over her mouth. "Ohmygod, all this time I thought it was only one man who did that to her."

"No, it was like six or seven of 'em involved."

Porsha, Paris and I gasp, clutching our chests. "Ohmygod," we say in unison.

"I can see one or two niggas kidnapping someone," Porsha states, disgusted. "But you talking six niggas, and she got beat..." She pauses, letting her words float around the room. "I'm sorry, but the more I'm hearing, the more I'm convinced that wasn't some random act. No, it was personal."

Felecia tosses back her drink. "You said it. Not me. But, between us..." she looks around the room like she's expecting someone else to walk into the room. She leans in. "There was a lot of crazy shit happening a few months prior to her being kidnapped."

Porsha cuts her eye at me. I tilt my head. "What kind of crazy shit?" Paris asks. Felecia sits back in her seat and pours the dirt. Tells us about some strange man constantly calling the shop asking for her, and when she'd hang up on him, he'd keep calling back. She tells us about someone throwing a brick through the back window of her car. Then, a week or so later, someone smashing out the shop's window with a steel pipe.

"My God," I say, shaking my head. "The plot thickens."

"Girl, let me get another drink," Felecia says, reaching for the pitcher. I've lost count of how many this is for her, at least eight or nine. But she's well on her way to finishing this pitcher practically all by herself. "You haven't heard the half of it."

"You mean to tell me there's more?"

"Chile, y'all did not hear any of this from me. Pasha would

have my head for sure. But, a few months before she got kidnapped, some young nigga came up in the shop and straight disrespected her in front of all of us."

Ohmygod, Felecia's splashing some juicy shit up on us tonight. I knew Pasha's ass was a hot-ass mess!

She goes into full detail about a guy walking into the shop, requesting a deep throat special from Pasha. Telling her he had heard had she sucked a good dick. That she had sucked one of his boys in his car while he was driving down Route 22. Then she tells us about her being attacked by some masked man who jumped out of the bushes when she was putting her key in her front door. And how she didn't report it, or want Jasper to know about it. Paris, Porsha and I are sitting here with our jaws dropped as she tells us this. By the time Felecia finishes dishing the dirt, it's almost one o'clock in the damn morning and my head is literally spinning.

CHAPTER THIRTY-FIVE

"Girl, you know I still can't get over what Felecia told us the other night." I'm on the phone talking to Paris, sitting behind my desk with my feet propped up. We've been on the phone for almost forty minutes recapping that whole evening. Since Felecia's visit, we hadn't really talked about it until now.

"Me either. I'm just glad Pasha's okay."

"Is she really?" I ask, wondering how she could be. I mean, if what Felecia said is true, then I don't know how anyone could be okay. Not without some kind of counseling at least. And the truth of the matter is we haven't had a chance to really talk to her. The times we've spoken have been real brief conversations about other things, like her being pregnant, then having the baby, and now her wedding.

"I hope she is," Paris says thoughtfully. "We used to all be so close growing up. It's sad how we've grown so far apart over the years."

Truth is Paris and I were the ones closest to Pasha growing up. She and Felecia would sometimes spend the weekends at our house when their grandmother worked the overnight shift at Beth Israel in Newark. She was a nurse and oftentimes would work double shifts on the weekends so that she could be home with Pasha and Felecia during the week. We'd be up laughing and playing with our dolls and other toys while Persia kept her distance. Persia wouldn't allow them to come into her bedroom, or play with any of her toys. She'd tolerate them if they were only visiting for the day. But, when they stayed over, she'd oftentimes be very mean and nasty toward them. I never understood why. Felecia one time said it was because Persia was jealous. That turned into a terrible fistfight between the two of them and with both of them getting ass whippings for fighting each other. We were expected to get along, and be there for each other. Not fight one another.

"Yeah, I know. Relationships might change, but the love doesn't ever have to."

"You're right. It's a shame, though." She pauses. "Promise me we'll never let anything come between us."

"Girl, please. We're thick as thieves. There's nothing that could ever break our bond." My phone beeps. I remove the phone my ear, glancing at the screen. It's our mother. "Mom is calling in; let me take this call."

"And try to be nice to her."

"Bye, hooker." She starts laughing and disconnects. "Well, this is a nice surprise," I answer. "How are you?"

"I'm doing fine. We haven't talked since brunch so I wanted to call to see how you were."

I smile. "That was sweet of you. I'm doing good; thanks. How are things with you?"

"I'm doing great. But of course you wouldn't have known that unless I called you, which is why I decided to reach out to you, first, instead of waiting for you to call *me*. Fanny thinks it's ridiculous that I have to—"

I shake my head. "Mother, stop," I say, cutting her off. I pause.

Think before I speak. "I'm happy to hear from you, okay. So let's not turn this into a situation where I wish I hadn't answered the phone, please."

"Porsha, I'm not looking to get into an argument with you. I'm simply saying it would be nice if you'd call me sometimes; that's all."

"You're right. I apologize. I promise I will try to do better."

"Apology accepted," she says. "I still don't understand why you treat me with such indifference. I'm your mother. It's like you let Persia turn you against me when I've done nothing but love you girls."

"And talk about us, Mother. Let's not forget that."

"I can't help it if I don't like some of the choices you and your sisters have made; especially with this whole sleeping with the same—"

I cut her off. I know this is my mother, and I love her, but I swear, sometimes I really don't like her. Like right now when she's getting ready to start her shit. "I know, Mother. We've heard this I-don't-like-the-nasty-shit-you-girls-are-doing speech a thousand times already. And it still hasn't changed anything. And you wanna know why? Because we don't care what you think."

"Porsha, I'm your mother. You girls should care about what I think. Does what your father thinks matter?"

"Mother, we're grown. You and Daddy and anyone else are entitled to your opinions. And none of you have to like what we do. But we're not living our lives for you, for Daddy, or for any-one else. I don't know how many times we have to keep having this conversation, but it's not going to change anything. At the end of the day, it really doesn't matter what you think. That doesn't mean that we don't love you. It simply means we want you to *please* keep your comments to yourself."

"Okay, Porsha," she says, sounding aggravated. "This is not why I called you."

"Then why did you call?"

"For three reasons: I was thinking about you. I wanted to see how you were doing."

Without thought, I smile. My attitude softens. Truth is I really do miss spending time with her. And I realize our—well, Paris's and mine because she and Persia have never gotten along—relationship with her deteriorated the minute she learned we were fucking the same men. She's said a lot of hurtful things because of it.

"Mom, I love you. And I don't wanna fight with you, anymore. But sometimes you make it hard to like you."

"It's terrible how you girls treat me," she says, disregarding everything I've said. "I made sure you girls had the best of everything."

"Yes, you did, Mom. And you don't have to keep reminding us of that, either. Trust me. We appreciate everything you and Daddy did for us. But, that doesn't mean we have to live our lives according to how you want us to, or how you think we should." Another call rings in. It's Emerson. I let out a sigh of relief. This conversation was starting to give me a headache. "Mom, I gotta go. I have another call I need to take. I'll call you toward the end of the week, okay?"

"Okay, go take your call. I need to get ready to meet Fanny, anyway." We say our goodbyes, then disconnect.

"Hello?"

"Hey, baby. How you?"

"I'm better now," I say, smiling.

"Oh yeah, why are you better?" In my mind's eye, I see him grinning ear to ear.

"'Cause I'm hearing your voice," I tell him, swiveling in my chair. I cross my legs, feeling my pussy tingle.

"Aaah, I like that, baby. What are you doing for lunch?"

I glance at the clock over on the shelf of my mahogany bookcase that's lined with rows of books on accounting and tax laws. It's almost eleven. The morning has been quiet, but I have several clients coming in to have their taxes done this afternoon, starting at one up until my last appointment at eight o'clock. One of the good things about being a tax preparer, it's seasonal. And with about twenty or more clients a week, I literally make thousands of dollars a month in a four-month span. However, when it's over it's over, which is why I also do accounting to ensure I have a steady flow of income throughout the year. Owning my own business was the best thing I could've ever done for myself. The whole idea of being chained to a desk, working for someone else and making them rich off of my hard work did not sit well with me. I tried it for two years and it was torture. So armed with a CPA and only twenty-five thousand dollars in savings, I stepped out on faith and started my own home-based accounting business. Then, two years later, I moved into an office space in West Orange. Now here I am, four years later, despite an uncertain economy, still standing.

I smile. "Nothing, why?"

"I was thinking I'd swing by and we could have lunch together."

"Em, I don't know if that's a good idea. What if Persia came here?"

He sighs. "So what if she did? She's going to find out sooner or later, anyway."

"I know, but...not like that. I want to tell her in my own time."

He sighs. "Okay, your sister; your way. Handle it how you want. But, I still wanna see you. So how you wanna handle lunch?" I tell him I'll come to him. "Is there anything specific you'd like to eat?"

I smile. "Yes...*you*."

"Then lunch is ready. I'll see you when you get here."

"I'll be there in twenty minutes," I say, logging off my computer, then grabbing my purse and keys.

"I'll be naked and ready."

"My mouth *and* pussy are already watering."

"Paradise Boutique. How can I help you?"

"Hey, beautiful," the voice on the other end says. "I wanna spend another day in Paradise." His masculinity oozes through the phone, causing my clit to tingle.

I press my thighs together, feeling the furnace between my legs ignite. "Umm, who am I speaking to?" I ask, playfully. "You might have the wrong number."

He laughs. "Nah, beautiful, I got the right number. And you know who it is; don't front, ma."

"No, seriously," I joke. "Who is this? Sammie? Laron? Craig?"

"Oh, damn, it's like that. That's how you doin' it?"

I laugh. "Let me stop messing with you. How are you?"

"I'm good. Thinking about you. You closin' at six, right?" I tell him yes. "I wanna take you out tonight."

Girl, don't do it. He'll be tryna turn this into a relationship. You've already fucked him more than enough times. Then laid up with his ass down in Atlantic City. Now he's tryna take you out, again. Not good. You see where this is going?

It's only a date. What harm can that do?

Girl, you're asking for trouble.

Sometimes a girl needs a little trouble. It'll be one last time for the road. I grin, ignoring the voices in my head. "And where would you like to take me?"

"Nowhere special; someplace simple to grab a bite to eat, then have a little fun. Uh, *you* do like to have fun, don't you?"

"That depends on the activity," I say coyly.

"It's whatever, baby. But for now, it's dinner. You wit' it or what?"

It's only dinner, I reason in my head. *It's not like he's asking me to marry him or anything.* "Listen. I'm not looking for a man," I decide to tell him. Not wanting there to be any room for confusion.

He laughs. "Yo, ma, breathe easy. We're kickin' it. I'm not looking for a man, either."

I laugh. "Real funny. You know what I mean."

"Relax, ma. You jumpin' way ahead of ya'self. All I'm tryna do is chill with you. Not turn this into a relationship. Not yet, anyway. I told you I wanted to snatch you up, but, uh…I need to see if you worthy of a man like me, first."

I suck my teeth, still laughing. "Oh, please. You may not be worthy of *me*."

"Yeah, aiight. Then I guess there's only one way for the both of us to find out. Isn't there?"

I smile. "I guess there is. But you already know this pussy's well worth it."

He laughs. "Oh, and this dick isn't?"

"Oh, the dick is definitely worth it," I say seductively. "Still doesn't mean you're worthy of being my man."

"Yeah, aiight. We'll see about all that. Where you want me to pick you up, at the store or ya crib?"

My crib? Oh hell no. I can't have him picking me up at the house. Persia and Porsha will think he's on the menu and wanna know when they can fuck him. They'll be ready to pounce on his ass real quick. And this one…I wanna keep him all to myself a little while longer. I tell him he can pick me up here at the boutique. He tells me he'll be here at six. "Okay, I'll see you later," I say as three middle-aged women walk through the door. "I have to get back to work."

"Oh, aiiight. Go do your thing. I'll see you in a few hours."

"Before I go...where did you say you were taking me?"

"I didn't," he says, lowering his voice.

"I need to know how to dress." He tells me to dress comfortable. That he's taking me into the city to a spot I've probably never been to. "Ohhhhkaaaaay, Mister Elusive. Do you mind elaborating a little more?"

"Nah. You'll see when we get there, aiiight?"

"And who is this again?" I joke.

He chuckles. "Yeah, aiiight. I'll refresh ya memory tonight when I see you." We exchange a few more words, then hang up. I tend to my customers, then for the rest of the day I find myself watching the clock, anxiously waiting for six o'clock to roll around.

Sitting in the passenger seat of Desmond's 2010 silver CL600 Benz on our way into the city, I feel completely comfortable. Drake's album *Thank Me Later* is playing out of the 600-watt sound system. And we're both kind of in our zones, bobbing our heads to "Over."

"Yo, you aiiight?" he asks, reaching over and touching my chin.

I shift in my seat, bring my attention to him. "I'm good."

He smiles, looking over at me. "So what you over there thinking about?"

"Nothing really," I lie, pulling my bag into my arms. I realize someone's trying to call me when I feel my phone vibrating. I fish it out of my bag, checking to see who's calling me. I have three missed calls. The first two are from my mother. And the last missed call is from Persia. *Shit, I forgot to call her to let her know I won't be home until later*, I think, sending her a text, letting her know I'm out and won't be home until late tonight.

Desmond looks over at me, smirking. "So who you texting, ya man?"

I laugh. "I don't have a man."

"You sure about that?"

"Trust me, if I had a man, I wouldn't be sitting here with you. I don't play the cheating game. Been there, done that."

"Oh, word?" he asks, shocked. "You don't seem like the cheating kind."

"I'm not. He cheated on me."

He shakes his head, focusing his attention back on the road ahead. "Damn, he's a real sucker for that. So is that why you done banned relationships?"

I laugh. "No, not at all. I wouldn't say I've *banned* relationships. I've put them on hold for a minute. I haven't found the right man, yet. And until I do, I'm not gonna settle. I'd rather be single than deal with a bunch of BS."

"I feel you." He glances over at me. "So, what's really good with you? You sexy as hell, and you don't have a man. You got friends? You got somebody you fuckin' wit' on a regular? Wassup?"

"I have a few friends," I tell him, gauging his reaction. There is none.

"Oh, word? And they all hittin' that?"

I laugh. "Unless you tryna put a ring on it, that's none of your business."

"You never know. If you're a good woman, I'll put a ring on it alright."

"I *know* I'm a good woman," I say confidently. "The issue is finding a man who can handle all of this goodness."

"Who knows, maybe ya luck's about to change, baby." I smile. Tell him I don't believe in luck. "Well, I do."

"Then maybe yours is about to change," I tease, shifting my body toward his. I reach over and grab at his cock. Knead it until it thickens.

"Damn, yo. Whatchu tryna do, have me run off the road?"

I kiss the tip of my finger, slip it into my mouth, slowly sucking before pulling it out and biting down on the tip of my fingernail. "What would you like me to do?" I ask, teasingly.

He leans over toward me with one hand on the wheel. He takes his eyes off the road and gazes at me. "Yo, you tell me. It's whatever."

I remove my hand, laughing. "Let me stop before you end up running down into a ditch and killing us. I need you to get me where we're going in one piece."

"Nah, I ain't tryna kill us, baby. But, uh, you killlin' me right now. You got my man down here throbbin' for real for real. What you gonna do about that?"

I grin. "Nothing," I say, shifting my body forward, getting comfortable in my seat, "for now, anyway."

"Yeah, aiight," he says, heading toward the Lincoln Tunnel into midtown New York.

"Wow, it's awfully busy in here," I say as we take our seats. We're at Dave & Buster's in Times Square. And he's right. I've never been here before.

"Yeah, it can get kinda hectic up in here. But, it's all good. It's actually one of my favorite spots. Sometimes when I ain't beat for a buncha of nonsense, I come here and get lost. I can spend hours up in here playing games." *Awww, how cute!* I smile, seeing this muscled-bodied, manly man light up like a kid at Christmas. "Yo, what can I say? I'm a big kid at heart."

I smile. "So I see."

When the waitress finally gets to our table, I order the chicken alfredo. Desmond orders a veggie burger and fries. He orders a Corona and I order an apple martini. In the forty-five minutes it takes for our food to arrive, the two of us talk like we've known each other for years. It feels nice. This time I tell him a little more about me. Let him know I grew up in East Orange. That I went to private schools. Then off to college.

The waitress returns with our drinks, then asks if we need anything else. We don't. So she floats over to the next table. He stares at me, taking a sip of his beer. He leans in, rests his arms on the table. "Beautiful, educated and mad sexy. I like that."

"My parents were big on education; especially my mother."

"Oh, word? Was she strict?"

I laugh. "She had her moments. But not really." He asks about my father. I tell him we're really close. That he was very involved in our lives. That he allowed us to make our own mistakes; yet was always there to help us figure it all out. "I love him to death."

He smiles. "Damn, that's wassup. That's the kinda relationship I wanna have with my daughters. Hell, with all of my kids. My pops worked all the time. He held down two jobs. So he didn't really have much time for us, growing up. My moms held shit down, though. She was the glue to our family. Pops was the bread-winner. But mom dukes ran the house. She spoiled us rotten; especially her boys."

I'm smiling, but I can't help but feel a tinge of envy that his mother was the kind of mother I wished for growing up. "And I bet you were her favorite."

He laughs. "How you know?"

I shrug. "Educated guess." I ask him who he looks more like, his mother or father. He tells me his father. Tells me he's the only one that took after him. The rest of his siblings look like his mother. I grin, "Well, your father must've been one fine man back in his day."

"Yo, what you mean 'back in his day'? Dude still got that swag juice."

I laugh as the waitress finally returns with our meals. The rest of the night, we eat, drink and laugh. Three apple martinis and four beers in, we finally make our way to the game room where we play rounds of Pacman, Centipede, and a few other video-games, then shoot a few rounds of pool. I surprise him when I beat him both times.

"I bet you didn't think a chick in heels could whoop you," I say, teasing him, "did you?"

He laughs. "Yeah aiight, baby. Think what you want. I let you win. But in the end I'm the one gettin' the prize. Believe that. And I play for keeps."

"No comment," I say, smiling.

"You ready?"

I nod, allowing him to take my hand into his and lead me out the door. I can't remember the last time I had so much fun with a man, laughing and talking. No airs, no extras. Simply two people enjoying each other's company. By the time we get to the car, I'm feeling frisky and free. And have already decided that the minute we get back to Jersey, he's getting some pussy before sending him on his way.

"I really had a nice time," I say as I fasten my seatbelt and settle back in my seat. "Thanks for inviting me out."

He flashes me a wide smile. And for the first time I notice how pretty his teeth are. "Nah, thank you. I enjoyed myself, too."

"So, was this a date?" I ask, coyly.

He grins. "It's whatever you'd like it to be, baby."

I smile. "Good answer." He reaches over and takes my hand into his. The rest of the ride we continue laughing and talking. By the time we turn onto Bloomfield Avenue it's almost midnight.

"Damn," he says, pulling up in front of Paradise. He brings my hand to his lips and kisses it. "I wish this night didn't have to end."

I lick my lips, letting go of his hand, then reaching over and grabbing his cock. I slowly rub it. "Who said it had to?" I unfasten my seatbelt, then open the car door. He's still sitting, with the car running. I glance at him. "Are you coming in for some *pleasure?*"

He smiles, quickly shutting off the engine. "Yo, you already know."

"Then welcome to Paradise."

Pleasure
CHAPTER THIRTY-SEVEN

P ushing him back on the desk, I grope him. Knead his cock; its width and length expanding beneath his jeans, thick fabric constricting its release. "Damn, girl...you sexy as fuck? You sure you don't have a man?"

I press the tip of my finger to his dark, full lips. "Ssssh, don't ask me a buncha questions." I squeeze his dick. "Mmmmm...you gotta nice fat dick..."

He grins. "You like that?"

"Yes," I say in a whisper, wrapping my arms around his thick neck. I stare into his eyes. Allow him to see the lust in mine. His hands find my waist, then my hips and my ass. He squeezes, pulling me into him; my hips pressing up against him. Without thought I grind into him. "I want some dick."

"Don't worry, baby, I'ma give it to you real good." His hands slide from my waist, gently glide up my body, caress the sides of my breasts. They are warm and soft against my skin, causing a sudden bolt of ecstasy to shoot through me. I shudder as he continues his journey, brushing the tips of his fingers along my neck. He cradles my chin, takes me in. "Damn, you so muthafuckin' fine. I wanna make love to you."

I swallow. Breathe in his desire for me. "And I wanna give you pleasure like no other. My pussy is on fire," I tell him, stroking his cock. It feels heavy and extra thick. He lowers his mouth, claiming my lips.

Desmond kisses me slowly at first, teasing the corners of my mouth before slipping his tongue between my lips. My mouth welcomes him in, allowing him to deepen the kiss. I close my eyes and get lost in the moment, sucking on his tongue. We kiss for what seems like an eternity before he moves to my neck, licking and sucking.

My nipples poke out stiff, like sweet Hershey kisses. He reaches for them, cups my breasts, then pulls them into his face. "Damn, you have some nice titties." I tell him to suck them. He unhooks my bra, lets my titties bounce and jiggle in front of him, then opens his mouth wide and devours them—one at a time. I toss my head back, letting out a soft moan. His tongue feels good swirling around my areolas. His fingers pinch my nipples, softly at first. then harder. And my clit pops out from under its hood; the moist heat from my pussy seeping through my panties.

"Oh, yes...mmmmm..."

"You got me so fuckin' horny, baby."

"You want me to suck on this dick?"

"Nah, I wanna eat that pussy, first," he whispers, slipping his fingers between my legs. I gasp, parting my legs wider. I want to feel his fingers inside me. "You got my muhfuckin' dick throbbin', ma."

I tug at his shirt, pulling it up over his torso. He raises his arms and I remove it, tossing it across the room. "I want you naked. Take the rest of these clothes off. I wanna feel this hard dick naked in my hand, against my body." I step back from him and he wastes no time in getting undressed. I smile, taking in his hard body and dick as I step out of my soaked panties. His dick jerks and bounces up and down. He grabs it at the base, then shakes it. "Yo, you see how hard you got this dick, right?"

I scoop my panties up, stepping back into him. "Oh, yeah, I see." I reach for it, stroking it with one hand while pressing my cum-stained underwear up to his lips. I tell him to eat my wet panties. He takes them from me. Holds them in his hands and cups them over his face and mouth, then inhales. He breathes in my essence. "Put 'em in your mouth," I say, slowly tracing his hard chest and abs with my fingertips. I pinch his nipples. He grunts, my panties hanging from his mouth.

Then in one swift motion he sweeps me up in his arms and carries me over to the sofa where he gently places me, then eases himself to the floor. He pushes my legs back, spitting my underwear out of his mouth. I pull open my lips for him. He kisses them; blows into my center; bursts of hot breath igniting me, setting my insides aflame.

"Damn, you have a pretty pussy." His lips go up and down my labia, left side, then right side. I moan, palming the back of his head. "Mmmm...you taste so damn good."

Licking my clit, my pussy milks his fingers in rhythmic spasms. With a grunt, he attacks my clit with his mouth and tongue. Fingers pushed in to knuckles, he curls them upward, sucking my clit deep into his mouth. He sucks me, nibbles me...until I erupt. He keeps his mouth planted over my sticky cunt, nursing himself on my juices. He doesn't pull back until he thinks he has sucked out the last of my cream. But, he's not aware that I'm an ever-flowing waterfall of lust. My juices continue seeping out.

I reach up and pull him into me, eager to taste myself on his lips, his tongue. Excited by the smell of myself, I lick and suck on his mouth feverishly, then inch my way down off the sofa, lowering myself in front of his throbbing cock. Precum oozes out of its slit. I lick. Take him into my mouth. Swirl my tongue over the head.

His head falls back, and he groans out loud. "Aaaah, shit...your lips feel so good around my dick...oooh, fuuuuck..."

I suck him balls deep. Suck him until his knees shake. Suck him until he shoots a thick, hot nut down in my throat. I swallow, stand up, licking my lips, then fingers.

"Daaaaaaaamn, baby, you the truth," he says, catching his breath. He grabs his cock. It's still hard. How I like it. He presses it up against me, sliding his tongue into my mouth. The mixture of my pussy and his nut on our breath, tongues hungrily twirling around the other, excites me. Any man comfortable enough to tongue me after I've swallowed his nut is a man after my own heart. My cunt creams and vibrates, ready to feel his thickness.

I skillfully roll a condom onto him and guide him inside me. He presses the head of his dick into my slit, then pushes in, slowly rotating his hips.

I gasp.

He slams his hips forward, shoves his dick all the way inside me. I gasp again.

He grunts, then pulls back, stirs my pussy nice and slow with the tip. "Damn, your pussy's so tight...and wet. Mmmmm, fuck... oh, shit..."

I clamp my legs around him and dig my heels into him. "Put that fat dick in me and stop teasing me," I demand, staring him in the eyes. "Fuck me."

He presses his body to mine, giving me what I've asked for. My orgasm vibrates through my clit, stretches out, the contractions causing my body to shake. "Aaaaah, shit...you so hot, baby... Mmmmm, this pussy's so wet..."

I whimper.

He moans.

My bliss, his bliss...becomes our pleasure, expanding, winging through the both of us. The heat we both feel urges us into harmonic thrusts; sweaty bodies colliding into the others. His yells of pleasure rising to match mine. Powerful waves wash over me. I lift my legs higher. Bend at the knees, pulling open my pussy, wider.

I welcome him into Paradise. Greet him with unadulterated pleasure.

He pumps me, moving inside of me with the right pace and rhythm. "Aaaaah, shit, baby…I'm gettin' ready to cum…Oooh, shiiiiit…uhhhh…uhhh…"

Trembling with utter ecstasy, he growls and grunts, and comes, flooding the condom. He gasps; his body still writhes in pleasure. "Ohhh shit, that was good."

I smile. "I'm glad you enjoyed it."

He kisses me. "You aiiight?"

I nod. Kiss him back. My pussy throbs with delight. Still, I want, need, more. His dick softens inside of me, slipping out. Desmond lifts up from me, shifts his body. I shift mine, lifting up from the sofa. I watch him as he removes the condom. I lick my lips. Drool gathers in the corners of my mouth. I want to drink him in. Want to roll his cum-filled condom into my mouth, then chew it like chewing gum. But I refrain from acting out my kinky thoughts.

Instead, I scoot up on my desk and spread my legs. I pat my clit. Caress my cunt. Desmond grins, licking his lips. "Come eat my pussy," I whisper, leaning back on my forearm. He walks over to me, leans in, presses his lips to my clit, and kisses it, then licks it. I let out a soft moan. He darts his tongue in and out of my slit, flapping it along the seams every so often.

"You like that?" he asks in between licks.

"Oh yessss…" His long tongue pushes its way deep inside of me, chin deep, it finds refuge in my slick cunt. He grunts and groans, lifting my hips up off the desk. "Yeah, like that," I coax, helping him find his way back to paradise.

"Don't forget Damon is coming through this Friday for another *tune-up*," Persia says, grinning as she flits about the kitchen, her heels clicking against the tiled floor. "He should be here around eight or so." She rinses her breakfast plate and silverware, then drinks the remainder of her hazelnut coffee before rinsing out her cup and sticking it in the dishwasher along with the rest of her dishes. I watch as she maneuvers around the kitchen, wiping the counters, then the table. She's so busy rattling on that she hasn't noticed that I haven't said a word. "Oooh, I can't wait to ride that nigga's back. My pussy juices at the thought."

I grunt, finally acknowledging that I've heard what she's said. "Mmmph, I forgot about him wanting to get that ass of his tore out the frame."

She chuckles. "Girl, be nice. All you need to do is worry about being the good little dick sucker you are."

I roll my eyes. "Oh, I'm being nice, boo." *And I'm gonna give him a nice, slow, wet dick suck, too.* Ugh. I'm such a damn contradiction when it comes to Damon. On one hand, I'm repulsed by the thought of him taking it in the ass. But, then on the other hand, I'm turned on by the thought of sucking his dick. He is so damn masculine. So damn hood. Between you and me, his cock cream does seem so much thicker when his ass is being stuffed. But, after all the shit I've talked, Persia will never hear that from *me*. "Don't worry. You know sucking a dick has never been a problem for me."

"Well…"

"Whose dick you getting ready to suck?" Paris asks, walking into the room. Her silk robe is open, revealing the pink teddy she's wearing.

I laugh. "It figures that would be the only part of the conversation you heard."

She gives me the finger.

"We're talking about Damon," Persia informs her. "He'll be here Friday. And Porsha was just saying how she can't wait to suck the nut outta his dick."

I laugh.

"Oooh goodie," Paris says sarcastically, clapping. "I get to see Porsha do what she does best while he gets fucked by you. What a treat."

"Whatever, smart-ass," Persia says, grabbing her car keys. "Make sure you're home, too. We wouldn't want to disappoint him." Paris asks her where she's off to so early. She tells her she's flying out to Atlanta to meet with a potential client who's interested in having her design their company's website, and meet their marketing needs. "It's a new research development company. I'm hoping to seal the deal before I get back tonight."

"Good luck," Paris and I say in unison.

"Thanks."

"Oh, before I forget," Paris says, taking a plate out of the cabinet, then scooping eggs out of the pan on the stove onto her plate. "I need one of you to cover the boutique tomorrow for me. Mom has invited me to drive out to the Dutch Country with her." She pulls out two slices of multigrain bread, then drops them into the toaster. She tells us how, since that incident at the diner, Mom has been really trying. "When we drove out to the outlets last month, *she*, of all people, apologized, which both of you know is no easy feat for her."

I glimpse over at Persia and see her rolling her eyes up in her head.

I chuckle. "So basically what you're saying is, once again, she's manipulated you. Made you feel guilty for your despicable outburst toward her. 'Cause you know she'll never let you live it down."

She huffs indignantly, placing a hand up on her hip. "She hasn't manipulated me into doing anything. What makes you say that?"

"Umm, let's see. You call her to apologize, and she turns around and invites you to spend the day shopping with her, and *you* were the one driving *her*. Now, she's inviting you out to the Dutch Country—to drive *again*. Hmmm…sounds like manipulation to me. She knows how you are."

Paris tilts her head, placing a hand up on her hip. "And what is that supposed to mean, 'she knows how you are'? Explain that to me."

"She knows you won't say no to her. It's not in your blood; especially since she knows how badly you want to have a better relationship with her."

Paris twists her face up. "And what's so wrong with that? I'd think you'd want to have a better relationship with her, too."

"I do," I admit.

Persia grunts, interjecting. "I find it interesting that she'll apologize to you for shit she says, but not once has she opened her mouth to apologize to me or to Porsha, for that matter, for anything offensive that has come out of her mouth to us. And she had ample opportunity the day we were all at brunch to do so. She didn't even call to see if Porsha or I wanted to drive out to Pennsylvania with her. No, she asked you."

"Oh, please. You're purposefully antagonistic toward her," Paris defends. "You like getting into confrontations with her. Look at how you make it your business to smear what we do in her face every chance you get. And she didn't ask either of you if you wanted to go because she knows both of you would've said no."

Persia glances at the clock. "Oh, please, now you're sounding exactly like her. Let's face it. You're her favorite. Always have been, always will be."

"I am not," Paris says indignantly. "She loves all three of us equally."

Persia pushes out a sarcastic laugh. "Please, you don't even believe that."

Paris sighs. "Okay, so she shows it differently. But she's never done anything extra for me. We've all always gotten the same things."

Persia rolls her eyes again. "It's not about material things. It's about the attention and praises she always gave you growing up." Paris disagrees. And I'm not sure if she's in denial, or extremely blind to the truth. But the truth is our mother has always favored her over Persia and me. And that's mostly due to her mild temperament. Persia has always been less tolerated because...well, she's always been the most difficult. She and Mom have always butted heads. But, of course, I don't say anything. I sit back and let the two of them duke this one out. Paris remains adamant that she has never been favored. "Whatever, girlfriend, I'm outta here. I have a plane to catch."

Finally I decide to comment. "Well, regardless of whether you were favored or not, after that stunt Mom pulled at the diner, I don't know why you'd want to put yourself through it. Besides, you said she started getting on your nerves when you spent the day with her up at the outlets."

"Well, true. But this time, I've made it very clear what I expect from her. And, like I said, she's really been trying."

Persia grunts. "Mmmph, well, let her know she has two other daughters she should be *trying* with. But, let me ask you this, since you seem to be all up on her bandwagon these days. What did she actually apologize for? Does she admit to any of the nasty shit she's said to us? Has she apologized for taking out her anger toward all of the women who she believes, in her twisted mind, wronged her by fucking Dad on us?"

Paris blinks. "Well, no; not really. But she did say she'd try to watch what she says."

I clap my hands together. "Bravo, bravo…once again she takes no responsibility for her actions. You already know, no matter how hard she *thinks* she's trying, she's going to say something to get under your skin. It's what she does. She can't help herself."

Persia rolls her eyes. "Oh, puhhhleeze. That woman can help herself if she wanted to."

"I'm not gonna let her get under my skin. Not this time."

"You need to cut your losses, honey. And feed her with a long-handled spoon, like I do."

"I'm not gonna stop trying," Paris says, eyeing Persia as she pours pomegranate juice into her travel mug. "She's still our mother."

Persia huffs. "Don't remind me."

"Whatever," Paris says dismissively. "So which one of you heifers is gonna cover the boutique for me?"

"I can't," I tell her. "I have appointments back to back up until eight o'clock tomorrow tonight."

Paris looks over at Persia. "What about you?"

She huffs. "Well, I guess it'll have to be me," she says over her shoulder as she's walking out of the kitchen. "I don't know why you don't hire someone part-time. It's not like you can't afford it."

Paris follows behind her. I overhear her saying, "Now why should I waste money on hiring someone I might not be able to trust when I have two beautiful sisters who I trust with my life?"

"Oh, please. You're such a kiss-ass."

I hear Paris laugh. "Love you, too, sweetie. Go seal that deal, then bring ya ass back here safe and sound."A few minutes later she shuffles back into the kitchen. "I really hope she lands that contract."

"Me too," I say, getting up to put my dishes in the dishwasher. "She's been working her ass off. She's good at what she does and no one deserves it more than she does. Knowing her, she will not board that plane back here until she has it in the bag." She agrees. I glance up at the wall clock over the sink. It's almost seven in the morning. "So what time are you going in today?" She runs her hands through her hair. Tells me she'll probably leave around a quarter to nine. "Uhhh, then you might wanna get a move on it, Sweetie. You know it takes you almost two hours to get dressed."

She waves me on. "Yeah, yeah, yeah; don't remind me. I swear. Today I would love to lie around and do absolutely nothing. Ummm…so what are you doing today?"

I laugh. "Not working the store so you can lay around today, boo. That's for sure."

She sucks her teeth. "You're such a bitch."

"Yep. But you know I always have your back when I'm not swamped. But, in the meantime, I agree with Persia. You need to put an ad in the paper for a part-time assistant."

The house phone rings. "I'll think about it," she says, walking over and picking it up from off the counter. She looks at the caller ID. "Speaking of the devil; it's Mom. I'm gonna put her on speakerphone." *Great*, I think, rolling my eyes up in my head. "Hello, Mom."

"Who's this, Porsha?"

"No, it's Paris."

"Oh good; I was hoping you'd answer. I called your cell but it went straight to voicemail. Why isn't your cell on?"

Paris frowns. "Mom, what difference does it make if my cell is off or not? You called the house. So, is everything okay?"

"Okay, Paris. Let's not turn this into another mess. I didn't call to argue with you. Where are your sisters?"

Paris looks over at me. I wave her on. "Persia left for a meeting. And Paris—"

"Hello, Mother," I interject.

"How are you, Porsha?" I tell her I'm good. "I don't know why you have me on speakerphone. You know I don't like being on that thing."

Paris shakes her head. "Well, Mom, if you call the house phone, you're gonna be put on speaker."

She huffs. "Well, then let me make this brief. What time are you going to be ready to head out to the Dutch Country tomorrow?" Paris glances over at me. I sit back in my seat, folding my arms, smirking. Last month it was the outlets in New York. Now this month she's traipsing out to Lancaster, Pennsylvania to hit up the Tanger Outlets. I'm convinced the woman is becoming an outlet junkie in her old age. "I'd like to get an early start so we can get up there as soon as the stores open. I want to beat the crowds. Afterward, we can have an early lunch, then spend the rest of the day relaxing before heading back in the morning."

"And we'll need to leave *early* in the morning, too. I need to be back by eleven to open the boutique."

"Oh, that's fine. But why aren't your sisters covering for you?"
Paris tells her Persia will cover tomorrow, but she still needs to
be back to open on Thursday.

"Well, what about Porsha?"

"Mother, I can't. I'm booked all this week. Paris already knows
if I could, I would."

"Oh, I see. Well, Paris, maybe you should think about hiring
someone." I smirk. Paris glances over at me, giving me the finger.

I laugh.

"I'll give it some thought. Look I gotta get ready for work. I'll
see you tomorrow morning."

"You never said what time you were going to be here."

"Like around eight."

"Make it seven," she has the audacity to say, "to make sure
we're there the minute the doors open."

I snicker. Persia sighs. "Mom, I'm the one driving. And I will
be picking you up at your house at eight o'clock; period."

"Well, I—"

"Eight o'clock, Mother," Paris says sternly. "That gives us plenty
of time." I smile. *It's about time she handles her*, I think, getting up
to make myself a cup of white tea. I pour water into the kettle,
then set it back on the stove, turning the burner on. "If that's not
good for you, then you can drive yourself."

She huffs. "Fine, then. I'll see you when you get here."

"Good. I love you. Now you enjoy the rest of your day. I have
to get ready for work."

"Love you, too. You, too, Porsha."

"Love you back," I say before she hangs up.

I burst out laughing. "Ooooh, she's hot with you right about
now."

Paris shrugs. "She'll get over it. I mean, really. I'm the one driving. And she's…" She stops herself, shaking her head. "She's still our mother."

"Who is never gonna change."

"Maybe not, but I'm still hoping it'll change how I deal with her so that I don't keep letting her disrupt my day."

I wave her on. "Good luck, boo-boo."

She sucks her teeth. "Whatever. Let me go jump in the shower so I can get out of here on time." I watch as she walks out of the kitchen, shaking my head. *Bless her heart*, I think, getting up to remove the whistling kettle from the stove. I glance up at the clock. *It's time to get my day started*, I think, dropping a teabag into my cup, then pouring hot water over it. *Yup, she's our mother alright, but she's still a mess!*

CHAPTER THIRTY-NINE

"Paradise Boutique, how can I help you?" I answer into the phone, glancing over at this chick messing up a table of assorted designer T-shirts that were neatly folded until her ass started ruffling through them. I want to charge over there and smack the shit out of her. But the deep, dreamy voice on the other end distracts me from kindly swinging Miss Messy Ass out the door.

"Hey, beautiful...I've been thinkin' about you all morning."

I blink. "Who is this?"

He laughs. "Oh, here you go wit' this again. You done forgot me that quick, *again*?"

It doesn't take long for me to realize that this deep, panty wet-ting voice on the other end isn't calling for *me*. It's for Paris. But, curiosity creeps up in me. And since he can't tell our voice patterns apart, I decide not to tell him he has the wrong one. Instead, I start to wonder if he's as sexy in person as he sounds on the phone. Wonder why Paris hasn't mentioned him. I need to see what this man looks like in the flesh. I smile. "Maybe, maybe not," I answer, coyly. My pussy comes alive.

"Yeah, aiight. Well, check this out. I haven't forgotten you; especially not after that last ep we had together."

My cunt purrs. *Ohmygod, that sneaky heifer has fucked this delicious-*

sounding motherfucker and hasn't said one word about it. "Is that so?" I ask, keeping my eye on Miss Messy, wishing she'd get the hell on up out of here while I talk to this dreamy delight on the other end. "Tell me what you've been thinking about?"

"Yo, don't front. You already know."

"Tell me, daaaady," I coo into the phone.

"I've been thinkin' 'bout that good pussy. My dick's been hard all day."

A tinge of jealousy sweeps through me, but is quickly replaced with lecherous thoughts of fucking him myself. I moan. "Mmmm, and I love me some hard dick." *I wonder how big it is. Is it fat and long, or short and stumpy?*

"And my dick loves how you make it feel. Damn. I wanna come to Paradise and get some more pleasure."

A smile creeps across my face. An opportunity presents itself. How can I resist?

I can't.

No, I have to.

Hmmm. I wonder why Paris never mentioned this one.

It's obvious. She wants him to herself.

Or maybe she's waiting for the right time to bring him to us so we can all feast on him, together.

Maybe not; maybe she's interested in him for herself.

Then she would've told us about him. She would've said he's off limits.

But we share everything. No one has ever been off limits.

"Why didn't you call my cell?" I ask, fishing to see exactly how well Paris and this mystery man know each other. Even though it's obvious she's already fucked and sucked him by the way he's talking, if Paris was really interested in him, he'd have her cell number, and he would've known she was out of town. I hold my breath. Wait for his answer.

He laughs. "Yo, you know you been frontin' hard. All the sexin' we do and you still haven't hit me with it. It's like you wanna see a nigga beg. Is that what you want, baby?"

Hmmm...she can't be too interested then.

But she's fucked him more than once.

That doesn't mean anything.

She still hasn't given him her number, so that says to me she has no intentions of giving it to him. And I can fuck him, too.

For a hot second, I consider my salacious thoughts. Think about Paris. Entertain the notion that perhaps she might really be interested in him, for herself. Think about how she might feel if she found out that I've sampled him, too. But then suddenly— I don't care. I want, need, to see who this man is. And why Paris has kept him a secret.

"No, I don't want you to beg."

"Then what you want me to do?"

I lower my voice. "Come here and fuck my pussy real good, and I'll make sure you finally get my number. But don't think I'm gonna make it easy for you." Miss Messy glances over at me, holding up a black Donna Karan dress. "Umm, can I help you?" I ask with more attitude than I probably should have. But, this bitch is trying to ear hustle on my time.

"Yes, I'd like to know if this dress is on sale."

Bitch, do you see a red tag on it? Is it on the sale rack? "Hold on," I tell him, annoyed that this bitch is fucking up my phone time.

"No, you good. Go handle ya business. I'ma come through as soon as you close. And you can finish all that slickness you were talkin' then."

"Ma'am," I say, holding a finger up. "Give me one second."

"Take your time," she says snidely.

I return back to my conversation, feeling my panties sticking to my pussy. "Oh, trust me. I'm gonna do more than talk. You make sure you're ready to put up, or get shut up. I want you to beat this pussy up."

He laughs. "Aaaah, shit. You done got my dick extra hard talkin' all that slick shit. I got you, though. We gonna see what's really good when I get there."

"Yes, we shall. Oh, and by the way, you've got my panties soaked." I hang up on him, pull down my panties and step out of them, sticking them in one of the drawers. I make my way over to Miss Messy. "Now, how can I help you?"

And this bitch better buy something, too!

"Damn, baby, you miss big daddy like that?" he asks the minute I pull him into the back office and pounce on him. The moment he walked through the door, grinning at me, I wanted to fuck and suck him. Envy swept through me. This is Paris's secret. Fine, dark chocolate wrapped around thick, bulging muscles. Her guilty pleasure would now become mine. It has been years since I've purposefully fucked a man who thought I was either Paris or Porsha. Boyfriends who loved them, or lusted them, wanting to be their firsts. But they weren't fucking. They weren't sucking. I was. And I was always eager to give them what they thought my sisters would. Good pussy, some ass, a good dick suck. Paris and Porsha were virgins doing boring shit—still making out, grinding, and kissing, and dick teasing. I was the one who gave the boys want they wanted. I'm the one who knew how to make them feel real good.

"Aaaaah, shit...suck that dick, baby..."

I look up, flutterin' my eyes and moanin' as I slowly run my tongue along the underside of his dick, then around the head. His dick pulses. I let go of it, standin' up. "Yo, why you stop? You got my dick hard as steel, right now."

"I'll be right back," I tell him, walking into the office closet to get my cherry-flavored head gel out of my purse. I scoop some out with a finger, put it into my mouth. He's now sitting on the sofa. I walk over to him, then drop down between his legs. I take his dick into my hand, then suck and slurp him until it starts to stretch and thicken. He closes his eyes. "Aaaah, fuck…that's right, baby…suck daddy's fat dick…"

He winds his hips, slow. Allows me to control the amount of dick I take into my mouth with my hands. "There you go…wet that shit…" I spit all over it, coating it with a glob of slob, then start jacking him off while I suck on his balls.

"Yeah, that's right, baby…"

"You like that? You like how your little cum-slut is sucking all over them balls?" I ask. I lift his dick up and lap at his balls, then roll my tongue around them.

He grunts. "Fuck yeah. Suck them balls for me."

I take his balls into my mouth. Pop them in and out, stroking his shaft.

"You want me to be your personal dick sucker? You like the way I coat your dick with my spit?" I ask, spitting on his dick, stroking it. He moans. "Tell ya little dick-sucking bitch how you want it." I tell him to grab my titties, twist them. Slap them.

He looks at me, seemingly shocked by my aggressive demeanor. "Damn, ma, you real wild tonight. I didn't know you like gettin' it in like this."

I grin, sly. "There's a whole lot you don't know about me, big daddy. Sometimes I like it real nasty. Sometimes I like it mild. Tonight, nigga, I want it wild." I tell him I want him to talk dirty to me; to call me filthy names and yank my hair. I let him know how I want him to fuck me. Tell him how I'm going to suck his fat dick nice and slow and wet, then suck the nut out of it. I tell him I want him to eat my ass out, toss this salad until I beg him to fuck me deep in it. I tell him no pussy tonight; ass and throat, only.

"Damn, ma. You wildin' for real; that's wassup. So that's how you wanna get it in, then that's how we get it in. So get back up on this muthafuckin' dick, bitch, and suck it like you love it."

"Mmmm, yeah, nigga. That's right. Talk nasty to a bitch."

He stands back up. "Suck daddy's muhfuckin' dick," he says, yanking me by the hair. The muscles in my pussy constrict. I take him back in my mouth. The head of his dick hits the back of my throat. He stands still; lets me feed on the dick. I gag, but keep on suckin'. He lets out a moan as I take him down to the base. I work my lips and tongue up and down the length of his shaft. "Yeah, baby…mmm, fuck…gobble that shit up…yeah, just like that…let daddy stroke ya throat, baby…yeah…mmmph…"

He feeds my hungry mouth with slow, deliberate thrusts. I sink my nails into his flesh. Urge him to bang my throat up. He wraps his thick hand into my hair, palms my head and fucks my throat. I close my eyes, but quickly open them when Paris's face enters my space. A tinge of guilt creeps up in me for doing this nigga in her office, behind her back, but I swallow it back along with this nigga's chocolate dick. I block out her image, making loud gurgling sounds. Spit and drool splash everywhere.

I reach beneath me, rapidly smack my pussy and pop my clit. I slip a finger, then two, into my slick cunt. "Yeah, play wit' that fat pussy, baby…" I look up at him. Tell him not to call me that. Direct him to call me dirty, harsh names: Bitch, Slut, Whore. "Aiiight, baby…shit, fuck…play in that pussy, bitch!" I moan. My pussy grips my fingers. I am wet and slick and ready. "You ready for me to fuck you in that fat ass, bitch?!" I moan again, rapidly sucking him off. He takes hold of my hair and yanks my head off of his dick, leaving my mouth vacant and lonely.

"Lean over on that desk and spread them ass cheeks." He drops down on his knees, shoves his face in between my thighs and eats my ass, tosses it like it's his last meal. He spits in my hole, runs his tongue in it.

I moan. Reach back and grab the sides of his face, pull him deeper in. I smother him with my ass. Grind up against his face and tongue until I feel weak. He stands, turns me around, then tells me to suck his dick. I do. Wet it up nice and slow. Spit all over it and jerk it as I lap at his balls. He asks if I have any KY. I tell him no. Tell him to fuck me like a prison whore. His eyes widen. "Say, what?"

I stand up. Bend back over the desk, planting my hands flat on top of it, glancing over my shoulder at him. "I said, fuck me. Like. A. Prison. Whore."

"Yo, you wildin' for real, baby."

"I'm not your baby. I'm your bitch, your whore." I slap my ass, hard. "Fuck me as such." I glance at his rock-hard dick still coated with spit. It bounces at the thought of fucking me in the ass, rough and dirty.

He spits in his fingers, rubbing them along the center of my asshole. He jabs a finger in. My ass and pussy muscles clench. My clitoris throbs. He leans into my ear, whispers, "You sure you want me to get up in this ass?"

I nod. "Yes. Pull my ass open and take it."

The tip of his thick dick presses into the entrance of my ass. Greeted with resistance, he slaps it, pushes his way through until something pops. A gasp escapes from the back of my throat. "Open this tight ass up. Let this dick in." He slaps me on the ass again. Pushes more of him in. I yelp. Writhe and wriggle under him, trying to manage his thickness; its stretch searing through my ass, causing moisture to seep from my chocolate walls, accommodating him; his dick.

"Oh, mmmm…fuck my ass…"

"Like this?" he questions, thrusting himself deep into me.

I groan. My words come out in a long string of syllables. "Yesssss...ohyesssssmotherfuckerfuckmehardanddeepwiththatfassdick..."

He reaches under me, finds my clit and presses on it, pinches it. It swells at his touch. He gently pushes more of his dick into my ass. "Ohhh, yessss..." The weight of him on top of me feels good. His hard body is hot against my back. His breath lost in my hair. I press my ass up against his hips; welcome his thrusts. "Fuck my ass deep, nigga." With each thrust, he stretches me. My ass melts around his dick. What he lacks in length, he makes up for in width and rhythm. I feel sparks shooting through my ass. He slips his fingers into my slit, then cups my pussy. "Oooooooh..." I push myself onto my elbows. Back my ass up on his dick. I rotate my hips, wide and urgent. I'm creaming. "Fuck me harder."

Another orgasm is creeping up in me, tickling the base of my spine, looping its way to my clit. I eye him over my shoulder. "Pull my hair, motherfucker, fuck me harder and smack my ass!"

"Aaaah, shit, baby, you real nasty tonight," he groans, yanking me by the hair and slapping my apple-bottom ass. I yelp and moan. He wedges his knee against my thigh and forces my legs open wider.

"I'm not your *baby*," I grunt, pushing my ass up against his hips. "I'm your slutty bitch. Say it!"

"Dirty, little slut! Ugh, fuck...nasty bitch..."

"Yeah, that's it, nigga. Fuck my slutty ass..."

He fucks me deep.

"Ohhh, yes...ooooh, you have my ass on fire..."

His fingers part the lips of my pussy.

"Aaaaaah, aaaaaaah...right there...ooooooh, yes...that's it..."

He fucks me hard.

I howl.

He groans as he pounds me, slipping his fingers into my silky slit.

"Yesssssss, fuuuuuuuuuck me, nigga!" I yell.

My ass is on fire.

My pussy is smoldering.

He kisses the back of my neck, bites my ear; his raw, naked cock fucking me in deep delicious strokes.

"Oh, shit...this ass feels so fuckin' good...tight...hot...oh, fuck...you like this rock hard dick in ya ass?"

"Yesssss! Ohsweetmotherfuckinggeezus...I love how good your dick feels in my tight...hot ass..."

"Whose ass is it?"

"Yourrrrrrrrrrrrrrrrrrrrrrrrrrrrrrrrrrrrrrrrrrrrrrrrrsssssssssssssssss," I hiss, bucking my hips to match his thrusts.

He fucks me harder, fucks me faster. "Is this what you want, nasty lil'bitch?"

"Yessssssssssssssssssssssssss, motherfucker! Fuck me harder!"

We've become two sweaty animals; frenzied lover-beasts racing toward a common goal of guttural release. Legs splayed as wide as possible, his thick dick beating up my ass, pounding my walls. I cream on his fingers.

His breathing becomes erratic, hurried. "Fuck...oh, shiiiiiiiit...this muthfuckin' ass's so gooooooooood...daaaaamn, baby..."

"Nut in me," I urge, knowing this act is risky, and dangerous. But it's a chance I'm recklessly willing to take. He's fucked Paris. He thinks he's still fucking her. This excites me. I think, change my mind. "Noooo, don't nut in me. Let me feel your hot cream shoot all over my ass..."

I watch him over my shoulder. Head jutted back, face contorted, eyes squished shut, he quickly pulls out; becomes an erupting volcano, spurting hot lava up against my ass and back. "Ohhhhhh, fuck!"

When he's done coming, he tries to pull me into him; wants to kiss me. I step away from him. Tell him to wash off. That he needs to go.

"Damn, it's like that?"

I nod, gathering my clothes up from the floor. "Yeah." I glance at the time. 8:46. *Ohmygod, I need to get home*, I think, watching him walk into the bathroom. I stare at his muscular, hairy ass, his hamstrings, and calves. *Damn, he has a nice body! No wonder Paris wants to keep his sexy ass a secret.*

"So, you just gonna toss a muhfucka out?" he asks, eyeing me. The way he looks at me...the way he holds my gaze.

A thought is conjured up as he locks his eyes onto mine. *This nigga is in love with her.*

I blink the notion from my mind before guilt takes root. "I have to get home," I tell him, feeling unnerved. I watch as he washes his dick in the sink. I hand him a clean hand towel to dry off with. The tips of his fingers graze my hand. I want to know more about him and Paris. "Who else you fucking besides me? I just let you hit it raw, and I hope you don't have anything. The last thing I need or *want* is a disease."

He glances at me, studies me. "Yo, I told you. I'm solo. I ain't out there like that. Shit, don't you think it's a little too late to be asking me that? I mean, shit. You know how we got down the first two times we got it in. We *both* were reckless. And here we go again." He shakes his head. "Damn, you got my head all fucked up. I'm the kinda cat who always wraps it up. And here I am, slipping with you. Shit." He steps back into his boxers, then his jeans. I watch as he slides his wife beater over his head, then puts on his shirt. "How many other cats you gettin' it in with?"

I blink. Hold back a smirk. Mmmph. That nasty little bitch done gave him raw pussy. And now he thinks she done gave him some ass, too. "A few," I tell him.

He stares at me. "They hittin' it raw?"

I shake my head, picking up my phone. There's a text from Paris. "No. I'm not normally so messy," I decide to tell him. Yes, half-truths. "But there's something about you that brings out the slutty side of me."

He grins. "So, what's good now? We tryna take this somewhere, or you wanna keep shit how it is—straight-up, no-strings fuckin'?"

I'm tempted to tell him that I've played a nasty little prank on him, but decide against it. I'll keep it hush-hush. "Let's keep it how it is." I walk him out into the front of the store. "And see how it all unfolds."

He grabs me, pulls my naked body into him. "Cool. But, yo, I'm not sure who you were in that office tonight. But she was mad nasty. And I liked that shit."

I smile. "Don't get used to her. She only comes out when I'm real horny." I grab at his dick.

"Oh, word?"

"Yup," I say, reaching for his zipper. "Let me suck your dick one more time, before I put you out."

He laughs, but allows me to fish his dick out of the slit in his boxers. "Yo, ma…you funny as…" I slip his dick into my mouth; suck it until he hardens. I cup his balls. "Aaaah, shiiiit…yeah, baby, suck that dick…"

Like a greedy little cum-slut, I suck his dick until he bucks his hips and shoots his load down into my throat. "Daaaaaaamn. Whew, you got a muhfucka's head spinnin'."

I suck his dick clean, swallow his load, then walk him to the door, stepping behind it to hide my nakedness as I open it. I tell him goodnight. And this time, when he leans into kiss me, I let him. Then I whisper my number in his ear.

He smiles. "So you ready to finally let me snatch you up?"

I grin, eyeing him sexily. "I've been ready," I tease, rubbing his dick over his jeans one last time. I don't even know this nigga's name. But what I do know is tonight's rendezvous will be my dirty little secret. And I *will* fuck him again.

CHAPTER FORTY-ONE

I'm in my hotel room, naked and sprawled out in the middle of the queen-size bed. I close my eyes, cross my arms and begin caressing my breasts, my left hand cupping the right tit, my right hand stroking the left. My nipples, stiff corks of chocolate, are extremely sensitive. I twist and knead them between my soft fingers. I let out a moan, eager to feel my swelling orgasm erupt and spurt out of my pussy.

I sit up and remove the towel from around my head, then grab one of the hotel's pillows and roll it in half, wrapping the towel around it. I straddle the pillow, pressing my hips into it, slowly grinding. I close my eyes, tighter. Think, imagine, conjure up a scenario that will bring me to the edge.

Behind my eyelids, there's a tall, dark-skinned man, stroking his dick into a long, thick erection. We're in an abandoned building. And there's a dozen or so other men standing in the room watching as well. Homeless, naked, and horny, they pull out their cocks and begin jerking off, too. I keep my eyes locked on the exotic-looking warrior with the rippled abs, muscular track legs and chiseled arms. The slit of his dick oozes precum. I'm licking my lips. He's licking his.

I grind onto the pillow, ride it, pressing my clit deep into my towel-wrapped lover. An inanimate object, along with my overactive imagination, will seduce me into a delicious orgasm. I hump the pillow with slow, rhythmic thrusts at first, then rock my hips faster against the damp towel. My pussy's overheating and leaking sticky juices. I reach down and pinch my clit, causing bolts of electricity to shoot through my body.

"Uhhh…oooh…you wanna fuck this hot, horny cunt?" I ask my naked admirer in a strained whisper. "You want this to be your cock I'm riding, instead of this pillow?"

My chocolate Adonis grins and grunts. He does not speak; just stares and strokes. It is the onlookers who sneer and speak lewdly at me. "Show us your cunt, bitch?"

"Pull open your ass. Let me fuck you in that slutty ass of yours?"

"Let me shoot this nut down in your throat, bitch."

Their harsh words cause my muscles to contract as I slide my slippery cunt down over the pillow. I'm making deep grunts, followed by groans.

"Yeah, you pretty bitch, let me split your pussy open with this big-ass dick," I hear in back of me. But I don't turn to look. I keep my eyes glued to the man in front of me. He is licking his lips, dipping at the knees, beating his dick in fierce, fiery strokes. Then in synchronized motion, they begin to move in toward me, encircling me. Their dicks, engorged and dripping with lust, are aimed at me. I can now smell a musky odor wafting through the air. My nipples are as hard as boulders. I can feel myself on the verge of an orgasm, and I can tell by the lusty glazes in their eyes, that they are, too. I hump, and grind, and buck my hips onto the pillow as they rapidly jerk their cocks. We're all grunting and moaning and panting with desperate anticipation for a sweet release.

And as if on cue, they aim their cocks directly at me and shoot hot wads of cum all over me—my back, my ass, my hips, the back of my head, my face; cum sticks to me, and dangles from my chin and strands of my hair.

Another wave of orgasms crash up against my inner walls, then rush out hard and rapid.

My body shudders.

I tighten my eyes closed.

I get up from off my knees, then walk toward the door, never looking back. When I get outside, it is dusk out. A few men from inside the apartment building have followed behind me. I can tell they want another round; maybe for now, perhaps for in the near future. They're sniffing and howling behind me like rabid dogs in heat. I see a picnic table setup off to the side and slightly out of view from the building. A smirk forms my crusty lips as I get an idea, walking over to the table. I decide to drop my jeans, then my G-string. I bend over the edge of the table, flashing them my round, bubble-ass. I wait for what seems like hours until some-one finally comes over to me. It takes almost forty-three seconds before I feel someone finally standing behind me, reaching for my ass. I crane my neck. Behind me is a thick, chocolate, cross-eyed nigga with dreads. He has a short, hairy dick, but it's extra fat. He's touching the area around my hole with it, tickling my slit before plunging inside of me, stretching me. I gasp. Moan. Back up on him. Throw this ass up on his dick.

Pump my hips.

Milk his dick.

Release guttural sounds deep from the back of my throat.

When he's done, seven other niggas take turns fucking me from the back, alternating from fucking my pussy to fucking my face. Some nut in my pussy, leaving it dripping and open. Others bust on my face adding to my already gooey mess. When they all have finished pumping and dumping their heavy loads out, I stand up, then shake my bare ass toward my car as cum oozes out of my hole and slides down the inner part of my thighs.

"Whew," I say as I collapse face-down on the bed, and wait for the room to stop spinning. My heart continues to pound as I attempt to catch my breath. I roll over on my side and reach for my ringing cell. It's Persia. I glance at the digital clock on the nightstand. 9:47 P.M. "Hey," I say into the phone.

"Ooooh, why you sound all out of breath?"

"I was in here doing aerobics," I tell her, touching my clit, then licking my fingers.

She laughs. "Unh-uh. Let me guess. Doing two-finger squats."

I suck my teeth, laughing with her. "Whatever, hooker. How were things down at the boutique?"

"Oh, good," she says quickly. "The day went by exceptionally fast. I couldn't believe it. I have to tell you. I really enjoyed manning the store for you today."

Mmmm, that's strange. Persia has never *enjoyed* covering for me anytime I've asked her to. Yet, tonight she's taken pleasure in it. I purse my lips. "That's good to hear. So what made it so *enjoyable?*" She tells me nothing specific. That she can't put her finger on what made the day at Paradise pleasurable. "Well, was it busy?"

"At times," she tells me, sounding distracted. "There was a steady flow of customers. And then there were a few hours where it was sort of slow. But, it gave me time to refold clothes and do some of my own work."

"That's good. How were sales?" I ask, walking into the bathroom and placing her on speakerphone while I wet a washcloth. I lather it up, then wash my face.

"Very good. I sold a few tees and a Judith Leiber piece."

"Oooh, which one?" I ask excitedly. She tells me The Grand Dutchess piece. I smile. That's a thirty-nine-hundred-dollar bag.

She tells me I pulled in close to six grand today. "Oh, that's great, girl. Shit, I need to have you cover for me more often."

"Girl, you know I got you. Annnnnytime, boo."

Unh-uh, something isn't right. "Oh, reaaaaaallly, now?" I walk back into the room, sitting on the bed. "Hmmm. Sounds like there was a whole lot more happening there than sales."

"Oh, no. Not at all," she responds, quickly again, still sounding preoccupied. "Other than those sales, it was a pretty uneventful day." Something's not right. It's in her tone. An uneasy feeling settles in my stomach. Desmond pops in my head. I ask her if there were any calls or messages for me. I didn't think to tell him I was going to be out of town for the night. Not that it's any of his business. Still, it would've kept him from calling for me at the store and Persia picking up. *Oh God, I hope he didn't call me today.* "No, nothing I couldn't handle. And there were no messages for you."

"Oh, okay," I say, surprised that I'm a little disappointed; yet, relieved at the same time that he didn't call. "Good."

"Why?" she asks, curiosity coursing through her tone. "Were you expecting a call from someone?"

"No. I was only asking."

"Oh. Well, enough shop talk. I wanna know how things are going in Lancaster with you and the Wicked Witch?"

I shake my head, sighing. "Don't start, Persia. She's really been trying. Actually, things have gone great. We've gotten along. And—"

"Whatever. How many times did you have to ignore something she's said sideways?"

"A few..." She laughs. "Look, that's beside the damn point. The fact is we've had a good day together." I tell her how we shopped and laughed and had dinner at this nice restaurant where we ate homemade chicken pot pies, then went to one of the local bakeries and gobbled up apple dumplings and shoo-fly pie for dessert. "We were like two greedy pigs," I say, laughing. "You should have seen us."

"Oh, joy; how exciting. Oink, oink, so glad I missed the pig show."

"You know, you can be such a bitch sometimes."

She laughs. "Takes one to know one, boo. So where is she now?"

"In her room knocked out."

She grunts. "Well, look. Let me go. I have a few more things to handle here before I head home."

"Home? Where are you?"

"Still here at the boutique."

I glance over at the digital clock on the nightstand. It's almost ten o'clock at night. I raise a brow. "What, this late? What in the world are you still doing there this time of the night?"

"Well, I straightened up, closed out the register, then ended up doing some website stuff."

"Girlfriend, that doesn't take all night," I state, frowning.

"And I worked on a few sites for three new clients while I was here. Time slipped by. But I was able to get a lot of work done today."

"Oh," I say, pausing. There's a lie floating around somewhere in all of this. I just don't know where it is, or what it is. But I'm sure, it'll be discovered. "Well, thanks again, for holding things down today."

"Anytime, Sis. You know I'll always have your back."

"I know you will," I say, trying to shake the unsettling feeling rising up in my stomach.

"Make sure you have your ass back here tomorrow. And don't forget about Damon this weekend; in case you try to make other plans."

"I haven't forgotten," I say, yawning. "Let me get off this phone and get in bed. We're leaving around six in the morning, so I need to get my beauty sleep."

"Yeah, you do that," she says, laughing. "We don't need you no uglier than you already are."

"Whatever, hooker. Get home safe."

"Thanks. Love you."

"Love you, too."

I press the end button, then sit the phone up on the nightstand, staring at it. I lie back on the bed, thoughts of Desmond wafting through my mind. *I should've given him my cell number*, I think, making a mental note to get his number from off of the caller ID and call him the minute I get to the store. *Stupid, stupid, stupid!* I let out a sigh, relieved he hadn't called while Persia was there.

Bright and early, I walk through Paradise's doors and head straight for the caller ID to get Desmond's number. I want to see him. Want to tell him that I would like to spend more time with him. I check the box, and almost faint. All of my numbers have been erased. *Ohmyfuckinggod, why the fuck did she erase the numbers off of the caller ID?* I pick up the store phone and dial her number.

"Hey."

"Persia, did you erase the caller ID yesterday?"

"Oh, yeah, I did," she says coolly. I feel like screaming on her. I take a deep breath. Calmly ask her why. "Girl, you had over three hundred numbers on that thing. I figured you were too busy to clear it out. So I did it for you. I went through all of the numbers to see if there were any from businesses and wrote those numbers down, in case you might need them in the future. Everything else got deleted."

I feel faint. And sick to my stomach. "Persia, you had no damn business erasing anything. Like, what the fuck?!"

"Whoa, girlfriend. What's up with all the hostility? They're only numbers. Is it *that* serious for you to get into a hissy-fit? Geesh. I apologize. I thought I was helping out."

I take another deep breath. "You know what. You're right. I shouldn't be screaming on you. You didn't know."

"I didn't know what?"

"That I needed a number to call back a customer about two handbags," I lie. "Those are guaranteed sales."

"Oh, damn. Well, if they want them bad enough, they'll call you back. Trust me. But I guess I shouldn't have deleted anything. I'm sorry. Like I said, I thought I was doing you a favor."

Bitch, you're always doing shit you have no business doing! I can't even talk to her right now. Thanks to her ass, I have to sit around and hope Desmond calls me sometime today. "You know what. You're absolutely right. If they want the bags, they'll call back for them."

"Exactly. I wouldn't sweat it if I were you."

"Trust me. I'm not going to," I say, pissed for not writing his number down, or committing it to memory. *Fuck!* "I'll talk to you later, girl."

"Okay. Talk to you tonight." The minute we disconnect, I feel a pounding headache surfacing. I glance at my watch. I have ninety minutes to go before the store opens. I decide to take a nap, walking into my office and plopping down onto the sofa. I lay my head back and close my eyes. *Porsha would've never done any bullshit like this!*

CHAPTER FORTY-TWO

W et heat floods the back of Porsha's mouth as I push the butt plug deep into Damon's tight, muscular ass. He's here for another round of Pain, Passion and Pleasure. And, tonight, we deliver like no other. "Aaah, fuuuuuuck..."

"You like having your hairy ass plugged while Passion gobbles up your cock and cream, don't you?" I ask, biting him on his shoulder, my nipples hard and erect against his back. He grunts and groans as his body trembles. Porsha slides her hands up his hips, pulling him deeper into her mouth. "That's right, Passion, suck out all that sweet cream, girl."

I pull the butt plug out of his ass, then push it back in. He moans. I brush lightly agains his balls. Tug at them from behind him. His body jerks. "Aaaaaah, shiiiiit...goddamn...y'all really know how to make a man feel good..."

"Oh this party's only getting started," I state, pulling the plug from his hole. I lick it, then press it up to his lips. Tell him to taste his ass. He sucks the plug as Porsha gets up off her knees. She lightly pushes my hand away from his mouth, removes the plug from his mouth, then replaces it with her sticky tongue. His hand slips between her thighs, brushes against her clit. She gasps. The cordless vibrating nipple clamps dangle snugly around her erect nipples, causing tingly vibrations to shoot through them.

"I wanna put my dick in you," he tells her, gliding his hand back and forth over her slit. "Your pussy's so wet."

Porsha moans, but doesn't seem interested in being fucked tonight. "Look how sexy Paris is over there playing in her pussy," I say, taking Damon by the hand, pulling him away from Porsha and walking him over to Paris. He grabs my ass, squeezes. "You like that fat ass, don't you?"

"Hell yeah," he says, slapping it.

I glance at him over my shoulder. "Be a good little boy, and I'll let you fuck me in it."

Paris is across the room. She has her legs spread wide with her jelly Chocolate Dream Vibe dildo stuffed deep in her pussy. It's vibrating G-spot curve and clit stimulator bringing her blissful delight. She moans loudly. Damon has his eyes locked on her as we walk over to her. "You wanna taste my pussy?" she asks him as she pulls her cum-coated toy out of her slit and hands it to him. He takes it, greedily sucks it, then reaches over and kisses her lightly on the lips, slipping his tongue into her mouth before bending over and licking her clit. He pulls open her swollen lips, rich brown skin and deep pink insides flash before him. He smiles. Tells her how pretty her pussy is, then dips his tongue in.

I crane my neck to see what Porsha is doing. She has left the room, quietly slipped out without a word. My attention is on the hunk in front of me, bent over with his ass sticking out and his face buried between Paris's thighs, to wonder why she has disappeared. I glance at Paris. Her eyes are closed. Her bottom lip pulled in. She's enjoying Damon's mouth and tongue.

I squat down in back of him, pull open his ass cheeks. I lap at his hole. Moan at the sweet muskiness that greets my nostrils. I inhale. Tongue probing the essence of forbidden desires, my pussy simmers with arousal. I force his thighs open wider, lick the back of his balls, finger his hole. He moans, loudly slurping Paris's pussy.

"Ohhh, yes…eat my pussy…ooooh, Damon. Your tongue is heaven…"

I pull Damon's dick to the back, lick around the head then wrap my warm lips over it and suck him until his dick swells in my mouth. He bucks his hips, a sign that he's ready to be fucked. And as bad as I want to strap up and grind into his tight, muscular ass, I have other plans. I stand up. Walk over to the closet and pull out a flogger, then walk back over to Damon and Paris, my eyes fixed on his ass. I bring the flogger up and around, then snap it against his ass—it suede multi-tails splaying across his ass like long, thin fingers, gently caressing his skin. He lets out a soft grunt, his mouth full with Paris's pussy. She grabs his head, lifts her hips. There is very little *sting* and *thud* as I snap it across his ass.

"Make her come," I say, striking his ass again. He moans. "Make her sweet pussy squirt in your mouth." I strike him again. He eats Paris's pussy in between hums and grunts, his tongue rapidly flicking across her clit, jabbing into her slit until she lifts her hips and grinds into his mouth, coming.

When he's finished, Paris pulls his face to hers and kisses him, then pushes him away. No words being said, she slips her dildo back into her pussy, rotating two fingers on her clit. She moans.

"Look how wet you got my sister's pussy," I say, wrapping my arms around his waist, my nipples pressing against his back; my pussy against his ass. I reach for his dick. Stroke it. He moans, watching as Paris pleasures herself. My own pussy is now on fire. I'm certain he can feel its smoldering heat. I smile as Damon turns to face me. He glances down at the flogger in my hand, then shifts his eyes between my thighs. He grins, knowingly. I want my titties and pussy whipped. Want to be called dirty names— slut, bitch, whore, wench. Want to be fucked rough.

He steps into me, yanks me by the back of my hair, then shoves his tongue deep into my mouth as he takes the flogger from me. I bite down on his lip. Paris watches as he throws me down on the bed. Excitement surges through me.

"Oh, yesssss," I coo, scooting back on the bed, spreading my legs, and exposing my smoothly waxed lips. "Whip my pussy."

Damon's eyes are fixed on my glistening cunt, admiringly and appreciatively. He swirls the flogger in around in the air in big circle. *Swish! Slap! Swish!* I yelp in delight as the suede lashes kiss my clit, the mouth of my pussy. He brings the flogger around again, striking my pussy harder this time.

Swish!

"You little nasty slut!"

I throw my head back, pinching my nipples.

"Fucking whore!"

Again, *swish!*

I yell out, on the verge of an orgasm.

"Dirty bitch!"

Swish!

He whips my clit and pussy and calls me names until I'm screaming and coming. Paris moans. She's coming, too. Desmond drops the flogger, then eases between my legs. He kisses my clit, my swollen lips. His tongue gently licks my cunt. This only seems to intensify my orgasms as my stomach strains against the lingering heat.

"Ooooooooooooh…"

Damon inches himself up over me, brings his sticky lips to mine. The scent of pussy—mine, Porsha's and Paris's—stained on his breath. "You ready for me to fuck you?" he whispers.

"Yes…"

In my peripheral vision, I see Paris getting up. See her opening the box of condoms. She rolls one down on her dildo, another condom in her hand. She walks over toward the bed. Tears open the condom as Damon shifts his body, lying beside me while she pulls out the condom. We continue our tongue dance in eagerness as she slowly rolls it down over his aching cock.

"Fuck my sister," Paris whispers in his ear, "while I fuck you with my dildo."

He moans. Hovering himself over me, I lift my legs, pull open my pussy and watch as he eases into me. Ooooh, his dick feels good going in. I let out a moan. He slowly twirls his dick inside my pussy as Paris opens his ass and inches her vibrating dildo into him. He grunts when she pushes the head in. She takes her time working his hole. I feel his dick thicken to capacity, stretching my walls.

"Aaaaaaah…ohhh, shiiiit," he says, thrusting in me. Paris matches his thrusts.

He alternates his hands and methodically strokes my clit, fucking me until I'm coming again. Paris rapidly plunges in and out of his ass until he's coming. He lets out a defeaning groan. His eyes are wide and fixed on mine as he grunts over and over. His body shudders. Then he collapses onto my chest, sweaty and spent, kissing along my shoulders and neck. Paris pulls her dildo out of him, then hands it to me. I slip it into my mouth, sucking his scent off while clenching his softening cock with my pussy muscles. I close my eyes as Paris walks out, listening to the light snores coming from Damon. I smile. *We fucked his ass to sleep.*

"I wanna see you tonight," Emerson says softly into the phone. There's tenderness in his tone that warms me. I really think I'm falling for this man. He makes me feel alive, and wanted, and desired.

I smile. "I wanna see you, too."

"Why you smiling?" he asks as if he can see through the phone, catching me by surprise.

"How you know I'm smiling?"

"I can feel it," he says, laughing.

"Yeah, right," I say, sucking my teeth.

"Oh, you weren't smiling?"

"I didn't say that."

"Aiight, then. So why you smiling?"

"The same reason you are," I shoot back, getting up and shutting my bedroom door. The fact that I still haven't said anything to Persia and Paris makes showing my excitement a little difficult. I want so badly to share this with them. Knowing Paris, she'll be happy for me. Persia is a whole other story. She'll try to talk me out of it. Plant shit in my head that will have me second-guessing my decision to give him, us, a chance.

After that night with Damon, I've decided I'm done. Decided that the only dick I want to be sucking and fucking is Emerson's.

After I sucked Damon's dick and fed him his nut that coated my tongue, Emerson's face kept flashing in my head. And I felt guilty. Felt sick to my stomach. So I quietly slipped out of the room. I went into the other room and watched him eat Paris's pussy, watched Persia flog him, then him flog her. I couldn't stand watching him as he whipped her titties and pussy like that; couldn't stand watching her enjoying it. I turned off the monitor, then I hopped in the shower and scrubbed my body until my skin felt raw. I'm done sharing men with my sisters—for now, at least. If things with Emerson don't work out, then maybe I'll pick back up where we left off—the three of us turning men out, together.

"Good answer," he says. "I wake up with a smile on my face every morning. And go to sleep with one every night, thinking about you. You've gotten all up in my heart."

I smile. "Awww, that's so sweet, Em. I feel the same about you."

"That's what I wanna hear. So, have you given any thought about what I asked you?"

"About what?"

"Going away with me." I tell him I have. "And?"

"I'm looking forward to it."

"Aaaah, shit. That's what I'm talking about, baby. You've made my day even better."

"Well, hold on. I can't go anywhere until the end of the summer. This month is really busy for me with work, and I have the Sade concert on the twenty-fifth. I won't miss that for anything. Then I have a lot of things going on in July and August."

"Damn, it's like that. Well, luckily I was able to swap my dates for the last weekend in December. But, um, you'd put Sade before me?"

"Sorry, but yes, I would. She only comes out every ten years, and there's no way in hell I'm going to wait another decade to see her live and direct."

He laughs. "Damn, wish I was going with you."

"There'll be other concerts," I tell him.

"And you know it. So when we gonna make this official, you and me? I'm ready to have you on my arm as my woman."

"I think I'm ready, too, Em."

"You *think*?"

"I know I am, but I have to wait until the right time. I want to tell my sisters in my own way. I'm going to tell Paris, first, instead of telling them together. She'll be genuinely happy for me, for us. Persia will take some work."

"I hear what you're sayin', babe. But, Persia's a grown woman. She'll have to get over it. I wanna build a life with you; not with her. So, whether she likes it or not, her feelings about us are of no consequence to me. I realize how close the three of you are, but if she's not going to be able to be happy for you, or us—"

"I understand," I say, cutting him off before he says something I don't want to hear. Choosing between him and my sisters is a no-brainer for me. Blood is always thicker than water. I'd have to let him go if it was going to put a wedge in my relationship with my sisters. The thought makes me sad. "She'll come around," I offer, hoping there's some truth to it.

He sighs. "I don't want you to get stressed about it. You already know if it were up to me, everyone would know. But, I realize how important it is for you to have your sisters' blessings. So however you want to do this is cool with me. I'm with you one hundred percent. Aiight?"

"Do you mean that?"

"Of course I do. I want you, Porsha."

I smile, nodding as if he can see me. "Thank you."

"Umm, I was gonna wait to bring this up later on, but since we're on the phone, I might as well ask...."

"What is it?"

"Are you still getting it in with other cats?"

"Em—"

"Hold on. Before you say anything, let me finish. I don't want there to be secrets between us. If we're gonna do this, we need to do it with us bein' able to trust each other to always be honest with the other, no matter what. Cool?"

"Yes. And I want that also, Em."

"Then we're good. So wassup?"

"To answer your question: yes." It gets quiet on the other end. "Hello?"

"I'm here," he says, sounding disappointed by my answer. "How long ago?"

"Em..."

"C'mon, Porsha, no explanations; keep shit real with me."

"Two nights ago."

"Oh, word?" I can tell I've hurt him. "And you're good with that?"

"No, I'm not."

"Did you enjoy it?"

"Em, please."

"Did you enjoy it?"

"Yes, but I felt horrible afterwards. I kept thinking about you, Em. I realized that I can't keep doing that. That I don't *want* to keep doing it."

"And you told your sisters this?"

"No, not yet. But I'm definitely not going to do it again. The only man I want to sleep with is you, Em. I mean that."

"Cool 'cause I don't wanna keep sharin' you, Porsh."

"You won't have to," I assure him.

"I hope not. You're the only woman I need, want, baby. And I hope that's gonna be the same for you. If we have to look outside of each other for satisfaction, then it's not gonna last. I need to know you're going to be as committed to this as I am."

I close my eyes. Try to remember the last time I felt like this, loved—by a man other than my father. Try to remember a time when I felt so emotionally full. This thing with Emerson doesn't complete me. And it definitely doesn't define me, nor does Emerson. No man has, or ever will. But, Emerson definitely adds value to my already enriched life. I can't deny that.

No matter how similar everything seemed, each one of them brought something remarkably different to the relationship. And I learned something about myself with each of them. With age and time and ongoing experiences, I'm so much different than I was five, ten years ago. Emotionally, I've grown. Sexually, I've blossomed and become secure in my sexuality. I know what I want, and need.

"You will be," I tell him, pulling my overnight bag out of my walk-in. I toss a negligee in, then a change of clothes for tomorrow along with some hygiene products.

"Good. Now what time am I gonna see *my* baby?"

"I'm leaving now."

"Cool. I wanna hold you in my arms."

"I can't wait," I say, grabbing my purse, then heading down the stairs. I don't bother looking for Persia, or saying anything to Paris. Why should I? I'm a grown-ass woman going to see *my* man.

CHAPTER FORTY-FOUR

Emerson kisses the back of my ankles, works his way over to my other foot, massages the soles of my feet, sucking my toes, then the back of my calves, pushing my legs back and burying his face between my thighs again. Slowly he pulls the crotch of my teddy to the side, snakes his tongue in between the fabric and licks my sweetness. I let out a moan. I grab him by the back of the head, pushing his face and tongue deeper into me. Against my will, my body shakes and I'm cumming and moaning. He cups the opening of my pussy with his mouth and swallows up my juices, then makes his way back over top of me. I grab him, stare into his brown eyes.

He grins. "You ready for this dick?

"Oh, yes," I whisper, lifting my hips. "Feed my pussy."

He presses the tip of his dick up against my blit. "Is this what you want?"

"Yes!"

He kisses my clit. "Pull open ya pussy for me, baby. Let me see those pretty pink insides." I take my hands, spread open my glistening lips. "Oh, damn! That's a pretty pussy..." He dips his tongue in. "And tastes good, too." He pushes more tongue in. "It's nice 'n sweet..." I moan. He darts his tongue in and out. "Mmmm, shit...I wanna make love to this pussy. You want this hard dick, baby?"

I grunt. He knows it's what I want, need. Yet, he asks the obvious, torturing me. "Yes. I need to feel you inside of me, *now*." He moves from between my legs, getting out of the bed. "Wait," I say, watching as he walks over to the pile of clothes in the middle of the floor. My pussy is frantic. "Where are you going?"

"To get a condom," he tells me, pulling out a red wrapper from out of his pants pocket. I pat my clit, pinch it, watching him tear it open, then roll it down on his dick. His sheathed cock bounces as he walks back over to the bed. "I'ma 'bout to give you this dick like you've never had dick before, baby. You ready for it?"

"Yes...oh, yes..."

He reaches up underneath me, pulls my hips up, then pushes the head of his dick in. I gasp. Dig my nails into his arms. He flicks his tongue against the corners of my mouth, trails along my neck, then up to my ear. He lightly blows in my ear; nibbles on my lobe. "You feel so fuckin' good, baby..."

His warm breath, his wet lips, they taunt my skin. His dick, slowly and deliberately, stirs inside of my honey pot, blending my sticky-sweet juices as they marinate his cock. I want him raw and naked inside of me. I want to suck my pussy cream off. Lick both sides of his thick shaft, then bury him deep into my mouth. I resist the urge to blurt it out. Defy the urgent yearning that gathers in the tip of my clit. I reach down; press on it. Bring it to life. Heat surges through me as one orgasm after another erupts.

"Damn, baby, you nuttin' on my dick? You got that pussy wet for me?"

I nod and moan. Grab him by the ass. Pull him into me.

He quickens his thrusts; positions himself so that his shaft hits my clit with each stroke. "C'mon, baby, that's right. Give me another nut..."

I scream.

"There you go...yeah, soak my dick, baby..." Emerson's cock pounds into me, his hands tucked beneath me, squeezing my ass as he fills me. I clench the width of him, crying out. Oh this man is fucking my pussy so deliciously deep. I hoist my legs up, right leg up over his shoulder, left wrapped around his waist.

"I love you, Porsh," Emerson gasps as he explodes inside me, filling the condom. He says it again, kissing me on the lips as he pulls himself out of me. He flops over onto his back and I quickly place his pussy stained, covered cock into my mouth and suck off my juices, then pull off the condom and squeeze out his nut, coating his dick with it. I feverishly suck him off, savoring the taste of his creamy nut. I lick his cock clean, swallowing the sweet-saltiness of his seeds. He pulls me up to him, then kisses me. I slip my tongue into his mouth, sharing what's left of his nut with him. "Damn, girl," he says, wrapping his arms around me. "You're something else."

I stare into his eyes. Kiss him, again, long and deep, then softly say, "You're not so bad yourself." He holds me tighter, closing his eyes. I close mine, too, smiling. I'm keenly aware that I've fallen for this man. And there's absolutely no turning back now.

Seven A.M., Emerson and I are in the shower together. I'm washing his back with a loofah scrub while he stands under the spigot, washing his front. His head's tilted back. "I could really get used to this."

"Get used to what?" I ask, feigning ignorance.

He turns to face me, kisses me on the tip of my nose. "This... waking up to you every morning and sharing the shower together."

"So you want a live-in backwasher?" I tease. He grins as I take his dick into my soapy hands and stroke it.

"Mmm, nah...I want more than that."

"What, a cockwasher?" I say, pulling in my lip as I continue stroking his dick while sudsing up his balls. I feel the heat escaping from between my legs. "Ooooh, I love how this big, beautiful dick feels in my hand."

He moans. "Damn, girl, you gonna fuck around and have me late for work."

I grin, looking up at him. I use my hand to milk the head of his dick. He dips at the knees. "You want me to stop?"

"Uhh, hell, no. Aaah, shit, that feels good…" I stroke him in slow motion. Reach between his legs; massage his balls. Jerk him until he nuts in my hand. "Now, it's my turn," he says, kissing me on the lips. He kneads my breasts, kisses my neck. "You feel so good, baby." He slips his hand between my thighs, pinches my clit.

I let out a moan as he brings me to the edge of an orgasm. He slips his fingers into my pussy. Hooks his arm up under my left leg and lifts it up. His two fingers are working my slit so good, they curve upward as his thumb presses on my clit.

He brings his lips to mine; kisses me passionately. I'm feeling things for this man I haven't felt for any other man. He pulls his fingers out of me, puts them into his mouth.

"You taste so good, baby." I'm pressed up against the tile. He drops to his knees, takes my pussy into his mouth and makes love to it with his tongue. I close my eyes. Get lost in the moment. He presses a finger on my asshole, then pushes it in.

"Ohhhh, yes…oh, shit…ooooh, your tongue feels so good…"

I give in to the sensations, give into my feelings, and come into the mouth of the man I've fallen for.

CHAPTER FORTY-FIVE

Yo, wats good? U feel like chillin 2nite?

I feel like sukin sum dick, I text back.

Word? Wat else u wanna do?

Swallow ur cream & feed u my pussy

Damn, wat x u wanna meet up?

N 30-40 mins, I text back, glancing over at Paris lying across the sofa, surfing the Internet. She looks over at me, then shifts her attention back to her laptop screen. For a fleeting moment, there's a wave of guilt that washes over me, but quickly ebbs as Mystery Man sends me another text telling me how much he can't wait to feel this pussy wrapped around his hard dick. I've fucked him four more times since that night down at the boutique. Each time, late at night when Paris is here back at home, moping around looking like she's lost her best friend. She couldn't have possibly been *that* into him. Otherwise, she wouldn't have let him slip through her fingers so easily. He would have her number, and be texting her instead of me for a night of hot, sweaty fucking. There's another text from him, wanting to know if we're meeting at our usual spot. I text back, tell him yes.

"Girl," I say, walking over and sitting on the arm of the sofa. "Why don't you get out and get some fresh air? For a while there you were out almost every night; what happened?"

She looks up at me. "Nothing happened. Just don't feel like going anywhere. Plus, I really haven't been feeling good." I ask her what's wrong. She tells me she feels drained, like she doesn't have any energy. That she's having trouble sleeping.

Mmmph, my God, she can't be depressed over some nigga she hardly knew. I touch her forehead. "Well, you don't feel like you have a fever so that's a good thing. Maybe you should try to get in to see the doctor so she can give you something to help you sleep."

"Yeah, you're right. Actually, I already made an appointment."

"Good," I say, glancing at my watch. It's almost ten-thirty. And I need to hurry up and jump in the shower, then head over to the boutique to meet Mystery Man. I stand up. "Well, I hope you feel better."

"Thanks. I hope so, too. Where are you off to?"

How'd she know I was going somewhere? Is it obvious? Did she overhear me saying something? I feel myself getting paranoid. "Oh, what made you think I was going somewhere?"

"Well, I saw you glancing at your watch, then quickly jump up, so I figured you had somewhere to be, or someone to do."

I push out a nervous chuckle. "Girl, I wish. I need to run out to the store real quick, but that's about it."

"Oh, what store?" I quickly tell her Pathmark without giving it much thought. She wants to know which one, glancing at her watch. I tell her the one in South Orange. She eyes me. "Not tonight, you're not."

I frown, giving her a confused look. "Why you say that?"

She shifts her body, sitting up. "Sweetie, if you're talking about the Pathmark over on Valley Street, it closes at eleven. So, unless you're leaving now, you're not going to make it."

"Oh, shit. That's right. Then I guess I won't be going there. I'll head over to Shoprite, then." She tells me they close at eleven as well. Then wants to know what it is I need from the store this time of night, anyway. Right now, I'm standing here feeling like a deer caught in headlights. "Oh, I have a taste for something chocolate."

"Well, hopefully you'll find a store open to feed your craving."

"Oh, trust me. I don't plan on going to sleep until I do," I shoot over my shoulder as I walk out the room. Mystery Man texts back.

HEY BABE. U LEFT YET?

GETTING READY 2

SUMTHNS COME UP. GOTTA GET A RAINCHECK. SORRY ☹

I blink at the text. *Oh, no. This nigga has got to be kidding me*, I think, quickly texting him back. AWWW. I WANTED SUM OF THAT CHOCOLATE ☹

I'MA MAKE IT UP 2 U 2MORROW

Mmmph, whatever, nigga! U BETTER

I GOT U

I don't respond back, instead I text Royce. HEY, U, WANT SUM PUSSY?

It doesn't take him long to respond back, which is what I like about him. He's young, but very consistent. Always responds back, always fucks great!

LOL...ALWAYS! ☺

WHAT X CAN U GET HERE?

I CAN LV NOW

MY PUSSY'S WET N WAITIN

NICE. C U IN 20

Since my night with Paris's mystery man feel through, I text Porsha to see if she wants to join me in fucking Royce down, then go down to the entertainment room to invite Paris to join in tonight's fucktivities. It's the least I can do. She turns her nose up, shaking her head. "No, thank you. I'm definitely not in the mood to have him and his horse cock anywhere near me."

"Oh, c'mon...Don't be a party pooper. We haven't bounced a man up and down on the bedsprings since Damon. And that's been weeks ago."

"Honestly," she says, getting up from her seat, stretching. Her bones crack. "I really haven't been in the mood. Besides, I told you before. Royce has too much dick for me. And I'm not keen on my pussy being stretched open tonight. And I'm definitely not interested in having him spray me with all that cum he shoots out, either."

I laugh. "Girl, you know that first nut isn't that bad. He can fuck you with just the head."

"No, thank you. The head on his dick is like a fat plum."

I lick my lips, feeling myself getting moist thinking about it. "Yes, it is—nice, fat and juicy."

"You can have at it. I'm going to bed. But I might stop in to watch, if I end up having trouble falling asleep." She reaches for the remote for the TV. "Are you staying down here?"

"No. You can turn it off."

Porsha texts back. NO THANKS. HAVE FUN 4 ME

I roll my eyes, following Paris up the stairs. *Oh well. More cock for me!* As she's walking into the kitchen, she asks what time Royce is coming over. I tell her he should be pulling up shortly. Tell her I need to hop in the shower. That if he should ring the doorbell before I finish to let him in.

"Will do," she says, opening up the refrigerator. I watch her pull out a cucumber, then frown. She tosses it back into the bin, pulling out an apple instead. I chuckle to myself. "You like him, don't you?"

"Who?"

"Royce," she says, washing her apple then biting into it.

I grin. "He's okay. But, I *love* his dick." The doorbell rings. *He must have sped over here for some of this good, wet pussy.* "Speaking of which, there he is now."

She waves me on, heading for the stairs. "Have fun."

"Oh, trust me. I plan on it. But, it'll be even more fun if you join us."

"I'm sure it would be," she says as I walk to the door. "But you're on your own tonight with that young stud." She disappears up the stairs as I open the door.

"You ready for me?" I ask, smiling.

He licks his lips. "I stay ready."

I pull him by the hand, slamming the door shut, then leading him downstairs to the Fuck 'em Down room where I plan on fucking him all night.

I have locked myself in my room to think, to wonder, to cry. To have my own private pity party away from the probing eyes of my sisters. *You're pregnant.* The words ring in my head. I'm still in shock.

After Desmond's disappearing act and my vomiting incident, I started panicking. My mind went back to the first night we fucked and I let him dick me raw. So stupid on my part, I know. I've been worrying myself sick, thinking he might've given me a disease, which would explain why I haven't heard from his ass.

I replay the visit in my head. "Wait, repeat what you just said?" I asked, shocked. I heard her the first time, but needed, wanted, her to confirm my ears weren't playing tricks on me. They weren't.

"You're very much pregnant." She smiled. I didn't. Still, I was relieved that I wasn't infected with anything—not yet, anyway. It's a fear that looms in the back of my mind every time I wonder why Desmond abruptly stopped calling me; stopped coming around. Maybe he's purposefully spreading HIV or some other disease, maliciously infecting women. I don't know. In my heart, I don't want to believe that that is the kind of man he is. But his actions don't leave much room for hope.

I'm pregnant! The next thing to do should be the easiest. It's a no-brainer. Get an abortion! Problem is I'm not a victim of rape, nor am I facing a life-or-death health crisis—situations *I* believe warrant an abortion if one so chooses. No, I'm a victim of my own careless choices. Whatever life crisis I'm in, it's by my own hand. And I have to deal with the consequences. Still, I'm torn. Aborting this life inside of me, or bringing it into this world, knowing there's no father.

Someone's at my door, turning the knob. When it doesn't open, they knock. When I don't respond, Persia's voice calls out. "Paris, why is the door locked? Are you okay in there?" I lie still. Turn my face into my pillow. Ignore the knocks. Ignore the pounding in my head.

I'm pregnant!

Persia

CHAPTER FORTY-SEVEN

It's been weeks since my sisters and I have fucked a man together. On four separate occasions, I've asked them if they wanted to fuck Royce with me, have asked them if they wanted to fuck Damon or Irwin, or anyone else we have on-call. Each time, they've both told me that they're not feeling up to it. When I've asked if they wanted to recruit some new dick to suck and fuck, they've both told me, "No."

Yesterday, Porsha came into my bedroom and told me she wouldn't be swapping men for a while. That she needed, wanted, to take some time for herself and not complicate her life with man sharing. "Is there anything in particular that has caused you to change your mind?' I asked, sitting up in my bed and taking her in.

"Yeah," she said, pulling her hair up into a ponytail. She was already dressed in her workout clothes. "I'm seeing someone."

I gave her a shocked look. "Since when? Who is he?"

"For about two months now. But, I've known him for a while."

"Well, who is he?" I asked again, curious. Although I'm not surprised to hear this since she's been staying out later, and not always coming home. Still…

"I'm not ready to say. But when I am, I'll tell you all about him. But for now, I wanted you to know that I've fucked my last man with you and Paris—for now, anyway. I really want to see what happens between me and this guy I'm seeing. I hope you understand."

"Of course I do," I said half-heartedly. I forced a smile. "A girl's gotta do what a girl's gotta do. Does he know about—"

She nodded, cutting me off before I could get the rest of my words out. "Yeah, he knows."

"Wow," I said surprised. "And he's okay with it."

"Yup. I'm not keeping any secrets from him."

I tilted my head. "Mmmm, just keeping them from me; interesting. Does Paris know?"

She shook her head. "No, I haven't said anything to her either. It's not like I want to keep this from you and Paris. I just don't want to speak too soon without being sure. I want the two of you to be happy for me."

"Mmmm, okay. You're my sister, and I love you. Of course I'm going to be happy for you. What kind of mess is that?" I wanted to be happy for her, but shit. Other than some mystery man who she felt the need to keep secret from me, she wasn't giving me much to be happy about. "But I won't deny that I'm offended that you didn't want to share that you've been seeing someone with me."

"Persia, it's not personal."

"Well, it feels personal to me. But, whatever, girl. When you're ready to share, I'll be here."

She smiled. "Thanks. I need to get up outta here. I'll talk to you later."

"Okay, then. Get it in for the both of us."

"I sure will. A girl's gotta keep this body tight."

"I know that's right," I said, waving her on. I watched as she walked out of the room, then plopped back down, covering my face with my sheets. And, yes, pissed and hurt that both of my sisters have been keeping shit from me. I mean, really, we're sisters. They should be able to trust *me* with everything. And keeping secrets shouldn't be an option between us. It wasn't when we were growing up. And it shouldn't be now, but it is. Then there's Paris. For the last three weeks, she hasn't been acting herself. She seems… I don't know, almost sad. Maybe sad isn't the right word. But she definitely seems different, and very preoccupied.

I catch her in the kitchen sitting at the table eating a fruit salad. She seems lost in space. I ask if everything is alright. "Yeah, of course. I've been really tired lately; that's all."

"Are you sure that's all? For the last few weeks, you haven't seemed like yourself. I'm worried about you."

She gives me a faint smile, shifting her eyes. "Thanks, but don't be. It's nothing serious; trust me. I'll be fine. Like I said, I've been real tired lately."

I walk over and give her a hug. "Well, if you want to talk about it, whatever it is—serious or not, I'm here for you. You know that, right?"

She nods, squeezes me tight. "Thanks. I know you are." She looks at me; takes in my outfit, then glances down at my feet. She frowns. I'm wearing her grape python Gucci four-inch platform T-strap heels. "Hooker, are those my heels?"

"Yeah," I say, profiling them for her. "I figured I'd break them in for you since they were still sitting waiting to be worn."

She grunts. "Mmmph, whatever. Where you off to today in *my* shoes?"

I chuckle, shifting my eyes. I can't stand looking at her at that moment. I hate the possibility, the probability, that her mood change might have something to do with her six-foot-something *secret*. The one I've been sneakily seeing behind her back. Yes, messy as it may be, it is inconsequential to me at this very moment.

I'm enjoying him. And he's enjoying me. Well, he *thinks* he's enjoying Paris, but that's not the point. The point is she should've mentioned him to me. Should've told me he was off limits, but she didn't. And now what I thought would be a few rounds of fucking, then sending him on his way, has turned into me wanting to spend more time with him, wanting to keep fucking him. I fuck him, suck him, give him my pussy and ass raw and have literally led him to believe that I'm Paris; that I want to be in an exclusive relationship with him. Truth is, I do. Well, okay, I'm lying. I simply want to keep fucking him. Fact is, I want to keep fucking Royce, too. I want them both.

I would've never thought in a million years, I'd be in this kind of predicament. Pretending to be one of my sisters has never been an issue for me. But trying to keep up this lie is becoming a bit more challenging the more time I spend with my—well, Paris's, mystery man. The way he looks at me, touches me, holds me, and calls my...uh, Paris's...name, leads me to believe he really cares about me. I mean her. But, *I* want him, too.

We've been talking on the phone and texting each other almost every day since the night I whispered my cell number in his ear. And I've been sneaking off to meet him down at the boutique late in the evening when I know Paris is already home. Or we've been fucking in hotel rooms. Then, in between fucking him, I'm still fucking Royce.

With Royce, what we share can't go anywhere other than in the sheets. He's my guilty pleasure. I've told him this. He fucks me good. I enjoy spending quality time with him in bed; that's it. He's too young for anything else. He still needs to find his way. He's a damn waiter, for Christ's sake! There's nothing he can offer me besides that big-ass dick. And I make sure to fuck him at least once a week. And if it's on a night that Paris's mystery man wants to see me, I suck mystery man's dick real good, then let him stuff my ass. It feels so good in my ass. He's the first man I've ever experienced creaming out of my ass with. But, he's not as adventurous as I'd like him to be. I like tonguing a man's ass. Like slipping my finger into his asshole, massaging his prostate. Mystery man isn't open to that. Royce is. I like handcuffing and blindfolding men. I like being in control. Mystery man isn't open to that. Royce is. Mystery man's dick isn't long and thick. Royce's is. Still, I want them both.

"You're dressed like you have a hot date or something."

"I wish," I say, moving around the kitchen. My cell buzzes. I pull it out of my bag. It's a text from Mystery Man. U STILL CUMMIN THRU?

I quickly text back: YES!

I slip my phone back into my bag, opening a cabinet and pulling out a glass. I open the 'fridge and pour myself some pomegranate juice. Do anything to keep from looking into her eyes. "So where are you off to?" she asks.

"I have a new client I'm trying to snag," I say, putting my glass to my lips, then gulping down my lie. I sit the glass in the sink. "I better get going."

"Not that you need it, but good luck. I hope you reel him or her in."

"Thanks. I think already have," I tell her, grabbing my bag off the counter, then heading out the kitchen. She stops me in my tracks.

"Persia, when you covered for me down at the boutique, are you certain there weren't any calls for me; from a man, in particular?"

My breath catches in my throat as I turn to face her. The moment of truth has presented itself. "No, not that I can recall," I state evenly, keeping my gaze on hers. "I would've told you if

there had been. Why? I thought you asked me this already."
She tilts her head, staring at me. "No reason; just checking."

"Oh, okay. Well, I better get going," I say, quickly turning around and walking toward the door. *I'm sorry, Sis*, I think, opening the door, then shutting it behind me. I hop in my car, catching my reflection in the rearview mirror. *I hope you'll forgive me.*

Forty minutes later, he's spread eagle in the middle of his bed, finger-fucking my pussy while I lick around his balls and stroke his dick. Before he starts calling me *baby* and other mushy shit, I remind him how I want it: Slutty. Tell him I want it rugged, raw and rough. He grins. "I got you."

"Call me a bitch," I snap, yanking his balls.

He grunts, slapping my ass—*hard*. "Bitch…" The stinging shoots through my pussy to my clit. "Put that dick back in ya muthafuckin' mouth." He slaps my ass again. I feel my cream rising from the back of my pussy as I put my lips over the head of his dick, then start sucking; slowly at first, then fast and hard, sucking his pipe real greedy like. Slobbering and spitting all over it. Damn, his dick tastes so good. "Yeah, suck that shit," he urges. "There's nothin' like a wet, sloppy dick suck wit' a buncha spit. That's how the fuck a slutty bitch is 'posed to suck a dick." He thrusts his hips upward. "Suck the shit harder." I rapidly bob my head up and down. Moan and groan. I smack and spit and gobble up his dick until my nose is mashed into his groin. The harder I slurp, the wetter my pussy gets. He stirs my insides with two fingers, twisting and plunging until my juices drip all over his hand. "Oh, shit. Wet-ass pussy. You a real greedy dick suckin' freak, ain't you? You ready to catch this nut?"

"Mmmm," I moan, nodding my head. "MmmhmmMmmmhm-mmm…"

He grabs me by the back of the neck. "Go all the way down on it." I gag. "Don't you throw up on my shit…" He slaps my ass again. I moan. "Take ya time, baby." *What the fuck is he calling me that baby shit for? He and Paris deserve each other, with all this mushy shit!* "Breathe through ya nose…" I stifle a giggle as my throat relaxes. Pretending to struggle with sucking his fat dick only intensifies my horniness. Little does he know, sucking a dick under eight inches is a breeze. I feign a gag, then swallow until I have him all the way down in my throat. "Yeah, that's it…oh, fuck… throat that shit…" I swallow; breathe through my nose. Gulp him down balls deep. Swallow again, then start bobbing my head, giving him the throat the way he wants it—tight and wet.

In one swift motion, I'm sucking his dick and shifting my body into the sixty-nine position, lowering my pussy down on his face. He inhales my scent. The sweet muskiness seems to make his dick harder. He licks and darts his tongue in and out of me. I'm moaning. He's moaning. I rock and roll my body, grind my pussy down on his face. *Ohhhhhgod, this nigga eats pussy good*, I think, coming in his mouth. He licks my cream from around my swollen lips. Tells me to come up off of his dick and kiss him. I shift my body around and kiss him, sucking the rest of my sticky juice off of his lips and tongue.

I grind on his cock, smear my wet pussy all over the head. "I want you to fuck me," I whisper into his ear, nibbling on his earlobe. "I wanna feel this fat dick in me…"

"Not until you finish suckin' it," he tells me, pinching my nipples. An inferno erupts in me, causing a wildfire to spread through me. I grind harder on his big mushroom head, causing my juices to shoot out of my pussy and coat his dick. "Now suck my dick," he says, pushing me down toward it. "I'm ready to bust this nut in your mouth." I inch my way down his body, leaving a trail of kisses down his chest to his navel. I slip two fingers into my creamy snatch. Lock my lips around the head of his dick, grab it at the base, then rapidly stroke it. "Aaaah, yeah…aaaah… aaaah…uhhh…here it comes," he says in between grunts and moans. "Caaaaatch it…baby."

His nut pumps into my mouth, shoots to the back of my throat, filling me up with a mouthful of warm dick milk. "Yeah, baby… aaah fuck…eat that nut up."

I stick out my tongue, show him my coated tongue, then roll my tongue back and swallow. He smiles, watching me guzzle and gulp it all down, like the greedy lil' whore I am.

"Yo, ma, on some real shit," he says, watching me climb out of his bed. I still don't know what the hell his name is after all the sucking and fucking we've done. But, now that I'm finally at his apartment, I'm hoping to stumble across something that has his name on it. I stretch. I've been laid up with him for almost four hours. He's fucked me three times, once in my pussy; twice in my ass. Both holes still throb. "What's really good wit' you?"

I tilt my head. "What do you mean?" I ask, feigning innocence.

"I'm sayin'…what's up wit' you always wantin' a muhfucka to call you bitches 'n shit and treat you all smutty?"

'Cause I am. I shrug. "It's only role-play."

"Yo, I can dig it. But, I'm kinda missin' that sweet, sexy shit we had goin' on when we first started kickin' it. You had a muhfucka wantin' to make love to you; not fuck you like you some bird 'n shit. It's like you flipped a switch on a muhfucka, and now all you wanna do is get it in on some aggressive-type shit. The first few times, it was all good and shit. So don't get it fucked up. I dig gettin' it in rough 'n shit, too. But, I ain't wit' it all the time. That's not my thing. Sometimes I wanna make love to whoever I'm vibin' wit'. Call you my baby 'n shit, feel me? I'm not wit' callin' a shorty I'm feelin' a buncha bitches 'n shit when we in the sheets—all the time. Feel me? That shit's for them smutty broads."

I shift my weight from one foot to the other. Sweep my bang across my forehead. "You're feeling me?"

No, bitch, he's feeling Paris.

He shakes his head. "Yo, do you even have to ask?"

Paris's face appears. I try to blink it away. She's scowling at me. "You fucking *bitch!*" I hear her screaming in my head. "You no-good, backstabbing, man-stealing, sneaky-ass *bitch!* I hate you!"

I feel a headache coming on. I really like this man. And I don't want to keep misleading him. But telling him the truth will make matters worse. Shit! I can't do this with him. I have to bow out of this mess gracefully. End this shit with him before he gets too caught up. Before he starts thinking about me all the time. Before he becomes consumed with wanting, needing, me all the time, I have to stop this now—before he ends up falling deeper into my web of lies. All this I know, but not today. I walk back over to the bed, lean over and kiss him softly on the lips. He grins. "Yo, what's that for?"

"For being you," I say, kissing him again. This time I slip my tongue into his mouth. Allow myself to get lost in his mouth, then pull away. *And for having good dick that's going to be hard to let go of.*

He reaches for me, pulling me on top of him. "Yo, when you gonna invite me over to ya spot so we can kick back 'n chill?"

Never, I think, pecking him on the lips. I decide to tell him that I'm in between places, temporarily staying with my sisters until I'm able to move into my own place. I tell him the minute I move in, he'll be the first person I have over to help me christen each room.

"Aiight, that's wassup," he says, running his hands over my body, palming my ass. I grind on him. He kisses me, then looks me in the eyes. "Yo, I wanna make love to you."

Paris's voice plays him my head. *You fucking, man-stealing bitch!*

I close my eyes and whisper against his ear, "Then make love to me."

CHAPTER FORTY-NINE

I t's been three months and still Desmond has not called me, or stopped by the shop. And there's still no way for me to get in touch with him, so I've finally let it go. Shit, what else is there for me to do? I don't even know his last name. Obviously something changed. I'm just not sure what. *You're pregnant and he doesn't even know it.* And, at this point, it really doesn't matter. Fuck him! I'm so over him. Truth is, Persia did me a favor deleting those numbers. *Niggas*, I think, slipping into a pair of faded Prada jeans. My baby bump is starting to show more, but not in a way that I can't cover it with a loose-fitting blouse or something. I bend over and roll the bottoms into big cuffs, tuck my blouse in, then step into a pair of five-inch Prada sandals. "Now where the hell is that belt?" I walk back into my walk-in closet, pulling open my belt drawer. It's missing. I head for Porsha's room. I walk in. "Do you have my black and talc Prada belt with the studs on it?" I ask as she's walking out of her bathroom. She's wrapped in a towel with her cell pressed up against her ear. She's smiling. She holds a finger up, signaling for me to wait.

"Okay...I'll see you when I get back from the city...Me too...I can't wait either. You enjoy yours, too..." I can tell by the tone in her voice that she's talking to her mystery boo. The one she's still not ready to tell Persia and me about. I'm fine with it. As long as she's happy, that's all that matters to me. And judging by her disposition the last few months, I'd say she's definitely happy. "Okay, now what are you in here asking me for, hooker? Coming up in here disrupting my conversation."

I wave her on. "Whatever. Where's my Prada belt?"

She drops her towel. "Look in my closet. I wore it a couple of weeks ago." I walk into her closet. Two minutes later, I walk out with my belt in hand.

"Ummm, why is it when I borrow your shit I put it back when I'm done, but you seem to forget where to put mine?"

She stops oiling her naked body. Her beautiful brown skin shimmers. "Ummm, have you returned that leather Prada bag that your ass took up outta here almost year ago?"

I laugh. "Girl, it hasn't been *that* long."

"Mmmmph; just what I thought. And it's been damn near close to it."

"Whatever, how much longer are you going to be? I wanna get into the city before it gets too hectic."

"Chile, relax. It's only ten-thirty. I'll be ready in like ten minutes. Don't you see me tryna get dressed? Geesh. Where's Persia?"

I sit on the leather ottoman situated by the window, peering out of it. "You know she's downstairs dressed and ready. I'm surprised she hasn't already called up here to see what's taking you so long. You know she has no patience for waiting."

"She'll be fine. If not, she can go on without me. You too, boo."

I give her the finger. We're driving into the city to look for something to wear for Pasha's upcoming wedding, then going somewhere to have an early dinner. "Nooooo, wrong answer. We're all going together. So, get your ass in gear, and let's get moving."

"Yeah, you're right," she says, clasping her red LaPerla bra, then slipping into a pair of matching panties. It's bright, bold color looks good against her skin. "I want to be home by nine."

I smile. "You and your mystery boo have a hot date or something?"

She grins. "Something like that."

"Well, you know I'm not going to pry. But I'm dying to know who he is."

"You already know," she quickly stops herself.

"What, I already…"

She puts a finger up to her lips to quiet me. She walks over to her door and quietly shuts it. "Paris, you have to swear to me that you will not repeat a single word of this to Persia."

"Girl, you know I—"

"I'm serious, Paris. Not a word. Swear to me."

"Oh, damn. Who is he?"

"Not until you promise me you'll keep what I say to yourself. Until I'm ready to tell Persia, you have to keep this between us. I mean it." I promise her. Tell her my lips are sealed. And she knows I mean it. She leans in and whispers, "It's Em."

"Who? I don't know an Em?"

"Sssssh, if I wanted a loud broadcast, I woulda kept the door open."

I wave her on. "Girl, please. Stop all this Secret Squirrel shit and tell me who the hell this man is who has you all head-over-heels."

"It's Emerson," she says, lowering her voice.

My jaw drops, my eyes pop open. "Saaaaaaay, what?! Emerson, Emerson? The Emerson we used to fuck?"

She rolls her eyes, sucking her teeth. "How many Emersons do you know? Geesh. Yes, that Emerson."

"Ohmygod. Get. Out. Since when?"

"Girl, will you quiet the hell down. We've been seeing each other for almost five months now."

I grin. "Oooooh, you sneaky bitch," I whisper, getting caught up in the secret. I stand up to give her a hug. "I looooooove it. And you know Persia is—"

"You know Persia is what?" Persia says, walking through the door, catching Porsha and me in our embrace. She tilts her head. "What you hookers up in here hugging about?" Porsha and I both look at her, then each other.

"I was telling her you were going to have a damn fit if she didn't hurry her ass up."

She eyes us suspiciously, then shoots a look at me. "And you had to hug her to tell her that?" I tell her she was asking me if I was okay. That she has been worried about me, like she has been. Telling me she's here for me, if needed, like she is; like we are for each other. She seems to have brought the lie. "Oh, how sweet," she says, folding her arms. "While you two hookers have been up here hugging it up, I've been downstairs waiting on your slow asses."

"Umm, don't look at me," I say, sitting back down. "I'm dressed and ready."

She rolls her eyes, turning to walk out of the room. "Whatever. But you're in here holding Porsha's slow ass up, so same difference. Let's go already, geesh!"

"I'll be ready in a sec," Porsha tells her as she's walking out the room. Persia threatens to leave in her own car if she's not. Porsha waits a few minutes more, then mouths, "Do you think she heard us?"

I shrug. With Persia, even though she didn't say anything, there's no telling if she heard us or not. But, at this point, who really gives a shit? If Porsha is happy with Emerson, then so be it. Like I said, I'm happy for her. And Persia will just have to get the hell over it. Besides, I have some news of my own to share.

"Now that I have the two of you together," I say once we're seated at our table. "There's something that I need to tell you both." We've finished our shopping and we're now having dinner at The Pink Tea Cup down on Seventh Avenue in the Village, waiting for the waitress to come take our orders.

"Uh-oh," Porsha says, eyeing me over her menu. "This sounds like something we need to hear over a drink."

"Or two," Persia adds.

I laugh. "Y'all lushes look for any excuse..." I stop myself in midsentence as the bubbly, blonde-haired waitress approaches us.

She introduces herself as Melonie. "Are you ladies ready to order? Can I start you off with some drinks and appetizers?"

"Yes, that's sounds delicious. Umm, let's see," Persia says, scanning the drinks menu. "I'll have a martini, dirty."

"And I'll have a mojito," Porsha says.

"You can bring me an iced tea, please. And I'd like an order of soul rolls and crab cakes." Porsha and Persia buck their eyes. I look at them. "What?"

"*Iced tea?*" Porsha questions, frowning as the waitress walks off.

I shrug. "I don't feel like drinking."

Persia purses her lips. "If you ask me, you haven't felt like doing much of anything, lately."

"I know. I—" I stop myself from saying more when the waitress returns with our drinks, then takes our dinner orders. Porsha orders meatloaf with smothered onions, string beans, and mac 'n cheese. Persia orders jumbo shrimp with collard greens. And I order the chicken and sweet potato waffles.

"Let's make a toast," Porsha says, lifting her glass. Persia and I do the same. "To sisterly bonds. May we always remain close; no matter what." We clink our glasses, then take sips from our drinks. "Now tell us, why the hell you drinking iced tea?"

I set my glass on the table, clasping my hands in front of me. "That's what I want to talk to the two of you about." I pause, taking a deep breath. "I'm pregnant."

Persia and Porsha spit out their drinks. Persia flops back in her seat, covering her mouth. Porsha shakes her head in disbelief, grabbing a napkin to wipe her mouth. "You're whaaaaat?" they both ask once they've gotten themselves together.

I repeat myself. "I'm pregnant."

Porsha places her hand up on her chest. "Wait a minute. *Pregnant?* When did you get pregnant, and how? Scratch that. I know how. I wanna know by whom."

The color in Persia's face seems to have drained. "Yes, please tell us. *Who* are you pregnant by?"

"I sorta, kinda, let myself get involved with a guy I really know nothing about. He came into the boutique a few months back, and I liked what I saw. And I wanted to have him, *alone*. And I did. The problem is it was more than once. Then I started really liking him."

"Ooooh, you sneaky bitch," Porsha teases. "Details, boo. So who is he?"

"His name is Desmond."

Persia places a hand up over her neck as if she's cluthing pearls. She stays quiet as Porsha rattles off a list of questions. What does he look like? When will we get to meet him? Is it serious? Does he know?"

I take another sip from my glass. "You won't be meeting him. And, no, he doesn't know."

Porsha gives me a confused look. "And why not?"

"Because he's stopped coming around and I don't have a way of getting in touch with him. He would call the store for me, then we'd make plans to see each other. I had planned on giving him my number when I got back from Pennsylvania. But, he never called again. Just like that..."—I snapped my fingers—"...he's vanished." Porsha wants to know why I can't get his number from off the caller ID. I tell her why.

"Mmmph," she grunts. "That's some bitch-ass bullshit. Maybe he had another woman."

I shake my head. "I don't know. He told me he didn't. And I believed him."

"Girl, you know niggas will tell you anything to get with you."

"I realize that, but he seemed different."

Persia quietly shifts in her seat. "Damn, girl, you alright over there?" Porsha asks, eyeing her. "You look like you're about to pass out."

She shakes her head. "I'm in shock; that's all." She brings her attention to me. "How many months are you?"

"Three," I say.

"Then you can still get rid of it," she says. Porsha and I look at her. "What? You are getting rid of it, right?"

I shake my head. "*No*...I'm keeping it."

"I can't do this anymore with you."

Desmond frowns. "Yo, you can't do what with me?"

"This," I say, sitting up on the edge of the bed. I've finished sucking his dick for the second time today and have been laid up in bed with him since this afternoon, savoring the last dose of dick I'll get from him after tonight. I'm cutting him off. I have to before this gets too out of hand. Okay, it's already out of hand, which is why I have to end this before it gets any worse than it already is. I can't stop thinking about what Paris dumped on Porsha and me last week. That she's pregnant. *Pregnant!* I honestly thought I was going to faint when she told us that. I literally broke out in a sweat. She's pregnant by *him* and he has no clue. I'm the one fucking him, and he has no clue. I can't stop thinking about Paris actually wanting to keep it. *Why in the hell would she want to keep a baby by a man she hardly knows?* This whole situation is a mess. One I created.

The only good thing out of all of this is that I got to have some of that thick chocolate between his legs, and now I finally know his name. Three months of fucking this man and I've had no clue who the hell he is.

He gives me a confused look. "Where's this comin' from? I thought we were vibin'."

I'm pregnant...I'm keeping it...

"Desmond, we were vibing. I mean, we are. It's just that..." I pause, trying to find the right words. Telling him what I know is not an option.

"You wanna fall back," he answers for me. I attempt to kiss him. He jerks his head back. "Nah, fuck that. I wanna know what you meant by that." He swings his legs around, and stands up. I try not to stare at his naked body. "Are you sayin' you wanna dead this?"

I nod, then shake my head. "No, I mean, yes. I don't want to, but I have to. I really like you," I say, pausing. I get up from the bed and walk over to him. Grab his hand. My small hand gets lost in his. *But I'm not who you think I am. And by the way, my sister's pregnant by you.*

"But?" he says, giving me a sideview stare.

"But my life is kind of complicated right now. There are things about me that you wouldn't understand."

"Like what?"

I slowly shake my head. "It doesn't matter. The fact is, as much as I want to be with you, I can't." He lets go of my hand. Walks over to the other side of the room and picks up his boxers. I watch as he slips them on. "I don't mean to hurt you."

He looks over at me. "Nah, I'm good, yo. I wish you woulda told me this shit sooner, instead of havin' a muhfucka gettin' all into you 'n shit. It's all good, though. It was fun while it lasted."

"I'm so sorry. I really, really like you."

He half-laughs. "You *like* me? Oh, shit. Well, check this out. I was really, really feelin' you, aiight? I wasn't only *likin'* you. I was diggin' you, hard. But, hey...it is what it is."

Persia, you owe this man the truth.

Truths aren't always what they appear to be.

You're right. Not when they're based on distorted realities. Give him the truth. That you're not Paris; that you've been misleading him. That she's carrying his baby.

The truth doesn't matter, anymore. The damage is already done. I'm not risking losing my sister over this.

The minute you tricked him and fucked him in her store, you lost her.

Dicks come a dime a dozen. Paris will meet someone else. I'm doing them both a favor.

But she's pregnant by this man.

Not for long. Hopefully I can convince her to have an abortion before it's too late.

"I swear, I never meant for this to happen."

He scowls at me, placing both hands up on his hips. "You never meant for what to happen?"

"To care about you the way I do." Truth is, I really have gotten attached to him. Well, not him, his dick. Actually, I love his dick. But, shit. I love Royce's dick, too. Why couldn't Paris stick to the fucking script instead of straying off with this man? All she had to do is bring him around for the three of us to share. And none of this would've happened. Now, he thinks I'm her. She's pregnant. He has deep feelings for her. She thinks he dissed her. And now I have to be the one to dump him.

"I'm seeing someone else," I finally offer, bringing him as close to the truth as I possibly can. A half-truth is better than none. He squints at me. His jaw tightens.

"You seein' someone? You mean as in fuckin'?"

I nod. "I'm so sorry. The last thing I've wanted to do was hurt you."

"Yo, I'm not hurt. I'm disappointed. But, it's all good. I'm glad you told me before I got in too deep." He gathers my clothes, walks over and hands them to me. "Yo, I think you should go."

I get up from his bed and slip on my bra and panties, then slide back into my clothes. He watches as I slip on my heels, then walks me to the door.

I reach for him, but he pulls away. I can tell he's hurt, even though he says he's not. He's an innocent victim in my sick-twisted game. I honestly feel bad. But, it's all for the best. He and Paris will both go on with their lives, never knowing anything different. Other than he stopped calling her, and she was fucking someone else. "I'm not the woman you think I am."

He eyes me, shaking his head. I see sadness. "Yeah, obviously not," he says, opening the door. He watches as I walk toward the elevators. He waits until I step in, then shuts the door. The elevator doors close and I'm left alone with my lies seeping from my pores, along with the musky fuck-smell that still oozes out from between my legs.

"Porsha, we have to convince Paris to get an abortion, and fast," Persia says in a hushed tone, looking over her shoulder to make sure Paris isn't in earshot. We're sitting at the kitchen table. Persia is seated in a chair next to me. "This whole situation is a mess."

I blink. "This whole situation is a mess for whom?"

She gives me an indignant look. "For Paris, who else? I mean, how could she be so careless, getting pregnant by some stray man?"

"Umm, I guess she got pregnant the same way you did when you screwed—"

"This isn't about me," she snaps, cutting me off. "Yes, I went off and fucked Brandon and his cousin. And I've apologized for that. I was fourteen and reckless. I can't believe you'd bring that up after all this time. And *that* situation was totally different than Paris's."

Brandon was a boy I dated my freshman year in high school. But unbeknownst to me, he was Persia's, too. They had been fucking for almost six months before I found out. One night, he asked her if his nineteen-year-old cousin, who was visiting for the summer, could watch the two of them fuck, then join in. She let him. And not only did she end up not knowing which one had gotten her pregnant, she ended up with gonorrhea as well.

"Look, I didn't mean to bring that up; wrong example. What I meant was we've all been careless at one time or another. Paris is a grown woman. And if she wants to keep this baby, then she should. And we should be there to help her through this. Not whispering behind her back, conspiring how to convince her to get rid of it."

She shoots me an incredulous look. "So you're actually telling me that you're okay with this?"

"Why wouldn't I be? She's our sister. I love her. And I respect her decision to know what she's doing. You should do the same."

"She's making a big mistake."

"Then it's one you don't have to live with," I remind her. "So let it go."

"Let what go?" Paris asks, walking into the kitchen. Persia and I look in her direction.

"The fact that you're pregnant," I say, glancing at Persia. "Persia thinks you should have an abortion."

Paris shakes her head, opening the refrigerator. "And how do you feel about it?"

"I'm going to love you no matter what you decide to do. And I'm going to love my little niece or nephew as if it were my own. Although, I hate to say, I'm so glad it's you pregnant and not me."

She shuffles over to the table, biting into an apple. I'm shocked at how big her stomach looks this morning. "I'm almost at the end of my first trimester. I'm not having an abortion; period. Yes, I made a mistake by not using a condom with Desmond. I was aware of what I was doing—living on the edge. But, this baby inside of me will not be born a mistake. I'm thankful I don't have HIV or some other disease." She eyes Persia. "Please, save your breath. You're going to be an aunt, so get used to it."

"Fine," she says, folding her arms across her chest. "When are you going to tell our parents?"

"Yeah, and what are you going to tell them?" I ask.

She sighs. "I really haven't thought about it. I'll tell them after Pasha's wedding next week."

"Umm," I say, pointing in the direction of her protruding baby knot. "Do you think you're going to be able to hide it?"

She looks at her stomach, pushing it out, then holding it in. "I'll wear a girdle and eat very light," she says, laughing at first, then busting out into tears. "I don't know what the hell I'm getting myself into. How does a man go from calling you every day, wanting to see you and sex you, to not calling you at all? No, 'I'm not interested,' no 'I've changed my mind,' nothing. It doesn't make sense to me."

I get up from my seat. "Girl, you know we're here for you." I look over at Persia. "Aren't *we*, Persia?"

"Of course we are. If he could disappear like that without a word, then obviously he was no good for you. If anything, he did you a favor."

"Yeah, you're right," Paris says, wiping her face with her napkin. She blows her nose. "It's still mindboggling, though. Niggas. He really seemed different."

"Obviously he wasn't," Persia says dismissively. "Sounds like he was a no-good, lying-ass nigga." I eye her. And she eyes me back. I can't put my finger on it, but, for some reason, Persia seems very uneasy about this whole pregnancy thing. "Who knows how many other women he's done this to. I say good riddance to his ass."

Paris sighs, wiping her face. She pats me on the hand. "Thanks. I'm a big girl, and I'm going to be okay. But, right now, I'm scared to death, bringing a baby into this world by myself, then having to raise it."

"Girl, plenty of women do it," I offer. "Men walk out and leave women to raise their kids every day by themselves. You're going to be fine. And you'll be a great mother."

"Thanks. I can do it. What bothers me the most is that he doesn't even know about it. If he walked out on me because of that, then I could swallow his disappearing act better. But, he stopped all communication without any warning. That's what I have difficulty with. If I ever run into him again, I'm going to slap the shit out of him."

Persia reaches over and grabs Paris's hand. "And this is why I really think you should reconsider having this baby. All it's going to be is a constant reminder of how fucked up he was. How he changed up on you. Every time you look at that baby, you're going to see that no-good nigga and start resenting it."

Paris shakes her head, rubbing her stomach. "I'm not doing it. This baby is going to be loved. And when he or she is old enough to understand, I'll tell them the truth. That he didn't know about them. That I love them in spite of not knowing their father."

"Well, that settles it," I say. "We need to start converting one of our bedrooms into a nursery. But, first, boo, you're going to need to buy a new dress for the wedding because I don't think you're going to be able to fit that little sexy number."

She laughs. "Oh, trust me. I'll stuff my ass into that thing, even if I have to wear a corset over a girdle. Come hell or high water, that dress is going to be worn."

Persia gets up from her seat. "I guess this'll be something else Mother can talk about."

Paris shrugs. "I guess it will be. Fact is I don't care what she thinks, or says."

"Ummm, speaking of which," I say, shifting in my seat. "Since I have the two of you here, I have some news of my own."

Persia flops back down in her seat. "Oh, God, please don't tell me you're pregnant, too."

I laugh. "Girl, hell no. Didn't you hear me when I said I was glad Paris was pregnant instead of me?"

"That's a relief," Persia says, letting out a deep breath. "Then what is it?"

I glance at Paris, then smile. "The mystery man in my life is Emerson."

She blinks. "You've got to be kidding me."

I shake my head. "No. I'm serious. Emerson and I have been going hot and heavy for a few months now."

Persia just stares at me, long and hard, then finally asks, "Why?"

O h, how I wish Persia could have seen the look on her face when Porsha revealed that she was seeing Emerson. It was…priceless!

"I don't fucking believe this. Tell me this is a joke."

Porsha shook her head. "It's not a joke. Emerson and I have been seeing each other for the last five months."

"I thought we had a pact to not see any men we cut off behind each other's backs?"

"We did," Porsha stated. "But I never wanted to cut him off. You did."

"And you agreed to it."

"Yeah, unfortunately I did."

"So you're the woman Emerson was talking about?"

Porsha nodded. Persia shook her head. "I can't believe both of you hookers have been keeping secrets from me. Are there any others that either of you might wanna share with me now?"

"Persia," I said. "I know you're upset that we didn't share this with you. But the fact of the matter is you spend too much time trying to micro-manage us. We're grown women, who are entitled to do what we want, with whomever we want as long as we're not maliciously or purposefully trying to hurt anyone else."

"Persia, Emerson is a really good man," Porsha offered. "And he loves me."

She stared at Porsha. "And the fact that"—She pointed around the room at Porsha and me—"all three of us have slept with him is okay with you?"

"No, at first it wasn't. I struggled with it. But, what we did with him was a mutual decision. I didn't know he had feelings for me. And I didn't know that I would have any for him. But I do. And he's not interested in fucking either of you, again. So, yes—now, I'm more than okay with it."

"I'm happy for you," I stated, giving her a hug. "I'm glad it's finally out in the open so you can finally bring him around."

Persia frowned. "I don't want him here."

Porsha raised her brow, placing a hand up on her hip. "And why not?"

"Because don't you think that having Emerson in our home after we've fucked him every which way is going to be a whole lot uncomfortable for all of us?"

"Not for me," I said. "I've always liked Emerson. I mean, it's unfortunate that I know what the man's dick looks and feels like…"

Porsha sucked her teeth, rolling her eyes. "Ugh! Gee, thanks. Don't remind me."

I laughed.

Persia frowned. "I don't think it's a good idea for him to come here."

"Well, this is my home, too. And eventually he will be here. So you're going to have to get used to the idea, or do your best to avoid him. But, we're a couple. I'm not going to keep staying the night at his house. Some nights, he's going to stay here. If that's not going to work for you, then I'll have to make other arrangements because I won't live someplace where my man isn't welcomed."

I gasped. The posssibility that the three of us would one day no longer live together had never dawned on me, or them. We customized this house with the understanding that the three of us would get married and live here with our husbands as one big, happy family. But nothing ever turns out the way we think it should.

Persia blinked. "You'd actually move out?"

Porsha nodded. "Yes, Persia, I will. I love this man. I want you to be happy for me. But, if you can't, then that's fine, too. I'm still going to be with him. If it doesn't work out between the two of us, then it doesn't. I was wrong for keeping my relationship with him from you. I apologize. I realize how stubborn and strong-willed you can be when you believe in something. And I didn't wanna fight with you about it."

Persia walked over to her. "I don't want you to move out. I don't want you to ever feel like you can't bring whomever you want here. This is our home. We built this place. We've shared a lot of memories here. I'll get over it. I'll be happy for you; just give me a minute to digest it all." They hugged. "Wait a minute. I'm not that stubborn, am I?" Persia asked, looking over at me.

I nodded my head. "Yeah, you are. You're actually almost as bad as Mother."

Persia groaned.

Paris and I laughed. Shit, that's all we could do. I'm pregnant by a man who I'll probably never see again. And Porsha's involved with a man the three of us have bounced up and down on. Definitely not how we envisioned our lives. But, it is what it is.

I walk over to the window and look out through the curtains. There's a very attractive couple walking with their two little girls. The father is pulling them in a red wagon with one hand, and holding the woman's hand with the other. She has her free hand up on her stomach, slowly rubbing it. She looks like she's almost ready to deliver any minute. I keep my eyes trained on them until they're no longer in sight—rubbing my own belly, wondering, imagining what life will be like as a single mother. Hoping I've made the right decision to keep it. At least I don't have to wonder who my child's father is. This baby was conceived out of lust; nothing more, nothing less. And sometimes I'm bothered by the fact that I didn't use protection with Desmond; that I put myself in this predicament. I'm so pissed at him for being such an asshole. For not being man enough to say he wasn't interested. I'm pissed at the fact that there was no closure. And yes, this baby growing inside of me will be a constant reminder of what I shared with him for those few months. Still, I have no regrets. If I could do it all over again, I would, but I'd use a damn condom.

My cell rings, snapping me out of my reverie. I smile, answering. "Hi, Daddy."

"Hey, babygirl, how's my beautiful daughter doing?"

I feel myself getting choked up. "I'm so happy to hear your voice."

"You sure know how to put a smile on your old man's face."

"Oh, Daddy," I tease. "You say that to Persia and Porsha, too."

He chuckles. "You're right. And it's true. Have I told you how proud I am of you lately?" Without any warning, I burst into tears. The idea of my son or daughter not ever experiencing the kind of love with Desmond in the way I experienced with my own father, tears me up inside. I'm so overwhelmed with emotions. Telling him I'm pregnant is going to be one of the hardest things I'll ever have to do. Not because he'll be hurt, or disappointed in me. It'll be looking into his eyes and seeing how he looks into mine. As if I'm still his precious little girl. "Baby, what's wrong? Why are you crying?"

"I love you so much, Daddy. I'm so happy to have you as a father."

"Aww, babygirl. Your old man loves you, too."

I decide that when I deliver my baby, I want him there with me. Just as he watched my mother give birth to my sisters and me, I want him to witness the birth of his first grandchild. I break down, crying again.

"Baby, are you sure everything's okay? Do you need me to come over there?"

"No, Daddy. I'm fine, really."

"No you're not," he says, concern etched in his tone. "Look, where are you?"

"I'm home."

"I'm on my way."

"Daddy, I'm pregnant," I say, placing a hand up on my stomach, sitting next to him on the sofa.

He stares at me, reaches over and takes my hand. He squeezes it. "How many months?"

"Four."

"Wow, four months." He smiles. "My little girl is gonna be a mother. Does your mother know?"

I shake my head. "No, and please don't tell her. I plan on telling her after Pasha's wedding. The last thing I want to be is the table discussion for the night."

He chuckles, knowingly. "My lips are sealed, babygirl. Now who's the lucky fella?"

"His name is Desmond."

"Is he one of the fellas the three of you—"

"No, not all."

I can tell he's relieved. He wants to know how we met. Wants to know what his intentions are. I tell him everything. When I'm done filling him in, he pulls me into him and kisses me on the head. "It's going to work out. I'm going to do whatever I can for you and my grandbaby."

I nod into his chest. "I know." We both welcome the silence as he holds me for what seems like forever until I finally sit up. "I couldn't have an abortion, Daddy. This baby is a part of me."

He smiles, cups the side of my face in his warm hands. Then strokes my cheek with the back of his hand the way he used to when I was a little girl. "Baby, you don't have to explain anything to me. That little baby is going to be smothered with love. And don't you worry about your mother. She'll come around. Trust me. The minute she sees him, she's going to melt."

I smile. "Daddy, how do you know it's going to be a boy? It could be a girl."

He shakes his head, reaching over and rubbing my stomach. "No, babygirl, you're carrying my grandson."

I start crying again. "I'm so sorry, Daddy."

"Sorry for what? You've done nothing wrong."

"For making you so ashamed of me."

He scoots closer to me and pulls me back into his arms. "Oh, babygirl, I'm not ashamed of you. I'm your father. And my love for you and your sisters will always be unconditional; no matter what. You hear me?"

I nod. Having my father here and hearing his words is the soothing balm I needed for my wounded spirit. I kiss him on his cheek. "I love you, Daddy."

He squeezes me. "I love you more."

"Mother...what are you doing here?"

She raises her perfectly arched brows, placing a neatly manicured hand on her hip. "Well, hello to you, too. Are you going to invite me in, or do I have to stand outside in this damn August heat?"

I take a deep breath. I'm inclined to shut the door in her face, but I can't. I step back and allow her in. "What brings you here? Paris is down at the store. And Porsha's over at her office."

She sits her handbag up on the coffee table. "I know where they are. I'm here to see you."

"*Me?*" I ask, frowning. "What for?" I eye her as she takes a seat on the sofa. Then she has the nerve to ask for something cold to drink like I'm in the mood to play hostess to her. "What would you like, water, cranberry juice or seltzer water?" She tells me seltzer water with very little ice. A few minutes later, I'm handing her a glass. I sit across from her; watch as she takes a sip. "So what is it you want to talk to me about?" I ask, wanting this to be over with as quickly as possible.

"I thought it was time you and I have a nice, long chat. Wouldn't you agree?"

I raise my brow. "A chat for what?"

"It's time for you and me to clear the air before Pasha's wedding next weekend. I'd hoped to do it a few months ago, but after how rude you were during brunch, I decided to ignore you."

"So then why are you here now?" I ask, folding my arms across my chest.

"Because I decided that it was time for me to confront you. There's going to be a lot of family at Pasha's wedding that we haven't seen in a long time. And the last thing I want is for there to be any mess."

"And what makes you think there would be any mess?"

"'Cause you can be messy, Persia. It doesn't take much for you to go off. We both know how nasty your attitude is."

"And we both know how messy your mouth is." I snap defensively. The nerve of her! "My attitude is fine as long as you don't say anything crazy."

She tsks. "*And* I'm hoping you leave it at home and not do or say anything to ruin Pasha's day. I realize how you can be when all the attention isn't on you."

My mouth drops open. *This fucking*…I stop myself from telling her to get the fuck out of my home. "She's our mother," I hear Paris say. *Big fucking deal!* "Excuse you? You're hoping *I* don't do anything to ruin it. Are you serious? You're the messy one. All you do is sit around and talk about everyone, including your own daughters. When have I ever said or done anything to ruin a family event?"

She tilts her head. "Persia, you heard what I said," she says, ignoring my question. "Leave your attitude here, or don't show up."

I laugh at her. "Who are you to tell me to stay home? It's not your wedding, nor are you in control of the guest list. And you're definitely not in any position to stop me from going anywhere. Sorry to burst your bubble, Mother. But I'm going to be there. Bottom line, the problem isn't me; it's you."

She glares at me. "You know what, I'm going to forget that I'm your mother for one minute and deal with you on the level you seem to want me to be on. So let's finally get this out in the open. Since you're so gully and wanna treat me like I'm some street bitch, from one *bitch* to another, what the *fuck* is your problem with me?"

I blink, shocked that she's come at me in this fashion. I watch as she slips out of her heels. Either her feet are hurting, or she's preparing to jump up and charge me. Either way, I brace myself, rising up in my seat as well. As I'm sitting here with her, it dawns on me that this is the first time she and I have been alone in a room together in years. There's no Porsha or Paris or Daddy to keep us from killing each other. There's nothing but space and air between us. She stares me down. I stare back. "Well, I'm waiting."

"You already know all of this."

"I want to hear it again," she says, shifting back in her seat.

I remain perched on the edge of mine; just in case. "I see you as a weak woman," I admit, staring directly into her eyes. She doesn't blink. "You sat around and let Daddy cheat on you, then you'd wanna run out to chase him down, banging on doors and confronting his whores instead of leaving him."

"Are you serious? The fact that I stayed with my husband, *your* father, and raised my daughters, made sure you all had the best of everything, and kept our home intact while he was out there cheating, makes me weak? I married your father knowing what kind of man he was. Yes, he had other women. But make no mistake, a fool I was not. And weak, I was not. Hurt, yes. But never anyone's fool. Your father did nothing I didn't allow him to do to me. He cheated on me because *I* let him. And leaving him was never an option, regardless of how many women he slept with. I chose to stay with him because I loved him then, and I love him now. He took care of home. And he took damn good care of you girls. Yes, I could've left him. Yes, I could've put him out. And I did pack his shit, numerous times. But he kept coming back."

"Because *you* kept taking him back," I state, rolling my eyes. "You acted like you couldn't live without him."

"*I* didn't want to," she snaps. "I took him back because I *wanted* him back. Not because I needed him. Not because I couldn't live without him. Our home, his business, everything we own, is in *my* name. If I wanted to be the messy wife, I could've divorced him and walked off with every-damn-thing and never looked back. And your father knew it. But I wanted my marriage. And, yes, I turned a blind eye to his other women as long as they stayed in their place and respected my space. That was our agreement. So forgive me for loving your father and for wanting to keep my marriage instead of walking out on everything we built together."

"Then that makes you no different from me. You willingly and knowingly shared him, period!"

"Girlfriend," she snaps, leaning forward in her seat with her hand on her hip. "I'm *nothing* like your nasty, trifling ass."

"Whatever. The fact is, for years, you shared him with other women, so you're just as nasty and trifling. Yet, you have a problem with what *we* do."

She lets out a disgusted grunt. "Ugh! Don't you dare sit there and compare what I did to the nastiness you've dragged your sisters into."

"Mother, you have no idea what you're talking about," I say, defensively. "I haven't dragged Porsha or Paris into *any*thing. They're grown women. They don't have to do anything they don't want to."

"And you've always been able to manipulate them."

"I haven't manipulated them into doing anything. You're delusional and jealous."

She snorts. "Jealous of what, the relationship you have with your sisters? The three of you are *supposed* to be close—you're sisters. That's how I raised you all to be. But that doesn't change the fact that you're a conniving, manipulative little *bitch*—excuse my French. But, the truth is the truth. Even when you were little girls, you always found a way to get Paris and Porsha to side with you. They idolized you. They've been so blinded by their love for you that they haven't been able to see what kind of sick hold you've had on them. But trust me. One day they'll see you for what you truly are. A nasty bitch! And you're going to end up losing both of them."

I'm literally stunned that she's called me a *bitch*, right here in my own home—not once, but twice. I take a deep breath to steady my nerves. But the truth is, I'm ready to go off on her. "Mother, it's time for you to grab your bag and go before I say or do something that *you'll* regret."

She remains in her seat. "I'm not leaving until we finish this conversation. So, if you feel like you wanna do or say something, then you do it. And I'll beat the shit out of you. Trust me on this, darling child of mine. I've had enough of your mouth and your disrespect. I'm your mother, whether you like it or not."

I clench my teeth. "I'm a grown-ass woman. I own my own business, and I *handle* my business. Look around you. Everything in here my sisters and I have worked for. I don't ask you for anything, and neither do they. So what we do with our lives is none of your business. You want respect, then respect *me*. You come up into my home and disrespect me. You call me a fucking bitch in my home."

"Well, you are," she snaps. "So get over it. I've accepted that you and I will never have any other type of relationship other than what we already have; strained."

I shift back in my seat, glaring at her. "Okay, *Mother*. And your point?"

"The point is, Persia, I know you don't like me; you never have. Every chance you've gotten, you've tried to make that little fact known. And, yes, it used to hurt, knowing that one of my daughters had so much disdain and hatred toward me. But it's okay 'cause you are an evil, miserable woman. You always will be."

"How dare you?" I snap, leaning forward in my seat. "You don't know a damn thing about me, Mother."

She shakes her head. "You were a sneaky, vindictive little bitch growing up, and you're sneaky and vindictive now. You're full of hate. That's what I know."

"Mother...get out!" I yell, jumping up from my seat. I storm over to the door, swinging it open. "Get out of my goddamn house, now!"

She stands up, slipping back into her heels, then grabbing her handbag. "Oh, I'll get out, but know this. Just like you went out and fucked Porsha's boyfriend and his cousin then got your little nasty ass pregnant, I know in my gut it was *you* who fucked all those boys out in the woods, then told them your name was Paris. It was because of *you* and your whorish-ass ways that the kids were whispering and calling Paris a whore and slut behind her back; a reputation that rightfully belonged to *you*. *You* fucked those boys. *You* let them run their dicks all up in you every-which-a-way. And *you* sat back and let your sister deal with the backlash. And, still, she forgave you. Because you're her sister and she loves you. But the shit you've done to them is despicable. If I were them, I wouldn't want anything to do with you."

I swallow, hard. She's bringing up my past, snatching my skeletons from out of their hiding place and throwing their bones back in my face. I have no words other than, "Get the fuck out of my house!"

"I'm leaving, but make no mistake. If you ever jump up like you're ready to fight, I'm going to forget that I gave birth to you and I'm gonna give you a good old-fashioned, Newark beatdown."

I stare at her as she walks by me. "I fucking hate you." The words come out in a low mumble, but audible enough for her to hear.

Slap!

I blink.

Slap!

"I know you hate me. And I don't give a *fuck* if you ever open your mouth to say another word to me. Because the truth is, I don't like you, either. And I never have. I love you because you're my child, but *bitch*, I'll beat you into the fucking ground if you *ever* talk to me like that again."

I'm literally paralyzed by shock. My ears ring, and I'm seeing stars. This woman has slapped me *and* admitted she doesn't like me! I am done!

Pain

CHAPTER FIFTY-FOUR

It's nine o'clock at night.

Royce's fingers dig into my hips as he thrusts in me; his humongous Mandingo cock piercing me to the seams, stretching my pussy beyond capacity. A sweet, delicious pain sweeps through my body like a wildfire. A moan bursts from my throat. "Ohh-hhhhhgod...this dick is so good..."

"Yeah, ma...this good dick is all yours..."

"You like fucking this pussy?"

"Aaaah, shit yeah...I love fuckin' this wet-ass pussy..." He pushes my legs up over my head, watches as his dick slides in and out of me. He pulls it out to the head, slowly stirs the opening of my slit. "Slap that clit for me..."

I smack and pop my clit. My cunt drools and nips at the head of his cock, like a hungry mouth as he teases me with it. He pulls it all the way out, then slams it back in. picking up his pace. I lift my hips; welcome him deep. The pressure of his dick pounds my G-spot, vibrating through my clit. My body is flush, my chest heaving. I pinch my tight nipples. Royce's relentless thrusting causes a ball of intense fire to erupt around the opening of my pussy. I moan, digging my nails into his flesh.

He moans. "Aaaah, shit you got some hot pussy..."

"Oh, yes...fuck me, little daddy...beat my pussy up...aaaaah-hhh..."

He rolls over onto his back, rolling me on top of him. His dick still stuffed deep inside of me. "I want you to ride this big dick," he tells me, squeezing a big chunk of my ass, then slapping it. "Cum all over it."

I reach in back of me, grab at his balls as I ride him. My ass going up and down, it doesn't take long before I feel a burning sensation ripping through my loins and I'm coming, long and hard.

Royce has become a regular in my bed. A three times a week fuck; sometimes four.

"Uhhhhhh…oooh…this big-ass, motherfucking dick…make my pussy so hot…slap my titties, motherfucker." It is his cue. I want it rough. He slaps each one, striking my nipples. I grunt, galloping up and down the length of his shaft. I slap his face. He slaps me back.

"Yeah, ride this dick, bitch…"

"Who's bitch am I?" I ask, pinching his nipples. He moans. Juts his hips upward, stabbing into me. I match him thrust for thrust.

"Mine," he says in a throaty whisper.

"Choke me then, nigga."

I have my hands around his throat. He places his hands around mine and squeezes until my eyes bulge. I start to feel light-headed. In a flash, the orgasm comes in hot, rapid waves. Gut-deep sensations surge through me. I lean in; bite Royce's bottom lip. He bites me back. We go at it rough and dirty for forty minutes before he's standing up, dipping at the knees, rapidly fucking me. A guttural bellow pushes out of me. I'm coming again. I wrap my arms around his neck and kiss him, my tongue probing deeply into his mouth. I close my eyes, then open them, staring into his young, handsome, sweaty face. My body trembles and Royce moans as hot, tight spasms milk his shaft. He's squeezing my ass, fucking me up and down over his cock. His mouth finds my left nipple. He bites it, causing me to cry out. Scream and buck up against him, my pussy juice squirting as he shudders, spurting his hot nut.

He falls back on the bed, panting hard and exhausted with his cock still tucked inside my sticky, slick cunt. I collapse on top of him, resting my head on his shoulder as I continue to shake. I'm still coming. I grind down on his dick nice and slow, then lift up off of it. I pull the condom off, then take his dick into my mouth, sucking his sweet creamy nut.

He wraps his hand in my hair, bouncing my head up and down. "Damn, ma…yeah, suck that dick…I'm gettin' ready to bust another nut right down in ya throat." I continue sucking his dick, then lapping at his balls, then licking his asshole. My fingers slip behind his balls while my wet tongue probes and dances against his tight manhole. When he relaxes, I slip a finger in. He gasps. I pop his dick back into my mouth, then "Aaaaahhh, shit…" I increase the suction on his dick, curling my finger until I am massaging his prostrate. I look up slantways at him. His eyes are rolling up in his head. I can tell he's starting to feel the pressure building up in his balls, his ass, in the pit of his stomach as he bucks his hips, and grabs at the sheets. He thrusts his hips upward, clogging my throat with his cock. In between loud grunts, he comes hard, flooding my mouth with his cum. I swallow as much as I can, allowing the overflow to spill out of my mouth and onto my chin.

I'm in love with this man's dick. And I'll continue to fuck him. I may have let Desmond go out of necessity, but not Royce. He stays. I lick my lips, scoop the cream that clings to my chin off with my fingers, then lift them to his mouth. He sucks them clean. Watching Royce eat his own cum has turned me on even more.

I smile.

And he smiles back. "I gotta 'nother nut for you." He pushes my head down. "Finish sucking it outta my dick."

I oblige him, wrapping my lips around his dick, then sucking and humming until I've sucked it clean as a whistle and he's fallen off to sleep.

"I swear I hope that woman doesn't open her mouth to say shit to me," Persia says, washing her Neutrogena face mask off. "I don't even want to look in her face."

I roll my eyes up in my head. "And what woman are you talking about?" I ask, knowingly. She's referring to our mother. It's been a week since the face-slapping incident and she's still harping on it. When I came home and saw her face bruised and she told me mother had slapped her, I knew she must have pushed the envelope with her.

Interestingly, Persia's version of the story is that Mother barged her way into the house demanding to talk to her, then started verbally attacking her. Then when she asked her to leave, she hauled off and smacked her. Of course Mother's version is somewhat different. And I believe hers over Persia's. I know our mother. And I know how her mouth can be. But, I also know Persia. And if Mother slapped her, it was for good damn cause.

"I'm talking about *your* mother, who else?" she states, brushing her teeth.

I get up from my seat and walk over to the bathroom, leaning up against the doorframe. "Umm, considering we're all sitting at the same table, I'm not sure how that's gonna work out for you. And I'm thinking this whole seating situation might be a bit uncomfortable with all the tension between the two of you."

She rinses her mouth. "Hopefully, I can switch seats with some-one and not have to be bothered with her."

I eye her. "Are you sure you want to go? I'm sure Pasha will understand. Actually, I'm sure she'd prefer you not be there if you and Mother are going to get into it. The last thing we need is the two of you tearing the place up."

She drops her towel, walking out of the bathroom. I watch her as she bounces around her bedroom naked, pulling out under-wear until she finds the right pair to wear. Then she tosses them all back in the drawer, deciding not to wear any. "Trust me. I have no intentions of saying anything to that woman. After that stunt she pulled, she's dead to me. So there's nothing to worry about. I'm not going to get into it with her. I'm going to the wedding. I'm going to have myself a damn good time, in spite of her. If I'm lucky enough, there'll be a fine-ass groomsman I can fuck in the backseat of one of the limos."

I shake my head, watching her lotion her body. "Persia, don't you think you need to take some responsibility for what happened?"

She stops what she's doing and stares at me. "So, you're saying I'm responsible for that woman coming up in here disrespecting me, then slapping me? I did nothing to her. She attacked *me*."

"No, that's not what I'm saying."

"Then what are you saying?" she asks defensively. She has her hand on her hip.

I glance at the crystal clock on her dresser. It's a quarter to three. The wedding is at five. "Persia, we both know you're not the victim here. Your attitude toward our mother has always been nasty. It's no wonder the two of you have never gotten along. If you ask me, both of you are stubborn, and overly opinionated. I can't help but to wonder what you said to her for her to slap you."

She huffs. "For the hundredth time, I said *nothing* to that woman. I mumbled something under my breath and she heard it."

"And what is it you mumbled, oh dearest sister, because up until now you've been adamant that you didn't do anything."

"I mumbled I fucking hated her."

I tilt my head, staring at her. I blink three times. Persia is a fucking mess. "Then, sweetie, you deserved to have your face slapped. And my advice to you is to apologize to her."

She gives me a look of indignation. "The hell if I will. *She* should be apologizing to *me*." Having this conversation is moot. I spin off on my heels and walk toward the door. "Where are you going?"

"To get ready."

"Ugh," Paris sighs, disgusted. "Of all days to get a fucking flat, it had to be today." We're on the shoulder of the Garden State Parkway, heading south waiting on a tow truck. The GPS says we're fifteen miles away from our destination. "And now we're going to miss the whole ceremony. We should've taken my car."

I suck my teeth. "There's still a chance we can make it in time."

She glances at her watch. "Mmmph."

I roll my eyes. "You act like I planned this or something. The tow truck should be here shortly. Then we'll be on our way."

Persia flips down the visor, checks her face and hair in the mirror. "This must be a sign," she says nonchalantly. She fusses with a curl until it is lying just so.

I'm looking out of my sideview mirror at the speeding cars flying by us, too aggravated to ask her what she means. And Paris is too caught up in her text from our mother stating the ceremony is about to start to be concerned either.

"Well, so much for that," Paris says, sitting back in her seat. "There's no way we'll make the ceremony now."

"Look on the bright side. We'll be there for the reception." Paris rolls her eyes up in her head. Persia grunts. I'm relieved when I see the tow truck finally pulling up behind us.

It is six o'clock when we finally pull up into Stillwell Estates, an exclusive gated community of magnificent estates in a cul-de-sac. When we find the address, I turn into the winding driveway and gasp.

"My God," Persia says, taking in the sprawling lawn. "Pasha's salon does well, but there's no way she's able to afford this unless there's a whole lot of dirty money up in here."

"Well," I say, driving up toward the valet area and pulling behind a Range Rover. "I ain't one to gossip, but we do know who she's marrying."

"Mmmph," Paris and Persia grunt as three young attendants open our car doors. They take our hands and help us out of the car, then loop their arms with ours and usher us down a long, white carpet that leads to the back of the estate. There are torches lit everywhere as we approach two large white tents. On the other side of the property, we see the bridal party over by a beautiful man-made lake, taking pictures. We spot Pasha in her gown but can't make out the rest of the group.

Ohmygod, this is beautiful, I think as the young attendants walk us to the entrance of the first tent where the guests mix and mingle and have cocktails until the bridal party arrives.

"Oh, she really outdid herself," Paris says, pulling out her camera and snapping pictures.

"Yes, she did," Persia agrees. "I hope those tents are air condi-tioned 'cause this damn heat is brutal today." We're relieved when one of the attendants tells us that both tents are. "My God, there are some fine men here tonight."

Even I have to cut my eyes and do a few double-takes. There are beautiful men and women all over the place prancing around in Gucci, Versace, and Armani. The sun's rays are hitting so much bling that it's blinding.

E *verything is breathtaking*, I think, feeling as if I've stepped into a paradise the minute we cross the entrance of the white-carpeted cocktail tent. Cool air greets us as we step in. The tent is adorned in white draperies, candles, and cube seating with gorgeous white couches arranged throughout the tent. Crisp and pristine, the whole setting is simply elegant. There are literally hundreds of gorgeous white roses and candles everywhere. *This is definitely going to be one wedding none of us will ever forget.*

I spot the wedding planner flitting around the room in a beautiful pale pink dress suit, giving orders to the wait staff. There's a handsome young man walking around with a 35-millimeter camera taking pictures of guests. "Oooh, look, there go Mother and Daddy over there," Porsha says, pointing.

"Oh, great," Persia groans. "I'm going over to the bar."

"Oh no, you're not," I state, grabbing her by the arm. "You're going to greet our parents. I wonder who that couple is they're talking to."

"I don't know, and I don't care. I don't wanna be anywhere near that woman."

"Well, too bad," I say through clenched teeth. "Now smile."

Dad spots us first, smiling. "There they are," he says, giving the three of us a hug and kisses on the cheeks.

"Fashionably late as usual," Mother says, glancing at her time-piece. She eyes me. "Looks like you've picked up some weight. I hope you're not going to let yourself get out of shape." Daddy shoots her a look.

I smile. "No, Mother, trust me. I'm not."

"Out of shape or not," the strapping man with the beautiful woman on his arm says, grinning. "You still look—"

The three of us scream as he faces us. "Garreeeeeeett, it's so good to see you." We hug and kiss him.

"And you must be Bianca," I say, extending my hand. "It's so good to finally meet you. I've heard so much about you."

She smiles. "Same here. Garrett tells me how close the four of you were growing up."

"Oh, please," Persia says teasingly. "We couldn't stand his big head. Hi, I'm Persia." She shakes her hand. Porsha introduces herself next.

Garrett pulls Persia into a big hug. "Yeah, right, Apple Head. Tell the truth. You couldn't stand not having me around." We share a laugh until this cocoa brown woman walks by, distracting all of us. She's wrapped in a form-fitting, white silk gown with thigh-high slits that leaves very little to the imagination. Her designer clutch is tucked under her arm. I glance down at her shoes as she sashays by. They're a gorgeous pair of high-heel, platform ankle-straps in white satin. But it's not her expensive wears or the blinding diamonds wrapped around her wrist or in her lobes that has us glued to her. It's her sculpted body, and her humongous ass that has us all mesmerized.

"My God, she's wearing that dress," Porsha says, eyeing her.

"Mmmmph, that chile has a whole lot of ass," Mother says, cutting her eyes over at Daddy who keeps them locked on her back-side until she's out of view. Garrett shifts his eyes when Bianca catches him staring too long.

"Oh, she stops traffic wherever she goes," Bianca states, stealing a sideways glance at her.

"You know her?" Garrett asks curiously.

"Not personally. I've seen her down at Pasha's salon a few times. Her name is Cassandra. But in the streets they call her Big Booty."

"And I see why," Persia says, shaking her head. "If I had her body, I'd be dangerous."

Mother grunts but is cut off by Daddy. "Oh, look," he says, pointing toward the back of the tent. "They're about to start the receiving line."

We spot Aunt Harriett dressed in a white, ankle-length dress-suit with a portrait collar bolero jacket. She's first in the receiving line, followed by another woman who I assume to be the groom's mother. She's smartly dressed in a bone-colored gown standing next to a man who looks like a taller version of the groom. Standing next to him is Pasha.

"Ohmygod, she looks beautiful," I whisper to Porsha and Persia. Mother and Father are in back of us, followed by Garrett and Bianca. Pasha looks gorgeous in a white silk, backless, beaded gown with a deep-pleated train. "Her gown looks absolutely stunning from here."

"I'm so glad she didn't wear a veil," Mother says to no one in particular.

Numerous waiters donned in crisp white tuxedo shirts, white slacks and white tuxedo vests walk by offering flutes of Krug, Clos Du Mesnil and Dom Rose—two of the most expensive champagnes—to guests as we wait to move through the line.

Standing next to Pasha is the handsome groom, Jasper, decked out in a black tux with white vest and tie. "I hate to say this, but her man is fine," Persia whispers in my ear. Porsha and I agree. "I wonder if he has any single brothers."

"I'm sure he has some in the wedding party," I say, craning my neck to look past him. Standing next to him is Felecia, who is Pasha's maid of honor. Next to her are three bridesmaids.

"I don't see any of the groomsmen," Porsha says, eyeing the line as she sips her champagne. I tell her it's optional to have all of the wedding party members in the line, or not.

"With all these guests," Persia adds, looking around at the line. "We'd be standing in this line for hours if they did." She grabs another flute of champagne, sitting her empty glass up on the tray when a waiter comes by. I take another glass as well.

As the guests move through the receiving line, they're then led through an archway that leads into another tent where dinner will be served. I watch as everyone in the bridal party stays focused, smiles painted on their faces, as each guest is greeted. Thirty people ahead of us, the woman with the big ass who Garrett's fiancée called *Big Booty*, shakes Aunt Harriett's hand, moving down the line. I watch as she hugs Pasha, then Jasper, kissing him on the cheek.

Porsha and I eye each other with a raised brow. "I bet you these eight-hundred-dollar heels they've fucked," she whispers.

"I hope not," I say.

"I wouldn't be surprised if he has, though, since he used to cheat on her before he went off to prison," Persia notes. I watch as she gives Felecia a hug, then says a few words to the three bridesmaids before walking off. "Speaking of groomsmen," she says in a hushed tone, "there's two of them right there. And they both look like they might be fine."

Two men, one tall and dark-skinned and the other the color of caramel, in white tuxedos, walk up to Jasper. The dark-skinned man leans in and whispers something into Jasper's ear. The three of them share a laugh. I can't make out who he is since my view is now being blocked by the other groomsmen and a thin woman and her extremely large date who are shaking hands with Pasha, then saying something to Jasper and the two groomsmen.

As we move closer to the line, the dark-skinned groomsman standing in front of Jasper turns slightly to the side, letting the couple go by. I catch a glimpse of his side profile. Persia abruptly gets out of line, almost knocking over one of the waiters and his tray. I turn in her direction, ask where she's going. "I gotta use the bathroom."

"Well, hurry up," I state, turning back toward the receiving line. I drop my drink, gasping. "Oh my God," I say in a whisper.

"What is it?" Porsha asks.

"It's *him*."

"Who?" Her eyes follow the direction of my stare.

"Desmond," I whisper as he turns his head in our direction and locks his eyes on mine.

"C hampagne?" the waiter asks as I rush by, almost bumping into him. I nod, taking my third flute as I grip my white satin Judith Leiber clutch and race out of the tent. I toss back my drink as I walk-run, gulping down my nervousness. I find refuge in the bathroom, a luxury air-conditioned mobile trailer unit, shutting myself in one of the private stalls. *Ohmyfuckinggod, I don't believe this shit! My worst nightmare is about to unfold!*

"How the fuck am I going to get myself out of this mess?" I ask myself, stepping out of the stall and walking over to the sink. I freshen my lipstick, then smack my lips together. Right now I wish I could click my heels three times and disappear.

Felecia and the girl with the big ass come into the bathroom. "Oh hey, cuz," Felecia says, walking over and giving me a hug. "I was wondering where you were. Paris and Porsha have been looking for you."

"Girl, I had to use the bathroom. I'll catch up to them in a minute."

"I don't know if the two of you have met, but this is Cassandra, one of the salon's most faithful clients. Cassandra, this here is my cousin, Persia." We exchange customary hellos.

"I spotted you earlier in the cocktail tent," I say, forcing a smile. "And girl, you're wearing the hell out of that dress."

"Oooh, thank you, boo," she says, smoothing out the front of her dress. "I had to get hit off with a few stacks from one of my young boy toys to…" she stops herself, giving me a confused look. "Wait a minute. I know Mother done tossed back a few rounds, but a bitch ain't sauced. Now, out there I met twins, right?"

"No, girl," Felecia says, laughing. "There are three of them."

I force a smile. "Yes, we're triplets."

"Oooh, girl, thank Gawd y'all cleared that up. For a minute I thought I was—"

"You sneaky, lying bitch!" Paris yells, swinging open the bathroom door. "You had to fuck him, didn't you?"

Felecia blinks.

Cassandra purses her cherry wine painted lips.

"Paris…I didn't," I stammer, shifting my weight from one foot to the other.

"You didn't what, Persia? Didn't mean to suck his dick? Didn't mean to fuck him? Didn't mean to trick him into thinking you were *me?* Or you didn't mean to get caught? Which one is it?"

"I'm—"

"What, *sorry?* Bitch, please. Not this time."

I cut my eyes over at Felecia and Cassandra, who opens her clutch and turns toward the sink, pulling out her lipstick while watching this whole mess unfold in the mirror. "Paris, let's not do this here," I plead. "We can talk about this somewhere more private."

"Oh, no, *bitch*. We're gonna talk about this right here, and right now. I don't give a damn who hears the shit."

Paris shoots a look over at Felecia whose mouth is wide open. "C'mon, Cassandra," she says, "Let's give them some privacy."

"Oh, no, Miss Fe-Fe, I was here first. You can run along, but I'm stayin' right here. This is 'bout to be some real juicy shit. And I ain't missin' one bit of it."

Felecia opens her mouth to say something to Paris, but she shuts her down, putting a hand up. "Don't; not a word. This is between me and my whorin'-ass sister." She tilts her head, narrowing her eyes. One hand is up on her hip and the other pointing a finger at me.

Porsha pushes open the door, racing in. "Paris, no, girl. Not here. This isn't the place to get into it."

Paris has a crazed look in her eyes. And if looks could kill, I'd already be dead. She ignores Porsha. "How many times did you fuck him? And where?"

"Paris, please. Let's not do this here. I promise you. I'll tell you everything. Let's go somewhere and talk in private."

"No, bitch, we're going to either talk here or fight here. You choose." I sigh, giving in. The last thing I want to do is get into a fist-fight with my pregnant sister. I tell her nine or ten times. She holds her stomach like she's going to be sick. "Oh, God. Where?"

I'm so embarrassed that she wants to air this out in front of Felecia and this nosey ass woman with the big ass. "Paris, I realize you're upset; you have every right to be. But I'm not going to do this with you here. What happened was a mistake."

"A fucking *mistake*?" she repeats incredulously. "Bitch, are you serious?! You purposefully slept with him. You pretended to be me, fucked him, then gave him *your* phone number and deliberately erased the numbers from my caller ID so I wouldn't be able to have contact with him. Yeah, bitch, that was Desmond—you know, the man you fucked—standing up there at the receiving line. And when I asked him why he'd stop calling me he told me that *I* broke it off with him. When the fuck did *I* break it off with him, Persia?" I am at a loss for words. "I'm waiting, bitch! I asked you if anyone had called for me and you told me *no*. Then after I told you I was pregnant by him, you still acted like you didn't know who or what the fuck I was talking about. You're a fucking lying-ass bitch! You looked me in my face, knowing you had fucked him behind my back."

"Paris, I swear to you, I stopped sleeping with him right after you told me and Porsha you were pregnant."

"And then you still didn't open your mouth and say shit. So tell me. Was sucking his dick and fucking him worth it to you?"

I steal a glance at Porsha. She glares back at me, eyes smoldering. I can tell she's pissed, too. Felecia decides she's heard enough and finally decides to leave. I'm sure so she can run off and start blabbing to everyone. Nosey-ass Cassandra leans back on the sink with her arms folded, determined not to miss a drop of dirt.

I've never seen Paris like this. I'm truly hurt, that I've hurt her. "Paris, you have to believe me when I say I'm so sorry. I know what I did was—"

"Fuck you, and fuck your goddamn apology, you selfish-ass bitch! I don't have to believe shit. All I wanna know is how many times you sucked his dick, or let him fuck you in that nasty, whore ass of yours?"

Three other women walk into the bathroom. "Paris, please," Porsha says, pulling her by the arm. "This is Pasha's wedding. Let's deal with this at home. We don't need anyone else hearing all this."

She stares at me long and hard. "You know what, you're right. Let me get the fuck away from this bitch. I don't know how the fuck she's getting home, but her ass is *not* riding in the same car with us. The bitch can walk or *suck* her way home as far as I'm concerned."

She swings open the bathroom door, storming out with Porsha hot on her heels. I turn to look at myself in the mirror, turning on the water. I'm wrecked.

Miss Nosey with the Big Ass toots her lips up. "Oooooh, Miss

Girl, you a real messy one, I see. And I looooove it!" She snaps her clutch shut and heads for the door. She glances over her sholder. "Good luck, boo-boo, 'cause girlfriend looks like she's gonna whoop that ass."

Bitch!

"For the love of God, what in the hell is going on?" Mother asks as soon as we approach the table. "Felecia came over here saying you were yelling and screaming at Persia."

"Mother, not now," Paris says, kissing her on the cheek. Then walks over and kisses our father. "We're leaving. If you want to know what's going on, ask your messy-ass daughter."

"Paris," Mother huffs.

Daddy gives Mother a stern look. "Let her be."

"I most certainly will not. I want to know what in the hell is this mess about you being pregnant and you fighting with your sister, airing your filth here."

Paris snatches her clutch from off the table. "Yes, Mother. I am *pregnant*. And I'm keeping it, okay?"

Everyone at the table gasps. Aunt Fanny and Aunt Lucky shoot each other the eye. Mother falls back in her seat, her jaw slack. Daddy lowers his head. This night has gone from bad to worse.

I open my mouth to say something when I spot Desmond walking over toward our table. But he's already in earshot of everything Paris is saying.

"And that fucking bitch pretended to be me so she could fuck the father of my baby behind my back. Let's go, Porsha. I'm through." She spins on her heels, stopping dead in her tracks.

Desmond's standing in back of her, frozen with shock, hearing that she's pregnant.

I glance over at the bridal table and see Felecia standing in back of Pasha, leaning in her ear, pointing over at us. I'm sure giving her all the juicy details of what happened in the bathroom. Pasha stares over in our direction as Paris runs out of the tent.

Right now, I'm too fucking pissed to be embarrassed over the scene I've caused. I have to get the hell out of here, and fast. I find myself running in heels out of the tent with Porsha chasing behind me, and Desmond calling out to me. But, I keep running.

"Paris, wait!" Porsha yells, trying to catch up to me. But I continue my stride as fast as I possibly can in six-inch heels. When I've gotten almost to the front of the property, I stop running, panting hard, out of breath. Porsha finally catches up to me.

"Girl, you have no damn business running in heels. What are you trying to do, break your damn ankles or fall and hurt the baby? You're not thinking straight. You're upset, but you're out here acting like a wild woman. You've let this entire thing take you out of character."

I take three deep breaths.

"No, that, sneaky bitch did this."

"Persia was dead wrong, but this wasn't the place or the time to address it."

"The hell if it wasn't," I snap. "Look, I don't want to talk about it. All I want to do is get—"

"Yo, we need to talk," Desmond says, running up to us. I feel like slapping his face, but I realize he's innocent in all of this.

"I'll go get the car," Porsha says, walking toward one of the valet attendants.

"Desmond, I can't. Not now."

He gives me a pained look. "Nah, fuck that. This whole night has been fuckin' crazy, yo. First, I find out your fam married my fam. Then I find out that you're an identical triplet and that it wasn't you who cut me off, but one of your sisters. And then I walk up on you and hear that you're pregnant. So you gotta tell me something, yo, 'cause right now my head is all fucked up."

He glances down at my stomach.

Instinctively, I place my hand over it. This whole night has drained me. "How do you think I feel? This whole time I thought you just stopped calling me and coming by the store because you lost interest in me, in us."

"Nah, yo, you—"

I stop him with my hand. "Let me finish. For almost four months, I've been pissed at you, thinking you were this fucked-up nigga who just disappeared. Not knowing that my sneaky-ass sister was lying up with you all that time, pretending to be me."

He holds his head in his hands. "This shit is crazy, yo. I still can't believe this shit. And this whole time, I thought it was you dissing me."

I see the attendant coming around with Porsha's car. "Look, I really have to go. Can we please talk about this tomorrow? This whole night has been exhausting. And I'm not feeling well."

He walks me toward the car. "Yeah, we can talk about this to-morrow, but I just need to know one thing." He eyes me.

I look up at him. "What's that?"

"Am I really the father?"

I nod. "Yes."

He runs his hand over his face. "Fuck. I need ya number, yo."

I rattle off my number. He types it into his phone, calls me, then hangs up. "Don't lose it." The valet opens the car door for me, then shuts it once I'm inside. I roll the window down and Desmond leans into the car. "I'm calling you first thing tomorrow, yo. You hear?"

I nod my head. He taps the hood of the car, then steps back and watches as Porsha drives off. I wait until he is out of view, then break down.

Eight a.m., I'm awakened by my ringing phone. Without glancing at the screen, I already know it's Desmond calling. I answer. "Hello."

"I keep playin' this whole shit in my head, yo. I'm fucked up like a muhfucka over this, yo."

I stretch and yawn, sitting up in bed. "I'm really sorry you had to go through that. What my sister, Persia, did was real fucked up. I blame myself. Had I given you my phone number, instead of playing games with you, all of this crazy shit could've been avoided."

"Nah, yo, don't blame ya'self. Ya sister gotta take responsibility for what the fuck she did. Yo, I felt something was different about you..." I cringe at the thought of him being with her. Fucking her the way he fucked me. "...but I couldn't put my finger on it. It was almost like you flipped into this whole other person."

"That's because I was."

"Yeah, no shit. I know that now. But, then...I really couldn't tell y'all apart. The only time you seemed different is when... damn, I thought you had a split personality or something."

"When what?" I ask, bracing myself for what I already know.

"When we were...you know, gettin' it in."

I groan. "Ugh. I'm so disgusted. I feel sick behind this."

"Yo, you don't know how bad I wanted to come down to ya store and talk shit out with you. But, I ain't never been the type of cat to sweat a chick who isn't interested in bein' sweated. Once you, I mean, she, told me she wasn't beat anymore, I fell back and played my position."

I have a pounding headache as images of them in bed flash through my head. I have to know. "Did you like fucking her?" I hold my breath, wait for his answer.

"Nah, I liked fuckin' *you*, ma. That's who I thought I was gettin' it in wit'. I was big on you, feel me? Even when you, I mean she, started flippin' the script, wantin' to be slapped up and choked and disrespected, I went wit' it 'cause it's what you, well she, wanted. She said she liked role-play. Yo, ya sister is a real snake for that shit; real talk."

I swallow back my anger. "Trust me. You're not telling me anything I don't already know. I'm so sorry you had to go through that. I can only imagine what was said after I ran up out of the reception last night."

"Yo, most of the peeps there were pretty lit the fuck up and didn't even really know what was goin' on." He chuckles. "Yo, I'm just glad to know my fam ain't the only ones all fucked up." He tells me when he got back to the tent, my mother, along with my aunts Fanny and Lucky, cornered him and drilled him until my father came and pulled her away from him.

"Ohmygod," I say, covering my face. "My mother and aunts are a mess."

He laughs. "Yo, they came at me like they were ready to get it in. Ya pops, though, seems mad cool. He and I had a chance to talk in private."

"What did y'all talk about?"

"You."

"What about me?"

"I told him that I was really big on you and wanted to work things out, if we could."

I can't believe my ears. A part of me is relieved, and happy to know this. But, then there's that other part of me who can't get past the thought that he's fucked Persia. "Even after all this mess with my sister?"

"Yeah. That shit still doesn't change how I've felt 'bout you, yo. I couldn't get you out my head."

"But it wasn't me."

"Nah, yo, it was *you* way before your sister stepped in. Listen. What happened, happened. I can't change that, and neither can you. But, we gotta deal wit' what's goin' on right now. I can't tell you what to do wit' ya body, but I need to know what are *we* gonna do about my seed you carryin'?" I tell him I'm having it. He gets quiet.

"Are you okay?"

"Yeah, I'm good."

"Are you bothered by that?" .

"Nah, I'm not. I've been wantin' a baby for a minute; just didn't connect wit' anyone I wanted to have one wit', until now. Yo, I wanna see you. "

I smile. "Tell me where, and I'm there."

"My place." He gives me the address. I tell him that I can be there in an hour or so; that I need to shower and get dressed. "Nah, that's too long. I need to see you *now*. Throw on some clothes and just come through. You can shower here."

I climb out of bed and go into my bathroom, then sit on the toilet. When I'm done, I flush, then wash my hands. I decide to take a quick sink-rinse. "I'll be there in thirty minutes."

"Cool."

"I'll text you when I'm leaving."

"Nah, fuck that. I wanna hear ya voice. Call me so we can talk while you drivin', aiight?"

I feel myself getting ready to cry. "I will."

"Cool. Oh, one more thing."

"What's that?"

"Pack a bag 'cause I'm taking you back to Connecticut with me."

"*Connecticut?* For what?"

"To meet my fam. But, first, I'm takin' you by my parents' spot. So my moms and pops can meet you."

"Oh, God. I'm sure she's going to have all kind of choice words to say about me."

He laughs. "Yeah, she might. But, don't sweat it. Her bark's louder than her bite. Once she gets to know you, she's gonna have mad love for ya. Trust me on this."

We talk a few minutes more, than hang up. I hurriedly wash up, throw on some clothes, then start tossing a few things into an overnight bag. I'm not sure what's going to happen between Desmond and me. It's been months since I've seen or talked to him, thanks to Persia. I'm not even sure if he's who I want to be with. But what I am sure of, I'm going to be a mother. And my baby's going to have a father in its life after all. And that's all that matters to me.

T he last three weeks have been hell. Okay, I know. A hell that I've created. Paris is still not speaking to me. Even Porsha is looking at me sideways for causing this riff between us. This whole situation has spiraled out of control. Paris hasn't been staying here; she's actually been avoiding me. I've become invisible to her.

And now I'm up in my room, standing in my window, watching as she moves some of her belongings out. I'm watching as Desmond helps her load things in her car and in his truck. I don't even know where she's going. Every so often, she looks up, stealing evil glances at me, rightfully so. I hurt her deeply. And for that, I'm so truly sorry.

It hurts standing here, watching her move her things out of our home. It hurts knowing that her forgiveness for what I've done may not come anytime soon. Yes, my actions caused this. But, eventually, she'll come around. She always does. We're sisters. And our bond will always be strong; no matter what. But, for now, I have to give her her space and weather the storm between us.

Mother was right. I'm a selfish bitch; always have been. I want what I want *and* who I want when I want it. If I'm completely honest with myself, the truth is I don't regret sleeping with Desmond. It sounds fucked up, but I simply don't. It's what I wanted to do. But that's something I'll never admit to Paris, or ever share with Porsha. However, I do regret Paris finding out. I regret seeing her hurt by my selfishness. Still, I believe I could've gotten away with it—as I have with all of her other boyfriends— had I fucked him only once instead of getting greedy. I should've never given him my number. I have offered to apologize to Desmond, but Paris simply laughed.

"Bitch, the damage is already done. What the fuck do you think an apology is going to do now? Make everything go away? No, bitch. Save your fucking apology. He's not interested in it. And neither am I. He was off limits to you, ho. The rule was we only share the men the three of us, or at least two of us, mutually agree on. Anyone else is off fucking limits, especially once we know he's interested in only one of us. Even if I didn't tell you about him, you *knew* he had feelings for *me*."

"Paris, if you would have told me that you've met someone that you wanted for yourself, then I wouldn't have done it."

"Bitch, you're so fucking full of yourself, it's a damn shame. If I didn't mention him to you, there must've had been a damn good reason. And when Desmond called the store looking for me, YOU should've told him I wasn't there. Then YOU should've simply asked me about him and I would've told you that I was keeping him for myself. So, don't give me that bullshit.

"Bitch, I forgave you when you slutted yourself out with all of them motherfucking boys and had the whole damn school calling me sluts and whores and shit. I took ass whippings and punishments for you, bitch. Why? Because I'm your sister and I loved you. And it would hurt me to see you always in trouble. I didn't want to accept that you were the problem. Not Mother, you. You've never given a fuck about anyone else but yourself. And I'm sick of it."

I went to walk toward her. "Paris, I know you're hurt, and —"

"Don't you fucking come near me," she warned, balling her fist up. "You have no fucking idea what I'm feeling. We've had our arguments and screaming matches over the years. And we've gotten over them. But, right now, if I wasn't pregnant, I'd beat the shit out of you. So the best thing you can do for the both of us is to stay THE FUCK away from me! Don't open your mouth to say shit!"

And with that said, she stormed out, slamming the door behind her.

Now I stand here watching as she and Porsha hug. I swipe the tear that has escaped from my eye and as she gets in her car and drives off with Desmond following behind her.

I take a deep breath. "Damn, she's fine as fuck," I had heard one of the guys say as I walked by the bleachers where they were all sitting, smoking weed. There were like eight of them. Three of them I recognized from school. The other five were boys from Newark. I had on a short skirt and a tight-fitting tee. I was itching to get into some trouble.

"Hey," this light-skinned guy with freckles called out. I knew him from school. "C'mere."

I walked back over to where they where all sitting and looked up at him. "Yeah?"

"Which triplet are you?"

I smiled. "Paris. Why, y'all want some pussy?"

They all started high-fiving each other, grabbing at their dicks. "Hell yeah." I was young and horny and wanted to fuck. I told them I knew where we could go to have some fun. They followed me as I led them to a path, that took us into the woods where— one after the other—they took turns fucking me, dumping cum into me. They all stood around cheering each other on until they all had their turn with me. I got up, picked up my panties and wiped my swollen, cum-soaked pussy with them, then walked out of the woods like nothing ever happened.

"You fucking bitch!" Porsha snaps, jolting me from my reverie as she swings open my bedroom door. I turn from the window and face Persia. "You see what you've done?! Because of you, Paris is moving out of this house. Because of you, there's a wedge between us now. That shit you did to Paris brings up old wounds for me, too. Like when you fucked Brandon, and fucked God knows how many other boyfriends of mine over the years. How many of them did you fuck, pretending to be me?"

I sit down. "Only him," I lie. Truth is I've fucked three of her boyfriends. But, I'll never tell her that.

She shakes her head. "I wish I could believe you, Persia."

"It's the truth."

Her intense stare tells me she isn't buying it one bit. "Whatever." She storms back out the room. My cell rings. I sigh. It's Mother. I press IGNORE. I call our father. He picks up on the third ring.

"Hey, baby girl," he says, his voice gentle and full of love. "I was wondering when I was going to hear from you."

"I'm sure you've heard the mess between Paris and me."

"Yeah, I got an earful the night of the reception. And you're mother has been beside herself; nonstop on the phone with your aunts."

"Ugh. I'm sure they're having a field day with this."

He chuckles. "It'll all die down soon.

"Daddy, I really messed up. Paris hates me. Porsha can't stand me right now. And Mother...well, she and I will never see eye to eye."

"Your sisters love you. Trust me. Paris'll come around. I've always tried to stay out of you and your sisters' squabbles. Y'all will work this through. I love you, Porsha, and Paris, equally the same. No, I don't agree with what happened. And I don't want to know why you did it. All I want is for you, the three of you, to get along. Hopefully, at some point, you and your mother as well." His tone is even and nonjudgmental.

Wiping my tear-streaked face with the back of my hand, I tell him how much I love him. Tell him how badly I want to make things right between my sisters and me; especially with Paris. I'm afraid I may have lost my sister this time. "I don't even know where she's staying," I say, sobbing into the phone. I'm relieved when he says she's temporarily staying with them.

"Your mother is enjoying every minute of it," he says with a laugh. *Yeah, that's because she's her favorite*, I hear myself saying in my head. There's a tinge of jealousy that sweeps through me from hearing this. Paris has always been the perfect one; the good girl. She was the triplet who always did everything right in our mother's eyes when we were growing up, followed by Porsha. And I'm the one who did everything wrong. Obviously, not much's changed.

"I'm sure she is," I push out, feeling myself getting emotional. I've caused this mess, and I have to fix it. I just don't know how. "Daddy, I have to go. I'll call you in a few days."

"Alright, baby girl. Your old man loves you; don't ever forget that."

I force a smile. "I love you, too, Daddy." I disconnect the call, then crawl up under my covers and cry myself to sleep.

"Bitch, you need to fix this mess between you and Paris," I hiss, glaring at Persia over my menu. We're sitting at the Mall at Short Hills getting ready to have lunch at the new Cheesecake Factory that opened back in July. I had wanted to spend the day shopping with *both* of my sisters, but thanks to this shit with Persia, that wasn't possible. It's been three months, and Paris is still not speaking to Persia. And everytime I think about it, it pisses me off; especially now that I'm planning her baby shower, alone. Persia may not be there to celebrate with us. I feel like slapping her face my damn self. "And you need to do it soon."

"I've tried," she offers, solemnly. For once, I see remorse in her eyes. "I've gone down to the shop three times, and she's told me to get out. She won't even take my calls."

"Well, this whole mess is a crock of bullshit, thanks to *you*."

She cringes. "Porsha, please. How many times are you going to keep reminding me?"

"Until *you* fix it. I don't give a damn what you have to do or say to make it right."

"There's nothing I can do. I've tried to apologize. I've left numerous messages. I've sent her cards. I've even asked Daddy to talk to her. She still won't have anything to do with me."

"Can you blame her?"

She shakes her head. "No. I wouldn't want anything to do with me, either."

"Mmmph. Well, you need to figure out something *before* she has her baby. And before this shower next month."

She sits back in her seat. "I can't believe she's almost eight months' pregnant. And I've missed out on most of her pregnancy."

"You'll miss out on a whole lot more if you don't make up with her."

Paris and I talk every day, and we've double-dated a few times. Desmond seems like a really nice guy. He seems like he's really into Paris. More than what I can say about any other man she's ever dated. He and Em even hit it off. Paris is still staying with our parents. And she's as miserable as ever; thanks to Mother constantly in her face, meddling and doting over her at the same time. Plus, she's ready to move back home with her sisters where she belongs.

So much has been going on since Pasha's wedding. Emerson and I have talked about moving in together, but I told him it's not going to happen until *after* we're married. I refuse to become a convenience. I give him all the pussy he wants. I stay over as often as he wants. But, a live-in girlfriend I will *not* be. I told him if he wants this woman in his life full-time, then he needs to put a ring on it *and* meet me down the aisle.

"So what you saying, you wanna get married?" he asked, rising up on his forearms, giving me a sideways glance.

I shifted my body so that I could face him on my side. "No, what I'm saying is, I'm not going to invest a lot of time and energy into being someone's girlfriend. At some point, we're going to have to know exactly where we're going with this. As a man, you should know what you want."

"I already know where I wanna go with it. And I know what I want. That's why I want you to move in with me. I want you."

I pulled him into me by the back of his neck, kissed him on the lips, then looked him in his eyes. "When you marry me, *then* I move in. Until then, we keep doing what we're doing."

He grinned, pulling me into his arms. "Say no more, baby. I hear you loud and clear." And three weeks later, he surprised me with an engagement ring. We haven't set a date, but I am officially engaged to the man of my dreams.

The waitress comes over to see if we're ready to order. I glance at my watch, tell her to give us ten more minutes, then change my mind when I see who I'm waiting for. "On second thought, we're ready."

I look over at Persia. "If you want to make it right, now's your chance."

She gives me a puzzled look. I get up from my seat to give Paris a hug before she gets to our table. "Hooker, what is *she* doing here?" she hisses in my ear. "I don't want to be anywhere around her."

"Paris, please," I whisper, helping her take off her coat. "Listen to what she has to say, for me."

She grunts, reluctantly walking back over to the table with me. I squeeze her hand. Persia gets up from her seat, bursting into tears as she wraps her arms around Paris. Paris and I look at each other, shocked. There are very few times either of us have ever seen her cry. Paris stiffens, keeps her arms down at her side while Persia tells her how much she's missed her; how sorry she is. Patrons in earshot are glancing over at us. I have to practically peel Persia away from Paris.

We take our seats while Persia continues sobbing. She goes to the bathroom to pull herself together. The waitress takes our drink orders. I order a cosmo for Persia and me. Paris orders a pineapple smoothie. For appetizers, I order the stuffed mushrooms.

"Paris, please work on putting this behind you and Persia. We both know she can be a bitch at times, but she's our sister. The holidays are coming up and I want to spend them with both of my sisters, together."

She waves her hand, dismissively. "You sound like Desmond. Trust me. I want nothing more than to put this behind me. But, it's not that easy."

"I know."

Persia returns to the table with her eyes swollen and red. "Paris, I'm so sorry for what I've done to you. I didn't think for one minute that you'd really care if I slept with him or not."

Paris tilts her head. "Exactly. You didn't think. Because, once again, the only person you were thinking about was yourself."

"You're right. Truth is, I did think about it. But I didn't care. I wanted him, too. I needed to see what it was about him that you wanted to keep to yourself."

Paris cringes as the waitress returns with our drinks. "And were you able to figure that all out?"

"Desmond seems like a really nice guy. And I knew how much he cared about you. I feel horrible for tricking him like that."

Paris raises her brow. "Do you really?"

Persia nods. "Yes, I do. Paris, the more I slept with him, the harder it was for me to tell him the truth. And it tore me up, knowing that the person he was falling for really wasn't you."

"You do realize you've made it very awkward for me to ever bring you around him."

"I understand that."

"The crazy thing is he wants me to have a relationship with you. Even after what you did to him, he's been encouraging me to talk to you."

Paris rubs her round belly. She looks beautiful pregnant. She has her thick, long hair pulled back into a ponytail. I glance at her hand and blink.

"Is that what I think it is?" I ask, gasping.

She flashes her hand. "Yes, Desmond proposed to me over the weekend at his parents' home."

"Congratulations," I squeal, digging into my bag, fishing out my own surprise "I didn't know how lunch was going to go, but I wanted both of you here. I have an announcement to make myself." I slip the ring over my finger, then flash them my hand. "Emerson asked me to marry him."

"Ohmygod," Paris says. Her voice filled with excitement. She takes my hand and inspects my ring. "Oooh, it's beautiful."

Persia looks stunned. "Wow, it is gorgeous. Both of you have beautiful rings. I'm happy for the both of you. Congratulations." She looks at Paris, then me. "So things between you and Desmond are really working out?"

Paris nods. "Yeah, things are great. If anything, this entire ordeal has brought us closer together. He wants a family, and he wants me."

"I'm happy for you." She looks over at me. "And you're happy with Emerson?"

"Yes, I am. I love him. And I would like to spend my life with him."

Tears well in her eyes. "I've missed so much over the last few months. I feel so empty not being a part of your lives. I feel so disconnected from the two of you. For anything that I've ever done to wrong either of you, I want you both to know how deeply sorry I am. Paris, things with us won't be the same, but I hope one day you can find it in your heart to forgive me."

Paris gives her a faint smile, then reaches over and squeezes her hand. "I miss my sister. I'm working on forgiveness. Not for you, but for me. I'm having a baby, and want my child to have both of his or her aunts in its life."

"And I'm getting married," I interject. "And I want both of my sisters in my wedding."

"Have you set a date?" Paris asks.

"No. Not exactly, but it'll be sometime in the fall of two-thousand-and-twelve. That'll give *you*—" I point to Persia—"enough time to fix what you broke. And you"—I point at Paris—"enough time to lose all that baby fat. I will not have a chunky bridesmaid in my wedding."

She laughs. "Oh, whatever, hooker."

"Have you and Desmond set a date yet?" Persia asks Paris.

"No. Not yet. We're not going to rush into getting married. We're still getting to know one another. He wants us to live together once the baby is born. But I told him, no. I told him the next man I live with—"

"Is going to be my husband," I finish for her.

She laughs. "Exactly. Sounds like someone else got that speech, too."

"Girl, please. How you think I got this engagement ring? I fuck Em good and suck him better, but I'll be damned if he's gonna get anymore than that until after we're married."

I lift my glass. "To new beginnings."

"And forgiveness," Paris adds, eyeing Persia.

"To new beginnings and forgiveness," the three of us say, clinking our glasses.

"Persia," Paris says, setting her drink back down on the table. She narrows her eyes. "You really hurt me. But the three of us have a home together, and we're partners in a business, so I'm going to have to get over what you did to me. Will I forget? Hell no. Will I ever trust you around my man? Hell fucking no! And even though Des isn't interested in being with you, I'm still going to watch you like a fucking hawk around him. If I ever catch you trying to flirt with him, or if I even think you're somewhere playing in your hot-ass pussy thinking about him, I'm going beat your ass, then cut you out of my life for good. Are we clear?"

"I promise you. That's something neither of you will ever have to worry about. I'm never going to let anything else come between us."

I gulp my drink. "Good. Now when the hell are you moving back home?"

"Not soon enough," Paris says, shaking her head. "Mother has been driving me crazy. I can't wait to get the hell up out of there. Love her dearly, but my welcome has worn thin."

The three of us share a laugh. Something we haven't done in a long time. I smile, feeling like there's hope for the three of us after all. I eye Persia. That's my sister, and I love her dearly. But, I'm with Paris. I'm going to be watching her ass, too.

Persia looks at me and smiles.

I smile back. *If she even sneezes wrong, I'm gonna beat her ass for the old and for the new.*

Paris
CHAPTER SIXTY-TWO

Tears roll unchecked down my cheeks. I'm bloated and miserable. This whole pregnancy thing is a lot more excruciating than I expected. Everything about Desmond makes me sick right now. The way he looks, the way he smells. I want to slap him. I'm already a week past my due date and I've only dilated three centimeters. I want this stubborn baby out of me, now. All it does is kick and squirm and make my life a living hell.

I'm so glad to be back here in my own bed. Living with my parents was…different, to say the least. But, here is where my heart is—for now at least. Persia and I are still on shaky ground, but we're talking and we're working things through. And she finally admitted to being jealous of me. Why I have no idea, but she said she's always envied me. One day when I feel like hearing it, I'll ask her to clarify. Right now, it's not that important to me. That's her issue, not mine. She realized I don't trust her as far as I can toss her, but she's still my sister.

Desmond just left here. I had to put him out. He was getting on my nerves, for no reason. I have to say, having him and Persia in the same room the first few times was definitely an uncomfortable feeling for all three of us. But we got through it. Persia apologized for her scandalous behavior. Surprisingly, Desmond accepted her apology. But, for some strange reason, there was something in his eyes that gave me the feeling that he's thought about her sexually. That he's fantasized about whatever little nasty deeds she used to perform on him. There's no telling with Persia. To this day, I don't know exactly what they did in bed, and I don't care to know. Even though I trust him when he says he loves me. Something deep in my gut tells me, if I offer him the opportunity to fuck the both of us, he would. Crazy thing is I've thought about it, watching the two of them together. I've masturbated to the notion of catching the two of them in the act.

There's a part of me that misses fucking men with my sisters. If I'm really honest with myself, there have been times when I've lain in bed with Desmond, fantasizing about Persia and Porsha and Emerson—all five of us in one bed, fucking the night away.

The three of us would have Emerson's and Desmond's hands and feet tied to the bedposts, taking turns riding down on their cocks, smothering their faces with our sweet, wet pussies while alternately sucking their dicks.

The baby kicks again, jolting me from my lascivious thoughts. "Ugh!"

"Here, sweetie," Porsha says, propping two pillows in back of me. "Let's see if this helps."

Persia is at the foot of my bed, rubbing my feet. Porsha takes a cold rag and places it up against my forehead. They've been tending to my every need for the last two weeks since my doctor placed me on bedrest. If I don't have this baby by the end of the week, the doctor says they're going to induce my labor. And that's fine by me. Daddy and Desmond know to be close by. They're the only ones I want in the delivery room with me. Mother wanted to be in there, but I told her absolutely not. I wanted the two special men in my life there. Surprisingly, she didn't make a big deal about it. She acted like she understood. And that's all I care about. I want this shit over with. I feel like a fat cow.

I steady my breathing. The baby kicks. And I groan. "Do the two of you..." Oh, God, this child is pressing down on my fucking bladder. I take short quick breaths, blowing in and out, rubbing my lower part of my stomach."...have any regrets doing what we've done with men?"

Persia and Porsha look at each other, then me. "No," they say in unison.

"We've had some good times man-swapping," Persia states, smiling. She quivers. "Whew, we've fucked the shit out of some fine-ass men."

"Yes, we have," I agree.

"Shit, I still think about it sometimes," Porsha admits. "Every now and then Emerson asks if I miss it."

"What do you tell him?" Persia asks.

"Shit, I tell him the truth. There are no secrets between us. But he also knows as long as I'm with him, I'm not sleeping with another man."

"If somewhere down the road he wants a threesome, would you allow another woman into your bed?"

"If that were the case, fortunately, I don't think it will be. But, if that's what he wanted, the only women I'd ever let him sleep with would be one of you. And I told him that." Persia wants to know what he said when she told him that. "He laughed, then told me that three of us together were too much for him; that I'm more than enough woman for him."

"Good answer," I say, shifting my body so I can lie on my side.

"Have you told Desmond?" Porsha wants to know.

It feels like this baby is kicking and punching me. "Aaah. Nooo..." Inhale. Exhale. I pat my stomach. Try to soothe this baby in any way possible. "I didn't have to." They both give me surprised looks. "Girl, you know after that whole fiasco at the reception, Jasper couldn't wait to get him alone and tell him all about the three of us."

They gasp. "Shut. Your. Mouth. What did he say to you?"

I groan again. "He asked me if it was true. And I told him yes."

"Then what?" Porsha inquires.

"Then he wanted to know how long we'd been sharing men, and how many. And of course he wanted to know if I used condoms. I told him always. That most times I only got my pussy eaten or laidback and masturbated while they watched me watch them fuck one of y'all."

"Ohhh, I bet you he thinks we're some nasty freaks."

I hold back a laugh, clutching my stomach. "Oh, it hurts when I laugh. But, yeah, he knows we're some real freaks. Hell, he walked in on me fucking myself in the back office one day when I thought I had the door locked. And, then, I fucked him. So yeah, he knows."

My cell rings. I have it lying beside me. I pick it up. "Speaking of him, now. Hey!"

"You still beefin' wit' me?"

"Nope. I just want this baby out of me."

"You and me both. My lil man has turned you into an evil woman. I miss the old you."

I suck my teeth, playfully. "Whatever. How you know it's going to be a boy, anyway?"

"Trust me. I know." I smile remembering, what Daddy said about knowing I was carrying his first grandson. As much as he loves my sisters and me, deep down he wishes he had at least one son. I remember the look in his eyes whenever Garrett spent the weekends at our house. The two of them would go out fishing or down to the courts to shoot hoops. I even see it now when he talks to Desmond. Daddy likes Desmond. And, Mother…well, she's still trying to get over the fact that I'm pregnant, and that Persia fucked him.

I groan. "Uhh. Remind me to never have sex with you again without using a condom."

He laughs. "Too late for all that. As soon as we're married, I'm pumpin' you up with two more."

"Yeah right, I don't think so. You better be the one carrying them."

He keeps laughing. "Yeah, aiight. We'll see." I groan. "Damn, I wish there was something I could do for you."

"There is."

"What's that?"

"Come lick my pussy. That seems to make it feel better."

He laughs. "Yo, you just threw me up outta there."

"Yeah, I know. But now I want my pussy eaten. I read somewhere that eating a woman's pussy while she's pregnant helps with the dilation process."

Porsha and Persia both fall out laughing at how ridiculous that sounded. Even I have to laugh. But he tells me he'll be back in an hour. We disconnect.

Persia stops rubbing my feet when she receives a text. She texts whoever it is back, then tosses her phone on the bed. "Royce wants to spend the night."

"I can't believe you're still messing with him," I say, shaking my head.

"Me either. I hate to admit it, but I kind of like him."

"Wow, isn't that something," Porsha says, laughing. "And I bet you have a big ole wide pussy now to show it."

She laughs with her. "Oh, fuck you. Let's simply say, he's stretched it to accommodate every inch of him."

I groan again, laughing. "So, in other words, you have a big pussy."

Porsha joins in my laughter.

"Whew, that boy has one huge-ass dick. Better you than me."

Persia fans herself. "Yes, indeed he does. My boy toy is a whole lot of man in between them sheets."

It's kind of crazy and sick that the three of us can sit here laughing about our sexapades while swapping sex notes on the men in our lives. The three of us have fucked Royce and Emerson. Persia's fucked Desmond, although that knowledge is still a sore spot for me. Still, we've passed men around and sampled the goods, like so many other women out there. Like my sisters, I have no regrets.

"So, what does that mean for you and the cute little waiter?" Porsha asks, eyeing her.

Persia shrugs. "Who knows? Only time will tell. For now, I'm having fun with him. Do you know I only recently found out that he graduated in May from Seton Hall with a degree in Business Management? And his father owns several businesses in Trinidad, and two Caribbean restaurants in Brooklyn. His father paid his tuition, but made him work for everything else he needed; hence, why he waited tables. But come January he's going to take over his father's two restaurants."

"That's great. Could you ever see yourself with him?" I ask, grimacing in pain.

She smiles. "Yeah, I think I could. He has a high sex drive, and is very open-minded sexually. But, more than that, he's intelligent and very caring. And he's exceptionally mature for his age. He's invited me to go to Trinidad with him in the spring"

I smile. "You should go."

"Oh, no, girl," she says, shaking her head. "I'm not ready for all that."

"Do you ever think you'll be satisfied with one man?" Porsha asks her.

She gives it some thought, then smiles. "Yeah, I definitely think I could. As much as I enjoy sharing men with the two of you, there's something nice about having a man you can call your very own."

A sharp contraction shoots through me, causing me to scream. Five minutes later, another one comes, sharper than the first. It feels like something is stabbing me. I clutch the sheets. "Ohmygod, I think it's time. Call Daddy and tell him to meet us at the hospital. Ahhh!" I yell in between contractions. Inhale. Exhale. Inhale. Exhale. This shit is excruciating. "This baby is ready to come."

"You want me to call Desmond for—" Persia stops in midsentence as I shoot her a look. "I know, I know. Hell no. I'll call Daddy."

"I'll call him for you," Porsha says, reaching for my cell. She locates his number, then dials it; tells him to meet us at the hospital. Persia tells Daddy the same thing. Then they both help me out of the bed and walk me down the stairs. Persia helps me into my coat. I scream as the contractions come quicker and last longer. "Ahhhhh!" I scream again when another contraction shoots through me. Persia helps get me into the backseat of the car while Porsha races over to the driver's side and gets in. She shuts my door, then hops into the front seat as Porsha speeds around our circular driveway.

My cell rings. It's Desmond. "Whaaaat?" I scream into the phone, panting.

"I'm a nervous wreck, baby. Where are you?"

"Ahhhh!" I yell into the phone. "On our way to the hospital."

"Baby, you remember how they told you to breath in that Lamaze class, right?"

I scream again. "Fuck Lamaze. You were supposed to come lick my pussy," I say in between contractions.

He laughs. "I know, baby. I'm gonna make it up to you." I yell again. "Yo, you my heart. I'll lick your pussy, suck them titties. Do whatever you want me to do to help you get through this, yo. You heard me, baby?"

I scream again, grabbing my stomach. "Bitch, press on that pedal and hurry up and get me to the hospital before I have this baby in the backseat of this car."

"Hold on," Persia says while on the phone with Mother, giving her minute-by-minute updates as to how far we are and what my condition is. "We're almost there."

I would smile if I wasn't in so much damn pain, happy to see them talking. It's the first time in months. Maybe there's hope for the two of them after all. I concentrate on my breathing. Close my eyes, try to block out the pain. Try to block out Desmond's voice as he tries to coach and calm me. It's not working. I scream.

I'm not sure what will happen once this baby comes into this world. And I'm not sure what the future really holds for Desmond and me. He loves me. And I love him. But I'm not *in love* with him. Yet, I want to be with him. He's a good man. And, if I marry him, it won't be for this baby's sake. It'll be because he's who I want to spend my life with. Still, there's a fleeting thought lingering around in my head that one day my sisters and I will sneak off to some sexy Caribbean island—before Porsha or I get married—and give one more man a weekend of sexual bliss, pleasuring him in ways he's never imagined, as Passion, Pain, and Pleasure—three sisters, three sets of hands, three pair of soft lips, wet tongues, and hot steamy pussies working together to drive him beyond the limits of ecstasy. Oh, yes…what a sweet, delicious thought it is. One I can't get lost in, not now. I let out another scream. *My baby's coming!*

ABOUT THE AUTHOR

Cairo is the author of *The Kat Trap, The Man Handler, Daddy Long Stroke, Deep Throat Diva* and *Kitty-Kitty, Bang-Bang.* He currently divides his time between northern New Jersey and California where he is working on his next literary masterpiece. His travels to Egypt are what inspired his pen name. If you'd like to know more about the man behind the pen, you can visit him at www. facebook.com/cairoblacktheauthor, www.planetzane.org., or on his website at www.booksbycairo.com.

IF YOU ENJOYED "MAN SWAPPERS," FIND OUT WHAT HAPPENS
BEFORE PASHA'S FAIRYTALE WEDDING IN

DEEP THROAT DIVA

BY CAIRO

AVAILABLE NOW FROM STREBOR BOOKS

2005

"Aye, yo, you need to let me know now if you're gonna ride this shit out with me 'cause I ain't beat to be up in this muhfucka stressin' 'bout dumb shit, feel me?"

"I'm not going anywhere. I'm with you, baby."

"Aiight, that's what it is. I'ma need you to hold it down out there. Keep that shit tight, ya heard? Don't have me snappin' out 'cause you done got caught up in some bullshit."

"Whatever."

"Whatever, nothin', yo. I'm tellin' you now, Pasha, don't have me fuck sumthin' up. I didn't ice ya hand up for nothin', yo."

"Jasper, please, I'm not beat for another nigga. Four years ain't shit. I keep telling you that."

"Yeah, and? I'm gonna keep sayin' the shit 'cause I know how hot in the ass broads are when a nigga gets behind the wall. They be on some ole other shit."

"Well, I'm not them."

"Oh, so you not hot in the ass?"

"Yeah, for you. But not for any other nigga."

"You better not be either, yo, word up. Let me find out you done had another muhfucka hittin' that shit and I'ma bust yo' ass."

"Nigga, please. The only thing you're gonna be bustin' is a bunch of nuts in them hands."

"Yeah, aiight. I gotta buncha nuts for ya ass, ya heard? Talk slick if you want, but I'm tellin' you, yo."

"I heard you. And I'm telling you. I'm all yours in mind, body and soul. This pussy and my heart are for you and you only. And I got it on lock until you get home."

"You better."

"I promise, baby. I do."

ONE

Y ou ready to cum? Imagine this: A pretty bitch down on her knees with a pair of soft, full lips wrapped around the head of your dick. A hot, wet tongue twirling all over it, then gliding up and down your shaft, wetting it up real slippery-like, then lapping at your balls; lightly licking your asshole. Mmmm, I'm using my tongue in places that will get you dizzy, urging you to give me your hot, creamy nut. Mmmmm, baby...you think you ready? If so, sit back, lie back, relax and let the Deep Throat Diva rock your cock, gargle your balls, and suck you straight to heaven.

I reread the ad, make sure it conveys exactly what I want, need, it to say, then press the PUBLISH tab. "There," I say aloud, glancing around my bedroom, then looking down at my left hand. "Let's see how many responses I get, this time."

Ummm, wait...before I say anything else. I already know some of you uptight bitches are shaking your heads and rolling your eyes. What I'm about to tell ya'll is going to make some of you disgusted, and that's fine by me. It is what it is. There's also going to be a bunch of you closeted, freaky bitches who are going to turn your noses up and twist up your lips, but secretly race to get home 'cause you're as nasty as I am. Hell, some of you are probably down on your knees as I speak, or maybe finishing up pulling a dick from out of your throat, or removing strands of pubic hair from in between your teeth. And that's fine by me as well. Do you, boo. But, let me say this: Don't any of you self-righteous hoes judge me.

So here goes. See. I have a man—dark chocolate, dreamy-eyed, sculpted and every woman's dream—who's been incarcerated for four years, and he's releasing from prison in less than nine months. And, *yes*, I'm excited and nervous and almost scared to death—you'll realize why in a minute. Annnywaaaay, not only is he a sexy-ass mother-fucker, he knows how to grind, and stack paper. And he is a splendid lover. My God! His dick and tongue game can make a woman forget her name. And all the chicks who know him either want him, or want him back. And they'll do anything they can to try to disrupt my flow. Hating-ass hoes!

Nevertheless, he's coming home to *me*. The collect calls, the long drives, the endless nights of sexless sleep have taken a toll on me, and will all be over very soon. Between the letters, visits and keeping money on his books, I've been holding him down, faithfully. And I've kept my promise to him to not fuck any other niggas. I've kept this pussy tight for him. And it's been hard, *really* hard—no, no, hard isn't an accurate description of the agony I've had to bear from not being fucked for over four years. It's been excruciating!

But I love Jasper, so I've made the sacrifice. For him, for us! Still, I have missed him immensely. And I need him so bad. My pussy needs him, aches for the width of his nine-inch, veiny dick thrusting in and out of it. It misses the long, deep strokes of his thick tongue caressing my clit and its lower lips. I miss lying in his arms, being held and caressed. But I have held out; denied any other niggas the privilege—*and* pleasure—of fucking this sweet, wet hole.

The problem is: Though I haven't been riding down on anything stiff, I've been doing a little anonymous dick sucking on the side from time-to-time—and, every now and then, getting my pussy ate—to take the edge off. Okay, okay, I'm lying. I've been sucking a lot of dick. But it wasn't supposed to be this way. I wasn't supposed to become hooked on the shit as if it were crack. But, I have. And I am.

Truth be told, it started out as inquisitiveness. I was bored. I was lonely. I was fucking horny and tired of sucking and fucking dildos, pretending they were Jasper's dick. So I went on Nastyfreaks4u.com, a new website that's been around for about two years or so. About eighteen months ago, I had overheard one of the regulars who gets her hair done down at my salon talking about a site where men and women post amateur sex videos, similar to that on Xtube, and also place sex ads. So, out of curiosity, I went onto their site and browsed around on it for almost a week before deciding to become a member and place my very own personal ad. I honestly wasn't expecting anything to come of it. And a part of me had hoped nothing would. But, lo and behold, my email became flooded with requests. And I responded back. I told myself that I'd do it one time, only. But once turned into twice, then twice became three more times, and now—a year-and-a-half later, I'm logged on *again*—still telling myself that *this* time will be the last time.

I stare at my ring finger. Take in the sparkling four-carat engagement ring. It's a nagging reminder of what I have; of what I could potentially end up losing. My reputation for one—as a successful, no-nonsense hairstylist and business owner of one the most upscale hair salons in the tri-state area; winner of two Bronner Brothers hair show competitions; numerous features in *Hype Hair* magazine, one of the leading hairstyle magazines for African-American women; and winner of the 2008 Global Salon Business Award, a prestigious award presented every two years to recognize excellence in the industry—could be tarnished. Everything I've worked so hard to achieve could be ruined in the blink of an eye.

My man, for another, could…will, walk out of my life. After he beats my ass, or worse—kills me. And I wouldn't blame him, not one damn bit. I know better than anyone that as passionate a lover as Jasper is, he can be just as ruthless if crossed. He has no problem punching a nigga's lights out, smacking up a chick—or breaking her jaw, so I already recognize what the outcome will be if he ever finds out about my indiscretions. Yet, I still choose to dance with deception, regardless of the outcome.

As hypocritical and deceitful as I've been, I can't ever forget it was Jasper who helped me get to where I am today. He's been the biggest part of my success, and I love him for that. Nappy No More wouldn't exist if it weren't for him believing in me, in my visions, and investing thousands of dollars into my salon eight years ago. Granted, I've paid him back and then some. And, yes, it's true. I put up with all the shit that comes with loving a man who's been caught up in the game. From his hustling and incarcerations to his fucking around on me in the early part of our relationship, I stood by him; loved him, no matter what. And I know more than anyone else that I've benefited from it. So as far as I'm concerned, I owe him. He's put all of his trust in me, has given me his heart, and has always been damn good to me. And, yes, *this* is how I've been showing my gratitude—by creeping on the internet.

He won't find out, I think, sighing as I remove my diamond ring from my hand, placing it in my jewelry case and then locking it in the safe with the rest of my valuables. Jasper gave me this engagement ring and proposed to me a month before he got sentenced while he was still out on bail. He wanted me to marry him before he got locked up, but I want to wait until he gets released. Having a half-assed wedding was not an option. But, there'll be no wedding if I don't get my mind right and stop this shit, soon! *I'll stop all this craziness once he gets home.* This is what I tell myself, this is what I want to believe. The fucked-up thing is that as hard as I have tried to get my urges under control, there are times when my "habit" overwhelms me; when it creeps up on me and lures me into its clutches and I have to sneak out and end up right back on my knees sucking down another nigga's dick.

See. Being a seasoned dick sucker, I can swallow any length or width without gagging, or puking. I relax, breathe through my nose, extend my tongue all the way out, and then swallow one inch at a time until I have the dick all the way down in my throat. Then I start swallowing while I give a nigga a nice, slow dick massage. The shit is bananas! And it drives a nigga crazy.

I sigh, remembering a time when I once was so obsessed with being a good dick sucker that I used to practice sucking on a dildo. I had bought myself a nice black, seven-inch dildo at an adult bookstore when I was barely twenty. At first, it was a little uncomfortable. My eyes would water and I'd gag as the head hit the back of my throat. But, I didn't give up. I was determined to become a dick-swallowing pro. Diligently, I kept practicing every night before I went to bed until I was finally able to deep throat that rubber cock balls deep. Then I purchased an eight-inch, and practiced religiously until I was also able to swallow it. Before long, I was able to move up to a nine-inch, then ten. And once I had them mastered, it was then, that I knew for certain I was ready to move on to the real thing. I've been sucking dick ever since.

The only difference is, back then I only sucked my boyfriends, men I loved; men who I wanted to be with. But now…now, I'm sucking a bunch of faceless, nameless men; men who I care nothing about. Men I have no emotional connection to. And that within itself makes what I'm doing that more dirty. I realize this. Still—as filthy and as raunchy and trifling as it is, it excites me. It entices me. And it keeps me wanting more.

As crazy as this will sound, when I'm down on my knees, or leaned over in a nigga's lap with a mouthful of dick while he's driving—it's not him I'm sucking; it's not his balls I'm wetting. It's Jasper's dick. It's Jasper's balls. It's Jasper's moans that I hear. It's Jasper's hands that I feel wrapped in my hair, holding the back of my neck. It's Jasper stretching my neck. Not any other nigga. I close my eyes, and pretend. I make believe them other niggas don't exist.

The *dinging* alerts me that I have new messages. I sit back in front of my screen, take a deep breath. Eight emails. I click on the first one:

Great ad! Good-looking married man here: 42, 5'9", 7" cut, medium thick. Looking for a discreet, kinky woman who likes to eat and play with nice, big sweaty balls, lick in my musty crotch, and chew on my foreskin while I kick back. Can't host.

I frown, disgusted. *What the fuck?!* I think, clicking DELETE.

I continue to the second email:

Hey baby, looking for a generous woman who likes to suck and get fucked in the back of her throat. I'm seven-inches cut, and I like the feel of a tight-ass throat gripping my dick when I nut. I'm 5'9, about 168 lbs, average build, dark-skinned. I'm a dominant brotha so I would like to meet a sub-missive woman. I'm disease free and HIV negative. Hope you are, too. Hit me back.

Generous? Submissive? "Nigga, puhleeze," I sigh aloud, rolling my eyes. *Delete.*

I open the next three, and want to vomit. They are mostly crude, or ridiculous; particularly this one:

Hi. I'm a clean, cool, horny, married Italian guy. I'm also well hung 'n thick. I'd love to put on my wife's g-string, maybe even her thigh-highs, and let you suck me off through her panties, then pull out my thick, hot cock and give me good oral. I'm 6'2", 180 lbs, good shape. Don't worry. I'm a straight man, but behind closed doors I love wearing my wife's panties and getting oral. I hope this interests you.

I suck my teeth. "No, motherfucker, it doesn't!" *Delete.* What the fuck I look like, sucking a nigga who wears women's panties? *Straight man, my ass!* Bitch, *you a Miss Honey!* I think, opening up the sixth email.

Yo, lookin' for a bitch who enjoys suckin' all kinds of cock. Hood nigga here, lookin' to tear a throat up. Not beat to hear whinin' 'bout achin' jaws and not wantin' a muhfucka to nut in her mouth. I'm lookin' to unzip, fuck a throat, then nut 'n bounce. If u wit' it, holla back.

Delete.

Ugh! The one downside of putting out sex ads on the internet, you never know what you're going to get. It's hit or miss. Some-times you luck up and get exactly what you're looking for. But most times you get shit even a dog wouldn't want. Truth be told, there's a bunch of nasty-ass kooks online. And judging by these emails, I'm already convinced tonight's going to be a bust. Try to convince myself that it's a sign that it's not meant to be, not tonight anyway; maybe not ever again.

My computer *dings* again. I have three new emails. My mind tells me to delete them without opening them; to log off and shut down my PC. But, of course, I don't. I open the first email:

5'11", 255 lbs, trim beard, stache, stocky build, moderately hairy, and aggressive. Always in need to have my dick sucked to the extreme! I love a woman who is into my cum. Show it to me in your mouth and all over your tongue, then go back down on my dick and try to suck out another load.

That's right up my alley, I think, deleting the note, *but not with you. Your ass is too damn fat!* I move onto the next email:

6'3", 190 lbs, 6" cut. Black hair, brown eyes. Here's a pic of my dick. If you like, hit me back. Before I even open his attachment, I'm already shaking my head, thinking, "no thank you" because of his stats. Don't get me wrong. I'm by no means a size whore, but let's face it…a nigga standing at six-three with only a six-inch dick. Hmmph. He better have a ripped body, a thick dick, and be extra damn fine! I click on the attachment, anyway. When it opens, I blink, blink again. Bring my face closer to the screen and squint. I sigh. His dick is as thin as a No. 2 pencil. Poor thing! I feel myself getting depressed for him. *Delete!* I click on the third email:

Do u really suck a good dick? If so, come over and wrap your lips around my 8-inch dick until I bust off on your face or down in your throat. 29, 6'1, decent build here. Horny as fuck for some mind-blowing head.

I smile. Maybe there's hope after all, I think, responding back. I type: *No, baby, I'm not a good dick sucker. I'm a great one! Send me a pic of your body and dick so that I know your stats are what you say they are. And if I like what I see, maybe you can find out for yourself.* Two minutes later, he replies back with an attachment. I open it, letting out a sigh of relief as I type. *Beautiful cock! Now when, where, and how can I get at it?*

I know, I know, aside from being risky and dangerous, I am aware that what I am doing is dead wrong. No, it's fucked up! However, I can't help myself. Okay, damn…maybe I can. But the selfish bitch in me doesn't want to. I mean, I do try. I'll go two or three days, even a week—sometimes, two—and I'll think I'm good; that I've kicked this nasty habit. It's like the minute the clock strikes midnight—the bewitching hour, I become possessed. I turn into a filthy cumslut. In a local park, dark alley, parking lot, public restroom, deserted street in the back of a truck—I want to drop down low and lick, taste, swallow, a thick, creamy nut. Either sucked out or jacked out; drink it from a used condom or a shot glass—I want it to coat my tonsils, and slide down into my throat. Not that I've gone to those extremes. Well, not to *all* those extras. But, I've come close enough.

And tonight is no different. Here it is almost one A.M. and I should have my ass in bed. Instead, once again, I'm looking to give some good-ass, sloppy, wet head; lick and suck on some balls; deep throat some dick, gag on it. And maybe swallow a nut. Yes, tonight I'm looking for someone who knows how to throat fuck a greedy, dick-sucking bitch like me. I'm looking for someone who knows how to fuck my mouth as if they were fucking my pussy, deep-stroking that pipe down into my gullet until my eyes start to water.

Ding! He replies back: *You can get this cock, now! No games, no BS, just a hot nut going down in your throat. I'm at the Edison Sheraton. Room 238.*

I respond, practically drooling: *I'm on my way. Be there in 30 mins.*

I get up from my computer desk, slip out of my silk robe, tossing it over onto my American Drew California-king sleigh bed. Standing naked in front of my full-length mirror, I like…no, love, what I see: full, luscious lips; perky, C-cup tits; small, tight waist; firm, plump ass; and smooth, shapely legs. I slip into a hot pink Juicy Couture tracksuit, then grab my black and pink Air Max's. I pin my hair up, before placing a black Juicy fitted on my head, pulling it down over my face and flipping up the hood of my jacket. I grab my bag and keys, then head down the stairs and out the door to suck down on some cock. I glance at my watch. It's 2:24 a.m. *Hope this nigga's dick is worth the trip.*